A Love Like No Other

Abigail and John Adams
A Modern Love Story

Nancy Taylor Robson

DEDICATION

For all the women who through the ages have fought with grace and
courage for their families, for their place in life
and for joy in every day

Head to Wind Publishing 2013

ISBN:1479358037
ISBN-13: 978-1479358038
Cover design: Kelly Parisi Castro

Prologue

"Are you there?"

He tried to rise off the bed. Unable to steady himself, he flopped back, eyes fogged with the delirium.

"I am here," Abigail said, gently taking the hand that lay like a withered leaf on the bedclothes.

"Are you there?" he repeated, trying once more to lift his head off the pillow.   Strength gone, he dropped back, exhausted.

"He's been doing that for a week now," his young wife said without inflection, coming across the room to stand at Abigail's shoulder and stare down at the wasted form on the bed.

Although he was only thirty, he looked fifty, eyes sunken and bloodshot, nose prominent where the skin had stretched gossamer thin across high cheekbones.

"A week?" Abigail's voice nearly broke, but she drew in a great draught of air, and with it, swallowed her pain. Her son, once bright-eyed and joyous - such wasted possibilities.

"Yes. The delirium has been on him before for as long as a week, but this time something's different...." Sally said, still gazing at the greenish face on the pillow. It looked almost ethereal, only half in this world. "I can't tell who he's calling for."

The young woman's tone was matter-of-fact, resigned.

Abigail's eyes widened. The shock of her daughter-in-law's words had pried open a door of guilt that she had locked long ago. His God? Is he searching for his God? Or for his parents? For his mother? What if we had held him closer, watched over him more?

Her two little granddaughters, clad in oft-mended clothes, stood by the window, watching the prostitutes below. It has come to this, Abigail thought bitterly. Waste begotten of waste. She wanted to call the children from the window, to tell them that life was not this morass of pain and squandered possibilities.

She felt a hand grip her arm.

"I've...I've... always been a disappointment to you and Par." The voice was rasping, the throat caked.

Jolted at her son's abrupt return to lucidity, Abigail pulled away for an instant.

"Aye," he whispered, as though her withdrawal confirmed his self-assessment. "I've always known it."

Gasping, Abigail leaned down toward the anguished face. No

evidence remained of the once cheerful, sweet-faced boy.   His
children will never know the good in him, will only know the stink of
drink and death and poverty, she thought, regret tearing at her
stomach. They will know only that their father left them destitute.

"You have not been a disappointment, to us," she lied, hating
herself for both the lie and for its necessity.   "You have been ever a
kind, joyful companion to us and to your friends alike..." she
hesitated, almost sobbed aloud, then continued.   "Your fault, if
indeed there is one, my dear son, is in your choice of companions.
You were ever one to judge too kindly. You have loved not wisely
but too well."

"Nay, nay..." he cried, distractedly, tears swelling out of the
corners of his eyes and streaking down his face. "I was ever a trouble
and a worry. And my girls, what's to become of my little girls?"

"Par and I will see to your daughters, as will your brother..."
John Quincy. Another rebuke. She wished she could call back
the name.

"Yes, yes, John Quincy..." he agreed, closing his eyes and moving
his head in a barely perceptible nod. "Of course. There is still John
Quincy. He is the son you deserved. It has been hard on Sally. She
deserved better..."

Abigail's family pride rose in rebellion at the thought that an
Adams would fail to measure up, but, glancing at Sally's haggard face,
she held her tongue.

"Nay, my dear," said the young woman softly, her tone an echo
of a happier time. "I deserved to be loved, and I always knew that
you loved me. Some things are beyond a man's control."

The compassion behind the words, an undeserved gift to the
man who had given much heartache and pain, nearly took Abigail's
breath.

"Whatever may happen," Abigail said looking hard into Sally's
haggard face, "you need not fear for your family. The Adamses look
after their own."

ACKNOWLEDGMENTS

The Adams Papers, containing the collected letters of Abigail
and John Adams and published by Belknap Press,
were invaluable.
They enabled me to hear the voices of John and Abigail, learn
the details of their daily lives, and grasp something of the
richness of their intellects and of the times.

Thanks to Mary Ann Bowers, Joan Enfield, Joan Smith Cramer,
Brenda Rocconi, and Abigail Robson, who read the manuscript
and encouraged me to carry on. And as always, thanks to Gary
whose love – made visible in work -- is a gift I treasure.

Chapter 1

Thus with the year
Seasons return; but not to me returns Day, or the sweet approach of even or
morn, John Milton Paradise Lost Bk III Line 11

1758

Leaning out of the velvet chair in Grandfather Quincy's study, fourteen-year-old Abigail Smith strained toward the waning light of the window. The words were almost indecipherable in the last pale rays that splotched the few remaining maple leaves on the tree outside. The seasons are changing without me, she thought.

The room was chilly. She closed the book and laid it on the windowsill then stretched stiff legs and rose. She had been at Mt. Wollaston for three months recovering from another of her recurring chest ailments under Grandmother Quincy's attentive eye. It felt as though she had spent half her life separated from her family, imprisoned by ill health. *But I have once again cheated death*, she thought. *Time to go home to Weymouth.*

Home. She loved her grandparents' Mt. Wollaston house, loved its air of intellect and prosperity. Colonel John Quincy had been a member of the Massachusetts House of Representatives for twenty-one years, fourteen of them as Speaker. Currency policies, legislation and trade were the stuff of daily conversation. Even in her grandfather's retirement, a steady stream of neighbors and acquaintances - magistrates, merchants, and farmers - came to ask his opinion on points of law, or for help in deciding a dispute.

It was stimulating and fed her keen sense of her family's importance. But she longed for the comfortable sounds of home and the companionship of her sisters (though not of her spoiled brother, Will), for her father, and – though less – her mother. But most of all, she missed Polly. Her elder sister, Mary, called Polly, Abigail viewed as both rival and confidante, the yardstick by which she measured her own dreams.

The front door opened followed by a man's heavy brogues on the bare hallway floors. Grandfather Quincy was home. She came to the door of the library, to meet him. As he came into the room, the old man smiled and reached out a hand to tug a wisp of hair that had

1

escaped her mobcap.

"How is my Nabby today? This crisp weather has revived your spirits, I trust?"

"I'm tolerable well, Grandfather. I wish you had let me come with you today. It is so beautiful outside. Please may I go tomorrow?"

"We'll ask your grandmother. Her judgment rules in these matters, though I agree, a walk may put some color in that cheek of yours." He smoothed his hand over his wig, ruffled in the autumn wind. "Do I smell supper?"

"I suppose so. I hadn't noticed. Mr. Milton and I have been closeted all afternoon."

"Yes, and neglecting your stitchery, no doubt. Husbands want wives who are well-bred not well-read, Nabby. A man desires the mending of his collars not his morals."

He spoke seriously, but there was a twinkle in his eye.

"Do you suppose any man will be so concerned with my stitches?" she retorted, tilting her head.

Her studied her for a moment. No beauty, he decided, though there is a spirit in her that a certain kind of man will appreciate -- if her will find her.

"You mock me, miss," he smiled.

She would not have used the same saucy tone with her father, he knew. For Colonel Quincy's minister son-in-law, life was a serious moral matter. The Reverend William Smith was a respectable if uninspiring match for Elizabeth Quincy, daughter of Colonel Quincy and Elizabeth Norton Quincy. If he was not a secular leader, he was, at least, a spiritual one, and so had a certain standing in the community.

The hallway smelled of warm bread and soup and drying herbs. In the kitchen, they found Grandmother Quincy in concentration over a piecrust while issuing sharp-tongued instructions to her young maid.

"Turn that bread dough again, girl," she snapped, nodding toward the hearth where a large bowl sat near the fire. "You want to raise it, not cook it in the bowl."

"Could a hungry traveler find a crust?" John Quincy asked as he came through the doorway.

"Sukey, fetch Colonel Quincy a bowl of soup and a slice of that first loaf," Elizabeth Quincy said, hardly looking up at her husband.

"Yes'm."

Sukey filled a bowl from the steaming pot on the trammel arm, and set it on the table.

"You'll be wantin' some too, won't you Miss Nabby?"

"Of course, feed the child, Girl!"

Orphaned, with six younger siblings, Sukey had lived with the Quincys for five years, long enough to grow accustomed to her mistress's tart tongue. The tolerance was born of gratitude. She knew too many girls who had been forced into prostitution by families who could not feed them. In the prosperous Quincy household, she wanted for nothing, and though Mrs. Colonel Quincy was impatient, she was also kind.

Obediently, Sukey ladled some steaming pea soup into a second bowl and put it on the table then cut thick slices of still-warm bread and slathered them with home-churned butter, while Abigail brought four cups from the sideboard for tea.

Grandfather Quincy had settled himself in a chair and begun to eat his soup loudly while the tea was made and poured.

"Colonel, you have forgotten to thank the Lord!" Grandmother Quincy snapped.

"The Lord knows how grateful I am, *and* how hungry," he replied, but he put down his spoon while his wife spoke a few words of blessing.

Slim, square-jawed and bright-eyed, Elizabeth Quincy was the same embodiment of spirit and determination John Quincy had married so many years before, but the years had worn away the polite veneer of youth along with what little extra flesh she had once possessed. Now, there was only skin stretched over bone, scant covering for the angular soul beneath. But while Elizabeth Quincy had never been beautiful, she still had a grace of movement, an energy and assurance that John Quincy admired.

"I walked over the top of the north hill and back after the council meeting," he said between slurped spoonfuls. "The trees have the aspect of a painting in their color. I would be glad of Mistress Nabby's company tomorrow."

He winked at Abigail.

"Well, perhaps if it is clear," his wife agreed.

She cast an appraising look at her fragile granddaughter. "But we'll not risk our Nabby so far as the north hill yet. Perhaps to the bottom of the lane and then back through the orchard. She's only now getting her strength back. Build it up slow, that's the way."

"Yes, build it up slow, but build it up!" Colonel Quincy replied.

"I feel much stronger, Grandmother," Abigail put in. "It won't be much longer before I shall be strong enough to return home."

"Speaking of Weymouth, Nabby, I had a letter from your mother today. Tom Tanner rode up with a basket of Bramleys from your parents' orchard and brought it with him," she said, dipping a crust of bread into the soup Sukey had put in front of her. "Sukey! Have you remembered to stir that stew?"

Immediately, Sukey put down her spoon, went to the hearth, and lifted the lid of the kettle that hung on the iron trammel. "Meat's nearly off the bones," she said, poking, surgeon-like, with a wooden spoon. "Umm. Smell's good! This summer's thyme was potent stuff."

"Put it to the back a bit, so it don't burn."

Sukey's tucked-up skirts suddenly escaped their binding and swept over the coals of the open fire.

"Mind your skirts, girl! " Mrs. Quincy cried, half rising from the chair, ready to grab the fire bucket and race to the well if need be.

Stepping back, Sukey reached down and rubbed the small smoking spot on her dress until it was snuffed out, then pulled the yards of material back into their confinement before pivoting the trammel back into the deep hearth.

"Mind yourself, girl!" Mrs. Quincy growled again. "There's too many go that a-way. Skirts ablaze, burnt to death - as though childbirth and disease weren't enough to contend with! Where was I? Oh yes! News!" she continued, businesslike. "Apparently one of the Boylstons brought a pipe into church in his pocket. Trouble was, it wasn't quite put out. The pocket caught fire. Right during your father's sermon it was, Nabby. He tried to put it out quietly, but it was too far gone so he had to run out and throw off the coat onto the ground and stamp it out! Your father had a difficult time regaining the congregation's attention after that! Your mother is most pricked at it."

Abigail could easily imagine her mother's indignation at the double sin against the Sabbath and her husband's preaching. That it was one of the Boylstons, who held themselves in such high regard, would make it the sharper wound in her mother's Quincy pride.

After supper, Abigail followed her grandfather down the dim corridor into the library. As she closed the door to keep in the warmth, she saw him bend down to stoke the smoldering embers, banked in their drift of ashes. He had the lean limbs of a farmer, despite a lifetime spent in court and study. She was proud of his physical vigor, but she was envious, too.

Under her grandfather's ministrations, the fire sprang back to life, licking up the edges of the split laburnum. Light danced up the opposite wall to the portraits of the Quincy ancestors in their gilt frames, heavy with respectability. Great-grandmother Quincy, regal in her laces and satins, was said to have had the same delicate chest as Abigail.

"Grandfather, why is mankind so weak?" Abigail asked softly, eyes still on the painting.

The old man looked at his granddaughter, his favorite grandchild. Although she had the dark eyes and oval face of the Smiths, she was slim and straight like the Quincys and loved learning - a boon to the generation she might bear. But the skin that covered her high cheekbones was transparent, a thin barrier between the soul and mortality. She might never be strong enough to marry let alone bear children. He settled himself into his chair by the hearth and lit his pipe with a taper from the fire.

"Do you mean weak in body or in spirit?" he asked finally.

"Both, I suppose," Abigail replied, frowning as she came to sit in the chair opposite. "Mother once said she had feared I would not reach my fifth year -- although here I am at the ripe old age of fourteen. Polly and Betsey and Will all have nary a sick day yet we all carry the same blood in our veins. What makes weakness?"

"I sometimes think that God made man weak in body to keep him from arrogance," he said, not answering her question. "Mankind is too arrogant by half. Can you imagine what he would be without the leveling scythe of mortality?"

"Is it arrogance to yearn for answers?" she persisted. "Adam only wanted to know about Creation. He was curious."

"I see you are reading Paradise Lost," he puffed thoughtfully on his pipe. "Curiosity is unending, Nabby. Man always wants to know more and more. *Some* is never enough."

"Not just *Man*," she murmured.

5

He sighed. She is so unlike her mother.

Elizabeth Quincy Smith had grown up amid the same discussions of law and politics, books and ideas. But in her, they had produced a feeling of moral and social superiority. Her Quincy and Norton forebears - judges, lawyers, and doctors, the minds and hearts of the colony's history - conferred importance. Abigail had absorbed a sense of inherited worth, but had also grown hungry for something more: she wanted to be counted in a wider world.

She will never be satisfied to be the wife of a country parson, Colonel Quincy thought. She conjures worlds where her mother imagines only villages. She will never find a husband.

In the Massachusetts Bay Colony a well-bred young woman should tend hearth and home while her husband tends to the outside world, a straightforward division of labor. Women deal with christening lace, pew money, the rental of the funeral carriages, the feeding and nursing and keeping of a family. Women who accepted that without question seemed most contented. Colonel Quincy had never considered that what looked like contentment might actually be resignation.

Abigail watched her grandfather, waiting for an answer, then finally repeated her question.

"Is it really weakness to want to know, Grandfather? Father always says to have faith. That it is impudence to question."

"You don't question the Almighty, do you Child?"

"No, I don't. I simply question why knowledge for anyone is a bad thing."

"It was the knowledge of good and evil that was forbidden," he reminded her.

"Yes. But why is it supposed that Eve alone is at fault for tempting Adam? Did he not take part too, by accepting the proffered bite?"

"You are too pert by half, Miss," Colonel Quincy replied. "And you are forgetting the serpent. Evil, dissatisfaction, temptation. Mankind must be contented with what God has given."

"Has God given evil and injustice?"

Her considered her for a moment, noting the straight carriage despite the weeks of illness. Shakespeare had such heroines - many of them doomed to tragedy by their own strengths.

"You are like Portia," he observed.

"Portia?"

"From Mr. Shakespeare's Merchant of Venice. Portia stepped out of her womanly calling to speak for right, for justice, and for mercy. She – a woman - defended a man who could not defend himself. And her faith and courage brought her her heart's desire - true love."

Abigail blushed. To be compared with this woman was high praise indeed.

"I would like to be like Portia," she murmured.

"You will be, my Child," her grandfather said, wondering whether or not she would live long enough. "In time."

They fell silent and stared into the fire, absently listening to the dry-leafed trees rustling in the wind. An autumn sound. It had a different cadence at year's end. Abigail suddenly felt the tug of time going, of life closing in once more to dark nights lit only by the wavering light of the candle.

The cabbages and potatoes were already lodged in the root cellar. Carrots and turnips and parsnips would follow, painstakingly blanketed in straw to be dug out gradually for winter meals. Grandmother's flowerbeds were dried brown except for the last stalwart chrysanthemums, which the old lady used to brighten the tables and fill the rooms with musky freshness. Abigail longed to wade through the piles of leaves the hired men had raked, and to gather Bramleys and Jonathans from the heavy-laden apple trees.

Grandfather Quincy stretched out his legs to studying the silver buckles on his shoes while he smoked. He did not move when Elizabeth Quincy, sewing basket over her arm, came in.

"Light the candles, child," she said as she took the seat Abigail had vacated for her. "Then search out your needlework. You'll not spend the whole day in study without regard to your stitches. I won't have it."

Abigail retrieved her embroidery from the chest by the window and pulled a chair beside the fire. The three had spent many an evening like this together until Grandfather nodded off to sleep and Grandmother roused him and sent him to bed.

"And how is your sampler coming, Nabby?" Grandmother Quincy asked after a time.

"Tolerable well, Grandmother, " Abigail sighed, "though I don't believe I'll ever have your touch with the needle."

"Nonsense. I have had a great many more years to practice. Let me see."

The old woman studied the stretched fabric. The ragged lines that created borders were only an approximation of their true course.

"You need to take more care, Nabby. Your attention wanders and along with it, your stitches. Come pull the chair closer and try again."

An hour later, when the old lady noticed that Abigail's head had drooped onto her chest and her needlework lay still in her lap, she gently woke the girl. Wandering out into the chilly hallway with the thin light of a candle to guide her, Abigail mounted the steps to her room.

She was relieved to see that Sukey had brought up an ember from the kitchen to kindle the fire in the room. Warmth ebbed out from the hearth, and shadows danced along the ceiling. She would miss the luxury at Mt. Wollaston. At home in Weymouth Parsonage, they were allowed to take a coal in the bedwarmer and run it over the sheets to take off the chill, but there was no fire in the bedroom. Wood was too costly. And, Abigail suspected, too self-indulgent for her straight-laced father. She slipped between chill sheets, pulled her knees to her chest and leaned over to blow out the candle. Slowly, her body spread warmth beneath the feather ticking and she inched her toes down until she lay stretched full length in the large bed.

When she woke it was well past dawn. As she lay there, arm across her eyes, enveloped in languid contemplation of the day before her, Sukey came in with a cup of hot chocolate. Setting the cup on the bed stand, she pushed open the drawn curtains.

"Shall I open the window a crack, Miss Nabby? It's a lovely warm day outside, as bright and shiny a one as we're like to see for a time, says your grandma. She says it'll rain tonight. Lord only knows how she knows it, but she's always right. You'll be walkin' out today I expect."

"I hope so, Sukey," Abigail murmured, sliding out of bed and padding barefoot to the window where the servant girl stood.

Sunlight splashed the tops of the trees and spread long fingers into the avenues of the orchard. Abigail smiled at Sukey. While she was not bright, Sukey was honest and willing and had a giving heart. Happy with her place in this world, Abigail decided with a twinge of envy.

When she looked toward the barn, she saw George, one of the hired men, leading Grandmother Quincy's gelding into the traces of the expensive little trap in which she 'went a'visitin".

"Where is Grandmother going?"

"Down to Cawley's. Mrs. Cawley's time's come and your grandma's goin' to take some food and such for the other little 'uns today while their ma's havin' her baby," Sukey replied, biting her lip nervously. "George said the midwife was there when he went by this mornin'. Miz Cawley's a might old to be still havin' little 'uns. Her husband should have..." she murmured, but didn't finish her thought.

Abigail heard a distant door slam and saw her grandmother stride out to the trap where George stood crooning to the horse. After handing George a heaped basket covered with an old piece of homespun, Mrs. Quincy climbed unaided into the trap. She settled herself then took the basket and the reins from George, whacked the reins on the horse's rump, and set off down the lane.

"You better get yourself dressed, Miss Nabby, before you catch your death standin' there barefoot like that!"

"Where is Grandfather?" Abigail asked while Sukey helped her into her clothes.

"Oh, I'm sure I don't know. Shall I go and find him?" the girl offered.

"No, I'll search him out."

Abigail gulped the chocolate then went down the front stairs. She found her grandfather sitting in his favorite chair in the library framed in the halo of light from the window behind him. A leather volume was open on his lap, and he puffed absently at his pipe.

"Ah, finally up, I see! Mornin's half gone," he said. "Go have your breakfast, then let us walk out together!"

While Abigail ate, Sukey bustled about humming. Dusting her hands off on her apron, she hung the battered soup kettle back over the trammel then poured a bowl of chopped vegetables into the pot. Abigail enjoyed Sukey's soups. What they lacked in subtlety, they made up in creative flair.

"What kind will it be tonight, Sukey?" Abigail asked, between bites of bread and butter and sips of tea.

"I put a bit of salt beef in the pot and I'll just fill it up with vegetables and such. I hope your grandma gets a pig from Mr. Cawley soon. It's been a while since we've had one," Sukey said as

9

she covered the pot and swung it over the fire, careful to draw her skirts aside.

"How old is Mrs. Cawley? " Abigail asked, suddenly imagining the scene in that cabin four miles down the road, the bloody bed linen, the screaming, muffled by the closed door, the youngest children huddled outside, waiting, terrified, whimpering for their ma.

"I don't rightly know - reckon maybe forty-six, forty-seven. Chancy havin' babies at any age let alone that old," she said. "My aunt nearly died birthin' last year - baby was breach - and she's twenty-eight. Though they's some just pop 'em out!"

Abigail shivered and pulled the shawl around her as though its thin material could insulate her from the harsh realities of life. She and Sukey fell silent when they heard Colonel Quincy's footsteps echo in the hall. He emerged carrying his winter cloak.

"I can't decide whether to wear this or not," he mused, brushing the nap down with one hand. "It's one of those contrary days when it could be warm all day or turn cold with an afternoon's breeze."

"Grandmother would probably tell you to take it, Grandfather," Abigail observed.

"Yes. I'm certain you are right. But she's not here and I don't want to carry such a heavy thing," he decided, suddenly delighted by the notion of disobeying his wife. "Are you ready, Miss?"

The two set off down the lane together, their steps bringing up little dust clouds in the dry earth. After walking down the rows of white pines, they turned north again to come around the barn and continue past the outbuildings toward the top of the rise where they stopped to rest. Puffing from the unaccustomed exertion, Abigail stood in a shaft of sunlight drinking in the richness of the autumn air. Colonel Quincy sat down in the shade of an old cherry tree and watched his granddaughter, whose pale face was turned to the sun.

"It's truly beautiful here, isn't it, Grandfather?" she burst out.

"Yes, Nabby. I come here when I want peace. Beauty helps us to forget the pain in life, sometimes, just as the intellect explores it."

"Have you ever brought Polly here?"

"I don't remember. Perhaps."

"I miss Polly - and Betsey and Willie too, of course," she added hastily.

Since Polly had turned seventeen, the family had begun to speak of her as a marriageable woman. Abigail hated it. She dreaded the thought of Polly leaving - of their lives changing, of the mortal risk of having children. And she felt jealous of the attention Polly was getting. She wanted to be considered marriageable too.

But if Polly were to marry, Abigail would marry, too, and perhaps even better. She wanted a husband, a companion for the mind. She did not yet realize how insistent the pull of carnal appetites would be. She heard only of the unwanted babies they produced. But she assumed those appetites were for other people, a different class; they would not touch her. She yearned for a mate for her soul.

It was a tall order, she knew. Mrs. Smith looked for men of property, with prospects and family. It was no guarantee of kindness. A bullying man could confine a woman to a life of near slavery. A husband virtually owned his wife, as he did his horse and buggy, and was free to use her as he pleased.

But Abigail, who had heard enough of that kind of marriage, had seen something of the pleasure of a good one. Not from the example of her parents' distantly correct union, but from her grandparents. She heard it in the respect in their voices as they sat together by the fire in the evening, sensed it in their comfortable affection, saw it in the surreptitious touch her grandfather sometimes gave his wife as he passed.

"Are you feeling all right, Child?" Grandfather Quincy broke into her reverie. "You look a bit feverish. Perhaps the walk was too far for the first day?"

"No, Grandfather, I am fine. I was only thinking..." she said.

"Ah, thinking again. Your mother will be angry if it has been about anything besides how you can please a husband. She believes I have spoiled you for domestic life."

"No, Grandfather," Abigail smiled, both uncomfortable and pleased at the way he seemed to read her thoughts. "Just a certain *kind* of domestic life."

"Your mother loves you, Nabby," her grandfather said, not for the first time. "She fears you will be an old maid if we make you too learned for all the men in Massachusetts Bay Colony."

"I know," Abigail sighed. " But I would rather be a spinster than marry a man who would not love my mind and character."

"Ah, so he must love your mind and character as well as your eyes? It is a tall order," he smiled, taking her by the arm. "Come, let

11

us go home."

By the time Abigail heard Grandmother Quincy drive up the lane, it had begun to rain. Supper had been cleared away hours before. Abigail met her grandmother at the kitchen door and took the sodden basket and shawl.

"Have Sukey bring me a cup of tea in the drawing room when she comes back in," Grandmother Quincy said wearily.

Abigail was laying a slice of bread and butter on a plate when Sukey, her shawl soaked, opened the back door and stepped inside.

"Grandmother wants tea."

Sukey nodded without comment, dumped her shawl on the table and put the kettle on while Abigail hurried to the drawing room. By the time, she opened the door, her grandmother had collapsed into a chair.

"What happened, Grandmother?" Abigail asked, fearfully guessing the answer.

"They both died," her grandmother replied, too tired to soften the shock.

Dead. Mother and babe gone in one stroke. Abigail stood rigid by the chair, listening to the crackling of the fire as it consumed the logs.

"It was a difficult lying-in," the old woman continued in a monotone. "Very difficult. And the mid-wife...I must speak with Dr. Warren. But there was nothing to be done. They're with their Maker now."

"What will the family do?" Abigail asked in a small voice.

"What is there TO do, child? They'll bury them Tuesday, I expect. I left food for them. The eldest girl can take care of the young 'uns, but it won't be easy. Cawley will be looking for a new wife soon. She had better be a sight younger, though that's no guarantee," she trailed off.

Abigail shuddered. A new wife. Like a new cow. Heartless.

Sukey arrived with the tray and laid it gently beside Mrs. Quincy's elbow. She handed her mistress a steaming cup, then wiped her eyes with the corner of her apron.

"Mrs. Cawley was good to me," Sukey whimpered.

"She was a good woman," Grandmother Quincy agreed without inflection. "Where is the Colonel, Nabby?

"Asleep in his chair in the study. Shall I wake him?"

"Yes. Tell him I'm home safe. Time to carry himself off to bed. I'll be up shortly. Sukey?"

"Yes M'am?"

"You go on to bed now, too."

Sukey left quietly, the sound of the door barely audible over the rain that now pelted the windows, an insistent staccato. Abigail crossed the room. Hand on the knob, she turned for a moment to look at her grandmother, head bent over the cup that she steadied in both veined hands. By the wavering light of the candle, Abigail could just discern the tear that made a slow, uneven course down the old woman's hollow cheek.

Chapter 2

With thee conversing I forget all time,
All seasons and their change. Paradise Lost Bk IV line 639

1761

The day dawned bright with a cloudless sky and a northwest wind that rattled the windows in their casings. Seated in the drawing room window seat in Weymouth Parsonage, seventeen-year-old Abigail watched as the heat of her hand traced its own outline on the frosted pane. Beyond the window, the landscape was bleak. The front garden was covered for the winter with straw and leaves. In a lonely corner of the yard, the pear tree reached arthritic limbs to the sky. The road that wound past the house was frozen.

The drawing room door swung open and twenty-year-old Polly swept into the room laden with cut evergreens. Betsey, who at age twelve was moving into a precocious adolescence, followed close on her heels.

"Why have you not stirred the fire, Nab?" Polly chided. "It's chill in here. Where is brother Will? Has he been in?"

"Not in the past half-hour," Abigail replied, rising. "I'm sorry, Polly. My mind was elsewhere. I hadn't noticed the fire going down."

She crossed the room with arms folded over her chest, shawl hunched up against her neck. Taking another log from the stack beside the hearth, she pitched it carelessly into the center of the mound of embers.

"How are you faring with the decorating, then?" she asked.

"Better since Will ran off," Polly replied. "He makes things so difficult. He's contrary just for the sake of it. I wish Ma would discipline him more. Although Miss Betsey, too, has a mind of her own."

"I will not be compared to Will," Betsey pouted. "Besides, you never let me decide how anything is to look, Polly."

"Decide in here, then," Polly said, "provided there are not pieces of holly in the chairs to prick the guests!"

"Polly! Whatever do you mean!" Betsey exclaimed in mock

horror.

Betsey, lively, warm, more unfettered than either of her sisters, was a practical joker. More than once she had overturned a guest's dignity to the consternation and embarrassment of the family.

"Is Mr. Cranch coming for dinner?" Abigail asked.

She liked Richard Cranch. Ten years older than Polly, he treated her with quiet respect, not the paternalism Abigail had seen in men who sought out young women. Perhaps it was his English manner. He had come from the Mother Country only a few years before and now repaired watches. He had made many friends in a short time with little effort, but the courtship of Mary Smith, eldest daughter of the parson of Weymouth, was harder going. He lacked family, money, and connections – the things most prized by Elizabeth Quincy Smith. All he could offer Mary was devotion.

Abigail was fond of Richard, and glad for Polly, but she was envious, too. For all her high-flown moralizing, she wanted a man to love her.

"No, Mr. Cranch was not invited for dinner," Polly replied, "but he will be here for tea. He is bringing Mr. Adams with him. You, too, will be glad to see them, I warrant."

Polly was testing. She had noted Abigail's growing interest in John Adams, her breathless attention to her toilet, her unnaturally shy silences in his presence. Abigail blushed to the ears. Polly missed neither the blush nor the quick shift of Abigail's gaze to the kindling fire. Nor did Betsey.

"Nabby has a beau!" she crowed.

"Codswallop!" Abigail cried, terrified that her sister might embarrass her before John, or alert their mother to her growing interest in him. "If you breathe a word..."

"Betsey, why don't you go see if Maggie has any hot cakes for you?" Polly urged.

"Nabby has a beau!" Betsey trilled as she skipped down the hall.

Polly pulled a piece of holly from the greens she had dropped on the floor. Each window was to be garnished with a small sprig wrapped in ribbon and held by a seal of wax. While pretending interest in the cluster she was arranging, Polly watched Abigail closely.

"You do have feelings for Mr. Adams, don't you, Nab?"

"Feelings? Why, if one finds a certain person's company

interesting, I suppose I do. He always brings reports of happenings in other parts - I have always found that stimulating." She reached for the ribbon, avoiding Polly's steady gaze.

Abigail was not prepared to admit, even to herself, what effect the blocky twenty-six-year-old lawyer had on her, how her heart raced at the sight of him hitching his horse out front, how she felt an unaccustomed warmth between her thighs at his presence beside her.

"Interesting? I would have supposed your feelings were more...personal."

"If they are," Abigail replied, struggling to convey indifference, "I don't suppose they would be of any consequence to him. He is too busy gallanting the ladies of Boston society to take notice of feelings in the provinces. I thought that perhaps when Hannah Quincy married Mr. Lincoln, we might see more of John Adams - because of Papa's suit over the title here, of course," she added hastily. "Yet he keeps himself busy at other things it seems. But what of it? My interest is purely intellectual. I find his mind stimulating."

Polly raised an eyebrow at her sister.

"Do you doubt?" Abigail demanded.

"I watch and observe," Polly replied gently. "I have seen how his visits bring color to your cheeks. I have seen, too, the dimming of that color at his interest in Esther Quincy."

"I have missed his company and his talk, nothing more," Abigail insisted.

In the past three years, John Adams had fallen in love with half the young ladies of Boston, pursuing one hopeless suit after another. His tastes seemed to run to flirtatious young women of wealth and position rather than character. Polly could see in those courtships John's mother's ambitions for her eldest son. Susanna Boylston Adams is family-proud, Polly thought. But then, half of Massachusetts Colony is family-proud. Yet if John Adams, too, is of that ilk, he will break Abigail's heart like fine china.

"Mr. Adams is perhaps too interested in chasing the fool's gold of position and fashion to appreciate sterling character," Polly ventured.

Abigail's eyes had widened. "I thought you liked Mr. Adams, Polly! You enjoy his discourse, I know you do!" Seeing the startled look on Polly's face, she paused, then spoke more reasonably. "I know Mr. Adams likes the ladies. I have seen him bask in their praise often enough. And they like him, too. He has wit and charm. But there is much more to him than that. He is a principled man, and one with a passionate desire to make a mark on the world, and a good mark at that. I grant he can be opinionated, but he is also knowledgeable and well-read."

"I only wondered..." Polly said, wrapping a protective arm around her sister. She was dismayed to discover that Abigail was trembling. "Nab!"

"Any woman of real discernment would be proud to call John Adams husband!" Abigail said, then added, softly: "I just doubt that his choice will be as plain a sparrow as me."

"John Adams would be the lucky one were he to have the sense to take you to wife," Polly whispered before releasing her.

The door slammed, and Betsey rushed into the room.

"They're here!" she blurted, keeping a keen eye on Abigail. "And Mr. Adams looks froze to the bone!"

Polly gripped her little sister's arm and pulled her close to look menacingly into the pretty oval face. "You are *not* to make any remarks that will embarrass our Nabby, Miss," she said through pursed lips. "Or you will answer not to Ma or Pa but to *me*! Do you hear?" Betsey nodded, eyes wide at her usually mild sister's threat. "That's better. Now. Have you shown them into the hall at least or are they still standing out in the cold?"

"Of course! I mean...! Papa is in the hall..." Betsey began but was interrupted by the Reverend Smith's entrance followed by the two blue-lipped visitors.

"Betsey, fetch your mother and advise her that our guests have arrived." Reverend Smith said. "Where is young Will?"

"I think he's out in back. Mama sent him to kill a chicken for supper," said Betsey. "Shall I fetch him?"

"Yes. Bring him in by the fire. His school books need tending to."

Before scurrying from the room, Betsey darted a swift glance at Abigail, who stood with hands clasped, eyes fixed on the floor.

"Sit ye by the fire, gentlemen," Reverend Smith said, waving his hand in the direction of the high-backed bench drawn near one side of the hearth. "Polly, get Mr. Cranch and Mr. Adams each a glass of Madeira."

"Yes, Papa," Polly replied, casting a fond look at Richard, whose

17

eyes had been on her since he first entered the room.

The two visitors crossed the room to stretch raw fingers toward the fire. With a pang of envy, Abigail noted the glances between Richard and her sister. I have no wiles to win a heart, she thought. No man will ever look at me with such warmth.

Quietly, she followed Polly to the sideboard where the large decanter sat flanked by a dozen crystal glasses. Though her father was frugal to the point of penny-pinching, her mother's love of fine things -- despite their budget -- occasionally won out. After pouring three measures of sweet wine, Polly handed two glasses to Abigail, and gave her an encouraging wink. Stone-faced, Abigail turned, and slowly traversed the room, her attention focused on the wine that threatened to slop over the sides and down onto her pale fingers.

"The ride from Braintree is a cold one this time of year," Reverend Smith observed.

"Indeed, Sir," Adams agreed, taking the glass from Abigail with a glance at her bent head. "'Tis only a half-hour taken at a canter, but long enough to freeze the limbs nearly solid! I fear it will be a hard winter. We are already worried about how to feed the livestock through 'til spring."

"Aye. There are many in my parish saying those very words. We must look to our neighbors in hard times. T'will be a winter spent cutting firewood. But then, politics provide heat in spite of the cold."

"It will get much hotter before the political fire is tempered, I warrant," Adams agreed.

"It will with such as you to stoke the fire," Abigail put in.

John smiled and shifted his gaze to her flushed face.

"I work not to inflame but to reason," he replied, earnestly. "It is simple right I advocate, nothing more."

"You are a reformer, Mr. Adams," Abigail retorted. "And all reformers are firebrands."

"Ah, perhaps, but even a reformed fire can warm the soul, can it not?" he laughed.

John had only lately begun to realize the intelligence hidden beneath Abigail's plain surface. She was not the feast to the eyes that the beautiful Quincy girls were, but she might, he was beginning to suspect, provide nourishment for the mind.

Abigail was about to respond when Mrs. Smith and Betsey

entered carrying trays laden with tea and small cakes, crossed the room and laid them on the sideboard. Rising, Richard and John bowed slightly when Mrs. Smith turned to speak —- warmly to Richard, but with icy correctness to John, though Rev. Smith had recruited him to help settle the dispute over the title to the parsonage. It was a trifling case, in Elizabeth Smith's view, which John Adams, a bumptious, opinionated upstart, was making too much over.

Though John Adams had inherited the family farm, there was little money. Additionally, she believed he had been weaned on self-regard. John Adams will live and die in obscurity, she thought, looking at his short legs, his round face and body. He will spend his life riding the country court circuits, and make himself notable only for his clambering ways and his unruly tongue.

"Ah, a fine repast, my dear!" Reverend Smith cried in an attempt to cover his wife's coldness. "Gentlemen, sit ye down. I was about to ask Mr. Adams how our case fares."

"It should not be much longer before it is resolved," John replied, tucking into a cake he had taken from the plate Mrs. Smith had offered.

"Well, that will be a blessing," Reverend Smith boomed. "I will be grateful to be required to think no more of the matter!"

"And do you have any work when Reverend Smith's case is done?" Mrs. Smith asked archly.

"Yes," John smiled, pretending to miss her implication. "In fact, since the case last year with Mr. James Otis over the Writs of Assistance, I have had many referrals and have been obliged to ride to Boston at least one day each week for cases in the town."

He was boasting and knew it but was fighting for his dignity. When Mrs. Smith fell into pursed-lipped silence, he felt a little thrill of triumph, but failed to note the significant look she shot her husband.

Heart pounding, terrified that her mother's hostility would discourage John, Abigail cast her mind frantically about for a way to turn the conversation. Weather, politics, what? Ah, The Bard! Thank you, Grandfather Quincy!

"With all those demands on your time, Mr. Adams, have you found the opportunity to read The Merchant of Venice?" she asked.

Her earnest recitations of line after line from Shakespeare's plays first piqued John Adams' interest, then admiration. Prodded by his own intellectual vanity, and by curiosity, he had begun to prepare for their meetings with a little study.

"I *made* the opportunity," John replied. "A marvelous effort. Especially Portia's courtroom speech. A masterpiece of intellect married to an expansive sensibility. Something to aspire to in my profession," he said.

The word "profession" hissed out of Mrs. Smith's mouth, but Abigail hurriedly began to recite:

" 'The quality of mercy is not strained. It droppeth as the gentle rain from heaven upon the place beneath: it is twice blest; It blesseth him that gives and him that takes...' " she paused at her mother's reproving glare.

" 'Tis mightiest in the mightiest:' " continued John taking a step toward her. " 'It becomes the throned monarch better than his crown: His sceptre shows the force of temporal power, the attribute, awe and majesty, Wherein doth sit the dread and fear of kings; but mercy is above this sceptred sway; It is enthroned in the hearts of kings, it is an attribute to God Himself; And earthly power doth then show likest to God's When mercy seasons justice.' "

"Well done, Mr. Adams!" Abigail laughed with delight, her shyness in his presence momentarily forgotten. The company clapped -- all but Mrs. Smith.

"I cannot compare my poor memory to yours, Miss Smith, but it was yours which inspired me to learn the most famous courtroom speech written -- so far!"

"A pretty compliment," Mrs. Smith remarked, noting those last ambitious words. He hopes to fly pretty high, she noted. Icarus, too, went above himself and fell. "A very pretty compliment. I shouldn't wonder you are popular with the ladies of Boston."

"Sincerity is never mistaken for merely pretty speech, Madam," John retorted, his temper beginning to fray. "Your daughter earns her compliments."

"Mama! I got the rooster!" Ten-year-old Will burst into the room. "I kilt him and strung him up outside the kitchen door."

"And just how are we meant to have poultry for dinner now?' his father demanded. "Eggs without a rooster do not a chicken dinner make!"

"The boy is learning how to butcher for me, Papa," Mrs. Smith said gently. "We will buy another rooster."

20

"If he was sent out for a chicken, a chicken he should have killed," the Reverend replied, unmoved. "Every other boy his age could have done the job well enough."

His wife's indulgence had begun to make itself apparent in Will's heedlessness.

"Now, Pa," Mrs. Smith murmured, reaching out to stroke Will's tousled blond hair. "He will learn."

Will was a handsome child, with a winning smile, but a cunning way. His father could not admit even to himself that there was something about the boy that he did not trust.

"My mother would have switched me for killing the wrong bird," John Adams remarked, a foolhardy step into family territory.

"Your mother and Will's are not the same woman!" Mrs. Smith informed John.

Abigail, who did not miss the triumphant grin Will shot John, made a silent vow. I will not so spoil my own children.

"I wish Mama could bring herself to like Mr. Adams even a little!" Abigail whispered to Polly that night when they were huddled in their beds listening to the wind whistling through the cracks in the walls.

"She will not be persuaded, I fear." Polly sympathized. Her mind was still on the lingering kiss Richard Cranch had given her just before he had stepped out the door, a promise of more to come.

"Mama shall come to see him as I do - in time," Abigail told the ceiling with quiet certainty.

Despite Mrs. Smith's chilliness, John's visits increased that winter. Two of three evenings during the week, he rode the four miles from Braintree, then came again on Sundays. At the sight of his thick, energetic figure knotting the reins of his horse's bridle Abigail's stomach fluttered. She looked for reasons to be near him, marveling at the electricity she felt at his surreptitious touch.

Her mother's disapproval had tempered - she still did not like John, but had begun to realize that John Adams would not, as she had first surmised, condemn his wife to a life of rural poverty. He had energy as well as ambition. He was willing to work, a quality Elizabeth Smith respected. And, despite his blunt and occasionally pedantic temperament, he had friends.

21

1762

Abigail brushed her brown hair gently then coiled it on top of her head before laying a dimity cap on top, her attempt to make the most of what looks she had been given. The room glowed with late afternoon sun by the time she heard hooves on the hard-packed road. Looking out the window, she watched John dismount and run a languid hand down the animal's neck before hitching it to the post in front of the parsonage. Her breath quickened in sudden memory of last Sunday behind the barn, the warmth of his hand against her back, fingers splayed over her ribs, his mouth pressed greedily on hers. Frightened by her own hungry response, the moment was both forbidden and intoxicating.

She tucked a stray tendril beneath her cap then came down the stairs to meet him at the door. When he stepped inside, instead of his usual clandestine kiss, he carefully withdrew a paper from his breast pocket and handed it to her with a courtly bow. Puzzled, she opened the letter and read:

Miss Adorable   *Octr 4th 1762*
By the same token that the bearer hereof satt up with you last night I hereby order you to give him as many Kisses, and as many Hours of your company after 9 'clock as he shall please to Demand and charge them to my Account: I have a good Right to draw upon you for the Kisses as I have given two or three Millions at least, when one has been received, and in consequence the Account between us is immensely in favour of your, John Adams.

Head still bowed from reading, heart beating so hard she imagined it echoed off the walls, Abigail carefully refolded the letter. Aurelia was the pet name Richard had for Polly; she was usually called Portia, both compliment and challenge. Elizabeth Smith had no patience with these affectations, but the young couples clung to them as private signs of connection. Abigail raised her eyes to fix John with a look of mocking reproof, a blush growing up her throat and spreading across pale cheeks.

"Mr. Adams, Aurelia is engaged to be married, while I am not. How can you imagine you have such a right to draw on me as Mr. Cranch has to draw on Polly?"

"Come, come, Miss Smith. No talk of rights!" he blustered in a half-whisper, eyes sparkling, leaning into her for a repeat of their meeting behind the barn. "You account is in arrears! Time for payment!" He wrapped one thick arm around her waist and drew her close. She could feel his heart thumping against her breast, an intimate rhythm; all that separated their naked bodies was a few layers of clothing.

Shyly, Abigail raised her head and pecked him on the cheek.

"Nay! That will never do! I needs must teach you to settle your accounts!" he whispered hoarsely, pressing full lips on hers.

The soft warmth of his mouth, the smell of horses and leather and the rich tonic of fallen leaves was like a drug. She leaned away, alarmed at the power of her own desire.

"Another," he said softly, hungrily.

"Nabby?" called Reverend Smith from the study. "Is someone there?"

John hastily released Abigail, straightened his waistcoat and smoothed one hand over his wig.

"Yes, Papa," Abigail called, trying to hide her breathlessness. "Mr. Adams has come to pay a call."

"Well bring him in here, Daughter. I wish to ask his opinion on a matter of my sheep."

"Yes, Papa." She leaned toward John again. "Mr. Cranch is in the drawing room with Polly and Mama sorting out the last of the wedding plans. Perhaps we may spend some time with them tonight."

I would as lief have you all to myself," John whispered, laying a possessive hand against her cheek, and leaning toward her again. Her skin tingled where he touched her, but she drew away, struggling to regain her composure.

She led him through the hallway to the dour-faced minister's study. Reverend Smith sat in his chair by the fire, his ledger open on his lap. John had followed Abigail into the room and stood with his hands folded behind his ample rump, waiting for the offer of a chair. After giving him a surreptitious smile, Abigail seated herself demurely beside her father's desk where pages of his partially written sermon spilled over the open Bible like autumn leaves.

"Sit ye down in that chair there, Mr. Adams," said the parson gesturing with his pipe toward an upholstered seat without looking

23

up from his figures, "and let me hear your views on the best way to prevent bloat in my sheep next year."

It pleased Abigail to have her father ask for John's advice. More than proof of respect for John's judgment, it offered hope for one day accepting him as a son-in-law. John sank into the deep chair and self-consciously straightened his clothes. He glanced at Abigail who had closed his note quietly into folded palms.

"Smoke if you wish, Mr. Adams," urged Reverend Smith glancing up momentarily from the ledger where the quill fluttered above columns of figures.

"Thank you, sir, no. I am once again trying to refrain from the use of tobacco," he replied, "though my intentions outstrip my discipline."

"You are not alone in that," Reverend Smith muttered as he closed the book. "Nabby, perhaps you would fetch us a small brandy?"

Without a word, Abigail rose and went out the door, her skirts whispering against the wall. Halfway down the hall, she stopped long enough to tuck John's note into the bosom of her dress, rubbing her hands fondly over the crackling paper, her body aching at the thought of physical contact with John.

Her mother had never spoken of the marriage bed. Never had Abigail seen her parents touch one another, never had either even hinted at what their children's very existence proved -- they had once, if not now, touched, caressed, made love. Or perhaps it had been a mere formality, a piece of physical commerce performed solely to produce children. Had they ever felt such urgency as she and John now felt?

What secrets passed between a man and woman? How did it change them? Polly will know before I do, Abigail thought with envy tinged with fear.

The end of the passage was warm where it opened into the kitchen. Elizabeth Smith sat at the long oak table, leafing through her tattered copy of E. Smith's Compleat Housewife while Maggie stirred the stew. Deftly, Mrs. Smith plucked out receipts, closely written on scraps of paper that she had gathered from friends and family over twenty-three years of marriage. Glancing up, she frowned as she watched Abigail pour out two measures of homemade plum brandy and set the glasses on a tray.

"Who is here?" she asked.

"Mr. Adams. In Papa's study. They are discussing sheep," Abigail explained.

"Sheep! Is Mr. Adams such an authority on sheep?"

"His mother does keep a small flock of her own, Mama," Abigail reminded her.

"Mmm. Susanna Adams is a hard-working woman. I will say that!" Mrs. Smith remarked, holding up a worn paper. "Here, Maggie, lemon cheesecakes. It would be a particular treat. I wonder if we could possibly find lemons this time of year?"

"We could always do with squash, M'am."

Abigail smiled, took up the tray, and went back through the passage. Her mother was happiest when planning a party. Entertaining took her back to the graciousness of her Quincy youth.

When Abigail handed the glass to John, he took it slowly, deliberately moving his fingers over hers before grasping the crystal. She glanced nervously at her father who was poking the fire, apparently unaware. After putting her father's glass beside him on the table, she took up her needlework, an embroidered collar for Mary's trousseau. Contentedly, she listened to the two men talk, only breaking her silence to ask a question or interject an observation. Each time his daughter spoke, Reverend Smith watched John's face, noting with approval the obvious pride the young man took in her intelligence. He knew that Abigail would only be happy with a man who appreciated her mind. While he viewed too much learning as a snare, a path to arrogance, he also knew that an attachment of both mind and heart together could last a lifetime, if not destroyed by broken trust. And, unwillingly, he sensed the physical yearning between them. How little young people know of what is to come in a life, he thought. On what little experience they choose a life's partner. If they knew what we know now... He pushed aside the thought and instead cast his eyes into the fire.

When they finished their brandies, Reverend Smith suggested they go through to the drawing room where Richard and Polly sat huddled close together on the high-backed pew set by the fire.

"I see you are taking advantage of the absence of a chaperone," Smith observed wryly.

Richard smiled, assuming camaraderie rather than rebuke in the remark. "It is chill," he said, still holding Polly's hand. "I have been refining my plans for carrying off Mistress Merry."

"It is hard to lose my eldest child," Mrs. Smith's voice came from the doorway as she entered carrying a brimming tray. "Even if it is to a man as good as Mr. Cranch. But I will still have my Nabby and Betsey to keep me company. And of course my dear, dear Will. I'll not so easily part with them." she shot John a pointed look.

"You cannot and I am sure, would not, detain them forever, Mrs. Smith," John admonished gently.

"Nabby is still only seventeen, Mr. Adams. There is time."

Mary Smith and Richard Cranch were married in Weymouth on a raw winter day in 1762. The church was hushed, all ears straining for the trembling whisper of Mary's voice as she repeated her wedding vows. Reverend Smith performed the sacrament while his wife daubed surreptitiously at her eyes. But her tears were gone by the time the newly married couple went outside to take their leave. Her guests were satisfactorily stuffed with saddle of mutton and venison and a dozen other delicacies. The party, her badge of refinement, had been a success.

Abigail stood in the twilight until she could no longer see the Richard and Mary, silhouetted against the sky as they rode side by side in the trap toward Braintree. An icy wind had sprung up. John took a step closer and reached his arm around her shoulders.

"Mr. Cranch will be a good husband to your sister."

Abigail nodded then sucked in a breath.

"I am only mourning a part of my life gone forever. Mary and I are no longer girls. She is no longer Polly, I no longer Nabby. We are Mary and Abigail now. Everything is changed."

"All things change, my dear," he said softly. "But for every loss, there is gain, too. Mary has exchanged her childhood home for her a home of her own, her childhood family for the one she and Richard will make together. There are joys they will know now that we can still only imagine."

She suddenly resented his presence, the insistence of his ardor. She wanted to be alone with her grief, alone with her fears of what the future held. A man can understand so little of what a woman must face, she thought. He sees only his pleasure, not her pain. She held her back straight, stood stiffly away from him.

The candles were guttering in their sconces by the time they returned to the warmth of the drawing room where the tables were laden with the remnants of the feast. On scattered plates along the tables and walls were a few lemon cheesecakes and dried fruits, and the crumbs of plum pies. Glasses, some still carrying the dregs of ruby-colored punch, sat on every surface. The guests were beginning to leave. Abigail picked up a plate and a glass, one of many borrowed from generous neighbors, and prepared to take them off to the kitchen. John caught her by the wrist.

"Our turn will be next," he whispered.

Fighting an urge to flee, Abigail remained silent.

"Mary, are you all right?" Richard asked anxiously as his wife steadied herself against the door jam. It was October 1763, only three weeks since the difficult birth of their first child, Elizabeth. A long, painful labor had worn down Mary's strength. The baby's head lodged in the birth canal and stayed, despite the midwife's determinedly kneading her fists into Mary's swollen belly. The doctor was summoned, and after slitting the birth opening wider, he reached in with his bare hand, managed to extract the slippery, wizened infant. The sheets, soaked in blood, had taken days to wash.

"I'm all right, Richard," Mary assured him. "Just a little tired. It will take me some time to get my strength back."

"You are up too soon, Mary," Abigail said, leading her sister to a chair at the kitchen table. "You should still be abed. Mr. Adams, pour Mary a cup of ale. It will put color back into her cheeks."

Over Mary's head, she and Richard exchanged concerned glances. Childbed fever had taken off many who survived labor and birth.

"I'm all right, Nab!" Mary sighed. "Don't fuss!"

John handed Mary a cup of homemade beer filled from the pitcher in the middle of the table. She took a long draught then turned a mischievous grin on John. "And when will you two be married?"

"I hope this year. Ah, winter evenings in Braintree," John replied, turning wistful eyes to Abigail. "Perhaps by this time next year, a little Betsey of our own?"

"Mama has not yet consented to the marriage," Abigail reminded him, sharply. "And there are sufficient Betseys in our family for now.

So please do not count our children before their parents have said their marriage vows!"

"She checks me with frowns and satirical speeches," John chuckled, turning to Richard Cranch, who was meticulously reassembling a customer's watch from scattered parts on the table.

"It is a Smith failing," Richard murmured, glancing at his wife.

"You men needs must be checked," Abigail retorted. She longed for marriage to John, but John's constant talk of a houseful of children fed her fears of childbirth and promised to shackle her to a life of drudgery.

"Mother does not wish to let you go, does she?" Mary remarked.

"No. I think not, but she will be persuaded," Abigail replied with a firmness that made John smile. I am perverse, Abigail thought. I want him, yet I fear him. Or perhaps I fear what part of myself will be buried in our union. Is every woman at war with herself?

"Your good mama does not believe an Adams to be worthy of the granddaughter of a Quincy," John observed.

"Perhaps not," Abigail agreed. "But she will yield in the end. You and I are made of tough metal, Mr. Adams. We shall endure."

"You are made of sterner stuff than I," John said, taking her hand in his. "For my part, the waiting is intolerable."

At his touch, all fears of childbirth and the burden of children withered in the heat of desire. Will carnal knowledge bring greater connection? she wondered. Or will it pall? Will he, like so many other men, tire of me and go in search of a new diversion?

"Perhaps Miss Abigail is testing your constancy," Richard mused, pushing aside the watch parts and lighting his pipe. "There was a time when your love changed with the seasons, John."

John was undaunted by his friend's reproof.

"I will be a rock, a mountain," he cried, thumping the table with his fist for emphasis. "Mrs. Reverend Smith and her daughter, Abigail, will see just how constant I am!"

"While you are proving your constancy, you should also be feathering your nest," Richard said. "Family does not come cheap. And Parliament is no help. We shall all have need of money when the crown gets through with us."

The crown had levied two and a half million pounds in taxes on the colonists in an effort to pay for the wars in Europe. The demand fueled bitter resentment among the colonists, a resentment inflamed by the mandate to provide food and sleeping quarters to the additional British soldiers who had been sent to guard the colonists. Many believed they were there not to guard but to intimidate.

"We will manage, Richard." Mary said without conviction.

"It is not only the money," John agreed, taking up Richard's complaint. "It is the principle. We have no representation, no one to voice our concerns and objections. Yet Parliament claims that the colonies have 'virtual representation.' Nonsense! We have none. Even Pitt, a former Prime Minister no less, agrees with us. Did you see the newspapers? He says virtual representation is, and I quote: 'the most contemptible idea that ever entered the head of man.' How does the English Parliament imagine it can continue with this?"

"And yet it does," Richard growled. "They demand money, we pay them. They tell us what to swallow, and we gulp it down. We have little recourse."

"We can refuse to pay," Abigail observed, "as with the Townshend Acts. But I fear this time more severe measures will be used against those who refuse to comply."

"You could be right, my dear," John nodded. "But the demand must be opposed, nonetheless. Yet in as orderly and legal manner as possible."

"There will still be bitter feelings," said Abigail.

"On both sides," agreed Richard. "It will be a long wrestle."

John and Abigail were not married that winter. Mrs. Smith continued to withhold her consent. Instead, in the spring of 1764, John was confined to a Boston boarding house with his brother, Peter, and two other patients enduring the new inoculation treatment against smallpox. The inoculation, made with pus from an infected sore of a recovering smallpox victim, deliberately induced a case of smallpox which, it was hoped, would produce a milder attack than the one left to contagion 'in the natural way.' It was a new and so far effective treatment against a deadly, age-old scourge. The patients who survived developed immunity. And most patients survived.

John had tried to persuade Abigail to join him, but her mother forbade it. She had not seen her daughter through a delicate childhood only to lose her to a deliberately induced infection. Mrs. Smith also suspected that John's urging stemmed from a selfish desire to have Abigail by him at all costs, not from a true concern for her welfare. No argument, no knowledge of Dr. Perkins's so far perfect record had swayed her. Abigail remained with her family in Weymouth, reading John's letters, tobacco-smoked in an effort to disinfect them, which revoltingly detailed each vomit and eruption and ache.

Laying John's latest missive on the table, Abigail took up her quill: Weymouth April 30 1764. Oh God, how much longer must we wait? she thought. Fears of childbirth and enforced domesticity were giving way to a fear of losing him. He was too precious a treasure to risk. How many men would enjoy her caustic wit? How many would ask her opinion on politics? And how many would she burn for? She had seen men, dressed in their finery, and tried to imagine climbing into a bed with them, to have their hands on her, give her body up to them, bear their children. The thought sickened her. Yet she wanted John with a passion that each day grew more insistent. Having watched the quiet joys her sister and Richard shared - the knowing looks, the small touches, the delight in their child - the fruit of their union - Abigail could not bear the thought of spinsterhood.

As she scribbled, the door opened softly and her mother entered. In the waning afternoon light, Elizabeth Smith looked creased, weary.

"May I come in, Nabby?" she asked softly.

"Of course, Mama."

She rose to give her mother the chair.

"Sit, Daughter. You are writing to Mr. Adams?" Mrs. Smith ventured.

"Yes. He says they are all doing pretty well under the circumstances. All their eruptions are filling well. They will have nary a mark."

"Well, that is good news. Pray send him my regards."

Mrs. Smith paused and shifted in the seat.

"Nabby, you have known of my objections to your engagement to John Adams...," she began.

Abigail nodded solemnly. Her heart leapt in a combination of dread and flickering hope at her mother's odd tone.

"It is not only his station, Nabby. His mother, Susanna... you would live side by side with her. She is not an easy woman...and with

30

his father gone, now she can concentrate her full attention on her sons...," Mrs. Smith continued haltingly.

Abigail smiled at her strong-willed mother's criticism of John's equally strong-willed mother.

"You find it amusing, my dear," Mrs. Smith said sharply. "But you do not know the kind of life a wife can lead, the degradation of a mother-in-law who will not release her hold on a son. It is that which I fear -- that and other things."

"What other things?"

Mrs. Smith drew a deep breath.

"You do not know what passes between a man and a woman... what a man.... needs. And what he will do when those needs are not met. A woman whose husband ... demands... can wear herself out in childbearing, while a man who ceases to ask...John would be away much of the time. He likes the ladies, Abigail. He likes their company very much. You would be left to his mother, to the running of everything, with the whole burden on you. He would be gone," she repeated.

"He is gone now, Mama, and our love remains," Abigail said uncomfortably.

"There will be other separations, other... temptations. Love does not always withstand the blows of life's circumstances."

Abigail could not let herself imagine that her mother was speaking from experience, or that her fears applied to the reality of life with John.

Shaken, but determined, she drew herself up.

"Mama, John Adams is not like other men. His principles are strong. And not all love ends. Mr. Shakespeare told of love that..."

"Mr. Shakespeare! Nabby!" her mother cried. "You have lived too long in books. Life does not echo books. Men do not act in accordance with their principles but with their appetites. Even St. Paul knew that a man knows what is right but does wrong anyway. It is a failure not of understanding, but of will. We are frail creatures, Daughter. Men are weak. I would not see you hurt."

Abigail's heart pounded. She knew of bastard children in the village, the whispers behind hands, the speculation on paternity.

"Mama, John has no bastards," she began, blushing to her ears.

"Yet!" her mother murmured. She looked at her daughter's earnest face, the innocent belief in the perfectibility of Man, of her man. Experience is the only real teacher, she thought. "Abigail, however good a man may be, he cannot help being a man. And we are women, the weaker vessel. Do not expect too much of your union. I see the love you bear John Adams. Do not give your heart completely. Hold a piece for yourself."

"Mama, Mr. Adams and I love one another. His love for me is equal to mine for him. Of that I am sure. It is not a simple, young love, but a strong bond that matures with each passing day. You must own we have waited patiently for your blessing, and for his mother's. Do you not think our lives have been difficult these two years? Our love is built not upon fancy, but upon the strongest possible foundation -- mutual respect and genuine affection and friendship. What stronger bonds are there? Surely you remember what it was to be in love and yet to wait."

"I remember well enough. That and more..." she sighed.

Rising, she touched her daughter's cheek with cold fingers. Light played against the walls, darting in and out of the corners as Elizabeth Smith turned and left the room. Abigail knew it was the only blessing she would ever have.

Chapter 3

Imparadis'd in one another's arms
John Milton Paradise Lost Bk IV Line 506

1764

John and Abigail were married by Reverend Smith in Weymouth Parsonage on October 25, 1764. Despite the long anticipation, the wedding was subdued. There had been no frantic sewing of trousseau, no invitations to family and friends, no preparations. Susanna Boylston Adams, the only member of John's family to attend, continually ran possessive hands over John's white satin vest before the ceremony. Her fingers plucked at the golden shafts of wheat she had embroidered, a reminder of her possessive love, a visible sign of her reluctance to let him go. Mrs. Smith remained sphinx-faced throughout the short ceremony, offering her cool cheek to the new bridegroom for a familial kiss.

In stark contrast to the abundant feast that celebrated Mary and Richard's nuptials, the wedding supper Elizabeth Smith had prepared for John and Abigail was spare. Susanna, whose sights for her eldest son had been set on the prosperous and social Quincys, doubly resented the slight the meagerness implied. Toasts were drunk, but there was more obligation than joy in them. Only the Reverend Smith's congratulations rang with sincerity.

Despite their mothers' unhappiness, John and Abigail stood before the minister filled with joy. This moment was a culmination of their three-year wait. Their love had not just endured; it had grown. Their mothers harbored doubts, but John and Abigail did not. Abigail stood straight-backed, chin lifted toward the future as she listened to the words that sealed their covenant. John, who had laid his hand over Abigail's where it rested on his arm, squeezed it now and again during the service, an unconscious right of possession. Even the pitiful meal could not wilt their anticipation of what was to come. When it was finished, they would go home to Braintree. Together.

Finally, they stood at the hitching post to take their leave.

33

Cloaked in red, Abigail stood beside the trap, unsure how to say goodbye. She had stepped off a precipice and into a life that was out of her parents' protective hands, a life she and John, for better or worse, would be responsible for. After hesitating for a few moments, she held out both hands to her father, a tentative smile on her lips.

"Goodbye..." The telltale tremor in her voice brought sudden tears to her mother's eyes.

Reverend Smith coughed, then spoke.

"May God always go with you, Nabby."

"And with you, Papa," she replied, feeling as though her chest would burst.

She heard her mother's swift intake of breath. Elizabeth Smith stood next to her husband, thin arms folded over the shawl wrapped around her shoulders.

"We have relinquished our daughter to you, Mr. Adams," she said with surprising tenderness. "You have the care of our Abigail, now."

"And she of my son," interjected Susanna sharply.

Susanna stood apart from the two Smiths, close to John, barely able to keep herself from clutching at his clothes. Suddenly chilled at the demands this woman could make on her life, Abigail tried to offer an olive branch.

"We will be neighbors, now," she began, carefully choosing her words. "You will see for yourself every day how my love teaches me to look to Mr. Adams' welfare. I can see the concern on both your faces," she continued, her voice growing stronger with conviction as she encompassed both women in her gaze. "Ye need not fear. Our constancy to one another is equal. Ye need not fear its diminishment."

"If love can guarantee its object's happiness, you can leave Abigail Adams in my care," John added patting Abigail's hand.

He handed Abigail up into the trap and climbed in beside her, then slapped the reins smartly on the mare's dappled flanks. The horse started, jerking the buggy on its way back down the road toward Braintree.

As they drove away from the parsonage, John and Abigail fell silent. Susanna Adams was to spend the night with the Smiths. John's brothers, Peter and Elihu, had gone to visit friends. Their new home and the house beside them -- Susanna's --would be empty. They were alone.

It was not until they had passed the pitted granite milestone on the road to Braintree that the reality of their vows hit Abigail. Tonight, for the first time, she and John would share a bed. He would touch her, caress her, and by a husband's right would take her. Now, with a strange mixture of apprehension and hunger, she looked forward to their joining. Her throat felt hot as she imagined John's touch, warm fingers sliding down her neck, her clothes opening, then her body...

As though he read her mind, John turned to her and, holding the reins in one hand, reached his arm around her back. Tenderly, he drew her to him, then kissed her long and greedily on the mouth. The warmth of his lips against hers kindled a fire between her legs. For the rest of the homeward ride, she marked with a thumping heart every tree, every wall that brought them closer to their home.

1765

The July heat was oppressive. The stifling days coupled with the blaze of the cooking fire made the little house at Braintree suffocating.

Cumbersome in her last month of pregnancy, Abigail dragged herself about in sweat-stained clothes, longing for a reprieve. While she feared the pain, the possibility of her own death or that of the child during the birth, she ached for it to be over. She was sick of being pregnant. It seemed unfair that their first few couplings had produced a baby. She wanted time to enjoy their nights alone together, to savor, without the burden of a baby, the naked desire on John's face and her own pleasure as they made love. Instead, she would be confined to a house and a squalling infant while John rode the circuits from town to town.

Although Abigail wanted to have her baby in her own home, in its conception bed while her husband waited below, John was leaving again. He wanted her to wait in Weymouth in case in the baby came in his absence.

"I would not leave you to anyone but your own mother," he had said firmly, "this being your first."

Though Abigail wanted to protest, make some sign of loyalty to

35

her mother-in-law, who had assisted at numerous births, she was relieved at John's insistence.

On the 13th of July, he drove her over the four miles of dusty, hard-packed road to Weymouth. They rode in silence, Abigail clinging to the seat and wincing at each lurch of the carriage. He does not understand what an ordeal this is, she thought miserably. Birth holds few fears for a man awaiting his first son. She was so uncomfortable, she almost wished she had not agreed to go, but when she saw the familiar rust-colored barn emerge from behind the trees, she felt glad to be home. Betsey, now sixteen, rushed out to meet them, babbling excitedly about the coming baby and the new colt Reverend Smith had bought that had thrown fourteen-year-old Will earlier that day.

"Oh DO calm yourself Betsey!" Abigail pleaded, irritated at the chatter. "I'm nearly fainting with the heat!"

"Mama has some lemonade," Betsey said, chastened at the rebuke. Taking Abigail's arm, she led her sister into the house.

The kitchen was cool and dark, the cooking fire a mere smoldering of coals at the back of the hearth.

"Well! I am glad you had the sense to bring our Nabby here, Mr. Adams," said Mrs. Smith when they came through the kitchen door. "I'd hate to think of my daughter being alone when her time came."

Abigail dropped heavily into a chair next to the lemonade and slices of cake Maggie had laid out.

"Mama," Abigail sighed, brushing damp hair off her forehead. "Mother Susanna is a stone's throw from our doorstep. I would certainly not have been alone."

It was exhausting to play the diplomat at every turn.

"Your mother means only that she is glad you will be here with her for the baby's birth. And so am I," John said gently. His look said: Do not tire yourself with trivialities.

"I *am* glad," Mrs. Smith agreed. "Susanna Adams is a capable woman, there is no doubt," she continued, softened by John's conciliatory words, "but you belong with your mother."

Although she liked having the direction of her own home, Abigail was relieved to let her mother take charge of her for now. No work to do, no decisions to make; it felt almost luxurious.

John stayed just one night then left, carefully putting his papers in the small leather bags slung across the saddle. He stuffed into his voluminous coat pockets the ration of bread and cheese and container of ale that Maggie packed for the first leg of the trip. A lump rising in her throat, Abigail watched him as he turned the mare's head north and rode away. When the labor pains started the following day, she wanted to send Will after him, to bring him back, but her mother forbade it.

"John can do no good here, Abigail," she told her daughter practically. "Gone, he can earn your bread and the baby's. Let him go and do what he can. We shall take care of you and your child."

It was a hard delivery. The birth was premature; the child was weak. Abigail lay stretched on the bed, bathed in sweat while Mrs. Smith rolled up the bloody sheets. Fearing the infant would die before she could be cleansed of original sin, Reverend Smith hastily wrapped his tiny, mewling granddaughter in a light blanket, carried her downstairs, and across the road to the meeting house where he christened her: Abigail Smith Adams. Having done what he could, he brought her back -- to let her die, he thought. But the baby refused to die. She clung to life with a will. And on the 1st of August, John returned to drive his family back home.

The ride back to Braintree together -- husband, wife and now child -- confirmed their marriage. The baby was visible proof of their carnal union. I am a whole woman now, Abigail thought, sun prickling on the back of her neck. She shielded tiny Nabby's face from the glare with the embroidered linen handkerchief her mother had given her. Now I am part of the march of generations.

Heat shimmered off the road. Beside her, John was crimson, despite the broad-brimmed hat. Perspiration ran from beneath his wig and dripped off his chin. When they reached the top of the rise, she could see the two saltbox houses sitting cheek by jowl like two confiding old aunts. Sun glinted off the flecks of mica in the stone wall that fronted the road. The zinnias that peeked overtop looked wilted.

Despite its proximity to John's mother, Abigail loved her house. She loved the barns, the outbuildings and privy, the single shared well, and the workshop where John's father had once made harnesses, shoes, leather breeches, and aprons for the surrounding villagers before the epidemic of 1759 had swept him away.

As John drove the carriage around behind the two houses,

Abigail felt a sudden maternal possessiveness of all that she could see. Laundry hung limp in the still air. The straw-stuffed ticking from their bed hung out an upstairs window. The herb beds, planted in neat thatches not far from the kitchen door, sprouted with gray-green sage and a shower of dainty camomile. In a far building a hammer clanged against an anvil -- John's youngest brother Elihu pounding a horseshoe into shape. The picket fence that separated the two yards showed bare spots. Perhaps brother-in-law Peter would paint it for her, she thought, mentally taking charge of the house again. She knew he could use the money.

Rachel, the servant girl Abigail had hired over her mother-in-law's irritated protests, crouched over the garden rows, her skirts spread wide about her like the blossom of a huge poppy. Deftly, she yanked carrots and snipped greens, flinging them into a basket at her side. She looked up when she heard the sound of the wooden wheels and gave Abigail a delighted wave.

John halted the horse and cart at the post beside the well and tied the reins to it. Reaching up, he took the baby and held it close while Abigail gingerly climbed down. Abigail took the baby and walked slowly into the house, grateful for John's steadying arm. With one hand, she untied the ribbons of her bonnet and flung it onto the kitchen table, then ran the handkerchief over her sticky forehead. Rachel came in with her basket of vegetables and a pail of water. Dropping her burdens at the door, she came over to peer at the baby's face, cooing.

"Favor's her papa already, eh. Mrs. A?"

"Yes, I think so too," Abigail smiled.

John beamed, and went to the table to pour a mug of beer from a sweat-beaded pitcher. The rocker that Reverend Smith had brought when he first learned of his daughter's pregnancy sat near the open window. Abigail eased herself down into it, unlaced her bodice with relief, and began to nurse the baby. Rachel stood at the table, washing greens in a basin.

Abigail watched Nabby's little face as it screwed itself up to take the milk. How fragile is the vessel that holds a life, she marveled.

"How much of the washing has been done?" she asked after a few minutes.

"Not as much as you'd a wanted, I fear," Rachel replied. "But I've had me hands full with the preservin' and tendin' the garden and such."

"Have you made any hard cider for Mr. Adams' morning tankard?"

"No 'm. We still have two more jugs and you're so partic'ler about it, I thought I'd better wait til you could see to it yourself. It's nice to have you back," she added.

"Thankee," Abigail smiled. "How many crocks of pickle and such do we have put up?"

"Ten of pickle -- purple cabbage, green walnuts, barberries, elder, mushroom, one of fish that old Mr. Corwell brought us one day last week when he heard about the babe's birth, and some cucumbers," the girl recited, squinting at the ceiling as she mentally ticked off the list. "There are about six of fruit out there and I've done another three of preserves."

"Good. We need to make some more cheeses," Abigail said, wincing as the baby pulled on her nipple. "Have ye dried any dill?"

Rachel nodded.

"Good. That will add good flavor to the cheese."

"I'll bring down the cradle," John said, watching his wife and child with satisfaction. "It will be much easier to sit by the window for a bit and mind her here will it not?"

Abigail nodded. John gulped down his ale and headed for the front stairs.

"Would you take a cool mug, Mrs. A?" Rachel asked pointing with her knife toward the jug. "I'll have dinner ready afore long."

They could hear John upstairs, clattering over the bare floors. He likes being a father, Abigail thought -- son or daughter it makes no difference. A crash echoed through the house as the cradle hit the wall halfway down the sharp turn of the stair. It was not until she went to bed that night that she saw the gouge he had taken out of the plaster.

The baby stopped suckling. Abigail looked down. Nabby was asleep, little lips parted. A droplet of milk stood on the rim of her mouth. Her face was just beginning to lose the puckered look of birth. Still, she was so tiny. In a rush of emotion, Abigail felt suddenly weighted by the responsibility of this new life. Gently bringing the child to her shoulder, Abigail burped her, then laced up her bodice.

"Oh! " Rachel cried, hands suddenly frozen over the wooden

trencher into which she was tearing lettuce. "Mrs. Susanna wanted to come over right away you came home. She's prob'ly right now peering out her windows to catch a glimpse, but I told her you'd be tired. It's not like she hasn't seen her granddaughter yet. Rode out to Weymouth every day, didn't she?"

John thumped through the narrow hallway, then brought the cradle into the room, carrying it like a bale of hay and dropping it onto the floor at Abigail's feet. She frowned. Men make such a clatter. She laid the sleeping baby in the cradle, and pulled the gauze over the rim to protect Nabby from flies.

"My mother-in-law would be mightily put out to be denied a first glimpse of her new granddaughter the day she comes home to Braintree," Abigail observed, her voice low to keep from disturbing the baby.

"That she would," John agreed. "I'll go next door and tell her she must come to welcome her first grandchild home!"

When Susanna came through the door, her face was unreadable. "Where's the child?"

Abigail pointed to the cradle. The older woman leaned down and lifted the gauze to gaze raptly at the little face. Nodding as she laid the netting back in place, she straightened and thrust her hands into her apron pockets.

"She's Adams all over!" she pronounced with satisfaction.

Abigail felt oddly resentful of being denied any part in her own flesh, but held her tongue.

"Abigail," Susanna ventured, turning the name over in her mouth like a bad taste. "It's likely to be mighty confusing to have two in one household. You couldn't have thought of a different name?"

"Such as Susanna?" Rachel muttered.

Susanna shot her a sharp glance.

"We will call her Nabby," John put in hastily, diverting his mother's resentment at having no part in the naming of the child. "There will be no confusion."

Susanna snorted and glared at Rachel.

"I've had to stay right *at* this girl to get her to work at all!" she told Abigail. "If I hadn't, you'd have been payin' her to set here the whole time you were away!"

"I thank you for attending to my household in my absence,"

Abigail told her mother-in-law, "but I am home now and can manage for us."

Her tone was quiet, but the command behind it was unmistakable.

"Well!" Susanna burst out. "I know when I'm not wanted!"

"Ma!" John cried, reaching a hand out to stop his mother, who had turned for the door.

"You are always welcome in our home," Abigail said to Susanna's back. " I pray that our daughter may be as close to her grandmother as I was to mine."

Susanna stopped for a moment and turned to look Abigail full in the face. There had been hard words between them over the past year. The adjustment on both sides had been difficult. But Abigail was determined to win Susanna's love and respect without losing her home in the process.

Carefully, Susanna assessed the young woman who had taken her son away. A son is a son 'til he takes him a wife.... Well, this girl's a match for my John, she conceded, and she will not stand in the way of his success. Yet he is still my John.

"I wish that as well," she said finally. "I would always have open doors between our homes. My grandchildren will be ever welcome under my roof."

Susanna turned at the door, and, shooting Rachel a triumphant look, marched back across the yard to her house.

Watching the older woman go, Rachel shook her head, but said nothing.

"What's for dinner?" John asked, ignoring the small drama that had just unfolded. He pecked Abigail on the cheek before dropping into a chair at the table.

"Sal'magundi." Rachel replied. "I thought a cool meal would be welcome after that dusty ride."

"Good," he said, pouring another mug of ale and holding it up in toast to Abigail. "Mrs. Adams, it is very good to have you home again!"

"No better than it is to be home, I assure you," Abigail smiled.

She had survived the birth. And the baby was -- so far -- alive if not thriving. Thank God for those most basic of blessings, she thought. She looked across the table at John. Sprawled in the chair, feet stuck out like a foundered horse, he looked utterly at ease with himself and his life.

"I have sorely missed hearing of your doings and your days, Mr. Adams," she said.

"And I have sorely missed your listening ear and good council, my dear," John replied affectionately, taking another swig from the mug. "In fact, I wish your opinion on a dissertation I am writing now. It is on canon and feudal law. I hope to have it published when I finish."

He will do fine things, she thought proudly. I have married well.

"Tell me about it, Mr. Adams."

"I want to make Parliament see they have no authority to tax the colonies without our consent. I cannot decide whether to sign my name or to publish it anonymously. What do you think?"

"I had better read it before I give my answer," she replied. "Does it touch on that infernal Stamp Act? I warrant that thing will succeed only in hurting trade. I doubt it will raise the revenue the Crown anticipates."

"Very perceptive, my dear. It is a wonder to me that Parliament failed to notice!" he snorted.

Rachel put a salad and two plates on the table. She bustled around the steamy kitchen, slicing a loaf of fresh, hot bread and lining up thick slabs of it on a plate beside a mound of fresh-churned butter. Going to the cupboard, she returned to plop down a dish of half-congealed raspberry preserves as Abigail came to the table and gingerly sat down.

"I like listening to you talk," Rachel said approvingly, hands on hips. "It always makes me feel so... I don't know... like I'm part of what's goin' on in the world. I wouldn't know half what's happenin' if it warn't for listening to you."

Abigail frowned.

"You are never to speak a word of what Mr. Adams, or anyone else in this house says to anyone else, Rachel. Is that clear?" she said, fear sharpening her words.

"Oh, yes'm! Sartinly, Mrs. A!" Rachel cried, anxious to reassure her mistress. "I'd sooner cut off me own ear than betray what's not mine to speak of, that's for sure."

Abigail hoped the girl spoke the truth, but she was growing wary of the times. "You have not told me of your last foray into Boston, Mr. Adams. What effect has the Quartering Act had?"

"The Quartering Act! " John spluttered, nearly losing a mouthful of lettuce. "I lately have wondered what lunatics occupy Parliament." He stabbed savagely at a piece of venison. "The Stamp Act taxes our every transaction. Now, the Quartering Act invades our very homes. If the crown needs quarters for its soldiers, let it rent barracks, warehouses. We should not be forced to open our homes to them. Parliament seems to have forgotten that we too, are Englishmen with Englishmen's rights. How can they be so shortsighted?" He had begun to shout in his vehemence. Abigail nodded agreement but put a finger to her lips.

"The New York Assembly has defied the act," he continued more softly, using the skewered meat on his fork to emphasize his points. "Massachusetts has called for an inter-colonial congress. It is scheduled for some time in fall. What this will bring in response from the Prime Minister, I do not know. But I do know this: We must fight the battle in the courts and the legislature -- not only to show Parliament that we as British subjects have a great respect for His Majesty's laws, but to be certain that we retain our right as Englishmen. It is the only way!" he concluded, stuffing the piece of venison into his mouth.

"I quite agree!" Abigail said vehemently. "Is that part of your dissertation? I must read it as soon as you have finished!"

He shall make a name for himself and for his family, she thought. But we shall not be safe.

They fell silent as they finished their meal while Rachel took the meat from the bones of a stewed pullet.

Chapter 4

Pandemonium, city and proud seat of Lucifer
John Milton Paradise Lost Bk X Line 424

1768

John's practice was steadily growing along with his stature in the community. In 1766, he was elected selectman, a gratifying vote of confidence from his friends and neighbors. His family was growing, too. His second child, John Quincy, had been born in July of 1767. This time, Abigail stayed in Braintree for the birth. Susanna and a midwife assisted. Abigail appreciated her mother-in-law's calm, sure hand. Though she was not deaf to the sharp tongue that still lashed at her occasionally, she knew that the implacable love Susanna bore John had begun to envelope her as well -- if only because she was the mother of John's children.

John still kept his office in the house, a matter of economy. But he sometimes worried that it did not reflect his growing position. Sitting on one side of the door, consulting a client, he could hear distracting, undignified clumpings on the other side.

Undignified or not, Abigail was happy to have John close. As he built up business in the community, he rode less often around the circuits. Yet she knew they could grow too comfortable in Braintree amidst the familiar -- the land disputes, the arbitration between contentious neighbors, the writing of titles and deeds. It was good and necessary work, but unchallenging. They both had bigger plans. Abigail had begun lately to speak of Boston.

"You must be nearer the hub of events, Mr. Adams," she told him. "No one ever made themselves heard from the provinces."

Her prodding fueled his ambition. In April of 1768, John and Abigail moved their growing family to a house on Brattle Square.

The day they left Braintree for Boston was warm, threatening a spring storm. The budding trees stood in sharp relief against a roiling, slatey sky. Rachel, and the Adamses new hired man, Joseph, had been sent ahead two weeks earlier to turn the Brattle Street house into a home fit to receive the family. John's brothers, Peter and Elihu, had left off their chores to give the couple a proper goodbye, helping to load the last boxes of flour and apples into the back of the wagon while John tied down the barrels of salt beef and butter.

Grim-faced and stiff, Susanna stood beside her new husband, John Hall. Mr. Hall had come into the household like a phantom, molding himself to his wife's life as completely as a well-worn suit of clothes.

When everything was ready, John leaned down to say goodbye to his mother, surreptitiously wiping a tear from the corner of her eye with his thumb. Abigail had climbed aboard the wagon holding nine-month-old John Quincy, named for her beloved Grandfather Quincy who had died at Mount Wollaston the very day of his great-grandson's birth, while Mr. Hall helped Nabby, nearly three, to scramble up beside her mother.

"G'bye, Gammar," the little girl lisped to Susanna, raising a small, fat hand in solemn salute.

Susanna Adams nodded briefly to her beloved granddaughter, rough hands thrust resolutely into her apron pockets. Though she has never acknowledged it, Abigail had been true to her word, generously sharing her children and her home. Now, that would all be gone. No more little feet running up to the back door with a handful of wildflowers, no more evenings together watching the sunset over the hills while she and Abigail rocked the children together. Another tear welled up at the image that absence conjured. Angry with herself at the sentiment, Susanna pushed the thought away like a dirty rag and lifted her square chin to look Abigail in the eye.

"I will miss my neighbors," she said brusquely. She could not bring herself to utter the words her heart cried: "You have a been a good daughter."

"I will miss you as well, Mother Adams," Abigail said, not trusting herself to say more to the woman she had come to love and respect despite their differences.

John had climbed up beside his family and taken up the reins. Peter and Elihu shuffled their feet aimlessly, kicking at little clods of damp earth. After a moment's awkward silence, Mr. Hall stepped forward and slapped the near horse's rump to send them on their way.

"May God be w'ye!" he cried, waving as the team jolted forward.

Neither John nor Abigail looked back as they started at a slow trot along the winding dirt road.

"You agree we are doing the right thing?" John finally asked his wife as the twin Adams houses fell out of sight behind a hill.

"Without doubt, Mr. Adams," Abigail nodded, wiping away the tears, which had begun to trickle down her cheeks. "Boston is where you belong, and your family belongs with you."

Reassured, John rode the rest of the ten miles in silence.

As they reached the crest of the last hill, Boston came into full view. The harbor was spread out before them, a broad, flat expanse of blue dotted with rocky islands. Two ships ghosted in on the late afternoon zephyr. Several others lay at anchor, riding with prows pointed into an outbound current. Wharves and warehouses lined the shores, and the white spire of the Old North Church rose above the roofs like a bony finger pointing the way to heaven.

"Will we be there soon, Par?" Nabby asked plaintively.

"Soon, Chick." He patted her tousled head.

"I hope Rachel has remembered to get milk into the spring house against our arrival," Abigail worried as she offered little Johnny a breast.

The large brick house faced on Brattle Square near the prestigious Anglican Brattle Church. Although the house was whitewashed and Rachel carefully closed the shutters each morning to keep out the sun, Abigail suffered from the heat. She was in the early stages of her third pregnancy. Her life, despite their move to Boston, was becoming what she had most feared. Drudgery. The children required constant attention; their trivial yet vital cares and obligations drained her. But she minded it less than she had anticipated. The joy of seeing Nabby learning to recognize letters and put their sounds together into words, the look of adoration on little Johnny's face as she fed him, the thought that she had in her hands the power to mold their lives -- these things now held more pleasure for her than she had once imagined.

Yet it was hard. Having left his growing practice in Braintree, John was forced to return to riding the circuits to support them. Gone for weeks at a time, he came home for only one or two days together, filled with stories of the cases he had won and lost, and burdened with news of the growing struggle between the colonies and Parliament. The conversations of politics and philosophy were lost in the tumult of clamoring children and overseeing servants' chores. Abigail missed the Braintree days when he was always in the next room, when his conversation at dinner encompassed law, politics, and the future of their lives. She missed their families, the companionship of her mother-in-law and quiet Mr. Hall, and the regular visits to and from her sisters and parents. Yet she felt a thrill at the bustle of Boston, at the sights her family in Weymouth and Braintree would know about only through her letters.

Men reeled by at all hours, bawling drunken songs on their way home from the taverns. Carts bearing all manner of humanity rolled by their door. Some were laden with the wares of traveling salesmen. Others were filled with smuggled goods, their contents sold on side streets in low voices. Carriages passed, the wheels rolling on dry, oaken shafts, the brittle sound echoing off the houses in the surrounding square. Horses' hooves clopped on the paving stones and the sound of heavy, leather-soled shoes could be heard rushing purposefully past the front windows.

Then in July, there was a new sound that heralded a new time -- the slap of hands on rifle stocks and the dull thud of leather boots on the grass. British soldiers were drilling on Brattle Square. For a week, shouted orders woke little Johnny from his afternoon naps. Holding the screaming child, Abigail would croon softly and squint through the slats of the shutters at the soldiers, sweat-soaked in their woolen uniforms, who marched in phalanx back and forth across the green below.

Summer 1768

Abigail sat at the little scrivener's table in her bedroom writing a letter to her mother. Little John Quincy lay asleep under the fly netting in the cradle beside her, starting in his sleep at each shouted order below. As she paused, pen in mid-air, Abigail heard a door slam and the sound of feet pounding up the stair. When John burst into the room, the baby's eyes flew open, but for only second. Automatically, he put his thumb in his mouth, and, still asleep, began sucking contentedly. Seeing the child, John beckoned to Abigail who followed him from the room, closing the door.

"I did not expect you from Plymouth 'til tomorrow," she

whispered as they went down the front stairs.

"Why did you not write me? What are they doing there?" John cried, his voice rising.

"Shh! 'Tis hard enough to get the baby to sleep! The soldiers arrived the day after you left. Did you not receive my last letter?"

"I don't know -- no letter made mention of His Majesty's troops in our yard," John said, trying to keep his voice low. Abigail led him into the parlor.

"You must not have received it then. I told you what I could. They drill morning and night without pause. It drives us all to distraction."

"No doubt. And what response has there been in the town? What do Cousin Sam and Mr. Hancock say?"

"I have seen no one. Rachel has been to the shops, but we are otherwise shut up in the house. I write to friends, and tend children, and wait for a husband who comes solely to shout and talk politics!" she cried, her voice rising. "Mr. Adams, a moment, please, for your wife who has missed you."

"Oh, my dear!" John said, immediately contrite. "I have sorely missed you and the chicks!"

He swept her into his thick arms and held her close despite the heat. The dust from his clothes nearly made her sneeze, but she sank into his embrace gratefully, and laid her head on his shoulder.

"Have you found another girl yet, my dear?" he asked, finally.

"No," she said without raising her head. "I am afraid there is very little to choose from. The girls who apply to my advertisements are either too young or women of such character that I would not have them in the house. One even arrived drunk!"

"I see," he said, only half listening to her as he cupped a hand around her enlarging belly.

"You need not take liberties, Mr. Adams!" Abigail said sharply, breaking away from him. "I will find someone before December. We will need help only after the baby comes. Come tell me about your week," she said, turning to walk down the dim passage to the back of the house.

"Do you realize I am coming to be known as one of Boston's foremost lawyers?" John boasted from behind her.

"And did I not tell you it would be so?" she responded without looking back.

In the kitchen, three-year-old Nabby perched on a tall stool watching Rachel roll out molasses cookies on the pastry cloth. Surreptitiously, the child snatched a piece of dough and crammed it into her mouth.

"You will ruin your supper, my girl!" Abigail said sharply to Nabby who dropped her arms at her sides and stared at the floor, but continued to chew her cookie dough. "And what have you to say to your father?"

"Par!" Nabby burst out when she caught sight of John. Running to him, she threw fat little arms up to be picked up and cuddled.

John chuckled and swung Nabby up to his chest. Grasping his collar, she planted a gummy kiss on his cheek.

"We're makin' gingermen, Par!" she crowed.

"So I see, Chick. There looks to be more on your face than in the oven!"

John replaced Nabby on the stool, poured himself a mug of beer from a pitcher on the pantry shelf then returned to lean against the door jamb farthest from the fire. He swigged the cool ale, and pulled out a large, dirt-streaked handkerchief to wiped his face.

"I nearly forgot," he said, extracting a folded paper from his pocket. "I have a missive from Mrs. Warren."

"And how is she?" Abigail asked taking the letter John held out to her.

Mercy Otis Warren, sixteen years Abigail's senior, had become a treasured friend. Her poetry, published anonymously, had first caught John's attention. A laudatory letter from John to the publisher had eventually reached the author, Mercy Warren, sister to his friend the firebrand lawyer James Otis. Mercy and John had begun a correspondence that eventually produced a standing invitation for John to stay at the Warren house whenever he rode to Provincetown on circuit court business. It had not been long before Mercy and Abigail had developed a confiding friendship through their own correspondence.

"Mrs. Warren is well, though as opinionated as ever!" John chuckled.

"And how are her sons?" Abigail asked as she broke the seal.

John drank the last of his beer and poured himself another before answering.

"She is beginning to worry over Winston's drinking. She worries too, about her brother, James..." he glanced at Rachel who gave no indication she was listening.

He left the kitchen and stepped out the back door, waiting for Abigail to follow. She had opened the letter and was scanning down the page as she slowly came out to stand beside him.

"She mentions none of this," she said with a mixture of surprise and hurt.

"I think she had no intention of saying anything to me, my dear, but my presence and her worries coincided."

"Her worries are the same as mine," Abigail said, still stung by Mercy's withholding a confidence that had been shared with John. "How can an unschooled woman teach children without the help of their father?"

"You are hardly unschooled, my dear. Well, perhaps unschooled but certainly not uneducated. Your reading would daunt half of Harvard's best graduates."

His voice trailed off, and he rubbed his forehead. His eyes held a faraway look.

"Mr. Adams, you are not listening to me," Abigail observed with annoyance. "Where are your thoughts?"

He turned to look her full in the face.

"Things are hotting up, my dear. I don't like it. Those troops," he said, gesturing toward the front of the house, "are sent as a threat. Governor Bernard must have requested Parliament to send them since he and the Boston legislature have been so much at odds over the Townshend Acts. It is a struggle for control. I don't like it."

He looked at Abigail's pale, oval face. Droplets of perspiration meandered down her forehead beneath her white linen cap. Smiling, he took her chin in one hand, and drew her mouth to his. Abigail yielded to his gentle pressure and they stood together on the step in a soft, lingering kiss. She imagined their urgent lovemaking that night, sticky, frantic, hungry. It was no wonder she had had three pregnancies in as many years.

"I miss you very much while I am away," he murmured.

"No more than you are missed, my dear friend," she replied and held her mouth up for another kiss.

"Abigail," John said presently. "Jonathan Sewall is leaving his post as Advocate General of the Court of the Admiralty."

"I know, Mr. Adams. It was one of the things I wrote to you in that letter that miscarried. It has been rumored that you will be asked to take his place," Abigail said, watching his face for reaction.

John frowned and rubbed his chin with one hand.

"It could be a very great honor," he said thoughtfully, almost to himself. "Or, it could be an attempt by the Governor to drive a wedge between me and Cousin Sam and James Otis. Our writings are a threat to him. The Governor contends that we foment rebellion, when all *I* want is an Englishman's justice." She noted that he had not remarked on what Sam Adams and James Otis might want. "I do not like the idea of being muzzled. And, at the moment, I have a good practice, and I am free to defend whom I choose. But it is nonetheless a tempting position. Good pay, and a step up the ladder. I have mouths to feed. I must give it a good deal of thought before I am asked -- *if* I am asked," he added ruefully.

After supper, John had a bath in the tin tub by the hearth. By the time he entered the parlor where Abigail rocked John Quincy in the cradle her father had given her and Nabby played toss on the floor, John was nearly asleep on his feet.

"I see Nabby delivered your pipe," Abigail observed.

"She did," John nodded, drawing on it as he flopped into his favorite chair by the empty hearth.

"Mr. Hancock has been pestering me about your return, Mr. Adams. He wishes words with you." Abigail frowned.

"You do not like Mr. Hancock, do you, Wife?"

Abigail glanced at Nabby, apparently absorbed in the objects she had scattered across the bare floor.

"Little pitchers," she warned, shaking her head.

"Do you have big ears, Chick?" John asked Nabby. The child lifted an adoring gaze to her father.

There was a sharp rap on the front door and John hauled himself to his feet, went into the hallway and opened the broad oak door. John Hancock, a mischievous look dimpling his cheeks, stood outside.

"Speak of the devil and he doth appear!" John chuckled, standing back so that Hancock might pass. "Come in, come in! We are in the parlor. Have a glass of ale with me, I can offer no punch tonight, I fear."

The two men walked into the spacious room, lit, now that the

51

sun had set, by several flickering candles. As the door opened, Abigail rose and gathered up the sleeping baby. Taking up the candle beside her, she spoke softly to Nabby.

"Come Child. It is time for bed."

"Mrs. Adams," John Hancock bowed and spread a vacuous smile across his face.

"Mr. Hancock. You must excuse me as I have to put my babes to bed. Do sit."

"Mama! No! I don't want to go to bed! I want to stay with Par!" Nabby wailed.

"Hush, Child! You will wake your brother. You will say goodnight to Par like a lady. Now collect your toys and come!"

Nabby, rising reluctantly, did as she was told, then followed her mother out into the hall.

"Mrs. Adams, would you send Rachel in with something to drink?" John called after her.

"Of course," she replied without looking back.

Holding the dozing baby, Abigail trudged up the stairs behind Nabby. She opened the door to the nursery, and laid the candle on the dresser. After putting Johnny in his cradle and drawing the netting over top, she turned wearily to her daughter and began undressing her for bed. The child offered no resistance and stood quietly on the stool before the washstand to have her face and hands cleaned. She was a sweet-tempered little thing, Abigail thought, contrite at the resentment she felt over her children's constant care. Rachel opened the door softly and peered into the dim room.

"I thought I heard your step on the stair, Mrs. A. Do you want me to do that?"

"No, thankee, Rachel. Go draw two mugs of cider for Mr. Adams and Mr. Hancock. I'll be down presently. Oh, and draw me a drink -- from the well, mind, so it will be cool."

"Yes'm. 'G'night, my little one," Rachel said softly to the child who climbed off the stool to give the young servant a hug.

Abigail tucked her daughter in bed and smoothed wispy hair around the sweet, plump face, so like John's. As she did every night, she asked: "Shall we say your prayers together?"

The child nodded, struggling to keep her blue eyes open. Heavily, Abigail lowered herself to her knees beside the cot and folded her hands. Nabby laced stubby fingers in imitation of her mother and closed her eyes. By the time the Lord's Prayer was finished, Nabby was breathing in soft, even rhythm, her hands still folded together on the top of the light coverlet.

Abigail pushed herself to her feet again. The heat coupled with her pregnancy tired her unmercifully. She dragged herself through the last hours of each day by sheer force of will. Descending the stairs, she paused outside the parlor door. The voices were low, calm. Nothing untoward, Abigail thought, relieved. When she entered, the two men rose, each holding an earthenware mug.

"Mr. Hancock has come to ask me to defend him against a suit the crown has brought against him," John said.

"I see," she said not looking at Hancock.

"You see, Mrs. Adams, there is some problem over my ship, the *Liberty*, and its cargo. The crown and I disagree," John Hancock explained, eyes glimmering.

"Oh?"

John thought Abigail suddenly looked very like her mother about to deliver a caustic remark.

"Yes, you see..." Hancock began again, but John cut him off.

"I have only just this afternoon returned, John," he said hastily, "and am weary from travel. Forgive me if I beg leave to speak with you tomorrow."

Realizing he was being dismissed, Hancock rose graciously, smiled, and laid his mug on the table.

"Remember what I said, John," Hancock said, playing unconsciously with his hat as he turned toward Adams. "I will pay handsomely for the best lawyer in Boston."

Adams smiled with pleasure at the flattery and followed Hancock into the hall to see him out. When he returned he noted that Abigail's grim expression had not altered.

"You might be a little more hospitable to Mr. Hancock," he admonished, realizing he was in all likelihood stirring a hornet's nest that would send off a battalion of stings. "Hancock can pay my fees in coin not chickens."

"He is a smuggler and a dandified opportunist," she retorted. "And I do not wish him to feel freely welcome in this house."

"John is not a bad sort. And," he reminded her, "there are many others whom you like who are also involved in smuggling, or so it is rumored."

"And what exactly does he want you to do?" she asked, ignoring his rebuke.

"The crown has brought him up on charges of smuggling. He wants me to defend him. He says I am the best lawyer in Boston. AND he will pay me well for my services."

"He flatters you to secure your help," she said sourly, taking up her mending. "You *are* the best lawyer in Boston, but he said that to coax your vanity into saying yes."

"Ah, Abigail! You are one in a thousand!" John burst out, jumping up from his chair and embracing his wife with a laugh. He would never be at the complete mercy of the slings and arrows of fortune with Abigail to guard his flank.

"You have already decided to defend him, have you not, Mr. Adams?" Abigail asked, stolidly squirming from his grasp.

She still had no love of needlework, but the economy of mending was necessary. And renewing something appealed to her frugal Yankee temperament. John chuckled and nodded an affirmative. She shook her head with a frown.

"Then you have also decided to decline the appointment to Advocate General?"

"Should I be asked," he reminded her, a smile playing around his mouth.

"Should you be asked," she acceded.

"Yes, I suppose I have. Do you believe I am making a mistake?" he asked, looking at her seriously.

"Not at all. I think you could only be happy with the freedom to support causes you think right. But about Mr. Hancock..."

"Let's hear no more of Mr. Hancock tonight," he broke in with an affectionate smile. "After all, I have been away a whole week. Are we not entitled to time alone without Mr. Hancock interrupting?" He nuzzled her and slid his hand slowly down her neck. "Let us go up to bed."

Chapter 5

Nor love thy life, nor hate; but what thou liv'st, Live well.
John Milton Paradise Lost Bk XI Line 553

1769

In the spring of 1769, the Adamses moved to a white clapboard house in quiet, maple-lined Cole Lane to escape the noise of Brattle Square. It was a year of struggle and fear. Boston's temperature was rising. The Sons of Liberty brawled in the streets with anyone whose sympathies they found suspect. A sailor, accused of being a British spy, was tarred and feathered then burned alive in Brattle Square. The brutality sickened John and Abigail. John was determined to be a voice of reason amidst the mad storm.

Early that year he had managed to get the charges against John Hancock dropped. Then he defended four sailors accused of murdering a British lieutenant in charge of an impressment party. Both cases were fought on the "right" side -- the revolutionary side. But, in the name of blind justice, John was just as ready to defend those opposed to the Sons of Liberty. While Abigail cheered his principles, she feared the retribution of the mob.

John and Abigail's third child, Susanna Adams, born in December of 1768, was so sickly she could still not walk by her first birthday. Simply feeding her required hours of patient labor, while Nabby and Johnny, bursting with health, shrieked up and down the stairs in rambunctious play. Exhausted with the move, the children, and the worry over John's safety, Abigail struggled to parcel out her waning strength. In December of 1769 she realized that she was three months pregnant with her fourth child. Strained to her limit, she hoped perhaps she would miscarry, a greater possibility, she thought, when Baby Susanna came down with a cough and intermittent fever, but even as she trudged up and down the stairs, exhausted, she watched her belly grow.

1770

At her desk, Abigail took the quill from the inkwell. 4th Feb.

Snow hissed through the bare branches outside. Inside, despite the flames that leapt up the back of the fireplace like shimmering woodland sprites, the room was cold.

The cradle that held Susanna sat close to the fire. Abigail had held her most of the day, rocking and soothing until the child dropped into a fretful sleep. Susanna's occasional gasps and moans were indistinguishable from the crackling fire, but her periodic spasms of coughing echoed hollowly through the room. The sound made Abigail's stomach lurch. The doctor had been no help. He recommended leeches, but Abigail, rebelling against what her instinct said was cruel, forbade it. Together she and Rachel had tried every remedy, every potion and tonic to no avail.

Homesick, nearly crushed with care, Abigail felt trapped in the constancy of motherhood. A woman's lot, she told herself with what she knew was an unholy measure of resentment. I must bear up. Letters to and from Mary, struggling to raise her own small family on Richard's meager income, helped. Writing was an exercise of intellect in a life sadly devoid of it. Abigail dipped the pen again.

A tiny, mournful cry escaped the baby's lips. Putting the pen back in the well, Abigail rose, crossed the room, and crouched down to peer into the cradle.

She listened to Susanna's rasping breath, like a far-distant saw on dry wood. Now I understand my mother's clinging, she thought.

Little Susanna smelled of the camphor rub Rachel had smeared on her thin chest at suppertime. When Abigail knelt, the baby's eyes opened and fixed on her. More than the coughing and the crying, this mute supplication tore at Abigail's heart. Susanna's trust was silent condemnation.

Despite the danger of sparks, Abigail shifted the cradle closer to the fire and rocked it, humming. The little head moved gently back and forth until the eyes closed again. Rising heavily, Abigail rubbed her swelling belly and said a swift prayer for the health of this new life growing unbidden in her womb. She felt clumsy and confined.

She thought of her cousin, Isaac Smith, in London for nearly three months. They had grown up side by side.

He now explores the world, walks in stimulating company. We were destined from birth for such different things, and only because of our sex. Many women are happy with hearth and home alone, why not me? Why must a woman have as many children as come her way? Men are no so encumbered.

Yet she was powerless to resist John's warm body, urgent, promising, beside her for only two nights in every seven. She longed for him when he was gone, for his touch, warm and insistent, exploring her body, running over every forbidden inch, the heat between her thighs, the cresting ecstacy when they both came together, transporting, if only for those few moments, was too tempting to resist.

I begin to understand weakness, she thought. *And thy desire shall be to thy husband and he shall rule over thee. There are many ways a man can rule without tyranny.*

Returning to her letter, she poured her frustrations onto the paper, grateful for Mary's sympathetic heart. When she finished, she scattered some blotter over the sheet, poured it off the page back into the container on her desk, then folded the letter in half twice and sealed it with wax. Propping it up against the inkwell, she rose, shivering, and went to the window. The thickly frosted pane obscured the snow falling outside. Slowly, she scratched her name in the icy whiteness just as she had done in childhood at Grandfather Quincy's.

The baby coughed, then whimpered. Abigail scooped her up and sat in Grandmother Quincy's old upholstered chair cradling Susanna in her arms. So small, the hands like those of an infant. Born with the Quincy chest, Abigail thought helplessly. Susanna coughed again, a wracking, dry rustle, like the last leaves of autumn scattering before a wind. Beneath the swaddling, Abigail could feel the little body contort violently. She sat with her daughter held close against her bosom, trying to protect the little life by sheer force of will. The fire danced up the chimney, its mesmerizing spirits leaping across the room.

She did not realize she had dozed until the door creaked open.

"Mrs. A? I just peeked in to check," whispered Rachel. "Don't you want to go to bed?"

The candle had guttered and died. Only the light of the low fire flickered, casting Rachel's shadow onto the wall opposite, an eavesdropping specter. Abigail felt cold and stiff.

"What time is it?" she asked.

"Near midnight. Mr. A's still out with his meetin', " Rachel replied, stirring the fire for her mistress.

"I think I'll wait for Mr. Adams," Abigail replied, yawning.

Gently, she pulled the blanket around Susanna. The coughing had stopped. The little body felt relaxed. Perhaps she's turned the corner, Abigail thought sleepily, but almost immediately, cold fingers clutched at her heart. She sat up in the chair, lowered the baby, and looked at the little face. The eyes were fixed in a blind stare.

"No."

A whispered denial. Susanna could not be gone. There would have been more warning, more of a struggle. She began to shake the baby. "No no no no no no!" Like an incantation. She could not be dead. I had a weak chest. I survived.

She thumped the little back, frantically trying to make it draw a breath. No response. Feverishly, she opened the blankets. The baby's chest, still warm, lay motionless.

"Oh my God!" Rachel shrieked, her hands reaching then withdrawing spasmodically from the child. "Slap her! Slap her on the back!"

Abigail turned the baby over and whacked her several times. Nothing. The body was like a rag doll, empty and limp. Rachel had begun to moan, hands at her mouth, nervously rubbing her lips as she watched Abigail try to will life back into her child. For twenty minutes, Abigail worked in panic, alternately massaging and shaking the little body.

"No use," Rachel whispered through a half-suppressed sob. "No use."

Finally, tears streaming down her face, Abigail laid the dead child across her lap and looked down on her once more. Susanna's life had gone out like the slow burning down of the candle, its ending a gradual diminishment of light until it flickered out. The tiny mouth had fallen partly open, revealing eight perfect teeth.

"She's gone." Rachel murmured, panting with the hard beating of her heart. "Susanna's with God now."

Rachel knelt beside Abigail and put an arm around her mistress's trembling shoulders. Abigail had turned her face to the fire, staring past the lifeless form she clutched unconsciously to her breast. She threw her head back against the chair and sucked in a long breath. It was well past two in the morning by the time John came home and discovered Rachel and Abigail weeping together by the dying fire.

The baby was buried in Braintree. John rode the ten snow-covered miles from Boston alone, the little casket held across his saddle. He watched, tears freezing on his cheeks while his brothers, Peter and Elihu, dug the grave, pickaxes ringing against the frozen ground. They lowered the pathetically small box into the hole, then, without a word, John jammed his hat back on his head, swung up into the saddle and rode back to Boston. On his return, he found Abigail sitting on the edge of their bed staring at the empty cradle. He sat down beside her.

"My Dear, you must accept it as God's Will," he said softly, laying a half-frozen hand on hers. "This new baby's coming will help you to overcome your grief, in time. It may not seem so now, " he hastily added at seeing the look of horror and disbelief she shot him. "It is hard. Our life on this mortal coil is strewn with sorrows. But we must trust that the Almighty who sees even a sparrow's fall sees our pain and loss. He will take Susanna to Him."

Abigail's eyes flashed at him.

"My faith tells me to trust, but that faith does not ease the stab I feel every time I look into that empty cradle! To bear a child – alive and to survive myself - to watch it grow, smiling, cooing at your breast, to spend all these months in tender care only to lose the life, as though all – all! – were a waste... The pain of a mother is a hard pain to bear!" she sobbed, tears coursing down hollow cheeks.

"Abigail. I beg you!" John cried, helplessly gathering Abigail to him, pressing her close. "You must try not to fret yourself overmuch. Please. For the sake of the child you carry if not for your own. "

"I cannot control what my heart feels!" she wailed.

She covered her face with thin hands, clutching until the fingers left white streaks in the flesh. John buried his face in her neck, reaching a stubby hand out to grasp a few strands of her hair between thumb and forefinger. He pressed the wisp hard, watching the tips of his fingers whiten with the pressure, and rubbed it against the tear that meandered down his cheek.

The 5th of March 1770 was cold and sharp, slicing through every crack and alleyway. Icicles hung from the eaves and tinkled a chillingly thin melody at the wind's whim. The snow was hard-packed, scrunching under the feet of passers-by. Youths raced by outside, shouting names at the red-coated soldiers, throwing snowballs and chunks of ice at patrolling sentries. The cold only served to sharpen Boston's bitterness. And the Sons of Liberty, a bubbling stew made up of the North and South End gangs stirred by John's cousin, Sam Adams, and the mercurial James Otis, readily boiled over into violence.

The entire household huddled around the blazing kitchen fire. Abigail mended sheets and pillowcases while sipping the cup of liberty tea Rachel had brewed from dried loosestrife. Joseph warmed his hands after having brought in another load of firewood. Tansy, the young black maid Abigail had hired at the end of February, stood side by side with Rachel rolling out cookies on the broad oak table. The room was filled with the fragrance of warm muffins bursting with currants and nuts, and the sweet-acrid smell of molasses cookies. Little John Quincy, two and a half, played blocks on the floor with four-year-old Nabby.

Abigail dropped her mending into the old reed basket her mother had given her and sipped the last of the bitter herb tea. Her body ached and she shivered with chills though the fireside was hot. In the distance, she heard the heavy clang of the town crier's bell approaching. She felt irritated with the children's high spirits and was impatient for John's return from his meeting in the South End.

Though she often had friends for tea or supper, it was John whose companionship she most craved. She missed him less in the morning when she spent an hour or two writing letters to friends and family. But in the evening, with the darkness closing, the children finally asleep, she felt bereft. As much as the comfort of his body, she loved the exchange of ideas. With John, she could test her perceptions of events, sharpen her reasoning, cling to knowledge of a wider world that felt more and more closed to her.

A muffled Crack! brought her to stiff attention. Oblivious, the children continued to play, but Rachel stopped stirring and lifted her ear inquiringly. She raised a questioning eyebrow at Abigail who sat immobile for a moment, listening. Putting a finger to her lips, Abigail rose and went to the front hall where she peered out a window into the street.

Men and boys raced by, shouting in urgent voices. Some were drunk, with horrible, leering faces lit by the promise of yet another bloody spectacle. Abigail turned away, her stomach churning sickeningly at the sight of these brutes, who were her fellow

Bostonians. When she returned to the warmth of the kitchen, Rachel greeted her with a silent curious look, but Abigail shook her head, shrugged, and sank into the chair, wrapping her shawl tighter.

John arrived home several hours later, stamping the snow from his shoes in the hallway before coming through the house to find his wife. She was curled in a chair by the parlor fire desultorily reading a volume of Molière, but started and dropped the book in her lap when John entered the room.

"What happened tonight, John? I thought I heard shots!" she cried, relieved to see him safely home.

He crossed the small room quickly, wafting cold and something more -- something unsettling in his wake. He kissed Abigail quickly then extended raw hands to the warmth.

"There have been terrible doings tonight," he said grimly, staring into the fire as though watching bloodshed in the leaping red flames. "It was between a group of soldiers and some of the local men. Three are dead, I believe."

Abigail gasped. "What was the cause? How did it happen? Did you see? I see you are sound and whole, thank God!"

He shook his head.

"I did not see. It happened while I was in the tavern. I did not leave the meeting until after the whole to-do was finished, but I might just as easily have been a passer-by inadvertently shot."

He turned his back to the fire to look at Abigail's stricken face. "They are calling it a massacre. His Majesty's soldiers opened fire on unarmed citizens, and killed three outright. Two more are wounded so they say. More than that I do not know."

"Who is calling it a massacre?"

"Several of those shouting the news in the streets. I found Cousin Sam and James Otis cooking up articles, working the political engine. I should be able to glean more tomorrow at the tavern. It is a nasty business, and will bring more, mark my words."

"Oh, John!" Abigail cried in panic, her eyes brimmed with tears.

She shivered, passed a hand over her sweating brow, and fell back in the chair.

"My Dear!" John exclaimed, dropping to his knees and throwing his arms around her. "I had not meant to alarm you."

"I am not alarmed, Mr. Adams," Abigail insisted, pursing her lips in an effort to regain control of herself. "It is the fever weeping, not

I. You must take no notice of the tears. Please. I would not be kept in the dark, no matter how harsh the light. The terrible fears one's imagination conjures are far worse than reality. Always tell me." The words spilled out one over the other. She treasured his candor, and could not bear to be relegated to the ignorance of so many other wives. She wanted him to believe her strong enough to bear any pain, any fear.

"You are my heart's joy, my dear," John murmured. "Was ever a man so fortunate in the choice of his life's partner as I? But enough for now. Politics in the morning. You need a warm posset and sleep to knit up the raveled sleeve."

"Not just yet Mr. Adams. I have dreadfully missed your company. You have been so busy of late. A little time and conversation would physick me."

Releasing her, John poured himself a brandy, and returned to the fireside where he slumped into a chair.

"Methinks you have been working too hard, my friend," she observed softly.

"No harder than need be," John replied. "There is much to be done. We moved here to improve my practice. It has. I have almost more business now than I can manage."

"It is because you are becoming known for your excellent council," she said. "Even so, I miss your company. You no sooner get home from a circuit than you are at the Admiralty Court or with the Sons of Liberty, or writing treatises." She sighed. "Your babes miss you too. I sometimes fear they will grow up and not know their own Par."

"Nonsense!" John bellowed good-naturedly. "How could anyone forget me?"

"I know as well as anyone that Boston needs her best sons now. My concern is for your health, Mr. Adams. You neglect yourself in the service of your country."

"Perhaps I do, my dearest. And I doubt the sacrifice will ever be appreciated. But I could no more decline the honor than I could decline to breathe."

Abigail sighed. He looked haggard. There were dark circles under his eyes and his skin had taken on a waxy, opaqueness that no amount of hard cider and brandy could cure.

The following evening, John came home after dark, cast his cloak into a chair in the hall and scampered up the two flights of stairs to the nursery. Bursting into the room, his face still wind-reddened, he swept Johnny and Nabby into his arms, laughing at their squeals as he rubbed his cold cheeks into theirs.

"Mr. Adams, *Please!* You will stir them both up again, and I was just coaxing them into bed!" Abigail cried in exasperation.

"I have missed my chicks!" John roared, while the children shouted, "Par! Par!"

While the children fired a barrage of questions, Abigail watched from a small wooden chair. Her pregnancy had grown increasingly uncomfortable, an added burden, and she felt her strength, which had started to return after Susanna's death, ebbing again with this latest fever.

"Your Mar wants you both in bed," John said to the children finally. "Quiet now, and she will not think so badly of my interruption. *Hush,*" he said, dropping Johnny into his cot. He took Nabby to her bed where he kissed her loudly on one fat cheek. "Lie down, and go to sleep," he instructed waving his forefinger in mock seriousness.

Bright eyes dancing, the two children lay stiff and solemn while John took Abigail's hand and pulled her from the low chair. As they turned to go, John stopped and smiled at his son.

"Can you tell us a story, Par?" Nabby asked softly.

"Story, Par - pease?' Johnny echoed.

John raised an eyebrow to Abigail who shrugged in resignation.

"A very short one, then," he said, taking the book Abigail handed him as she started out the door.

"I shall wait for you in the parlor, Mr. Adams. Supper will be nearly ready so do make it a short one. The children have had a long, exhausting day."

"As have you, I warrant. I shan't be long," he promised.

"Night Mar," Nabby called as her mother started out the door.

"Goodnight, Child. Mr. Adams, do not neglect their prayers."

As John opened the book, the nursery door quietly closed.

Tansy had laid their supper, roast mutton and bread and butter, close to the fire in the dining room. Abigail collapsed into a chair and sipped at her ale until John arrived. While they ate, John spoke of the children, their education, proposed futures for them. Abigail nodded and listened, but she could sense his mind was elsewhere. Finally, Tansy brought Indian pudding and two small glasses of plum brandy. When the door closed behind her, John raised his eyes to fix her with a steady gaze.

"I spoke with Josiah Quincy today, Abigail."

"Yes?" she responded, irritated at having to wait for him to come to the point.

"He has something of a dilemma to solve," John paused, weighing his words.

"And what is that?"

"He has been asked to defend Captain Preston. He has said he will not accept the case unless I join him."

He fell silent. Her face had frozen at the mention of the British soldier responsible for the Boston Massacre.

"There are now four men dead," she said evenly, trying to calm the panic rising in her throat. "The papers are inflaming the mob. Would it willingly massacre the man who defends Captain Preston?"

She let the question hang on the air for a moment; John remained silent.

"There is, I take it, another side to the tale," she said finally. "Tell me, Mr. Adams."

John drew a long breath, stuffed his pipe full, and lit it before continuing.

"I believe him to be worthy of defense, Abigail."

"Of course, or you would not consider it," she retorted with some impatience.

He nodded.

"According to Preston, Private Hugh White was walking at his post down King Street from the Town House. A group of apprentices, rabble really, began mocking and taunting White. They threw several snowballs and chunks of ice. Finally, White lost his temper and hit one of them with his rifle butt. The boys shouted until they raised a crowd. White was attacked by the mob. He fell back to the Customs House steps and pounded on the door to be let in, but the door held fast. According to White, the crowd threatened to kill him and dared him to fire his rifle. Captain Preston marched a relief party, a corporal and six privates, to the scene, in file, with empty muskets. By the time they got to White, the crowd was large and would not let Preston and his men through to him. Instead, it turned on Preston and his men -- catcalls, more missiles, several soldiers hit by rocks and chunks of ice.

"Captain Preston gave the order to load their muskets, and while doing so, someone hit him with a cudgel. His arm is broken. A private Montgomery was knocked down by the mob. He fired in anger, but fortunately missed hitting anyone. There were then sporadic shots fired. The captain says he turned on his men and demanded to know why they had fired. Preston admits he was in a rage. The men said they had heard the command "Fire!" and thought it had been *his* order. The charge against Preston is murder. Four men dead, and a fifth soon to follow according to reports."

John had recounted this story in the clinical tone of a surgeon examining a wound for infection. But when he had finished, he leaned forward earnestly, and reached across the little table to take both of her hands in his.

"Abigail, Captain Preston is known as a sober, honest man. I believe his story. What is more, I fear if I do not help Mr. Quincy with his defense, Preston and his men will not only not get a fair trial, but the mob will deal out retribution. You remember the poor soul who was burned alive..." he shuddered. "It will confirm to those in England that Bostonians are barbarians. I must help restore law and order."

Abigail watched him carefully for a moment. There was something else, she could feel it. Then it came to her. He has already agreed! she realized, shocked. He does not ask my permission, but only explains his reasons. Bursting into tears, she covered her face with both hands and bowed her head to the table.

"My Dearest!" John cried in alarm. "Please, do not fret."

"You mock me! You have already taken the case!" she cried, raising her eyes in accusation.

"I never mock you, my Rock! I knew you would feel as I do. I know that it may be dangerous, but I fear if I do not help Mr. Quincy, he will refuse the case. If he does, those men are lost. And so is all hope of maintaining our laws. We must for our own sakes ensure a fair trial."

An image of John, tarred and feathered by a frenzied mob flashed into her mind. A horrible fate. Destitution for herself and her children. What would she be required to sacrifice on the altar of John's duty and service? She suddenly realized that devotion to what they saw as John's destiny could also mean the loss of everything. Perilous times. Could my husband be killed in doing a lawyer's duty? A vision of her life without John, of loneliness and struggle, crowded. She pushed it away. Pregnancy makes me vulnerable. A man would not have these fears, she reminded herself. All life is uncertain. Abigail lifted her head, and looked at him through the tears, wiping them from her cheeks brusquely.

"How proud I am to have such a courageous Friend!" she said finally. "I understand your reasons, John. I admire and share them."

She drew in a deep breath, then dabbing her eyes with a linen handkerchief she had pulled from her sleeve, she asked: "But do you think there will be any reprisals against you?"

"That I cannot say," John answered, leaning back in his chair to sip at the brandy, his eyes still fixed on Abigail's lined face. "But we must at least try to conduct business here with reason. The rest of the colonies have no sympathy for the violence we have had in Massachusetts these past ten years. The papers have been scathing. It diminishes support for the cause. If we can persuade the mob that law and order is our very best hope, and further, that my sentiments remain patriotic, I should be safe enough. After all, Nabby," he said softly, using her childhood name, "I am well known by the Sons of Liberty as a fair man. Cousin Sam and Mr. Otis will remind them of that," he said then added thoughtfully, "I only pray God that Jamie Otis's mind is in a fit state to reason."

"Mrs. Warren is very worried about her brother," Abigail agreed. "I had a visit from her earlier in the week. She fears for his sanity. It seems he is more and more out of his senses and in his cups. Can he still be an effective instrument?"

"I do not know. He grows wild in his accusations against Governor Hutchinson and Parliament. He sees conspiracies around each corner. Tonight he seemed in a frenzy, although his words made sense enough."

"We need cool heads such as yours," Abigail said, her voice strengthening with her resolve. "To think of all the senseless violence undertaken in the name of our cause! Governor Hutchinson's house burned and looted, men killed, or horribly beaten. You must stand up for Law."

She had tucked her handkerchief back into her sleeve, her fears overtaken by her self-righteous faith in John's place in history.

At the end of May in 1770, Charles Adams was born. Abigail breathed a deep sigh of relief when she saw her newborn son, plump and rosy, squalling with health in the mid-wife's arms. This one shall be safe, she thought. This one, I shall not lose before his time. She thanked God for the healthy delivery, then fell back onto the sweat-stained pillows in exhaustion.

She had been out of bed only a week when John returned home with the news that he had been elected to the Massachusetts House of Representatives. She sat in their bedroom, rocking the cradle with her foot while she sewed a piece of torn lace back onto one of Nabby's dresses.

"But Mr. Adams, the Governor has forbidden the Assembly to meet. How can anyone be elected to that phantom body?"

"In *Boston*, " he reminded her, smugly. "The Governor has forbidden it to meet in *Boston*. Do you think that would stop the exercise of our English rights? We are not phantoms. We are alive and well and meeting in Harvard College across the river."

"I see. But just how do you expect to manage your law practice *and* serve in the Assembly?" she inquired, taking a stitch so forcefully she snapped the thread. "Travel alone will take up a great deal of your time each day. Does your family have no claim on your time?"

"Are you not pleased they have elected me?" he demanded, annoyed that she should throw obstacles in the path of his triumph.

"I am proud they have seen your merit," she replied, biting off another piece of thread with her teeth. "It is especially gratifying to know they have such confidence in you regardless of your accepting Captain Preston's defense -- especially as they are so keen to stretch the man's neck. I ask merely whether there are sufficient hours in the day to accomplish all the tasks you are setting yourself. Do you wish to make yourself ill?"

"And what do you suggest I do? Shall I leave my duty to someone else? Or perhaps you would be so kind as to find someone to earn this family's bread whilst I carry on with my political duties. I see no one else stepping into my shoes on either score."

" I see there is no talking of this to you now," she said, her tone icy. "But you must believe this: I am proud that you have been elected. I only meant to point out to you that your health is already suffering from the strains of work. But, I see you are in no mood to listen."

The baby, awakened by their rising voices, wailed. Abigail gave John a reproving frown and lifted Charly from the cradle to her shoulder. John leaned over the infant and rubbed the fat little chin with one finger, cooing softly. The baby quieted immediately, staring with fascination at his father's round face. Abigail marveled at his sudden calm, so unlike John's mercurial temper.

"I am sorry to shout, my dear," John said, still admiring the baby. "Perhaps I *have* been working too hard lately. My nerves are frayed, but it this is an honor I must accept. I know that you understand," he finished, looking sidelong into her pensive face.

"I do, Mr. Adams. And *you* understand that my opposition is in the name of your welfare."

John smiled, noting for the first time the silver strands that threaded through her brown hair, the hollowness of the once-round cheeks. She has had a difficult two years, and is likely to have more, he thought ruefully.

Four pregnancies in six years had taken their toll, although her spirit remained as strong as ever. Twenty-six and she was already beginning to look matronly. He kissed her softly on the mouth, brushing his face against hers. She forced a smile, smothering her resentment at his more frequent flashes of temper.

It was not until November that Captain Preston and his men were finally brought before the judges. John and Josiah Quincy had done their work well. Acquitted of the murder charges, Preston and his men were sentenced to a relatively mild punishment on the charge of manslaughter -- branding on the thumbs.

Despite his jubilation at their victory, John was exhausted. Abigail called in Dr. Joseph Warren. His diagnosis was extreme fatigue. The prescription: an absence from all worries of public and professional life. Buttressed by this pronouncement, Abigail persuaded John to move back to Braintree, away from the danger -- and the intoxicating glory -- of public life.

Chapter 6

That which before us lies in daily life Is the prime wisdom.
John Milton Paradise Lost Bk VIII Line 192

1771

September of 1771 was warm and dry. Blue skies were blotched with cottonwool clouds whose silhouettes moved over the rolling, rock-strewn land like a troop of restless angels. The heat bred swarming clouds of insects. Flies congregated in thick clumps on manure piles and cicadas rent the air in frantic alarm.

In the Adams's Braintree kitchen, a kettle of soup, steam rising in curling wisps, hung on the long trammel over the fire. Tansy, alone while Rachel stayed in Weymouth to nurse her ailing mother, stitched apple slices onto long strings to dry in the sun. Ringed around the table's end, the three Adams children ate their lunch of bread and cheese and apples while Abigail read a letter from John that a neighbor had just delivered from Boston. Although exiled to Braintree for his health, he kept an office in Boston to which he traveled every several weeks.

"When's Par comin' home?" Four-year-old Johnny asked, his mouth crammed with bread.

"John Quincy! Mind your manners!" Abigail snapped. "How many times must I remind you never to talk with your mouth full?"

"Yes, Mar," the little boy said, hanging his head in shame.

"Nabby, cut your brother a piece of cheese," Abigail instructed the six-year-old, who sat at the head of the table, a look of prim authority on her face.

"Mind the knife!" Abigail cried, as Nabby picked it up by the blade.

A look of shock and hurt crossed the child's face. Regretting her sharpness, Abigail changed her tone. "Take care, Child. We want you to reach a ripe age with all fingers and toes intact."

Nabby smiled tentatively and made a second attempt at the loaf while two-year-old Charly, confined to a high chair, squealed and reached toward the loaf with both hands and feet.

A wave of nausea washed over Abigail and she stopped reading for a moment to suck in deep, warm draughts of fresh air. The nausea receded. Another month and that stage will be passed, she thought. Pregnant. Again. This heat is unbearable and the children are driving me to distraction. Too many children in too short a time. I am chained.

"When's Par getting home?" Johnny asked again, having carefully finished chewing and swallowing.

"I have a letter he wrote in his office not five hours ago," Abigail replied. " Mr. Cranshaw left it when he stopped. See if you can read it."

She handed her son the piece of paper with John's familiar scrawl on it.

Johnny squinted at the paper, but could make out only several of the words: "There is no.... here... And I... " He hung his head again, and handed it back to his mother. "I can't, Mar."

"It will come with work, Johnny."

She took the letter from him and folded it back into her apron pocket.

"Par says he shall come home tomorrow."

"Mrs. Adams?"

The hired man, dressed in breeches and shirt with the sleeves rolled to his elbows, stood just outside the open kitchen door. Abigail rose and went to the door. Another wave of nausea washed over her and she leaned against the doorjamb.

"Mrs. Adams, we've done croppin' the dead and diseased stuff off all the apple trees," he said, wiping the sweat and dirt from his face with a lean forearm. "Jacob's burning the boughs now." He gestured out to where Abigail could see a youth stirring a smoking pyre of branches and leaves.

"I hope you haven't had to cut too many limbs, Mr. Palmer, " she said, frowning.

"No'm. Not too many, I think. We only took them's that had too many worms on them to scrape off. I raised a torch to some, an' burnt 'em where they lay. I know how partic'lar Mr. Adams is about his trees. But there's a lot of caterpillars out there this year, M'am. We should have got 'em earlier. They'll eat the whole orchard if we don't get rid of 'em all -- take them out root and branch so to speak."

"Yes, you're quite right, of course. Well, continue throughout

70

the orchard. And check the other trees. Mr. Adams has once again sent instructions to be sure to get every last worm."

"Yes'm. Might we have a drink afore we get on with it? It's mighty hot out."

" Tansy, fetch a pitcher of ale from the shelf and give Mr. Palmer a cup."

"Mar, can I go cut trees, too?" Johnny pleaded.

"Not until you get a better grasp of your letters, John Quincy," Abigail replied. "Your education comes first. Par will teach you husbandry, but you needs must look to your reading and ciphers."

"I can help teach him, Mar. I can read right good now," Nabby piped up. She handed Charly another ragged slice of bread, and watched as he stuffed it greedily into his mouth with a satisfied snort.

"Mind he doesn't choke on that. Yes, Nab, your reading is not going badly, but your understanding needs improvement. Pronouncing the words is little use if you don't grasp the meaning."

Abigail, frustrated and tired, did not see the look of dejection on her daughter's face, did not guess the girl's aching need for approval. Tansy returned and handed the pitcher and cup to the hired man, who took it without a word and set off toward Jacob. She then went to cut herself a slice of bread from the loaf for her own lunch. Waving the flies off the butter, she took the knife and slathered a generous lump on the bread, then pulled a stool near the doorway where she could watch the men working while she ate.

"Want some cheese, Tansy?" Nabby asked, hoping to practice her slicing.

"A bit, Miss," Tansy smiled. She was fond of the Adams children. They were high-spirited without being arrogant, a trait she had found seldom enough in her short life in service. "I like yer mama's cheese."

"Mar makes the best cheese," Nabby agreed proudly. "She'll teach me how to make it soon."

"I am gratified it finds approval here," Abigail observed, "but I am even more gratified that Mr. Tufts wishes four more cheeses for his shop. That will help fill the Adams family coffers a bit in these hard times."

John's practice was doing well, but not so well that they didn't use every penny. More mouths to feed, more work, more money. A never-ending treadmill.

71

"I done," Charly cried struggling to escape from his chair. "See cows."

"Oh, very well. Have you children had enough to eat? Nabby, take your brother down to the barn for a visit with the cows. And mind he doesn't get into the muck pile as he did last time."

"Yes, Mar," Nabby replied, taking her squirming brother from the chair and wiping his mouth with her apron in imitation of her mother.

"Come, Charly, you can hold my hand," Nabby said, reaching out for her brother.

Charly stared at the offered hand for a moment, made a face, and started for the door alone.

"Looks like that young 'un has a mind of his own," Tansy observed with a smile.

"I thank God for children who are whole and well, but there are times when I could wish for more malleable spirits and less independence," Abigail sighed.

"Whole and strong's a lot to be thankful for."

Struck by her tone, Abigail looked up. The girl was uneducated, but intelligent. Abigail was happy to note that since she had come to work for the Adamses, Tansy no longer seemed cowed.

"My brother, Will," Tansy continued half to herself, "was never right, not from the time he was born. Pa beat him near half to death tryin' to get him to do chores, but poor Will jus' couldn't learn. Never made sense to him I expect -- like he'd only half-come from heaven and still had one foot back there."

"What happened to him?"

"Don't know, rightly. Pa said he wandered off and got lost. He jus' went off one night and never came home. I always suspected Pa had took him somewheres so he couldn't find his way home. Warn't no badness in Will nowhere. He jus' couldn't learn. Had no brain for it."

"How terrible!" Abigail cried. "Your father should have been horsewhipped!"

Tansy nodded agreement. "It was kinda a blessin' on us when Pa left, at least some ways. I miss Will. I hope he's with God now -- but I'd like to see him once more," she said pensively.

Abigail shuddered, imagining that unfortunate creature's terror when he discovered his own father had abandoned him. How cruel we can be to our children. Even those of us who intend good, she thought, chastising herself for her impatience. Yet how much is too much? They cannot go without correction. When is correction discouragement? Spare the rod and spoil the child. The Scriptures give only rough guidance, few details.

"Suffer the little children to come unto me," Tansy murmured, as though in answer to Abigail's thoughts. "I felt so glad when I heard that bit o' Bible in meetin' for the first time. I jus' KNEW then that's what happened to Will. Jesus jus' took Will to Him with all the other little children that can't live in this world."

Abigail nodded silently. Losing Susanna still ached, and she felt a stab of guilt for her ingratitude at yet another pregnancy. It suddenly seemed like blasphemy.

In early March 1772, Abigail took her first vacation away from the children. John had business in Plymouth and Mercy Warren's invitation to stay with them was too tempting to refuse. As she struggled to settle the children at the parsonage with her parents, with Charley clinging to her skirts plaintively, she almost lost her resolve. But her father urged her on, picking up the toddler and chucking him under the chin. By the time the parsonage had disappeared around the first bend in the road, she had begun to feel less guilty.

"They will have a wonderful time," John said reassuringly. "Their Smith grandparents love to spoil them. It is us who will suffer for it upon our return."

Abigail laughed, feeling lighter, freer than she had since Nabby's birth. There was no child hanging onto her, no demanding voice at her elbow, only the palpable closeness of John, and the vast panorama of the countryside -- simple pleasures, but how rare. John put his arm around her.

"I am very glad of your company, my dear," he said, a smile playing with the lines at the corners of his eyes.

"And I yours."

She looked at the man she had married only eight years before. At thirty-seven his compact body was still firm, thanks to daily exercise, but the face had aged. The plump cheeks betrayed a jowl, the furrow in his chin had deepened, and the lines around his eyes, once fleeting in anger or mirth, were now firmly etched.

"You study me with such care, Wife," John said, giving her a sidelong glance.

"I was thinking of our first ride together as husband and wife, Husband," she replied.

"It seems yesterday and yet a lifetime ago," John said.

"It is nearly five lifetimes ago," Abigail reminded him, rubbing her bulging belly.

"Yes, five," John agreed, his mind touching on the bitter ride he had taken with Susanna's coffin held across his saddle.

He looked at Abigail's pregnancy with pride. Their fifth child together. Their coupling was no longer frantic urgency, but was still passionate, and deeply satisfying. Despite his pride at their children, and his joy in their physical life together, John worried at the obvious toll it was taking on Abigail's constitution. After this child, they would endeavor to have no more, he decided.

It was a warm day for March, but the fields and hills still wore the muted colors of winter. The trees were naked, the slopes and valleys still tufted with dead grass. But the scent on the air held the promise of spring, a hint of greening and opening earth. Shimmering blue ponds mirrored the sky, and the season's first songbirds flitted overhead. Abigail sucked in a deep breath, then exhaled, slowly.

"You sigh, my dear?" John asked, his eyes on the road.

"I was thinking."

"When are you not?" He chuckled, urging the horse faster to pull them through a mound of mud. "And wither has your mind wandered?"

"I fear I will make a poor showing for you beside Mercy Warren's brightly shining star," she replied.

"You? You cannot believe that."

"I am but a poor country lawyer's wife, unschooled and unsophisticated. I am a pale moon beside the brilliance of Mrs. Warren's sun."

"You are whining," he teased.

"I assure you I am not," she replied.

Mercy Warren had recently published a play satirizing the British, an accomplishment that provided a ticket into the highest and most powerful circles of colonial society. She published anonymously, but everyone who was anyone knew the name of Mercy Otis Warren and strived to be counted among her friends. She and Abigail corresponded often, which conferred satisfying – if minor – celebrity in Braintree. But she would be nearly invisible in Plymouth. And, while Mercy commiserated with her over the thousand details of a woman's life, it was John's whose opinion that mattered.

"It seems to me that the moon was *envious* of the sun," John remarked.

"Is that what you think?" Abigail demanded, straightening.

"I think you are no moon 'sick and pale with grief,' but a sun in your own right," he replied with unusual diplomacy and no small measure of loyalty. "No woman in the colonies can outshine you."

They rode for a few minutes in silence before John added:

"I would judge you to be of equal intellect and ability to Mrs. Warren. "You simply have no ambition to thrust yourself before the public eye as she does."

Women are not allowed ambition, Abigail thought. Or perhaps I am not.

"Mrs. Warren writes anonymously," Abigail pointed out. "A woman may use her mind without an unseemly show."

"She makes it very easy to discover the identity," John retorted. "I wonder: does she neglect her children in her pursuit of the intellect? The colonies have need of strong voices for the cause, but it mayhap her family needs her more."

"Can a woman not take part in a life outside her own doors without being accused of neglecting her children?"

"There are ways to take part," John replied. " Your support of me, for example. You can thereby support the cause without dividing your attention."

"I have not noticed that *her* attention is divided," Abigail replied, "if her letters are the true measure of her devotion, then she is as committed to her family as I. And you cannot deny that you enjoy a woman with opinions, Mr. Adams, a woman of learned discourse."

"I enjoy *your* discourse, and I enjoy women," John corrected her. "It does not mean I wish them to take such a public role. It demeans them to strut across the stage."

"Portia was not demeaned."

"Portia is a fiction. Life is fact."

"Life may imitate art," she replied tartly.

John looked stolidly ahead, jaw clamped shut. He could appreciate Mercy Warren's mind, listen to her opinions, he could even flutter around the flame of her glowing talent, but he refused to view her as anything but a notable exception to an immutable rule.

The twenty-five mile journey to Plymouth took seven hours. As they entered the town, Abigail was once again assailed by doubts at the figure she would cut -- pregnant, provincial, hemmed in by house and nursery. But when they arrived and Mercy flung the door wide to welcome them in, she forgot her fears in the face of her friend's enthusiasm.

"Come sit ye down, Mrs. Adams," Mercy cried, leading them through a spacious hallway to a large, well-appointed parlor in which a fire blazed.

She gestured to a wing chair pulled close to the hearth. On a table at its side sat a silver tray laden with small cakes and bread and butter.

"I am honored that Mrs. Adams would drive all this way to grace my humble home," she said, touching Abigail's forearm. "Mr. Adams is a much-prized guest, but to have the redoubtable Mrs. Adams as well is indeed a boon. I am glad to return hospitality to a lady who has shown me such favor with her letters."

Doubts dispelled, Abigail, smiled and hugged her friend. Mercy was richly dressed in a gray taffeta gown trimmed with lace. She swept around the room like a young woman, her carriage graceful, her face, plain, yet beautiful in its clean, spare lines. James Warren, who had joined them in the parlor, watched his loquacious wife indulgently. While she took command of Abigail, he poured two large measures of rum into crystal glasses and handed one to John.

"A dram will help revive your spirits," he said, raising his glass in salute.

"The ladies have no need of such spirits," Mercy said, smiling as she reached for an embroidered cord hanging beside the mantelpiece. "Our company is tonic enough for now. You will take tea, Mrs. Adams?"

"I will, and gladly."

Mercy pulled the cord and a moment later, a young woman with a freckled face and wisps of red hair that stuck out under her cap like broom corn appeared at the door.

"You may bring the tea now, Brigid."

Yes, M'am," the girl replied, managing in two syllables to reveal a thick Irish accent, as she dipped in a quick curtsey.

"How was your journey, Mrs. Adams?"

"The scenery was beautiful, though were I to make the trip as often as Mr. Adams, I suspect I should tire of it," Abigail laughed.

Mercy was about to ask another question when the door burst open and a boy about six years old clattered up to his mother.

"Nathan..." Mercy began, lips pursed, but the boy broke in.

"Winston is..." he glanced at the guests and paused.

Mercy nodded, frowning, bent down and whispered something into the boy's ear.

"I don't think he'll go up for Augustus," the child replied earnestly. "He's awful wild. It's Papa we need."

Mercy looked imploringly at her husband. James set his glass down on the sideboard, with a barely perceptible shake of his head, murmured, "Please excuse me," and left the room followed by Nathan.

John raised an eyebrow at Abigail but made no remark.

"I apologize for my son's rudeness, Mrs. Adams. I fear there is still some distance between Nathan's knowledge of manners and the application."

"I find it the same with my little ones, Mrs. Warren," Abigail smiled, relieved to see that Mercy Warren's children were no more perfect than hers.

Raised voices followed the muffled sound of a plate being smashed at the back of the house, but Mercy's expression did not change as she lifted the tray of cakes and offered it once again to the Adamses.

"I will see what is keeping Brigid with the tea," she said when everyone had been served. "Then perhaps you would like a rest before dinner. You must be fatigued. Tonight's party includes some of Plymouth's patriots that I think you should meet."

Smiling, she replaced the tray and swept from the room in a rustle of taffeta and lace.

It was a rather poor company of 'patriots' by Boston standards, Abigail decided. There were eight at table. Edmund Nichols, richly dressed in satin and his wife, Rosamund, plump and fussy, was trimmed with so many bows that she looked as though she were being attacked by a swarm of butterflies. At the other end of the table on either side of Mercy were the Claymoors, a couple whose conversation took the form of a duet, each one getting part way through a sentence only to have the other finish. Throughout the dinner, Edmund Nichols made a series of ungenerous and mostly ill-founded pronouncements on the character of the Sons of Liberty and such pot-stirring Bostonians as Mercy's brother, James, and John's cousin, Sam Adams. Mercy appeared unperturbed, even laughing at some of the more obtuse slanders, but Abigail, who suspected that Nichols's pompous disapproval was tinged with more than a little envy, struggled to hold her tongue.

The Plymouth contingent's patriotism appeared to be commercial their objections to Parliament founded on local business rather than principle. Convinced that they would prosper only if the colonies were severed from the 'gangrenous limb' of England, they discussed dissolution with the eagerness of schoolboys anticipating the end of term.

"I doubt we will see a separation from the mother country in my lifetime," John said. "There is strong opinion against it."

"But what about those marvelous firebrands Otis and Sam Adams? They have rejected England entirely!" Nichols bellowed. "They have carried the cause this far on their backs. Why not to freedom?"

"They do not hold the whole of the colonies in their hands," John replied, annoyed. "The south has markets in England. They have little taste for independence. Parliament has behaved shamefully, make no mistake. It has ignored the rights of its citizens. It taxes us without due process and creates hardship where none need exist. Yet our nation is still tied to the mother country."

"I would expect the man who defended Captain Preston to say such things," Nichols spat out. "But the Sons of Liberty will separate us, mark my words."

"The Sons of Liberty respond to injustices," John said, his face reddening. "As do I."

"Our own Mrs. Warren does the same thing," Mrs. Claymoor bubbled. "Why, she is as much a voice for the colonies..."

"...as the Sons of Liberty," her husband finished.

Abigail looked at Mercy, who sat at one end of the table, face glowing rose in the candlelight. She has chosen her friends for their flattery, not their principles, Abigail thought.

"I merely toll a warning," Mercy demurred. "Along with all the other bells clanging away. Is that not right, Mr. Adams?"

"Only a cacophony will make Parliament sit up and take notice," John said, belying his words on the journey there. "Your published work serves the colonies well."

Jealousy and anger jabbed Abigail. He will admire Mrs. Warren but wants his own wife at home, she thought.

"You publish for the cause, but remain a lady," said Nichols, stuffing his mouth full of veal. "It is for the men to sign their names and take the lumps that come."

"Do not women receive lumps for their opinions as well?" Abigail asked with deceptive sweetness.

"How can she? It is not only modesty that demands her anonymity, but a knowledge of her own inferior credentials, her lack of education, even so learned a woman as Mrs. Warren," Nichols responded, bowing toward his hostess.

"Once again it is education!" Abigail cried. "First men deny it to us then they denigrate us for lacking it. Women may serve in a different sphere, but we too need the tools to serve well."

"Quite right, Mrs. Adams," Mercy agreed, clapping her hands together. "If men were to afford women an education, how many more able minds would join in the work at hand?"

"Well said, my dear," James Warren said, amiably. "Yet I would not wish to add the expense of educating a daughter to that of five sons. Here, let us have some more of the veal at this end if you please."

"Exactly," Nichols continued. "What need has a woman for education? All she need learn is the tricks of her trade -- kitchen and the nursery…and the bedroom," he finished, winking at the men.

Tricks of the trade! As though we were common prostitutes! Abigail thought her head would explode from bottled anger, but she fought back her temper to make her point.

"What do men fear from well-educated marriage partners?" she demanded, ignoring John's glowering look. "Surely our knowledge could only benefit? Think, sir, how better prepared we should be to mother the next generation of men. How can a woman make decisions about her sons' educations when she has none herself?"

"Those are men's decisions for men's lives. Her husband will make those decisions," Nichols rejoined smoothly.

79

"Oh, yes, Mr. Nichols has ably provided for all our sons," Mrs. Nichols chirped.

"And what about a woman whose husband is dead or absent?" Abigail persisted.

"Then her sons do not need an education. They needs must work to feed the family for the man who cannot or will not."

"So those sons may not have a chance to better themselves?"

"Not every man is destined for the courts, or for trade, my dear Mrs. Adams," he said. "Some must till the soil and bend their backs. The cream rises naturally to the top; our own Mrs. Warren is a fine example."

Abigail was livid but before she could continue, the door swung open and the top of a dark head appeared around it. The Warrens' nineteen-year-old son, Winston, lurched into the room. Mercy, who sat facing the door, went pale and sat bolt upright. For a second, unable to focus, Winston swung his head around the room, apparently searching for a familiar face.

"Winston, your brothers have all had their supper in the kitchen," Mercy said firmly. "Brigid has set yours aside for you."

"Oh, I'm not hungry, Ma," the youth drawled, swaying a little. His handsome face was flushed. "Jus' a li'l thirsty. Brigid hid the ale," he whispered hoarsely.

James Warren, who had risen from his chair, took a step toward his eldest son.

"You are interrupting your mother's company," he said, sharply. "Make your apologies. You will find your supper in the kitchen."

The boy's smile, a crooked echo of his mother's, vanished, and a look of anger flashed across his even features. "I did not intend to disturb the good folks of Plymouth," he said, bowing unsteadily.

"Let us see if Brigid has remembered to keep supper warm for you," Warren said, taking his son by the arm.

"Pa..." Winston started to object, but James Warren's grip tightened and he lead his son forcibly from the room.

The door closed and as soon as the latch had clicked, Winston's voice could be heard shouting: "You needn't push me! I am no mewling calf to be corralled!"

Mercy began an animated conversation, but her voice was not loud enough to drown the argument that ensued on the other side of the door. The guests pretended ignorance, but the party, already foundering, was at an end. By 10 o'clock, the Warrens and Adamses sat in subdued silence in the parlor, sipping sweetened wine.

"You held your tongue well, Mrs. Adams," Mercy smiled as she leaned back into the folds of an armchair.

"I did not hold it as I should have," Abigail apologized. "I did not mean to become embroiled in a war of words with your guests, but education is a subject on which I hold particular opinions."

"As do I," Mercy agreed. "You spoke my mind as well as your own, so make no apologies. Besides, such discussion serves to enliven a dinner party. It would be so dull were we all to agree."

"Still..." Abigail began.

"No, I know how they appear," Mercy broke in. "They are simple people, perhaps a bit pompous in their certainty, but kind. And it is they who are the support for the cause. I thought Mr. Adams would enjoy hearing what stripe of patriot populates the provinces."

"Indeed," John agreed absently.

He and James Warren sat in hard chairs drawn close by the fire, sucking on pipes. Though he had answered Mercy, his mind was on Winston. What produces a son who destroys himself and so wounds a family, he wondered. How is it that good homes can make bad children?

The four of them fell silent for a moment and Mercy stared into the fire. Finally, she drew a deep breath, as though drawing air straight into her soul.

"It is I who must apologize -- for my son's behavior," she said softly, watching the flames lick up the sides of the logs.

James Warren looked at his wife, his kind face mournful.

"The vagaries of youth can visit even the most upright of families at times," Abigail put in.

Mercy shook her head. "If it were merely that -- youth. But I fear not. It is so like my brother, James. Our parents prayed that his indiscretions were merely youthful high spirits. He was so full of promise. But drink was like a plague, perverting his sanity, and now.... I am thankful our parents can no longer witness either James or Winston." Mercy's face had fallen into hard lines, and her cheeks held none of the lively blush they had at dinner.

Compassion and affection for Mercy swept over Abigail. She knew what it was to watch a loved one drown in the bottle. Her brother, Will, had begun to frequent the taverns while still in his teens. Now, nearly grown, he owed money all over Braintree and Weymouth, and, to her shame, made no attempt to pay it back.

"It is hard to know..." Abigail said softly. "My own brother, Will.... He is not a bad man, you understand. He is..."

"Spoiled," John put in sourly. He had watched with frustration the indulgence and excuses for Will's wantonness.

Mercy was jolted at John's harsh words and darted a look to see what effect they had on Abigail.

"Yes," Abigail sighed, eyes on the fire. "I regret to use the word, but it is true. Will is spoiled. My parents have tried. They have found him work, which he refuses to do, have secured a place at school for him, which he thrusts away like a child with a toy he no longer desires. Instead, he ruins his chances with gaming and..." she could not bring herself to say 'whoring.' "They have tried," she repeated, "but Will has always been without discipline -- his own or theirs. And now it is too late."

It was a family secret offered as solace to friends grieving over their own mistakes. Alcoholic Will was, by tacit agreement, rarely mentioned even within the family circle. Abigail's admission was born of a generous impulse. Yet the word 'spoiled' carried an implied accusation for the Warrens as well. Mercy had spoiled Winston, her handsome, charming firstborn. But if Mercy heard it as an accusation, she ignored it.

"Winston was such a charming child, Mrs. Adams. Always happy, and filled with life. I hope you will see him in a better light while you are here. He has many admirable qualities."

She adores him, Abigail thought. As my mother adores Will.

"It would indeed be surprising if he did not have admirable qualities, Mrs. Warren, considering the character and mettle of his parents," Abigail said. "The apple does not fall far from the tree."

"That is, in part, what we fear," James Warren murmured, still staring into the fire. "From which branch is Winston sprung?"

By June of 1772, John's health had returned. He had submitted for nearly two years to his doctor's prescribed Braintree cure. He spent his days lopping his apple trees, comparing his manure piles with those of his neighbors, but itching to return to public life. Finally, with Dr. Joseph Warren's blessing, he made plans to move back to Boston. John and Abigail purchased, for £553 6s 8d, a substantial house on Queen Street, big enough for his growing family and his growing reputation, yet small enough to prevent envy. Once again, Abigail packed up the family's belongings -- children, servants, and a cartload of wood and vegetables -- and made the trip back into the center of the conflagration.

Chapter 7

Revenge, at first though sweet, Bitter ere long back on itself recoils
John Milton Paradise Lost Bk

1773

With her ledger in her arms, Abigail marched into the warm, brick-floored kitchen, filled with the aroma of baking bread. A pair of rabbits roasted over the fire, the fat sizzling onto the logs. The churn between Tansy's knees slurped in time to her rhythmic plunging. Rachel checked the loaves in the brick oven then plopped into a chair near Tansy. The two servants, eager for their wages, watched as Abigail dusted a layer of flour off the table with the corner of her apron, then put down the ledger and set the ink and quill beside it. They exchanged glances as their mistress drew coins from her pocket and stacked them in columns on one side of the table.

"Those rabbits are good and fat," Rachel remarked.

"Umm," Abigail nodded, only half-hearing as she sat and began ticking off each name in the ledger as she counted the coins.

"Rachel, thankee for your services," Abigail said, sliding a stack she had made toward the end of the table.

Rachel rose and slid the stack off the table into her palm. She counted as she dropped them one by one into her apron pocket.

"I thankee, Mrs. A.," she said, satisfied as the last piece of silver clinked on top of the others.

Although she had noted with irritation Rachel's counting, Abigail's eyes never left the columns of figures as she turned the ledger around for the servant to sign.

"You may come collect yours, Tansy," she said after Rachel had stepped back toward the hearth to stir a pot of soup.

Tansy scrambled off the stool, her eyes fixed on the coins. She took the coins in skinny brown hands, spreading the few pieces of silver out in her palm. Fascinated, she fingered each one, turning them over to scrutinize both sides before wrapping them in a ragged handkerchief and carefully depositing them in her apron pocket. Taking the quill Abigail held toward her, the girl scrawled a 'T' beside Abigail's finger in the record book, then trotted back to the stool,

84

pleased at the money slapping heavily against her thigh.

"Where are Joe and Walter?"

"Joe's gone to haul the load of firewood from Mr. Evans, and Walter ought to be comin' in any second. He's hanging a ham in the smokehouse," Rachel replied.

As they spoke, they heard the dull clump of leather soles on the back steps, then the rasping of shoes on the iron boot scrape. Walter opened the door and came in with a gust of wind that scurried around the room, rushing at the pages of the ledger. He slammed the door behind him and unwrapped a greasy muffler. When he spied the coins on the table, a gap-toothed grin spread across his face and he stepped forward.

"Piercin' cold today, Mrs. Adams," he observed, hulking over the table. "Nice in here, though."

He pulled dirty mittens from raw, lean hands and stuffed them into his coat pocket.

Abigail handed the young man his wages, and put a finger beside his name in the ledger, indicating where to sign for them. Walter took the quill awkwardly, accidentally dropping a blot of ink onto the figures before marking a quavering "X" on the line.

"Thankee, M'am," he mumbled, stuffing the money into his pocket.

"Have you replaced that broken window pane in the shed yet?" she asked.

"No'm. I couldn't find any panes of the proper size to fit. That is, Mr. Tencher was out o' glass," he corrected himself. "But I slapped a board over it, temporary-like."

"I see."

She distrusted Walter, but could not bring herself to dismiss him without evidence, especially in these hard times. Too many hungry, unemployed youths already roamed the streets. She slammed the ledger shut and gathered up the remaining coins.

"Rachel, tell Joseph when he comes in that I'll pay him tonight, and I want him to stack some of the dry wood by each of the fires after he has his supper."

"Yes'm."

"Walter, fetch my large basket from the pantry. We'll go to the shops when I come back downstairs," she told the youth.

Walter waited until Abigail had left, then darted into the cold pantry where he found a plate piled high with slabs of smoked ham. Picking up a piece, he wolfed it down, then stuffed two more into his pocket before taking the large market basket from the shelf and coming back into the kitchen.

"Tansy, fetch me a mug o' ale," he demanded.

"She don't have to fetch for you," Rachel snapped.

Walter pulled a chair close to the fire, and flopped into it, stretching his feet toward the blaze languorously.

"Well now, maybe she don't and just maybe she do," he said, an evil gleam coming into his eye. "If she knows what's good for her, she'll fetch that ale."

Tansy skittered into the pantry and returned with a full mug, which she handed to Walter with downcast eyes. He took it and slapped her on the rump, laughing when she hastily retreated.

"Leave her alone," Rachel growled, rummaging in the cutlery drawer.

"Aw, she likes it, don't you Tansy-girl? All them that color like it," Walter crooned, licking the ale from his upper lip, his eyes moving familiarly over Tansy's body.

"Mrs. A. wouldn't like to hear you talk like that to her girl," Rachel told him, peeling an apple.

"Mrs. A. ain't goin' to hear me," he retorted, taking another long swig. "What's the matter? You jealous?"

Rachel spat on the floor in answer and reached for another apple.

Abigail had mounted the stairs to the front bedroom where the children were playing in a bright pool of light. Nabby and Johnny, seven and five, sat on the floor, assembling a puzzle. Two-year-old Charly grabbed a puzzle piece and stuffed it into his mouth then grinned defiantly at Nabby, who patiently worked a finger between his lips and took the piece away from him. As soon as Abigail opened the door, Nabby came across the room, hands on hips.

"Mama, Johnny says he'll go to school but I shan't. He's wrong, ain't he?"

Abigail sighed. "Par and I shall do our best for all our children," she replied evasively.

How do I explain to my bright, eager daughter that the world does not consider her worth the cost of an education?

"Nabby shan't go to Harvard, shall she?" five-year-old Johnny demanded.

"I fear women are not admitted to Harvard," Abigail answered.

"See? See? I told you so!" Johnny crowed, skipping around the room.

"John Quincy Adams, stop that this instant," Abigail snapped. "An education at Harvard is a privilege, but brings with it responsibility. More will be expected of you."

She was lying, and knew it. More might be expected of Johnny, but more would be offered to him, too – more opportunities, intellectual challenges, accolades. Men do not want to share, she thought ruefully. But she could not admit even to herself the relief at being spared the expense of educating a daughter. It would be hard enough to find the school fees for three sons.

She left the children to their play, and went to her bedchamber where little Tommy slept in a cradle by the fire. Another baby. Another responsibility. Well, thank God for his health at least. After locking the ledger inside a cabinet, she went to the dresser to pull out gray kid gloves and her drawstring purse. It was still heavy with what remained of the money John had given her Friday night on his return from Provincetown. He had been home only one night before setting off for New Hampshire. Though she missed him, she knew his absences were the only thing that kept her from another pregnancy.

Wrapping her squirrel-trimmed cloak around her shoulders, she stood before the mirror and examined herself. More lines, more gray hair. I was never beautiful and I shall be old soon. Twenty-nine my next birthday. Will I still hold my husband's heart? She remembered the Quincy girls, beautiful and flirtatious, enough to tempt any man. There are many who would happily lie with my husband, she thought. It would break my heart.

She checked little Tommy, who lay curled in feline contentment, then went back downstairs.

"Walter, do you have the basket?" she demanded, marching into the kitchen.

"Yes, Mrs. Adams," he said, hastily gulping the last of his ale and shoving the mug away.

"We shan't be very long, Rachel. Tommy's sleeping the sleep of the innocent, and the others are playing in the front room. They'll be wanting food before long, I warrant."

Without another word, she strode out the back door. Walter followed close on her heels, hunching at a blast of icy wind.

"Do you have the measurements?" she asked.

"Yes'm. I mean, no'm."

Cloaks flailing, they went down the brick path. At the clapboard shed, Walter wrestled the door open and held it while Abigail ducked inside. The dim interior smelled of damp and rats. Abigail stamped her feet while Walter laboriously cut two lengths of sisal to the window's dimensions.

Finally, they set off down the road toward King Street and the shops. Walter walked beside Abigail, matching her brisk stride, and darting surreptitious looks at her face, which was nearly obscured by the deep, fur-trimmed hood.

At the first corner, she turned into the dimly lit candle shop where she paid the bill, then bought four new tallow candles. They slowly continued down the row of shops where Abigail either paid whole accounts or left partial payments with a promise to return with more at the first opportunity. In addition to the candles, the basket Walter carried soon filled with bits of ribbon, spices, a stack of writing paper, fresh-caught fish wrapped in newsprint and already half-frozen in the cold.

At Arthur Trencher's shop, Abigail opened the door reluctantly. She dreaded his sly insults and surly manner, usually preferring to leave that bill to John to pay on the way to one of his meetings with the Sons of Liberty. But John had been too much away, and the bill was long-owing. Walter had begun to drag his feet as they neared the shop. Instead of following Abigail inside, he seated himself on the steps.

A quick pint at the tavern on the corner would go down a treat, he thought, jingling the pay in his pocket. It was tempting, the thought of a drink before that blazing hearth, but he decided against it. Instead, he huddled outside the shop and waited.

When Abigail opened the warped door, the bell jangled. Mr. Trencher, who sat with feet propped on the dusty counter, a long, foul-smelling pipe clenched between yellowed teeth, never moved.

"Good afternoon, Mrs. Adams. And what brings you out on such a cold day? Need something else put on yer bill?"

She went to the counter, annoyed that he had not stood.

"I wish to pay some money on account and to purchase a new

pane of glass for the shed," she said.

"Well now, let's see..." he said, dropping his feet onto the floor with a thud and rummaging underneath the counter. He pulled out a stained ledger and slapped it onto the counter with a smack that made Abigail start.

"Mighty jumpy today, eh, Mrs. Adams?" he chuckled slyly. "Your husband shouldn't leave you alone so much. A woman needs regular servicing. The lack makes even the best of 'em skitterish as rabbits."

"The account if you please," she snapped.

"Let's see," he said, dragging a crooked finger down the rows of figures. "How much do you owe me this time? Ah yes, here we are. Seems you've had rather bad luck with windows this month, eh?"

"What's that?"

"Well, I see your man came in here last week, Friday it was, and bought a pane of glass to replace one that was broke. By a rock, I think he said. Boston's a dangerous place for windows. This one broke by a rock too?" he grinned showing wide gaps between his teeth.

"My man bought a pane and put it down to the account?"
He nodded.

"Walter? The boy out there on the step?" She pointed.

Trencher came out from behind the counter, crossed the bare floor and peered out through the glass at the back of Walter's head. Silently, he returned to his place behind the counter.

"Well?"

"Yep. That's the one. Here it is, right here," he said, showing her the entry. "Friday, 12 Feb 1773, for one pane glass 2 shillings. Right good amount to take to the alehouse, ain't it?" he remarked archly.

"Alehouse!" Abigail cried.

"Well, now, he wouldn't be the first boy in service to charge something to a master's billet and sell it on the streets for his own pocket money, would he?"

Boiling, Abigail pulled money from her purse.

"I have one pound ten to give you on account, Mr. Trencher. And if you would be so good as to cut me another pane to these measurements," she said curtly, producing the two pieces of sisal, "I would be grateful."

89

"How grateful, I wonder?" he muttered before turning aside.

Abigail burned, but bit her tongue. There were few places in town where she could find the same kind of goods Tencher carried, and few places where, despite the sneering and leering, she could leave an account so long unpaid.

The mysterious windowpane explained why Walter was freezing on the step. What to do about him? John would not be home until the end of the week, and she knew if she let the matter ride for that long, her authority would be completely undermined. Yet she dreaded a confrontation - her accusations, his denials. Her mind ran swiftly through several possible scenes, all distasteful. Trencher returned carrying the glass, laid it carefully on the counter and handed Abigail her pieces of twine. While he marked the entry in the ledger, Abigail deliberately measured the sisal against the pane, to ensure he had not cheated her.

"I ain't cheated you yet, Mrs. Adams," Trencher growled as he wrapped the pane in newsprint.

"To be sure, Mr. Trencher."

Taking the pane in her hands, she turned and strode from the shop. When the door opened, Walter rose, trying to discern whether or not she had discovered his larceny. Unable to read anything in her detached, tight-lipped expression, he smiled tentatively as he tucked the glass in a piece of old linsey-woolsey in the basket.

As an antidote to her black mood, she decided to stop at the bookshop. Her face was scarlet with cold by the time she stepped into Cole's Compleat Bookseller. The shop's spare interior smelled cozily of mildew and ink and fine leather bindings. Walter sat in a wooden chair by the window and laid the basket gingerly on the floor while Abigail strode around the little shop, gazing longingly at the new volumes on the shelves.

"Ah, my dear Mrs. Adams," Mrs. Cole sang out cheerily from the recesses of the storeroom as she bustled through to the counter. "And what can we do for you today?"

"I had wished to bring you something on account before I returned here, but I fear my greed for another volume of The Spectator has overcome my scruples," Abigail said.

"Certainly, Mrs. Adams," Mrs. Cole replied. "I have no fear for the money. Not from you. And when does Mr. Adams return this time?"

"End of the week, as far as I know. He's up to New Hampshire on the Superior Circuit."

"Yes. He stopped here to collect a copy of Pope, a gift for his next trip to Plymouth and the Warrens, if memory serves. I suspect he wished to reread it himself before handing it along," she smiled confidingly. "And how are all your little ones?"

"Very well at present, thankee."

"You have a fine little brood," Mrs. Cole said with warm sincerity. "But it's as they get older the problems arise. Take my Joseph. He's a good lad, truly, but he can't settle. Mr. Cole and I have been urging him since he was a boy to go into the business, you know. But he'll have none of it. He graduates from Harvard this year, and is talking of the law. I don't know, I'm sure! I wonder, Mrs. Adams," she said, brightening as though she had just now landed on the happy thought, "might he talk with your husband sometime soon? Mr. Adams could tell him a thing or two about what it is to read the law and what sort of life it is. We'd be ever so grateful."

"I'm quite sure Mr. Adams would be happy to talk with your Joseph," Abigail smiled, glad of an opportunity to repay their kindness. The Coles continually extended credit to them without ever making them feel in debt. "Perhaps Joseph could come round one day next week if Mr. Adams is home. How would that be?"

"Oh, wonderful! I will speak with him. How difficult it is to give one's children sound guidance with so few credentials."

"Precisely," Abigail agreed. "My friend Mrs. Warren and I have often complained of the difficulty of raising children without the benefit of a formal education."

"Mrs. Warren..." Mrs. Cole said. She had not missed Abigail's surge of pride at the name. "Even such as Mrs. Warren has her cross to bear."

Winston's debauchery was known even in Boston -- the price Mercy paid for her fame.

Mrs. Cole turned and bustled to the shelf where she found a new volume of *The Spectator Papers*, bound in brown leather and embossed in gold. Returning to the counter, she pulled out a sheet of paper with which she began to wrap the book.

"Oh, Mrs. Cole, you need not wrap it. Paper is far too dear these days," Abigail admonished, shocked at the extravagance.

91

"Nonsense, Mrs. Adams," the other woman said jovially. "The little ones may use it for drawing."

"That is very kind indeed," Abigail smiled, touched at the generosity of this ordinarily thrifty New England shopkeeper. "I will pay the entire bill owing as soon as Mr. Adams returns home with funds," she promised.

"People who love books the way you and Mr. Adams do always manage to pay their bills. We are not worried over your credit, my dear," Mrs. Cole informed her as she knotted string around the parcel.

"You are very good, Mrs. Cole," Abigail said, taking the packet. "Don't forget to tell Joseph we will expect him next week. I'll have Mr. Adams call round to set the day. I thankee."

Her encounter with Mrs. Cole had lifted her spirits, made her feel a little less alone. As she left, Walter scrambled to his feet and followed her out the door. Outside, the cold air scalded her throat and lungs. Yet buoyed by Mrs. Cole's kindness, she set off toward home at a swift pace, her skirts and cloak lashing her legs in the wind. Walter hurried along beside her, increasingly more hopeful that his theft had gone undetected.

When they reached the back fence of the Adams home, Abigail took the basket from Walter and sent him off to the well to draw water to fill the ewers in the chambers. Grumbling, he turned down along the path, scarf flying behind him like a tattered flag.

"A cup of tea would not be amiss, Rachel," Abigail said as she came into the warmth of the kitchen and stretched her hands toward the fire.

Rachel had taken the rabbits from the roasting stand and stood over a huge platter, carving them into joints and arranging them carefully. Abigail put the basket down in the pantry and withdrew from it the writing paper and other sundries, leaving the pane of glass and the fish.

"I've just made a pot of tea, Mrs. A. It's ribwort this time. Not the best, but not too bad," Rachel, informed her. "Will ye take some?"

"Yes. It's hot at least," Abigail sighed.

Rachel nodded in reluctant agreement. She had fewer scruples than her employers and would have been grateful for a fresh-brewed pot of smuggled real China tea, but knew enough to hold her tongue in this political household.

"Do ye want milk?"

"No, I'll grit my teeth and bear it as 'tis," Abigail chuckled as both women stared ruefully at the pot of virtuous brew. "The main thing is heat. I'm nearly froze clean through. Have the children et their supper?"

Rachel nodded.

"Walter will be in to fill the ewers in a moment. Rachel, do you know anything about the pane of glass he bought at Trencher's?" she asked.

Rachel kept her head down, sipping at her cup.

"Little enough," she murmured.

"Well?"

"Friday evening Walter came home from the tavern with some trinket he said the woman there had given him. He was in his cups a bit, and I thought he'd stolen it. But I said nothing. I..." she paused, searching for a way to explain her silence on the matter. "I don't like to be near him when he's had too much to drink, Mrs. A. I don't know what he might do."

Abigail watched Rachel over the rim of her cup. Walter had come to them in need of a job, and Abigail's sense of Christian charity would not let her turn him away, but she had always been uneasy about him. His father had beaten Walter's mother to death in a drunken fit, so they said, but there was never any prosecution, no witnesses. He followed his wife soon after leaving his only living child to fend for himself. Heaven alone knew where Walter's father had gotten the money to buy drink, but somehow there was always money for that when there was no money for food for the boy. Abigail had taken Walter in the year before, as much to help him as to help herself. She was beginning to think it was a mistake.

"Is the fire in the parlor stirred?"

"Yes'm. Should be fair warm in there by now."

Taking her cup and two cookies, Abigail walked through the chill hallway. If she had not decided to lace her tea with brandy, she might never have discovered him. When she opened the door to the dining room, she was shocked to see Walter standing beside the table, glass in hand, a bottle of John's rum open on the table. He must have left the front door unlatched earlier and come in there.

"How dare you!" she cried.

Walter started at her voice and nearly dropped the glass, accidentally slopping the rum over the side.

"I never..." he faltered.

"I said: how dare you steal Mr. Adams' rum?" Abigail repeated, heart thumping.

"Uh... I just wanted a little nip fer the cold..." Walter stammered.

"And is that what happened to the first pane of glass you charged to our account? Did you sell it for drink?" she demanded.

"Well, uh, I don't know... No! I never! That pane got broke... on the way home."

"Do not lie to me, Walter Bolt. I will not tolerate a liar -- or a thief. Is this how you repay us for a roof over your head, and fair treatment? You are released from service. Now get out! I will have Rachel pack your things and leave them on the kitchen stoop."

The young man stood immobile, his gaze the hooded eyes of a cornered dog.

"Mr. Adams hired me. Mr. Adams must fire me, not you," he said slowly straightening. Glaring at her, he deliberately downed the rum he still held in his hand before slamming the glass onto the table. Abigail wavered between fear and indignation then drew herself up.

"Insolent boy! Who pays your wages? Who pays the shopkeepers? Who manages this house? Mr. Adams? No! I do. Leave now or I shall fetch the sheriff to throw you in jail."

For one long moment, Walter stared at her defiantly. Then, his eyes flickered.

"All right, I'll go. But you'll be sorry you turned me out into the cold, I warrant you," he growled.

He pushed past Abigail, who stood in the doorway, and went out the front door. Tea and cookies still in hand, Abigail hurriedly locked the front door then went back down the dim corridor to the kitchen.

"Rachel, I have just let Walter go. Please pack his things in a bundle and put them on the back step. I do not want him in this house again."

Trembling, she gulped the bitter tea, and laid the empty cup on the table.

It had been dark for hours by the time she had listened to John Quincy's lessons and read three pages of *The Spectator* with Nabby. She scooped up Charly, who was curled like a possum at her feet near the hearth, and took the children to bed. When she returned to the kitchen, she found Rachel asleep at the table, her head on her folded arms.

"Go to bed, Rachel," Abigail said as she jostled the young woman.

Tansy was already asleep on her pallet in the pantry.

"Yes, Mrs. A," Rachel yawned.

"Is Joseph in yet?" Abigail asked.

"I don't know. I haven't yet seen him," the young woman replied sleepily.

"I want to bolt the door," Abigail murmured, frowning, "but I'd hate to lock Joseph out on a night such as this. Yet I don't want to leave the house unlocked, neither."

"Walter probably won't be back tonight, Mrs. A. Especially not if he's already had a few. He'll have gone off to the tavern to drink up the rest of his wages. Afterwards, he won't have enough sense to find his way back here."

"Perhaps you're right," Abigail agreed.

Rachel banked the fire for the night then moved off toward the tiny servants' room at the back of the house. Abigail trudged to the front door to check the bolt. Although she never minded the days when John was traveling, she dreaded the nights. In the dark she felt alone and fearful. She plodded upstairs and put the candle on the chest beside her mirror. After letting her hair down, she brushed it through with a dusting of powder. Still too cold to wash it yet. Perhaps next month. Fumbling out of her day clothes, she carried the candle to her bedside, climbed into the cold sheets and blew out the light.

She awoke from a fearful dream, not knowing the time, but certain someone was moving inside the house. One of the children? Rachel? She raised herself upon an elbow, and listened. The fire had burned low, a smoldering of coals on the hearth. Nothing. Dimly she could hear the ticking of the hall clock. Her neck ached from the awkward position held so long. A dream, she told herself. Imagination. She started to lie back down when a thud followed by the muffled sound of a man's voice brought her straight upright in bed. Heart pounding, she waited. A rat? No, there *had* been a voice. Surely, it was Joe. Wasn't it?

Tensed in every muscle, she slid from bed and stepped barefooted onto the cold floor. She stood, groaning inwardly at the creak. What should she do? Trembling, she took the heavy candlestick in hand, lit the candle from what was left of the fire, and tiptoed toward the door. At the top of the stair, she waited, listening. There was no sound. Carefully, she went down the stairs. Silence. I imagined it all.

A loud creak, a footfall, unmistakable this time. Her heart hammered against her ribs. Please let it be Joseph, she prayed, knowing that he would never have been foraging in the dining room in the middle of the night. At the door, she stopped, waiting. What shall I do? Confront the intruder? Suppose there is more than one? Oh John, where are you when I need you most? The blood pulsed in her ears, almost drowning out the sounds coming from behind the door. Shall I run for help? Where? No, I must do this. Sucking in a breath, she swung the door wide.

For a moment, she did not recognize the figure, then by the single wavering candle she saw Walter hunched over a bulging sack, the foot of a silver candlestick sticking out of the corner of it. Walter held the brandy bottle in his hand. When he heard Abigail lurch into the room, he looked up to stare stupidly into her face. Then an impudent smile of recognition slid across his features.

"Evenin'," he said, squinting.

"Get out!" Abigail hissed through her shock and fear.

"Thought you owed me one last drink just to warm the bones, like. You throwed me out into the cold," he slurred, ignoring her command.

"Get out!" she said again, teeth clenched so hard her head hurt. "How dare you come..."

"You take a lot on yoursef don't ya, woman?" the youth interrupted weaving slightly, his jaw thrust out at her. "My ma would never dare to speak to a man as you do. She knew her place, least w' me dad around. He broke two o' her teeth once when she nagged at him. *He* taught her. It was soo easy," he continued almost in reverie. "He was big, ya know. Big. I was there. I saw. She were tryin' to make him feel small. Some women are like that. *You're* like that. But it was so easy. Pa just reached out his hand...."

He swished at the air with the back of his hand with a force that made her heart jolt. The motion knocked him slightly off balance and he grabbed the corner of the table to steady himself.

"He was a big man," Walter repeated, thinking back to the night he had watched, motionless, while his father beat his mother unconscious. "And she just fell limp, like a rag doll. And her mouth started to bleed. She just sat there all crumpled in the corner with her hand kinda coverin' her mouth and blood oozin' out between the fingers. Didn't say nothin'. He had shut her up all right, ya see. Women like you want shuttin' up."

He glared at her through bleary eyes and tried to take a swig of the bottle only to discover it was empty. Distracted, he turned to rummage in the cabinet.

Clutching her candlestick, Abigail edged sideways until the full bulk of the table stood between the two of them. What am I to do? she thought. Please God, help me. Walter continued his search through the cabinet, finally emerging with a large bottle of rum in his fist. Uncorking it, he swung it to his mouth, dribbling half of it over his tattered clothes and onto the table and floor.

"Women like you want shuttin' up," he repeated, suddenly lurching toward Abigail.

"You havin' trouble, Mrs. Adams?"

Covered with mud and snow, Joseph's bulk filled the doorway.

"Not if Walter leaves quietly, " Abigail said with an evenness that surprised her.

"I can easily get the gun to shoot him for you, Mrs. A," Joseph said matter-of-factly. "It would make a terrible mess, but then you wouldn't have no more dealings with him, either. Gone!"

He said the last word with a force that imitated the sound of a gun going off.

"No! Don't shoot me!" Walter cried, his eyes darting around the room for a weapon, or a means of escape.

"Git out, Walter," Joseph commanded.

He came in, seized the drunken youth by the collar, and dragged him out into the hall. When he reached the front door, he pulled Walter's face close.

"If you ever come round here again, I'll shoot you dead for sure. You'd just be another sad body felled for liberty."

Eyes wide, Walter nodded dumbly.

Joseph opened the front door and pitched Walter headlong down the front steps. The youth sprawled, making vain attempts to shout obscenities at the closed door, then puked loudly into the road.

Joseph closed and bolted the door, then came to Abigail who had half-collapsed against the wall, face white in the candlelight.

"Are you all right, M'am?"

She nodded. "Your arrival was very timely. Where were you 'til this hour?"

"The old lady down the road, Mrs. Bright -- you know in the blue clapboard? -- asked me to collect a load of wood for her. As you weren't here, I figured you wouldn't mind, not for a old widow-lady, so I was off again. Cart got stuck, and it took me til now to pull it out and get back. I won't ever thaw," he said, shivering in his sodden, stiff clothes.

"Here. Come take a dram of brandy, then get yourself into dry clothes by the kitchen fire," Abigail said. "We'll be burying you if you're not careful. And you're far too valuable to lose."

Joseph took the glass and gratefully drank the contents at a gulp.

"Thankee for the help," she said softly, both relieved at his coming and frustrated at her own impotence.

Joseph nodded, and turned to walk down the hall to the kitchen. Taking the candle in hand, Abigail remounted the steps alone.

Chapter 8

And out of good still to find means of evil
John Milton Paradise Lost Bk I line 165

1774

"The first essay, Johnny," Abigail said, as the seven-year-old turned pages in a copy of *The Spectator.*

The June sun splashed buttery pools across their Boston yard and a gentle breeze carried with it pear blossoms coupled with the salty stench of a Boston low tide. Nabby sat on the grass stitching quilt squares while watching her brothers, four-year-old Charly and two-year-old Tommy, who tried unsuccessfully to catch a robin prospecting for worms. Johnny, hopes of play dashed, sat at his mother's knee, her book on his lap.

Despite gratitude for their lively good health, their inquisitive minds, Abigail chaffed at the shackles of her children's needs. She longed for freedom -- to read for days, to discuss philosophy or politics uninterrupted, to write letters or visit friends. A man's life, she thought. I want a man's life. Yet as a woman... no, because I am a woman, I am blessed. I should be ashamed.

"Here, Ma?" Johnny asked, ready to begin his lesson.

She sighed, and looked down at the innocent face. There was a hint of Grandfather Quincy in the wide blue eyes. Raising up a man like Colonel Quincy is hard, important work, she thought, but work without credit. I wish some credit.

"Right there." She put her finger on a page. "Begin."

"The Spectator, No. CDLXXIV," the boy began.

"You do not say 'No.', Johnny," Abigail instructed. "You say *number*. What is Mr. Thaxter teaching you? And you read that string of letters as a number. That is a Roman numeral. C is one hundred, and D is five hundred. When the smaller number is in front of the larger number, you subtract. Take one hundred from five hundred which leaves..."

"Four hundred," he responded, baffled.

"Correct. And the L is fifty, the X is ten, so that is fifty plus ten plus ten equals..." she waited.

Johnny paused, thinking, then "Seventy."

"Yes. And IV means one taken from five..."

"Four."

"So, you read the number...?"

His brow furrowed, he repeated the instructions to himself softly, twice, while Abigail pursed her lips impatiently.

After consideration, he replied, tentatively, "Four hundred and seventy four?"

"Yes." She nodded. It was a triumph of reasoning, but she refused to acknowledge it as such lest it breed conceit in her son -- and herself.

"Proceed, Johnny."

John Quincy read the page aloud, stumbling only twice. When he had finished, he looked up at his mother hopefully.

"That was not badly done, Johnny. Read another page and try to improve your grace in the reading of it. You needs must improve your grasp of the words so you do not stumble over them and make your listeners lose their train of thought. It interrupts the ideas."

"Yes, Mar," Johnny mumbled, stung.

For an instant, Abigail thought she saw hurt flit across his face. *Am I making him strong or callous? I cannot be soft on him; I would not raise up another Will.*

The kitchen door swung wide and John strode out into the yard.

"Ah, my brood, gathered together. Good."

Blood-shot, dark-rimmed eyes were the only evidence of John's punishing workload -- circuit court schedules, local clients, meetings of the Assembly and the Sons of Liberty. A wearing schedule that left little time for home, yet, except for his eyes, he looked prosperous and happy. *He looks,* Abigail suddenly realized, *like a cat, who has just drunk the cream. He has a secret.*

"And how is your reading coming, my boy?" John boomed at Johnny.

"You had best ask my mother, Sir," Johnny replied, glancing at Abigail for approbation.

But Abigail's attention was on John.

"Your father has news," she said shrewdly.

"Mar knows me too well," John laughed. "General Gage has dissolved the Assembly."

"What does it mean, Par?" Nabby asked, sitting up.

"It means he can, if we do not comply, send his troops, forcibly eject us from our assembly, and lock us out," he explained.

"Oh."

"And did you comply?" Abigail asked.

"Yes," John replied, smiling.

"One month in office and he is wielding a large political sword," Abigail observed, on edge, waiting.

John wore the same look as when he told her he had accepted Captain Preston's defense following the Boston Massacre. She hated the cat and mouse game he played with news. He holds all our lives in his hands, yet he makes me beg for each morsel, she though bitterly. But her pride kept her from seeming eager.

"Gage plays the strong commander," John agreed with Abigail's observation.

"Then are we to have no other government than General Gage?" Johnny asked.

"Not if the citizens of the colonies have anything to say about it," John cried at last. "Only hours before the Assembly was dissolved, we elected five delegates to the First Continental Congress in the colonies!"

"And you are one of them," Abigail finished for him.

John nodded, eyes dancing.

"And where will this Continental Congress meet?" she asked.

John's face faltered only slightly.

"Philadelphia."

"What will it mean, Par?" Nabby asked again.

"It means he will be away even more and be paid even less," Abigail answered sourly.

"Undoubtedly," John agreed, unfazed. "It will also mean that I will help decide our country's fate. I pray I am equal to the task," he added, suddenly remembering to pretend humility.

"It is an honor you are imminently qualified to receive, Mr. Adams," Abigail said flatly. "You have earned your place in history. But it is won at the expense of your family. Posterity, however kind it may prove, cannot recompense us for the loss of your company."

"I know, my dear," John replied, softening at her acknowledgment of his 'place in history,' something he allowed himself to reflect on only in his most private thoughts.

He put his hand on her shoulder but withdrew it when he felt her stiffen.

"I sorely miss you and the chicks," he said gently. "But I do this not only for us now, but for our children's children. I study politics and war that my sons may study mathematics and philosophy, so that their sons may study painting and poetry and music."

"We miss you all the same, Par," Johnny said earnestly.

John spent much of the six weeks between his appointment and his departure riding the Superior Court circuit in Maine, trying to fill the family coffers. He stopped at home for only three days before leaving for Philadelphia on the 18th of August, three weeks before the First Continental Congress would convene. Her pride at war with her resentment, Abigail watched John's receding back as he trotted off with his cousin Sam Adams, James Bowdoin, Thomas Cushing, and Robert Treat Paine. He leaves for adventures. I tend home fires, she thought.

But the home fires in Boston would soon explode into a conflagration, fanned by General Gage. He had ordered cannon mounted on Beacon Hill. Entrenchments and breastworks cut through the commons of Boston, and troops, housed in a canvas city constructed throughout town, marched through the streets.

In preparation for the conflict, the Sons of Liberty and their friends scoured the town for gunpowder, hiding it in barns, houses, cellars, and the rafters of taverns, a surreptitious magazine dispersed among a hundred Whig sympathizers.

Hearing the stealthy rustle of feet outside her window one evening, Abigail flung up the sash. A troop of minutemen, arms loaded with casks of gunpowder, marched softly past. The commander stepped out of line, and came to the window on moccasined feet.

"Do ye want some powder, Missus?" he whispered. "We may all have need."

Shuddering, Abigail shook her head. Will there be house-to-house fighting? She watched silently as the man stepped back into line and the column of grim-faced patriots filed away. We must return to the safety of Braintree.

She could find no one to rent the house, but her fears overcame her prudent management. If it be burned to the ground, at least we will not be inside. She hired an agent to oversee the property, and moved back to Braintree.

The September day, dry and hot, like the curling leaves that had fallen prematurely, only added to the apprehension, the sense of foreboding. The cellars, by now usually chock-full of barrels of pickle and potatoes, apples and onions and huge mounds of saw-dust-packed root vegetables, showed gaps, a promise of hunger that made housewives snap at neighbors and clutch at their children impatiently.

The Crown rained down punishments. Each measure brought a countermeasure from the colonies. Boston Harbor was thick with the bristling masts of British warships like the remains of a fire-ravaged forest. Conflict was only a matter of time.

Abigail, dreading their arrival at the barracks in Boston, sat in a trap beside her father. Impatiently, Reverend Smith slapped the reins on the horse's flanks, willing the journey to be over. The overheated animal took two or three desultory trots then fell back into a slow walk.

"I only hope Will can be made to come with us," Reverend Smith said, breaking the silence of the past three miles.

"Will may believe Mother's illness to be merely a return of one of her old complaints and believe he need not come," Abigail remarked, wondering even as she spoke why she was trying to make excuses for Will. He will make his own excuses soon enough, she thought.

Reverend Smith remained tight-lipped.

"In that event, what shall we do?"

"We shall insist," Rev. Smith replied quietly. "At present, the army has less need of Will than his family."

Earlier that summer, the Massachusetts Provincial Congress had voted to enlist twelve thousand recruits. Will, married and the father of two small children, had immediately joined up; whether to redeem himself or to escape his responsibilities was unclear. On that point, he was silent. He had simply come to the parsonage one day and dropped off his family.

"Suppose Will is not sober?" she asked.

Squinting into the distance, her father murmured, almost apologetically: "Will was ever the apple of your mother's eye. A mother sees God's hopes where others see imperfection."

The old jealousy jabbed. Will had done little to earn their mother's love, while Abigail and her sisters had done their duty at every turn. Yet it was Will who held Elizabeth Smith's heart, as though by divine right. Will's presence, when sober, lit an unadulterated joy in Elizabeth Smith's eyes, a flame that stood in stark contrast to the distant affection she showed her daughters. The Prodigal Son was ever doted upon, Abigail thought. Duty must be its own reward, a bitter lesson.

Yet for the sake of the love she bore her mother, Abigail would do her utmost to ensure Will's presence, however much it rankled.

The drought-hardened ruts stretched like concrete ribbons from Weymouth to Boston, turning the ten-mile ride into a bone-rattling trial. Carts loaded with milk and eggs and meat from the outlying farms choked the highway. Some were relieving Boston's acute food shortages; others were profiteers seeking hefty gain. Their carriage passed the body of a dog on the side of the road, its stinking, swollen carcass covered with flies.

As they drew closer to town, gaunt boys and old men began to approach the carriage begging, their clothes in tatters. The drought had brought as many people low as had the British embargo, and Abigail trembled to think that but for the grace of God and her own shrewd management, she and her children would starve this winter.

After several inquiries, they found William in an old warehouse that had been converted to a barracks. Unpainted and withered with neglect, the building's clapboard sides sagged despondently, an echo of the limp discipline in the ragtag militia. Inside, William sat with five other men in a rectangle of light that spilled through a window onto the ale-soaked boards of a rough table.

For a moment, as Abigail and her father approached, the men looked like a huddled remnant of the Last Supper, curiously transplanted. But when they reached the little knot, Abigail's heart sank. Several bottles of whiskey, two empty, stood on the table. A sticky deck of cards was being dealt by one of the men, and a pile of coins sat in the middle of the table. If the Reverend Smith felt grief over the lost promise of his only son, his voice gave no hint of it. There was only barely controlled rage.

"William, it is midday! And see how we find you!" he bellowed as though reaching the last pew with a warning of damnation.

"You find me very well, Father," William replied leaning back to survey his father through slitted eyes.

Although Will Smith feared his father, his flippancy did not betray so much as a hint. The others laughed at their comrade's apparent quip.

Emboldened by his friends' laughter, Will continued, "In fact, I am surprised that you found me at all. I could easily have been drilling on the commons, or off to a meal, or showing the troops how to clean muskets...."

"Enough!" Reverend Smith thundered. "I need to speak with you. Privately."

Reverend Smith glared around the ring of upturned faces, defying any to interfere.

"Privately? These are my friends. I have no secrets from my friends. Why, Bill, here -- same name as me, you notice, except I am not an officer -- yet -- Bill here is our senior commander. At least while Tom Guthry is out."

"You show your officers such disrespect as to call them by Christian names?" Abigail blurted incredulously.

"And why not?" her brother sneered. "Are we not all colonists together? Did we not elect our officers? What need have we of setting another Lord or King above us?"

"Hear! hear!" the half-drunken men around the table agreed.

"I pray our entire army is not so corrupt as this fragment appears," Abigail said, heartsick at the fragility of what supported John's efforts.

Her father laid a hand on her arm to silence her.

"William, I needs must speak with you -- alone -- if your officer will give me leave," he said in voice that brooked no obstruction.

"Why certainly," Bill, the officer, agreed, tucking his cards into his open jacket and leaning back comfortably in the rickety wooden chair.

William hesitated. He had wanted to force his father to stand alone, while he held forth surrounded by his friends. Or better still, force the old man to leave without speaking at all. Now, he had little choice but to follow his father to a remote part of the warehouse and listen, resentfully, as he had on so many other occasions.

"Your mother is not well, Will," Reverend Smith began. "We have come, your sister and I, to return you home in hopes your presence will revive her spirit."

William looked sideways at his father, a glint in his red-rimmed eyes.

"Mother has spells each autumn. It lies in the humors of the change of season. And each year, she returns to health, as regular as the ticking of a clock. Perhaps it is simply a way to return me to the fold."

"You accuse us of dissembling while your mother may lie at death's door? Have a care, William," Reverend Smith said low, through gritted teeth. "Our Maker numbers our days on earth. Your mother is no longer young, or strong. It is your Christian duty as well as your duty as a beloved son to return to lighten her remaining days."

"My duty lies here, Father," William replied.

"Then for the sake of your family..." Reverend Smith began, his temper rising.

"No one questions that Abigail's husband is so much away," William broke in plaintively. "Of course not. John Adams is our light and shining star. Glory be to John on high. He may leave home and family in the hands of others without a second's thought and no one speaks to him of duty. Why may I not be treated with that same respect?"

"People will respect a respectable man!" his father exploded. "A man *earns* respect and not by swilling spirits and gambling the sun away neither!"

"Ah! And you are such a *respectable* man!" William said sarcastically.

Reverend Smith reached out a hand to slap his son, but stopped himself. He drew a deep breath, and studied the floor for a moment, forcing himself to a calm he did not feel. Then he looked up into Will's once-handsome face, now puffed and mottled with drink.

"William, your mother ails. It could well be her last illness. Does that not touch you?"

A defiant expression crossed the younger man's features, followed by something Abigail could not read. Sorrow? Regret?

"I cannot, Father. I *will* come. But not today."

"So be it," Reverend Smith replied angrily.

Without another word, he strode out of the building.

"How can you hurt our parents so, Will?" Abigail cried, tears starting. "If your duty does not call you, then does not your love?"

106

"I will have none of your sanctimonious preaching, Sister," William growled. Turning his back on her, he returned to his comrades. Angry and ashamed, Abigail followed her father outside to climb into the carriage. They rode back to Weymouth in silence.

By tacit agreement, Reverend Smith and Abigail contrived a story to explain William's absence: too important, people depending on him, crucial to the regiment's morale. The words nearly choked Abigail, but Mrs. Smith's eyes brightened with pride.

"Perhaps Will was right," her mother said, coughing convulsively for a moment as she struggled to bring up phlegm.

Abigail leaned over and held a handkerchief to Elizabeth Smith's mouth, withdrawing it when her mother had finished her fit.

"Perhaps my Will was right," the older woman rasped finally. "He will earn accolades and glory in the army. He had no chance here, no opportunities. Joining the struggle for freedom will be the making of him."

"Yes, Mother," Abigail agreed softly, her heart writhing at the lie. "Perhaps so."

Despite their fears, Elizabeth Smith recovered. Buttressed by the belief that her son was finally learning to honor a commitment, she could look unashamed into the faces of her daughter-in-law and grandchildren. And, because his mother still lived, Will was vindicated in his refusal to come home.

In late autumn, John left the debates in Congress only to take up another battle of words on his return to Braintree. A loyalist pamphleteer written under the pseudonym, *Massachusettensis*, had charged the Whigs with fomenting revolution – treason, a hanging offense. Incensed, John fired off a reply under the pseudonym *Novangulus*. Neither nor Whigs and Loyalists, he insisted, were subject to Parliament since they had no representation within that body. It was possible to remain loyal to King George yet reject Parliament's unconstitutional edicts. About two-thirds of the colonists, John estimated, resisted Parliament but all were loyal to the king –this assertion despite the fact that he had recently persuaded Congress to appoint George Washington as Commander-in-Chief of the newly forming Continental Army.

John was writing a *Novangulus* paper on April 19, 1775, when

British troops sent to confiscate a store of munitions and powder fired on colonial militia at Lexington and Concord. That act killed several men, and with them, John's loyalty to the British Crown.

While Abigail's indignation matched John's, her fears outstripped his. He would be consumed with the tantalizing prospect of building a new nation, but she would be left alone to run the farm, raise their children and keep their precarious finances intact. He was stimulated; she was besieged.

John left for Philadelphia and the Second Continental Congress in May 1775. Abigail watched him trot away on the gelding, listening to the rasping cough that he had not been able to shake. His eye infections had grown worse. God keep him, she thought. All our lives are in your hands now.

Although he had been given enthusiastic receptions all along the way, John wrote from Princeton that he worried there was more smoke in public support than fire, that it would evaporate at the first true test. Abigail thought of her brother, Will, and his drunken friends in the militia. Will they bolt at the first shot? If they do, and the British capture the Congress, they will all be hanged. Would the British Regulars march over Penns Hill and capture the families of the patriots who had begun it all? Destitution – or worse --would be the family's fate.

Though it was the anniversary of John's appointment to the Continental Congress, there were no celebrations, the honor overshadowed by fear of what lay ahead.

The June day dawned hot and still. The younger Adams children followed Nabby to the barn to milk the cow. They loved to squirt the milk fresh from the teat into the mouths of the hungry barn cats, who waited nearby, meowing like a Greek chorus. Only Johnny sat at the long kitchen table, his head bent over a copy of *Rollin's Ancient History*, reading aloud while his mother worked.

Their household had altered. Joseph had left for the army in July. The following month, Rachel had married and left, and Tansy returned home to raise her youngest siblings when her father died. Finding new servants that didn't lie, steal, or drink was a burden, though the gossip that followed even the most circumspect family in the village, made it easier. Secrets were short-lived.

In September, Abigail hired Patty, the daughter of Mr. Cawley's second wife. True to Grandmother Quincy's prediction, he had found another wife, a new mother for his children, not a year after his first wife died in childbirth. Now, with children of her own, Abigail understood both the loneliness and the practicality. The third of five more children born to Cawley and his young second wife, Patty had been working since she was nine. In these hard times, parents everywhere viewed service as a means of feeding their families.

Patty, accustomed to living in other people's homes for most of her life, knew how to become part of a family, yet remain on the outside. She stood churning butter beside Suzy, who shelled peas at the table.

Abigail's father had brought Suzy, nearly Abigail's age, to them. Suzy had spent her life on a farm in Lexington on the other side of Boston, a place Reverend Smith had traveled on business years before.

"She comes of a good family, but like many, they have fallen on hard times. I will help with her wages, if that is needed," he had told Abigail when she had opened her mouth to protest.

It was an odd offer, but Abigail, who was glad of a sober, sensible woman, and of the extra money, agreed without examining it further. Able and willing, Suzy was a quiet presence in the house, and though she had no children of her own, was good with Abigail's brood.

On June 17, Suzy and Abigail stood side by side kneading bread dough. Suddenly a sound, ghostly, like half-imagined thunder, caught Abigail's attention. She stopped and lifted her head.

"Did ye hear that?"

Johnny stopped reading. "I heard nothing, Mar."

An echo, slight, but distinct, repeated.

"I heard something, Mrs. Adams," Patty agreed, frozen in mid-churn.

Abigail wiped off her hands then stepped outside the kitchen door into the shadow of the house. Birds chirruped happily through the trees and the sun beat down on the roof, making the upstairs like an oven.

In the distance, Abigail thought she could see a puff of smoke rising over Boston. Johnny left his book and came outside to stand beside her.

"I think I heard something, Mar. What could it be?"

"See that little cloud rising?" she asked, leaning down beside the eight-year-old and sighting down a finger pointed northwest "What think you -- smoke?"

Johnny looked at his mother, his eyes wide for a moment. "If we climb the hill, we might could see."

Together they set off at a half-trot toward Penn's Hill. The sounds of thunder became more pronounced, the belching of a distant, muffled colossus. By the time they had reached the low summit, they were panting. Straw-colored tendrils of hair stuck to Johnny's forehead and Abigail's dress stuck to her back.

"Look!" Johnny cried, squinting toward Boston where a blossom of smoke opened above the miniature peaks of the buildings.

Another bloom opened and another, an ephemeral garden rising in a purple haze toward the blue overhead. The belching had grown louder, and each new burst of smoke was followed after a few minutes by the echoed boom of the cannon rumbling over the hills toward Braintree.

"It's war, Mar, ain't it?" Johnny asked wonderingly.

"Yes, son. It's war."

Her stomach lurched as she spoke the words. No turning back now.

"Are we a new nation?"

"Not yet," she said somberly. "Many will die before we may call ourselves a nation, if indeed God grant it at all."

"I pray no one we know may die in it," Johnny said quietly.

"There will be many we know who will fall," Abigail predicted. "May God give them rest in a just cause."

That evening, Abigail learned that their dear friend, Dr. Joseph Warren of Boston, had died in the Battle of Bunker Hill.

Fear and famine drove a steady stream of families to the countryside. Many moved in with relatives, others paid acquaintances or strangers to take them in. The Adamses had already given curmudgeonly Isaac Hayden, whose two sons had enlisted in the militia, two rooms off the kitchen by the time Tott, the Boston jeweler, arrived with his wife and six children. They had escaped Boston just before the British soldiers had closed the town. Hayden, ensconced rent-free, refused to make more room for the Totts.

"I must keep the space open if any of my family should come to visit," he insisted.

"The Totts are many more than you and need the space."

Hayden had merely slammed the door in her face and thrown the bolt.

Furious but impotent, Abigail packed up John's books and papers and installed all eight of the Totts in John's one-room office.

Worse than the battles in Boston was the dysentery epidemic that followed. It spread long, groping fingers into the countryside. In one week, eighteen friends and neighbors in Braintree were buried. As she lay in bed, Abigail fought rising panic. *How will I keep it out? I could not bear to lose another child.*

On the 5th of August, an exhausted soldier from Elihu Adams's regiment brought him home from Cambridge in the back of a buckboard. Sweating, half-delirious, Elihu was covered with a tattered blanket and stank of the plague. With a tenderness that touched Abigail's heart, the soldier helped to carry him upstairs to the small room in Susanna's house that Elihu shared with his wife and children. For five days, Susanna nursed her son in turns with Elihu's young wife, but in the end, all they could do was watch him die. By the time John returned to Braintree for three weeks in August 1775, Elihu's youngest daughter had been buried, too.

More than ever, Abigail resented the crowded household. There was no time alone. Then, three days after John mounted his horse and set off on the four hundred mile journey between Braintree and Philadelphia, the plague crossed their threshold.

It was early, not long after cockcrow, when Charly crashed down the stairs and through the doors of the hall that led to the kitchen searching for his mother. Hayden, locked behind the dairy room door, still lying in his cot, banged on the wall with his fist for quiet. Abigail stood at the back door drinking in the peace of the morning sky when Charly, fat face flushed, charged through the door.

"Mar! Mar! Tommy's real hot and he can't get up. Johnny says to hurry and fetch you!"

Dear God, thought Abigail, *spare my child!* In momentary panic, her mind fell on Joseph and Mariah Hawkins who had buried all five of their children, felled in quick succession like young saplings before a logger's ax.

Snatching her skirts in both fists, Abigail rushed upstairs behind Charly. The room, though sparsely furnished, was crammed with books and papers, the contents of John's office. A narrow path led to the bed. Johnny sat beside Tommy on the low cot that the two younger boys shared, dabbing his brother's forehead with a handkerchief he had dipped into the water pitcher on the night stand, and holding the wash basin for his brother. A thin pool of vomit swished in the basin.

"You stand away from him, John Quincy," Abigail said, breathless. "Let me have the towel."

Obediently, Johnny stood and handed his mother the basin and the wet scrap of linen.

"Run tell the Totts," she ordered, swabbing three-year-old Tommy's forehead. "They need to know the dysentery's come into this house so they'd best keep away from us as much as they can. Charly, go get Suzy to empty this basin and the chamber pot. And tell Patty I want a bowl of gruel."

Abigail looked down at her youngest child's usually merry face. A frightening image of little Susanna flashed across her mind but she pushed it away. "And Johnny, once you tell the Totts, then go to Grandmother Smith's. Tell her I ask that you all stay there unless you show signs of the sickness."

Johnny nodded, his face grim while five-year-old Charly, eyes wide with fear, watched his mother's quick movements.

"Now be out, boys!"

They bolted down the stairs. After a few moments, she heard bare feet coming slowly up the stair and turned to see Patty standing in the door, swaying slightly. Her blue eyes were glazed and her shoulders slumped as though under a weight.

"What ails you, Patty?" Abigail asked, dreading the answer.

"I don't know, M'am. I just don't feel good. It's so hot!"

"Take the basin and empty it, then get a cool cloth and lie down."

"Yes'm."

Abigail watched as Patty staggered across the room, took the basin and the chamber pot, and started down the stairs with them.

"If you can't manage, stop and put them on the stair then get some help," Abigail called, fearful of her spilling the vile contents down the stairs.

She listened as the girl crept down the tightly winding staircase, dragging the handled chamber pot along the wall to steady herself. Then the front door slammed and she could hear the dry grass rustle as Patty carried the two containers out back to empty them.

Through the floorboards, she heard Johnny's high-pitched conversation with Mr. Tott. She did not hear Suzy until she came through the doorway carrying a tray with a bowl of gruel and a jar of hot vinegar.

"Are you all right?" Abigail asked, looking sharply at Suzy's red face.

"Yes," Suzy replied, putting the tray down at the foot of the bed and wiping a bare arm across her brow. "It's hot in the kitchen is all. Patty don't look any good, though."

Abigail nodded.

"I brought the vinegar," Suzy continued. "Thought you might want me to wash down the chamber a bit. It stinks already."

Abigail nodded again, her eyes still on the woman's face. "Are you sure you're well?"

Suzy shrugged and pushed her sleeves up higher on strong, freckled arms.

"As sure as we can know in this life, Mrs. Adams," she replied carelessly.

Dipping a rag into the hot vinegar Suzy began scrubbing the floor by the bed where vomit had slopped out of the basin. While Suzy scrubbed, Abigail swabbed Tommy's face. He lay back on the pillow, moaning softly in a half-delirious sleep. He cried out once, swinging his arms wildly. Abigail held the little body, crooning, then laid him back on the sheet. When she had used all the vinegar, Suzy stood, stretched her back and leaned against the door.

"It's powerful hot today," she observed softly, squinting at the dazzling square of light in the window. Bees buzzed in the apple tree outside and the sound of birds in carefree chorus wafted across the fields.

Abigail shot her an appraising look.

"I fear Patty may have taken the dysentery. She'll need help."

Suzy nodded noncommittally, pushing herself away from the doorframe with one hand. "I thought she looked kinda peaked this mornin'."

Turning, she padded back down the stairs on callused bare feet.

Tommy tossed in his sleep, then suddenly woke again and leaned over to vomit. Abigail grabbed the vinegar bowl and held it under his mouth. The wrenching convulsions held the child so long, she feared he would faint for lack of air, but finally, he gasped and gulped in breath, then fell back on the bed, his eyes closed again, whining softly.

"You lie here, I'll be right back," she said after wiping his mouth with a cloth.

Going down the stairs, she went through the living room and around to the long hall at the back of the house. When she entered the kitchen, her heart nearly stopped. Patty lay on her small pallet at the side of the room, doubled in pain with a bowl filled with vomit at her side, while Suzy slumped in a chair at the table.

Abigail crossed the room and laid a hand against the girl's forehead. "You're on fire."

"It came on me sudden-like. I just didn't' have any more strength to climb the stairs. I'm sorry, Mrs. Adams. Maybe if I rest a bit here...." The rinsed washbasin sat on the table at her elbow.

"Lie down," Abigail said firmly. "I'll empty Patty's bowl and bring you both cool cloths.

As she rinsed out another scrap of linsey-woolsey, she heard the back door slam. Ten-year-old Nabby, just in from milking, stood transfixed at the scene before her, her eyes sweeping the room in shock.

"Pour out a pitcher of milk then put the rest in the spring house. We won't have need of it right now. Tommy's took sick and so are Suzy and Patty."

Nabby's face went white. "Is it the pestilence?"

"I fear so," Abigail said, helping Suzy to lie down on the pallet she had taken from a cupboard. "Johnny's gone to Grandmother Smith's to tell her. I want you children to go to the parsonage."

Nabby trembled, her eyes wide with fear. "I can't leave you here alone, Mar," she said softly, as though testing the assertion for merit. "You'll get it too."

"I can't expose you to the sickness, Nabby."

"You can't be here alone, Mar," Nabby repeated, more certain now. "Jake has his hands full with the fields. I'll stay and help you nurse."

Abigail sucked in a deep breath and gazed thoughtfully at her daughter. The child's courage filled her with pride.

"Very well," she agreed. "But you're not to wear yourself out."

Abigail and Nabby had settled the two servant girls in the kitchen, boiled a large kettle of vinegar for cleansing and had a crust of bread and some milk together for breakfast. As Nabby laid out Jake's mid-morning meal of bread and cheese, covering it with a cloth to keep off the flies, Abigail suddenly asked: "Did Charly go with Johnny?"

"I don't know, Mar."

The front door slammed, and Abigail heard the tramp of heavy shoes on the bare hallway. Elizabeth Smith appeared in the doorway. Her dark eyes, set hawk-like in the oval face, took in the two young women sprawled on their pallets on the floor, the vomit, the fear on her granddaughter's face, the exhausted pallor of her daughter.

The sight of her mother, coupled with the smell of dysentery and vinegar, transported Abigail to a night twenty years before when at age eleven she lay in bed, bathed in sweat despite the bitter cold, her thin arms limp on the bedclothes. She had overheard the doctor's whispered prognosis: little hope. Then, as though in a dream, she saw her mother framed in the doorway holding a bowl of steaming broth. She could still hear her mother's words, spoken with such certainty that Abigail had known it must be true: "You *will* recover, Abigail."

Although twenty years had elapsed, Abigail saw her mother once again as an angelic presence, straw bonnet tied firmly, mouth set in determination. Elizabeth Smith carried a basket laden with medicinal herbs.

"You must have whipped the horse all the way here," Abigail said, fighting back tears.

"You had need," Mrs. Smith replied matter-of-factly. "I will brew up a tisane."

For five days, Abigail, Nabby, and Elizabeth Smith nursed their charges, holding heads, washing a never-ending stream of filthy linen, sitting by Tommy and Suzy and Patty's bedsides, snatching naps, spooning gruel down throats raw from retching.

Abigail had collapsed against the kitchen wall, nearly asleep on her feet, when Suzy's voice rose from the cot in the kitchen.

"Mrs. Adams?"

Wondering if she had heard the voice in her dreams, Abigail opened her eyes and peered into the twilight. A moon shone through the window, splashing light on the pallet on which Suzy lay.

"Mrs. Adams?"

Abigail got up and went to kneel by the bed.

"What do ye need?" she asked wearily.

"Nothing," the woman replied weakly. Her hair was plastered to her face and she lay calm beneath a thin blanket. "I just wanted to say thankee for all you've done for me."

"It's not more than any Christian woman would have done," Abigail said, her voice flat.

Though she said it and, knew, somewhere in her heart that she meant it, all she really felt at that moment was a fervent wish to be left alone.

"No," Suzy said, shaking her head on the ticking that served for her pillow. "No, you went a long way past Christian when you took me in. Knowin' what I was to you."

A warning somewhere at the back of Abigail's heart sounded an alarm. Don't ask, she told herself. Let it be. But she ignored her instinct, and leaned closer.

"What do you mean 'what you were to me'?"

Suzy turned her face full upon Abigail with a look of horror.

"You don't...? But he promised me he'd... that he would never...Your father never told you?"

Abigail, heart pounding in her chest, shook her head.

Suzy sucked in a shallow breath and hesitated, then exhaled the words.

"I am your natural sister. I was to be the son your mother could not give him. Then, when I was born female...."

Abigail's heart caught. My natural sister? She is my father's bastard child? Not possible. She cannot be the child of the man who preaches against the sin of adultery. The man who castigates men who spend nights with the tavern wenches, who collects for the natural children of the nameless neighbors everyone knows. Can it all be a pretense, a sham?

"It's not possible." Abigail said.

"How not possible?" Suzy inquired softly.

"My father could not have done that." Abigail insisted, softly,

116

for she heard her mother's footsteps overhead.

"Look at me, and deny the truth," Suzy whispered. Her face wore an expression of anger and pain, and bitterness at years of having to deny her own paternity.

Abigail's mind reeled. He had lied to them. Though he had never spoken a word, he had lied.

"Have you always known?"

Suzy nodded, the movement of her head barely perceptible.

"Does my mother know?"

"I cannot say. Does she know that I am the child that she so long has wondered about? I doubt it. Does she know that one exists? What woman does not know in her heart if her husband has been unfaithful?"

She let the question hang on the air between them.

Her father had betrayed them all, had brought this bastard daughter here, for his own legitimate daughter to employ, had left his shame on her doorstep. A wave of rage and hatred boiled over her. Her mind reeled. She must push the sin away, exile it to the farthest reaches of her world.

"I cannot have you here once you recover. I cannot for the sake of my mother. I will not," she said, ashamed at her own wish to escape.

Suzy nodded, her face unreadable.

"I did not want to deceive you. He said he told you, that you accepted. My mother has died. I have nothing. I inherit nothing, I have no brother to act as my protector."

And when my mother gave him a son ... but such a son, Abigail thought bitterly.

Suzy went on, her voice trailing to a whisper as her strength died.

"I had not seen him for many years. He came when I sent word. I would not have called upon him, but I was desperate. Yet I hoped he could place me with some acquaintance, someone who would let me live close enough to see him, to know my own father, yet not..."

"You are on the mend," Abigail whispered hoarsely, as she heard her mother's footfalls coming down the stairs. "When you are well enough, you will find another position. I will give you a good recommendation -- provided you leave Weymouth."

Abigail's harsh words were not for the woman who, innocent of

117

the circumstances of her own birth, struggled to make a life for herself, but for the father whose cowardly deception had in one stroke, shattered her faith in men.

Abigail was sitting on the bed beside Tommy, swaying slightly when Elizabeth Smith came into the room carrying a cup of chamomile tea.

"Suzy is on the mend I believe," she said, handing the cup to Abigail.

Abigail scanned her mother's face for some sign that she knew Suzy's secret, but there was none.

"That is good news," Elizabeth Smith replied, but her words lacked conviction.

As soon as she is well enough, she is away from here, Abigail thought determinedly. My life will be as before.

"How is your son?" Elizabeth Smith asked, unaware of the turmoil in Abigail's mind.

Grateful to turn her attention to Tommy, Abigail ran a shaking hand over the boy's forehead and smoothed down a hair.

"The dysentery seems to be leaving him, but look at his face, see how the bones show through? Will he have enough strength to survive?"

Involuntarily, she began to sob, tears coursing down her cheeks and onto her stained cotton dress. Filled with weariness, anger, confusion, she wanted to fold herself into a ball and wait until John came home, to have him take her in his arms, promise he would never do to her what her father had done to her mother, to make the world come right again. She covered her face with her hands and cried uncontrollably.

"Abigail, calm yourself," Mrs. Smith said firmly, sitting down beside her daughter. "It is the fatigue crying. Tommy has begun to show a bloom in his cheek, I think. Look, there. There is proper color beneath the skin now. And he has not puked nor his bowels run for a day. It may be a time before he is able..." she stopped and looked at the pallor of daughter's skin.

Abigail raised a shaking hand to wipe the sweat from her forehead as her mother reached out to put her hand against Abigail's flushed cheek.

"Dear God, you are burning, Daughter! Get ye to bed,"

Elizabeth Smith said, her voice low. "I will have Nabby brew more tea."

"Do not have her up here!" Abigail cried. "I would not infect her too!"

"No, you are right. I will nurse you myself. Do not fear for your daughter, Daughter. I will see to everything."

Obediently, Abigail trudged across the hall to her room, cluttered with papers and books, and flopped onto the bed. For three days and nights, her mother brought her trea, swabbed her head, carried off bowls and pots of puke and diarrhea. As in the fevered dreams of her childhood, her mother's presence filled the room with comfort and hope.

On the third day, Abigail rose and came down the stairs unsteadily. In the kitchen, she found her mother and Patty sitting together, elbows on the table, each sipping a cup of tea while Tommy sat on the floor, leaning against his grandmother's skirts.

"Thank God," Abigail breathed when she saw her son.

"Mar! Mar!" Tommy cried, attempting to rise.

"No, Tommy, you sit," his grandmother said. "Your Mother is right here. She will sit with us and we shall all be together."

In the eight days of his fever, Tommy's plump face had grown wan, his cheeks hollow. His eyes were large blue saucers set in deep sockets.

"Where is Suzy?" Abigail asked, suddenly noticing the empty corner where a single, whispered conversation had turned her world on its ear.

"Gone, poor soul. We thought she was mending then suddenly it was as though a putrescence took hold of her body and ate her up. We buried her yesterday. And the Tott's eldest and youngest children are both gone, too."

Patty nodded, mute.

Abigail flopped down at the table. Gone. And with her, the secret of my father's betrayal, his carnal lust. At least I need not fear for my mother now, she thought. She will be protected. She looked at her mother, the worn face gray with fatigue but with a faint flush beneath the pale skin.

"You have once again brought me back from the dead," Abigail said. "I owe you my life."

"That's true," Elizabeth Smith said, rising unsteadily, but with her eyes on Abigail. "I give the keeping of it back into your own hands once again."

"Mar!" Nabby was coming in from the well. Spying her mother, she dropped the bucket of water and rushed over to throw her arms around Abigail's neck. "Oh, Mar! I was so afraid you was going to die! Hannah Slaughter buried her mother Tuesday, the day you came down with it, and I was so scared! I couldn't bear it!"

Abigail endured the hug. "Your grandmother's skills have nursed me through worse than this," she said, her eyes still on her mother's face.

"You should be proud of your daughter, Abigail. She has done well," Mrs. Smith said, turning toward the door, her shawl clutched tightly round her thin shoulders.

"Mother?" Abigail asked. "Are you unwell?"

"It is fatigue, and the heat," her mother said, reaching for the bonnet that sat on the table, yellow ribbons snaking away from the crown. "I am just in need of rest. I have asked Jake to drive me home. I will send him back with your children. Patty, be sure to scrub down the house top to bottom with boiled vinegar before they arrive."

"Yes'm" Patty replied wanly.

"Thank you, Mother." Abigail said, making a weak effort to rise, and failing. "I am more grateful for your help than I can tell."

"It is no more than my duty, " Mrs. Smith replied. "You would do the same."

"Aye, Mother. I am grateful nonetheless."

She loves me but without the warmth she feels for Will, Abigail thought. I will never see the joy in my presence that Will's presence instills.

"Goodbye, Grandmother," Nabby said, stepping forward to kiss the older woman, but her grandmother fended her off.

"Goodbye, Nab. You have worked well. You are a capable young woman."

A compliment she has never paid me, Abigail thought sadly, but brushed the resentment away. No mean thoughts. I am well. My son is well. She dared not admit even to her innermost mind her relief that Suzy had died.

It was two days later that Reverend Smith came to give Abigail the news. Elizabeth Smith had come down with dysentery the day after she had arrived home. He gave no hint that Suzy's death meant anything to him, or that he feared that Abigail had learned his secret. If he saw a difference in her demeanor, noticed her drawing away when he came near, he gave no sign. His mind was on his wife.

This time, Will came from his regiment and sat, sober, at his mother's bedside, holding her hand, offering words of encouragement and love. But Elizabeth Smith, beyond even Will's reach, neither smiled nor frowned. She died on the first of October 1775.

Chapter 9

But still bear up and steer right onward
John Milton sonnet XXI

1775

By the time John returned for Christmas, an edgy uncertainty infected the town. Rumors that marauding bands of loyalists were burning Whig homes, that Whigs would be hanged as traitors, that the regulars would commandeer food leaving colonists to starve ignited fears that ran from house to house like wildfires. The Totts, struggling to recover from the loss of their children and anxious to save what they had left, packed up and moved farther inland. John had his office back, but now it was crammed with friends and neighbors, frantic to learn the mind of the Continental Congress.

The cannons that Ethan Allen had captured at Ticonderoga were brought to Boston and mounted on Dorchester Hill, one of the few promontories General Gage had neglected to fortify. Under cover of darkness on March 2, 1776, George Washington crept up the hill with 4000 men and 37 teams of horses and in a single night erected a battery of breastworks and cannon. Finally, they had a position from which to fight for Boston.

On the following day, Abigail, alone again after John's return to Philadelphia, sat by the fire darning a sock. Methodically, she wove the thread through the sock's heel, tamping each threaded line down against the ones before. Patty stretched gratefully on her pallet in the kitchen, asleep for an hour. Through the dairy door, Abigail could hear the muffled snore of Isaac Hayden, still in defiant possession of his two rooms, his own private fortification against Abigail's continuing efforts to dislodge him. Resentment had long ago overtaken her charity. She wanted him gone.

A twig in the fire snapped. The northwest wind, which had keened through the hills and fields for days, was finally silent. Perhaps I should move my household farther inland, away from the threat of capture, burning, and God alone knows what else, she thought. John says they would not dare to touch us, but who is to speak for us if a band of drunken soldiers rampages through our village? His letters hide as much as they reveal -- though I cannot blame his caution. Who knows what hands they may pass through between Philadelphia and Braintree? But I want some word of guidance. Where is my partner in life? Why must it all fall to me?

The fire spat, and she rose to stir the flame up higher. The warped step at the top of the stair creaked. Bare feet padded down to the front hall. Then the parlor door opened. Nabby, dressed in shift and nightcap with nothing covering her but a shawl, peered round the door.

"I could not sleep," she said, coming into the room.

"Come and stand by the fire, Nab," Abigail said. "What brings you down? Did I not give you enough work to do that you are still so full of energy?"

"You needs must give me more work?" Nabby replied mischievously.

She of all the children most resembles John, Abigail thought. She has his humor, but also his vanity.

"Work is always there to do," her mother rejoined. "Come and warm, yourself. Why could ye not sleep?"

"I am afraid."

As am I, Abigail thought.

"All this talk of another great battle. Mrs. Craddick says that if it comes, they will burn all our homes and us in them. Is it true, Mar?"

"I cannot believe that they would destroy women and children," Abigail replied with more certainty than she felt. "The Regulars have wives and children of their own. We still share a language, a motherland."

Is a lie protection or cowardice? She wondered as she spoke, her mind lighting on her father's betrayal of his marriage vows. In keeping Pa's secret I am joined to the betrayal? She did not let herself acknowledge that her silence also protected her family's reputation. But to Nabby, perhaps I am not lying, but merely speaking my prayers.

"Mrs. Craddick says that when men are in war, they think neither of their homes nor their families, but bloodlust and plunder," Nabby said.

Abigail silently cursed Mrs. Craddick for her unthinking tongue.

"And how, exactly, would Mrs. Craddick know?" she demanded.

"How many wars has she attended?"

"None I s'pose," Nabby replied thoughtfully.

BOOM! The windows shook. Abigail dropped the sock she was darning.

"It must be Boston," she said, starting up from her chair.

BOOM! BOOM! BOOM!

The painting of her parents that hung by the fire rattled, threatening to leap from the plaster wall.

Patty came scurrying around the corner in her shift and shawl, eyes huge.

"What it is Mrs. Adams? It ain't the end of the world?"

"It may be the end of *our* world," Abigail said, heart pounding. "Let us go outside, perhaps in the darkness we can see whence it comes. It *must* be Boston."

Behind her, Abigail could hear the dairy room door unlatch and Hayden's heavy footsteps follow them out through the kitchen and into the night. The thought occurred to her that she could rush in and lock Hayden out of the house for good. Tempting, but impractical. She could not have done it. Above the indigo horizon, rosy bursts lit the sky. The northwest breeze carried a tattoo of gunfire and the heavy, thundering boom of cannon.

"My boys must be givin' 'em hell," Hayden cried, gleefully.

He smelled of ale and tobacco and sweat. Abigail ground her teeth. Why will this man not leave? He would be useless in time of trouble.

"Will they come this far to fight, Mrs. Adams?" Patty asked, breathless.

"I don't know. I pray not."

"Naw, they won't come here," Hayden asserted confidently. "It's the loyalists we've got to fear this far out! Those Tory neighbors, like the Calendars, who might burn us out of our homes."

"*Our* homes Mr. Hayden?"

Hayden ignored her.

BOOM! BOOM! BOOM!

A starburst spread across the night sky.

"Well, we ain't goin' to change the course of the battle from here," Hayden observed. "And I'm freezin'."

Hayden turned on his heel and went back inside, slamming the door behind him.

"Go to bed, Patty," Abigail advised, shivering. "Mr. Hayden's right. We can do nothing. If they come closer, we shall hear."

"We shall hear and RUN!" Patty said solemnly, hitching her shawl closer around her shoulders.

Abigail nodded agreement. Out of the darkness, two figures came through the stone wall between the houses.

"I cannot credit it," said Susanna Adams Hall, shaking her head in a mixture of amazement and disgust. "Mr. Hall is sound asleep. He has heard nothing. "

" 'Tis as well," observed John's brother, Peter, who had come outside with his mother. "T'will do his heart no good."

"And you would do your mother's heart no good to enter that fray," Susanna retorted. "I've lost one son already. And I worry myself sick over John's safety. Two men were attacked on their way to the last Continental Congress. Suppose it had been our John? Is he not in enough danger for you both? You must run John's farm while he fights for liberty. That is your part in this battle. You need not join the army. Fight instead to keep our country fed."

She stamped her feet and beat her arms in an effort to keep warm. Peter, arms clamped across his chest, mouth pursed angrily, said nothing.

BOOM! BOOM! BOOM! BOOM! BOOM! BOOM!

"Will they come so far, think you?" Susanna mused.

"I don't know," Abigail replied, eyes on the colors splattered like blood across the black horizon.

"Mother, may I sleep with you tonight?" Nabby asked suddenly clutching at her mother's arm.

"Yes, Nab. You run inside. The night air will do you no good. I'll just bank the fire and come up. Check the boys afore you climb in."

"What think you, Mrs. Adams?" Susanna repeated. "Will they come this far?"

Abigail shook her head again and shrugged. "If they come with such noise and fanfare as this before them, at least we shall be warned."

By the time Abigail had climbed the twisting wooden steps, Nabby was asleep, coverlet pulled to her chin. But, despite her confident pronouncement, Abigail lay in bed trembling while the battle that raged ten miles away shook their home.

The siege of Boston was terrifying, even in Braintree. Window-shattering cannon blasts continued for days until finally they fell silent. By then, Charlestown lay in charred ruins, homes and shops destroyed, the dead and dying lying in the streets. But the colonists had won. On the 17th of March, 1776, with Johnny and Nabby in tow, Abigail climbed Penn's Hill to watch the 170 British ships that had been scattered at anchor over the harbor hoist sail and slide out the channel.

In Congress, the delegates were hammering out the principles of new government. John fought to retain the property-based right to vote -- otherwise, he insisted, *'new claims will arise; women will demand a vote; lads from twelve to twenty-one will think their rights not closely enough attended to; and every man who has not a farthing will demand an equal voice with any other in all acts of state.'*

Portia-like, Abigail disagreed. *'That your sex are naturally tyrannical is a truth so thoroughly established as to admit of no dispute,'* she wrote from Braintree, *'but such of you as wish to be happy willingly give up the harsh title of Master for the more tender and endearing one of friend. Why then, not put it out of the power of the vicious and the lawless to use us with cruelty and indignity?'*

'..In practice you know we are the subjects,' John had replied, unmoved by her persuasion. *'We have only the name of masters.'*

Abigail was furious.

July, 1776

"Oh Mother, to think, Father had such a great hand in making that document, in deciding the fate of our country!" Nabby cried breathlessly.

By the 18th of July, Abigail, the four children, Johnny's tutor John Thaxter, Will's daughter, eight-year-old Louisa Smith, Abigail's sister Betsey Smith, and Patty had all been at Uncle Isaac Smith's house in Boston for a week. Bearing beds, linen, and a cow, they had come to be inoculated by Dr. Bullfinch against the smallpox which was scything through village and town, leaving hundreds of dead in its wake like so much threshed wheat. This time, Abigail thought, I shall be inoculated. My mother can no longer prevent it. They were inoculated on the 11th. The news of the Declaration of Independence arrived on the 14th.

"We show no signs of the disease, and I will not be deprived of hearing that glorious document read out for all of Boston," Abigail said.

Signed on July 2nd and ratified on July 4th by the Continental Congress, the Declaration was to be read out at the government seats in all thirteen colonies.

The sun, a thick globe that dripped crimson over the harbor's still surface, was high in the sky by the time they began walking toward Kings Street. A teeming river of people, fed by the tributaries of each passing block, gradually washed like a human tide to the shore of the State House steps. Faces were joyful, strangers saluted each other in excitement; women's eyes shone, and they waved handkerchiefs like banners above their heads. Reverend Smith, who drove a second cow from Braintree to provide their milk, clutched thirteen-year-old Nabby's hand, dragging her along behind him.

On the subject of Suzy, Reverend Smith had remained mute. Only at Abigail's insistence had he driven the body back to Lexington to be buried there. I will not have her gravestone mocking me from the Weymouth churchyard, Abigail decided. But her only words to her father were of Suzy's right to be buried on her family's farm. Were I to ask, I believe Pa would deny it, she thought. If he did deny, would I believe him? Stay silent. It is past mending.

Following her father through the crowd, Abigail clung tightly to eleven-year-old Johnny's hand.

"Will we have a special place to listen?" Johnny wanted to know.

"I should think we will be lucky to get close enough to hear, the throng will be so great," his Grandfather replied. "Everyone wants to hear the words that have changed our fate."

His pride at John's part in the Declaration could not have been greater if John had been his own son. He had need of a son to be proud of. Will had not been heard from since Elizabeth Smith's death. Will's wife and children, now numbering three thanks to a baby conceived during the few days Will had spent at Weymouth for his mother's funeral, had had no money from him in nine months. They were supported entirely by Reverend Smith, penance for his own sins.

"It is a document to make the spirit soar," Abigail said,

remembering the draft of the Declaration that John had enclosed with his last letter. "John speaks highly of Mr. Jefferson's abilities and intellect. It is Mr. Jefferson's hand that framed the words -- though he draws on many of Mr. Adams's ideas, of course," she added quickly.

"Mother, will there be a place for women in our new country?" Nabby asked.

"What manner of question is that?" Reverend Smith demanded. "Woman has her place, always."

Nabby blushed, and fell silent.

"I believe my daughter meant a vote for the ladies," Abigail said, not wanting to start an argument yet unwilling to desert her daughter's hopes -- or her own.

"Vote? Nonsense!" Smith bellowed over the noise of the crowd. "Why should a woman vote? Has her husband not a voice? If she disagrees with the head of their house, her vote would cancel his. We want liberty, not anarchy."

"Perhaps it would strengthen his vote," Nabby offered. "Two voices from one home united?" She loved her grandfather, and wanted his love, but refused to gainsay her own opinion.

"Union is declared in the marriage," Reverend Smith replied dismissively. "Two lives are joined as one. One vote. Woman is the heart, but man is the head of the household. Never forget that."

"Yes, Grandfather," Nabby sighed.

Abigail raised an eyebrow at her daughter but said nothing. Neither she nor Nabby stated the obvious, that with the men gone to war, women were the de facto heads of households everywhere. They bore all of the responsibilities, yet held none of the power.

They passed several pieces of field cannon. As they approached the State House, they saw men in uniform bearing muskets, shoulders thrust back, eyes focused intently on the figure of Colonel Crafts who stood in the belcona of the building.

"Is he reading it yet?" Johnny asked, trying to see over his mother's shoulder.

"I think not," Abigail replied, raising her voice over the din of excitement. "He looks as though he is holding the proclamation, waiting for the throng to settle."

Reverend Smith called over his shoulder, "Follow me, Abigail, and I shall break through to a place for us that is worthy of John

Adams's wife!"

"Oh, Mother! " Nabby cried, giggling in excitement. "Isn't it wonderful? Our Par signed the Declaration of Independence for the whole American colonies! I want everyone here to know!"

"They will if you continue to shout so, Nab," her mother retorted acidly in an effort to still her own welling pride.

"I think Colonel Crafts has begun to read. He's holding up his hands for silence," Reverend Smith said loudly.

He pushed through to a spot nearly beneath the belcona. Abigail struggled to keep up with him, her skirts dragging against the skirts of the other women who rushed forward to catch every word. Her straw bonnet slid off her head and jounced against her shoulder, but crushed in the crowd, she could not lift her hands to put it back on. Sunlight baked her cheeks and perspiration ran down her face.

By the time they reached the spot the Reverend Smith had claimed on the steps, the tall, round-bellied figure of Colonel Crafts, uniform brushed and pressed, stood above them, arms outstretched in benediction. Beside him holding a scroll, stood a small, self-important orderly.

"Here ye! here ye!" the orderly shouted.

"Sh sh," ran through the crowd like small spurts of escaping steam until the entire body had fallen silent.

"I will not waste time in preambles," Colonel Crafts began, perspiration streaming down his florid face. "We all want to hear the words that have made us free."

A roar arose, but he held his hands up again and it quickly died. Without shifting his gaze from the faces beneath him, he put out his hand. The orderly carefully placed a document in it. Unrolling it, the colonel began to read.

Beautiful words, inspiring words swept out over the crowd, clasping Abigail's heart in their grip. Johnny squeezed her hand in silent joy, his face shining.

"This is what we have missed Par so much for, ain't it Mar?" Nabby asked, leaning around the bulk of her grandfather. "We have given him over for the greatness of our country."

"Yes, Nab. His work decides all our lives," said Abigail. She wanted everyone within hearing distance to know who she was and that it was her John, her ambitious, hard-working, dedicated John, who had had a hand in framing this new nation's cry for freedom.

If only her mother could have seen this day, the fruits of John Adams's labors, a vindication of Abigail's decision to marry an upstart country lawyer all those years ago.

The crowd listened in silence as the colonel read down to the last sentence: *"'And for the support of this declaration, with a firm reliance on the protection of divine Providence, we mutually pledge to each other our lives, our fortunes and our sacred honor.' "*

He stopped, dropped his hands and looked out over the sea of rapt faces.

"GOD SAVE OUR AMERICAN STATES!"

"Huzzah! Huzzah! Huzzah!" burst from the crowd. The bells in the Old North Church steeple began to toll. They were followed by each church in turn, the peals echoing through the alleyways of the town, and spilling out onto the glassy harbor where privateers began firing their cannon. The forts and batteries followed suit, and the soldiers fired their muskets in the air, shouting, faces jubilant.

One soldier, standing on a ladder supported by two others, began to pry the king's coat of arms from the door of the State house with his musket barrel. When it hit the ground, the crowd sent up a triumphant shout, surging forward to break the crest to pieces. Militiamen arrived carrying crests and images of King George III, which they dumped in a pile and set alight in the middle of Kings Street, the funeral pyre for a monarchy.

"What are they doing, Mar?" Johnny asked as he watched the now-frenzied faces.

"They are preparing to expunge all evidence of tyranny from our country," Reverend Smith answered the boy.

"I wish Colonel Crafts had read out the names of the signers," Nabby muttered in disappointment. "I had hoped to hear Par's name for all the world to hear."

"Pride goeth before destruction and a haughty spirit before a fall," Abigail admonished, though she, too, had wanted to hear her John's name read, perhaps even be recognized as Mrs. John Adams. The flames licked up over the collection of relics that was growing higher with each passing minute.

"Thus ends royal authority in this state," she cried no longer able to contain herself. "And all the people shall say amen!"

John finally returned home in November. The war had been

going badly for America. Defeat followed defeat. Hungry, cold, and exhausted, militiamen were deserting in droves. Others were waiting only until their enlistment was up at the beginning of the new year. Discouraged, exhausted with the separations and sacrifices, John had almost decided to give up public life. He reclaimed his book-lined office, and set about trying to revive his moribund law practice.

An icy rain tattooed the windowpanes and drummed rhythmically on the roof. After knocking gently, Abigail opened the door between the office and the front hall and came through, carrying a steaming mug.

"I thought you might put this to good use, John," she said, putting aside a copy of Thomas Paine's incendiary pamphlet *Common Sense* in order to set down the drink.

She looked around the office, arms folded in satisfaction.

John pulled the spectacles off his nose, leaned back in his chair and looked at her. She was thinner, her nose more sharply outlined against her cheeks and the bones in her hands clearly defined beneath work-roughened skin. He realized with a start that he had hardly seen her in the past twelve months.

"And what potion have you made me, Wife?" he asked.

"A grog to lift your spirits and warm your bones," she replied, a wry smile turning up the corners of her mouth.

"What? Have you lost the means to do that yourself?" he asked, drawing her onto his lap.

"Mr. Adams! What if one of the children were to come in?"

"The elder ones know whence they came and the younger ones are not allowed without knocking!" he replied, holding her tightly.

"John! Suppose someone were to come?" she cried, struggling to stand up.

"Cease, Abigail," he said, loosening his grip but still encircling her with thick arms. "I have missed my wife. I would have a kiss from you."

After a quick glance through the sleet-glazed windows to the empty roads and fields, she turned to him and planted a kiss on his cheek.

"Nay, my dear. Not a sisterly peck. I wish a kiss," he said softly, reaching his full mouth up to her face.

Relenting, she met his lips, settling into the warmth of his body and letting his sensual embrace fill her. It had been too long. Too long that she had done without him. Too long that she had carefully avoided pregnancy. Her body yearned for his.

Without warning, the side door opened, and Sam Adams lurched into the room, shaking the sleet from his cloak and hat. Mortified, Abigail leapt off John's lap like a frightened cat.

"Cousin Sam," John said. "We did not hear you."

"Small wonder!" Sam replied, chuckling.

Abigail blushed to the ears.

"Sit ye down, Cousin. What brings you away out yonder in such miserable weather?" John asked.

Sam frowned for a moment and looked speculatively into the grog in the crockery mug by John's elbow.

"Is there something to warm the bones of a poor, frozen soul?"

"There is, Cousin, and I will fetch it in a moment," said Abigail, studying Sam's face. "Unless I mistake, you have come to bring news."

"I have," Sam sighed, collapsing into the large, round-backed wooden chair at the other end of the table, "and it is not good."

Abigail sucked in a breath involuntarily.

"General Lee is captured, and so ill-prepared that he was still in his bathrobe. He will be paraded in it," Sam said, shaking his head. "A shock for our troops, and a terrible defeat."

Abigail's throat caught in fear. Lee captured! General Charles Lee, the Englishman named third-in-command of the army by the Continental Congress. John's face had gone gray and his mouth hung open in disbelief.

"Aye," Sam nodded, looking at their stricken faces. "I can see ye felt much as I did when I heard the news. Many of our forces are taken. These are dark days."

"How can we hope to prevail?" John whispered, a moan to himself.

Sam nodded gravely. "It is bad indeed. Ten thousand of the enemy are encamped not thirty miles from Philadelphia. The Congress is moving to Baltimore."

"Baltimore!" Abigail breathed. Even farther from home. What would happen to John and the other delegates were they to be captured by the British? Would they be imprisoned? Hanged?

Guessing her fears, Sam added, "We can yet succeed if we do

not lose heart."

"We *must* succeed," Abigail said. "I shall get your grog while you draw your chair close to the fire. We need our strongest champions now."

She looked closely at both Adamses, thirteen years apart in age, but alike in bulk and intellect. John was the better read of the two, but Sam had an instinctive intelligence, and a kind of emotional stamina that would enable him to pluck up his own spirits so he might encourage others to carry on the fight.

As she closed the door, Abigail could hear Sam speculating about the best way to wrench victory from the jaws of defeat. He will never allow John to quit politics, she thought. Sighing, she went down the hall, her thick-soled brogues rhythmically hitting the bare floorboards.

1777

Bent over a letter he was composing to John Hancock, John only half-heard the galloping hooves that stopped abruptly outside his door. Joseph Stevens, their one-time servant, burst into his office, bringing with him a blast of cold air. Snow capped his shoulders like the peaks of the distant hills and melting flakes mingled in his hair.

"What's happened?" John demanded, starting from his chair.

"Washington," Joseph spat out the word through half-frozen lips. He fumbled with ragged mittens, striding to the fire as he yanked them from raw, wet hands. "Washington has won at Trenton."

"Won?" John repeated.

"Yes. Defeated the Hessians. Boston has just had the news. He crossed the Delaware under cover of night and attacked. It was the surprise that did it. They say he's captured a thousand men. Washington has brought us a victory!"

Quickly clasping Joseph in a jubilant embrace, John then turned and ran through the living room where Abigail sat listening to seven-year-old Charly read from Psalms while she reworked an old shirt of John's into a shirt for Johnny. Five-year-old Tommy sprawled on the floor by the fire, scratching his letters on the bricks with a piece of slate.

"Abigail," he cried, coming into the room. "He has done it!

Washington has delivered a victory at Trenton. "

"Thank God!" Abigail said, dropping her sewing in her lap.

"Will General Washington win the war for America, Par?" Charly wanted to know.

"I think he will, Charly," John said, scooping up his son and swinging him around the room. "I do think he will!"

The following week, John left for Baltimore. Hoisting himself up into the saddle, he cast a swift, surveying look around his property. Guilt assailed him. Bitter winds scoured the empty orchard and last season's flowers straggled dry and broken along the front wall. The scene was desolate.

"You need not fear for your little family."

Cloaked hunched over her shoulders, Abigail followed his gaze to the faces of Tommy, Charly, and Nabby at the window, then looked him in the face.

"But I do, my dear," John said, gripping the bare hand she rested on his leg. "If ever a woman could manage and make do, it is you. But times are hard, and likely to get harder before all is said and done. And I have little enough to leave you."

"You leave our children a great deal," she corrected him sharply. "The strength to fight for what is right. Honor and credit for your self-sacrifice. These are no mean things."

"They do not put bread on the table. And I cannot send you any money this time," he replied. "Congress's stipend does not even cover my expenses. It is a great pity that John Hancock will no longer invite me for meals, but ever since I nominated Washington instead of him for Commander-in-Chief, he has snubbed me."

Abigail snorted. "I shudder to think of the state of our army were John Hancock to be its head. A shallow peacock, and no true friend to you, John."

John laughed. "Perhaps, but for all that, his hospitality tastes as fine as any I have ever enjoyed."

"True friends are sweeter than mere hospitality," Abigail said. "We are not yet destitute. Do not let Congress forget the plight of Massachusetts. There are many here who are near to starving."

"I worry that you and our babes may one day be among those who face such straits if I continue this work to the neglect of my business."

"If you do not see this work through, you will not *have* a business," she told him. "Be off, Dearest Friend, before I freeze to death standing here taking endless leave of you."

"God be w'ye, Abigail," he cried, turning the horse's head south as he edged his heels into her flanks.

"And with you, John," she murmured, her throat constricting as she backed away from the horse.

The little mare set off down the hard road at a trot. Abigail had spoken with conviction, but hid her loneliness and fear. She suspected she was pregnant again. The memory of Mrs. Cawley, who died of a late pregnancy gone wrong, suddenly bubbled up, and she shuddered. Perhaps I am mistaken: I am not with child.

By February, she knew.

Despite the muddy, littered streets, John enjoyed Congress's time in Baltimore. Boards of War, Ordnance, Navy, and Treasury were established. Although he had been drafted to the Massachusetts Supreme Court, and the money would have been very welcome, he resigned without having served. He explained in a letter to Abigail that he could not be in two places at once. *'And I am not a formal man, not serious enough for such a position.'* Though she was chagrined at the money's loss, she understood.

In mid-February, Congress moved back to Philadelphia. Half the city had fled during the British occupation, leaving behind only Quakers. *'Boring as beadles'* was John's verdict. At the end of March, Silas Deane, Ben Franklin, and Arthur Lee, America's three commissioners, landed in France. Their mission: to negotiate a loan to continue the Revolution. They succeeded in obtaining 3 million-livres interest-free for the duration of the war. But it was still not enough.

Scrambling to pay the Continental Army, Congress printed more and more money. Inflation, as pernicious as plague, followed. Abigail struggled to find farm help, finally paying one hand the unheard-of sum of £14 for six months' work. Finding the cash to pay Chase, the agent in Boston who was looking after their vacant Brattle Street house, pay the real estate taxes, the servants, and the scores of sundries needed to run a household was a fulltime job. She sold apples and homemade cheeses, sold or traded lambs and sheep and calves, hired her hired men out at a profit, and bartered for whatever she could.

By the summer of 1777, John had been gone six months and was worn out. Yet his sense of duty, and his barely acknowledged sense of his place in history, kept him in Baltimore.

The July night was sticky, close. Bugs clung to the windowpanes and crawled up the walls into the pale glow of the sconce. A moth fluttered around the candle by her elbow. Abigail sat in John's office, household ledger opened on the table, the inkwell standing like a blue-coated soldier beside it. Running her finger down the columns, she studied the sums. To Dr. Benjamin Bullfinch, for inoculation, £72. He had waited a long time for his money, but she had finally paid it in full. Raising cash required perpetual jockeying. She had sold their share in a small barge John had bought years before, sold a field and an old sword -- a useless piece of hardware when cash was needed. From the money for those things, she had subtracted payment for the house in Boston and for hired help. It will at least keep us from bankruptcy, she thought, pulling out the £20 note that Dr. Church had delivered from John that morning. She laid it on the table beside her little pile of currency and coins.

A chill passed over her and she sat up straight for a moment, rubbing her swollen belly. A girl, she thought. I know this child to be a girl. She had felt unwell for a week --restless, ill at ease, as though her heart were beating out of time.

"Mother?" twelve-year-old Nabby opened the door. "I am brewing mint tea. Do you want some?"

"Yes, though I cannot imagine what possessed you to make hot tea in this heat," Abigail replied. "Where are the boys?"

"With Patty. Johnny is finishing the French translation you set for him. Tommy and Charly are playing."

"It's nearly time for them to be off to bed."

"I'll tell them you said so," Nabby replied.

She closed the door. Abigail bent over the book again. As she picked up the pen, she realized she was shaking. Her hands quivered. Holding the pen tighter, she touched it to the ledger. The writing trembled. Trying to steady her hands, she dipped the pen once again in the inkwell. A fit, like a current of electricity seized her. Her limbs shook, elbows rattling on the table where she tried to brace herself. She put her hands to her face, holding her head. The fingers were chilled. Clutching her arms, she made an effort to stop the shaking that now wracked her body so forcefully that the chair rattled against the bare floorboards.

The baby! she thought frantically. My little girl!

The door opened and Nabby came across the room, eyes on the cup of tea she carried. It was not until she put it on the table that she looked at her mother.

"Mar? Mar! What is it?"

Abigail shook her head, holding her arms tightly against her ribs. "I don't know. I fear it's the babe."

"Oh Mar! I'll run get Granmar Susanna!"

Nabby bolted from the room, skirts flying. The front door slammed shut. It seemed like hours until sixty-six-year-old Susanna Hall ran puffing into the room behind Nabby. Quickly, she wrapped her arms around her daughter-in-law and helped her to rise from the chair.

"We'll get you to your bed," she said firmly, still out of breath.

She and Nabby helped Abigail up the stairs. She sent Nabby back downstairs, but she pulled a chair close to keep watch over her daughter-in-law. Finally, at midnight, the fit subsided. By then, Susanna was asleep in the chair. Abigail lay bathed in sweat, the covers flung back. From the next room came the peaceful breathing of her three sons. Now and again, the wooden bed frames creaked as the boys turned in their sleep.

"Mother Susanna," Abigail whispered.

Susanna's eyes fluttered open.

"What is it? Are ye past the fit?"

"Yes, I believe so. It is stuffy, is it not?" Abigail started to rise.

"Lay back, Abigail. Lay back. I will open the window wider," the old woman said, rising stiffly. "I will send for the doctor in the morning."

Abigail nodded, silent.

"There was no blood," Susanna informed her. "Perhaps it was just some swiftly working ague."

Abigail shook her head, silent. She ran an arm over her forehead then let it drop by her side.

"No. It is the baby. I know it. My little girl."

She began to cry softly, large tears welling in her eyes and spilling silently down her thin cheeks.

"Hush, Child. If it be God's will, 'tis no use to cry."

Abigail lay weeping quietly, her arm flung up over her face as though to ward off a sharp blow.

The doctor broke her water two days later. For twelve hours, Abigail was in labor, frightened, sweating, praying to survive the delivery. Don't let me die, she prayed between contractions. The children cannot manage alone. Susanna is old. Thoughts of her children, hired out as servants, living with people who cared nothing for books, for principles, abused, or worse, flashed through her mind as she convulsed on the sodden bedclothes. Nabby sat downstairs, sobbing and trying to shut out her mother's moan.

Finally the baby was born: whole, perfect. But dead. A little girl. Abigail had been right. Susanna laid the little body, wrapped in swaddling clothes, in the cradle in the corner. Her fears now were for Abigail. Neither she nor the doctor could staunch the blood that gushed from Abigail's emptied womb. It soaked through the bedding to the ticking beneath and finally to the bare boards, life ebbing out in red ribbons.

I refuse to preside over two deaths in one night, Susanna told herself, gritting her teeth in anger. While the doctor applied leeches to Abigail's arm, Susanna frantically used every device her mind could conceive to save her daughter-in-law's life. She packed wool between her legs, bathed her in cold water, kneaded her belly, drew Abigail's knees up to her chest then put a cold compress soaked in comfrey on her forehead. Finally, the blood stopped. Only one death this time. Thank God.

Dawn reached rosy fingers into the room. Abigail opened her eyes and stared, white-faced, at her mother-in-law.

"Was it a nightmare?" she whispered.

Susanna glanced involuntarily at the cradle, now empty and shook her head without a word. Abigail turned her face into the pillow. Another daughter, gone, she thought. Another death to mourn. No more. No more children. I cannot bury another child.

Chapter 10

Long is the way, and hard, that out of hell leads up to light.
John Milton Paradise Lost Book II line 432

1777

Still believing Abigail to be carrying their fifth child, John sent a steady stream of letters home, solicitous for her health, rejoicing in their blessings, and praying for the safe delivery. At each new letter, she walked up the hill to the graveyard, a mournful pilgrimage to the graves of her dead daughters.

She struggled to raise her spirits, but nothing helped. Plodding through her days as though drugged, heavy with the heat, irritated at the demands of her children, and bitterly lonely for John, Abigail longed to be free of all life's encumbrances.

We are never free, she thought. From the moment we form our first attachment, we are shackled to one another, and to living. If John would only come home. I ache for his touch. I want – need -- to be held.

Congress was back in Philadelphia, entrenched, desperately scavenging for funds to continue the war, and arguing over the course of the fledgling government. In August, General Howe captured Philadelphia. Abigail panicked. If the delegates were captured, they would be hanged. Let him be safe, dear God. I will stop my complaints if only he is safe. Days went by without word. Rumors flew. Neighbors worried to her – is he captured? Imprisoned? Agony. The children, overhearing, were fretting.

Finally, a letter. The delegates had fled to Lancaster just ahead of the British troops. Safe. For now.

Their thirteenth anniversary on October 25, 1777 still did not bring John, but it brought a reason to celebrate -- Gentleman Johnny Burgoyne surrendered at Saratoga. A great victory for the American cause. John's absence once again had meaning. Abigail went to Boston to join friends in toasting the nation's health.

On November 7th, four days after Congress received official word of Burgoyne's surrender, John and Sam Adams took a leave of absence from Congress. Frustrated with the disagreements over money, with the wrangling between the northern and southern factions, and spurred by fears for the safety of their families, they set off for home. John had just flung his bag up behind the saddle when Sam caught sight of Elbridge Gerry taking long strides toward them over the bricks.

"I mislike his look," Sam remarked, eyeing the lanky Gerry's progress toward the hitching post where the two Adamses stood.

John finished tying a knot on his saddlebag and put one foot in the stirrup.

"If we hurry, he'll not be able to stop us."

"Ho! John!" Gerry shouted.

"We cannot stop, Mr. Gerry!" John replied, swinging himself into the saddle. "We have families who await us."

"Wait, John," Sam urged, feet still planted firmly on the cobbles. "Let us at least hear him out."

"No. I cannot chance being detained. We have spent nearly a year nursing our country. Now we must see to the health of our families."

"We can deny him if we must," Sam reminded him.

"When have we ever been able to deny a request?" John grumbled.

He dropped the reins against his thighs and waited.

"John," Gerry said, coming round behind Sam Adams's horse to stare up into John's weary face. "I will not hold ye long. We've just had news."

"What news?"

"It's Silas Deane. We now have proof that he has abused his position."

"Abused?"

"Stolen. He has been taking bribes and cutting money from the funds Congress sends for procurement."

"I feared as much," John said. "He was ever a bad choice. He is reedy; his character bends with the winds of desire. And France is the most tempting of countries, not a place for one who cannot say no to an offer of gain."

"Congress must recall him," Gerry said, his eyes on John's face. "I will propose it."

"You have my vote," John said, hoping to cut the conversation short.

"I want you to replace him."

"Me!" John burst out. "Me! NO! There are others who would do admirably. Not me. I cannot speak a word of French. How can I be expected to even communicate let alone persuade? And I have little use for the French people with their fripperies and self-conscious manners. I am no diplomat. I am too plain spoken. Surely our time together in Congress has taught you – everyone -- that. I would insult their ministers and jeopardize our cause. Besides, I need to be home. I have been a slave to my country for three years. I have given up business, family, home. My practice is in ruins. My wife runs our farm, educates our children, suffers privation alone. How can I be expected to desert her and go to France?"

He was ranting, waving his arms like a madman.

Sam had stayed silent, watching his cousin's face. He knew John was anxious to be home. Yet there was something else written on his countenance. Pride. His vanity has been pricked, Sam thought. He is pleased to be asked.

The road to Braintree seemed to stretch out for months. John and Sam stopped overnight with friends in Watertown, and checked the post office there for letters forwarded from either the Congress or family. Finding none, they continued north in a light snowfall. When John finally reined in his horse at his Braintree gate and tied her to the fence post, relief flooded through him. Home. My oasis. Without warning, the front door yawned wide and the children spilled out of the house, racing through the snow and shouting: "Par! Par! Mar! Par is home!" Abigail appeared at the door, then came skidding across the stones. Flinging her arms around his neck, she buried her face in his shoulder.

"Oh my Friend!" she cried, through the musty woolen collar of John's cloak. "My dearest, dearest Friend!"

John held her close.

"I have sorely missed my little flock, and my dear wife."

He pressed his cold face against the cap on Abigail's head.

"I have been studying with Johnny," Charly cried, "and I almost know as much Latin as he does!"

"You do not!" Johnny retorted, "I have gone much farther in the translations than you. Mr. Thaxter says so. I am completely finished with Rollins, Par."

141

"Our cat had kittens, Par!" Tommy chirped, tugging at his father's cloak, snowflakes landing in a milky halo around his blond curls.

"Oh, Par! I was so, so sorry you wasn't here when Mama lost the baby. My own little sister," Nabby cried. "But Mr. Thaxter was so good to us, and brought Mar tea and...

"Par doesn't want to talk about that!" Johnny pronounced. "Look, you've hurt Mar."

Abigail still clung to John, surrounded by the leaping children, tears standing on her lashes. She brushed them off with the back of her hand.

John held her out at arm's length and looked down at her flat belly.

"You have lost the babe?" he asked, disbelief on his face.

"You have not had my letters? Oh, John!"

"Oh Par, it was awful," Nabby began. "I had to wait..."

"Hush, now hush," John ordered, holding Abigail close. "Not now. You are safe. For that I give fervent thanks."

"Grandmother Susanna came..." Tommy began importantly.

"Enough, children! It is too cold for you all to be standing out here. Go in by the fire and tell Patty to make me a grog. Be off, now," John said looking sadly at Abigail.

"Yes, Par," Tommy said, turning on his heel and skating through the snow to the front door.

The others turned and followed him reluctantly, glancing back over their shoulders at their parents, locked in an embrace. When the door closed, John pressed his lips to hers in a long, hungry kiss.

"We may make another," he whispered in her ear.

Hurt and anger swept over her and she stiffened in his arms. He understands nothing of my grief, of my fear. John felt her pull back, but refused to release her.

"I grieve for our lost little one," he said. "But it was not meant to be."

"It was a daughter," Abigail said, her mouth trembling. "I give you sons, but I may not have daughter."

"You have Nabby."

"Yes. I have Nab," Abigail agreed. "I shall never let her slip from me."

You cannot clutch at them, John thought, but said: "I have made

142

a decision, Abigail. Our separations are too hard. I have done enough for my country. I am resigning Congress. I am home for good."

Welcome words. Abigail leaned back and looked into his face. Is it true? Will I have a husband now? Working in the office, writing, eating supper together while the children worked at their studies. He will oversee John Quincy's education, take Charly and Tommy in hand, hold me at night, his hands ... she shuddered involuntarily at the pleasure of their lovemaking. Perhaps another daughter ... no. It is too painful. We shall have no more.

"Who will take your place, John?" she asked, still not believing he could release to others the fledgling nation he had helped to midwife. "There are few who can claim your knowledge of law AND your strength of character."

"My place will be supplied, my dear," John replied. "It is the turn of others to step into the breach."

She heard the words, but suspected there was more weariness than conviction in them. What will his answer be once he has recouped his practice and grown bored with home? John was in New Hampshire on a law case for the Superior Court when the letter from Philadelphia came. Overcome by curiosity and anxiety, Abigail opened it. To her mingled horror and pride, Congress had voted that John replace Silas Deane as commissioner to France.

"I want to go with you, John."

Abigail stood in his office, arms folded defiantly across her chest, her eyes fixed firmly on his face. She had waited an interminable three days for him to return from New Hampshire and read the letter of his appointment. He had said nothing, only rubbed his thumb over the seal, slowly, as though testing its texture and depth.

"Did you hear what I said, Mr. Adams? I will go with you. I cannot bear to be parted from you again."

He sighed, put the paper down and looked at her.

"I have not even accepted yet," he said. "Do not put the cart before the horse."

Abigail cocked her head skeptically.

"You cannot refuse," she retorted.

"Can I not?"

"Not the John Adams I know."

He looked steadily at his thirty-three-year-old wife. Time and strain had begun to etch deeper lines in her face, strew silver through the brown hair. Evidence of time they might have spent together lost.

"What do you suggest we do with the children?" he asked.

"Johnny is enrolled with Mr. Moody in Boston beginning next April," she responded, ticking off their brood. "Nabby is with my father at the parsonage most days since Betsey wed Mr. Shaw. Father depends on Nab; he is lost without my mother, though Will's daughter Louisa is still with him. Nab can remain at Weymouth. Mary and Richard Cranch might keep the little boys, or perhaps Sister Betsey."

"Betsey? Leave our sons with Mr. Shaw?" John asked. "Have you so suddenly altered your opinion of him? You have hardly spoken to him since they were married. Ye gods, Wife. Do ye think he holds any great affection for you? You would not even attend their wedding!"

Abigail had taken an instant dislike to John Shaw, Betsey's new husband. Arrogant and aloof, she had decided, distrustful of the provincial virtues, entirely too anxious to take Betsey away from her family. He understands nothing of family ties, family duties. Additionally, Betsy's marriage had been planned and sealed in unseemly haste. It raised questions amongst the neighbors about whether it had been rushed of necessity. They would train keen eyes on Betsey's belly, ask pointed questions, count months until the birth of their first child, perhaps sully the family's reputation, a reputation that Abigail held very dear.

"Not Betsey, then," she cried, desperate to find a way to accompany John and unwilling to become embroiled in an argument. "There are others. Or we can take them. It would be an opportunity for their education. John, I will not be left without you again."

For a moment, John was tempted to say yes, despite the hardship and obstacles, despite the expense and fears. But he was tempted for only a moment.

"My dearest Friend," he began, choosing his words. "Without your partnership I could not serve our country. It is you who run the farm. I have virtually no law practice now. We cannot manage without the farm -- that and our few little investments. If you were to go with me, who would run it? How could we pay a manager and still pay our bills? And who would look to it as you do? You must remain here to protect it."

"But..."

"Abigail," he continued, cutting her off. "Were the farm and the children the only impediments to your coming, we might yet find a way. But there is a more compelling argument. The seas are full of British men-of-war. By now, the British know of my appointment. It is likely they will make some attempt to stop me, perhaps a fatal attempt. Our children would be orphaned. Or suppose we were to be captured? These dogs deal with prisoners in the most horrifying manner. Even women. Especially women. What pleasure would they take in tormenting the wife of John Adams? These are times of war, Abigail. I cannot risk it."

"Surely, the risk is mine to take?" she said, voice quavering. "Do you think I am not sensible of what savagery sailors could inflict on a defenseless woman? I will gladly risk it. I can no longer be without you."

"Abigail, enough! I beg of you, do not make this more difficult for me than it already is!" John implored, nearly shouting. "It is too dangerous. I need you here. You cannot go."

It hurt. He wants me here more than he wants me with him, she thought. His heart cannot yearn like mine. She gave a him a long angry look, then turned and marched off to the kitchen.

1778

In January, the Massachusetts General Court finally paid John £226 6s. 2d. for services as a delegate to the Continental Congress.

"Four years' service, Abigail. Four years!" John bellowed, as he stacked the silver on his desk. " And what do we have to show for it? Not enough payment to cover the cost of farm labor for that time let alone all the other expenses."

"Posterity will repay you, Husband," Abigail replied absently, her mind on the more immediate problem of procuring the stores to supply John and Joseph Stevens, who would accompany him on the voyage to France, without impoverishing the family he left behind. She sat in a chair opposite his desk and scribbled on the back of an envelope she had pulled from her apron pocket. "Chickens, I think, a sheep or two, salt meat, eggs, corn, rum, ale, wine, sugar," she said as she ticked down her list. "What else will you need?"

"Tobacco," John said without looking up, "and pipes. There will be long evenings during the crossing. I have arranged to meet the captain of the *Boston* offshore at Mt. Wollaston. It will not be so public a departure as one from town. In that way I hope to forestall any attempt to capture 'Minister Adams.' Many would gladly take me as hostage. It will be difficult to ferry the livestock out, especially in this weather," he observed, glancing out the window at the snow that was being chased sideways by a northwest gale.

"Paper! I pray you may find that paper is not as hard to come by in France as here. Write me long, long letters, John, full of effusions of the heart. And many of them. I will be in sore need of your company by post if I cannot have it in the flesh. Oh, I wish I could go!"

John kept his head down and made no remark. Abigail sighed and dipped her pen in the inkwell that stood between them on the table. There was a tentative knock on the door.

"Yes?"

"Par?"

Johnny came into the room by degrees, like a dog unsure of its welcome.

"What is it, lad?"

John laid down his quill when his son had reached his chair.

"Par, I've been thinking. You shouldn't go on that long voyage alone," he said, searching his father's face for a reaction.

"I am not alone, Johnny. I'm taking Joseph with me. He's ever been faithful in our welfare," John replied, smiling affectionately at his eldest son.

Johnny was ten now, and nearly as tall as his mother. A serious child, eager to please, though a little delicate in his looks. Too much time with women, John decided. He needs a man's guidance now, not a mother's care.

"Yes, but Joseph is not the same..." Johnny said, his eyes dropping to the pewter buckles on his shoes.

"Not the same as what?" John asked, baiting Johnny while he decided what his answer to the boy's still-unspoken question was to be.

Abigail watched the two of them, her heart pounding. Please

don't ask, she begged silently. Please. Please say no if he asks. It is too much send my best friend and my right hand on such a perilous voyage.

"You need someone who can help you with your French, Par," Johnny said, finally looking up at his father's face earnestly.

"Help me with my French! Listen to the young scamp, Abigail! He implies his father's understanding of the diplomatic language is not sufficient to the task at hand," John said, teasing.

Abigail remained tensed, a tigress ready to spring in defense of her young or perhaps in defense of her own happiness.

"You have been studying Mar's French grammar assiduously, Par. But...."

"But you think I am still not equal to the convoluted conversations of the French court," John finished for him. "Such cheek!"

"Par, I want to go with you," Johnny blurted. "I could help you. We could spend the voyage speaking French to prepare you for the court. I could... I could act as secretary to you. Surely you will need someone you can trust to transcribe letters, carry dispatches, messages…" Johnny said, warming to the argument.

"And what about your schooling young man," Abigail said, breaking her silence.

"It would be schooling enough to be with Par!" Johnny burbled on eagerly. "I am only part way through that list of books you gave me to read, Par. We could discuss them. I could read more. And your French..."

"Ah, yes, my French. My abominable French," John laughed. "Enough John Quincy. Enough. I will discuss it with your mother, and we will give you our decision at supper tonight. Now go back to your French grammar."

John Quincy's eyes lit up and he made an awkward bow then clattered out of the room, slamming the door behind him. Abigail had put the quill down on the table and folded her arms across her chest.

"Abigail..." John began, seeing NO written in every line of her body.

"John, the voyage is too dangerous! *I* may not go because it is too dangerous. Has that changed, suddenly, now that John Quincy has asked to go?"

"Abigail, the perils for a woman are far different from those for a man, or a boy. He has long missed a father's company. He is growing into a man without the manly guidance he needs. I do not know when I may be back, though I pray it may not be so long as the last Congress. He needs his father. And, in truth, I need him. He is quite right about my French," John laughed, hoping to soften his wife's mood.

"What about his education, John? We have already arranged with Mr. Moody to enroll him in school."

"There are schools in France, my dear. He was not to go to Moody's until April because the school is too full now. And think how he can improve his French with me in such a post. What opportunities might this open for our son? It is time I began to look to our boys' futures and their careers."

Abigail, mouth set in a grim line, stared hard at her husband. Resentment pounded in her chest. How little men know of women, she thought angrily. How little they care. He denies me the only comfort I want, and then thinks to repay me with the threatened loss of those I hold most dear. Men hold our lives in their hands so carelessly. For him and his son, it will be an adventure. He cares nothing for the risk to them, while the risk to me is too great. And does a woman not risk herself every time she makes love, every time she conceives and gives birth, or miscarries? Women face death every day. Does he not know I wish adventures, new experiences, challenges, too? My sacrifices are double his and he is oblivious. Does he even love me? Unconsciously, her hand went to the locket at her throat and she fingered its tooled face absently, searching for her next argument. Only later did she remember the locket's inscription: *I yield. Whatever is, is right.*

"Your mind is made up," she said, mouth pursed into a thin line.

"You know me so well."

He reached for her, but she backed away, refusing to be touched.

"Abigail, do not draw away from me," he urged. "Our time together is short. I do this for you as well as for me and for our son. It is too much to ask a mother, even a woman as excellent as you, to raise a son alone. There are things a father alone must impart."

She stared angrily.

"My dear, this is an opportunity for Johnny. You know that. And regardless of what Providence holds in store for us on this earth, we shall all meet again on that distant shore," he coaxed, his hand still close, waiting.

"We must not tempt Providence," she spat out.

"We are not tempting Providence when we do the tasks allotted us in this life, or when we make use of the opportunities afforded us."

"Your arguments are convenient to your purposes," she retorted. "Yet, I yield."

"To me?" he asked softly, raising an eyebrow, a glint in his eyes.

"No. To your judgment," she said angrily, once again taking up her pen and returning to her list.

For a long moment, he watched her, bent over the table just out of his reach.

The February landscape was blanketed in snow. Drifts obscured the contours of the buildings, and the garden was a pristine fairy village of wind-carved hollows and spires. Johnny, breathless in his eagerness to be off, danced around the sleigh. Wrapped in an old woolen shawl, Abigail stood stolidly beside Joseph, throat aching with unshed tears.

"Be good, Johnny, mind your manners, and be a good help to Par," she said, trying to grasp Johnny's shoulder to still him and focus his attention, but he skittered out from beneath her hand.

"Yes Mar," he replied distractedly, his mind on the adventure that sprawled ahead.

Abigail studied the son in whom she took such joy and pride. He cannot imagine a mother's fears, she thought, wanting to clutch at him, but too proud to put out a hand lest he refuse the contact. How long would they be parted? What trials would he face? Please, God, protect them both. Keep them honorable and whole. A sly doubt, a fleeting thought of her father's travels crept into her thoughts but she pushed it away. Let them travel safely and return home to me. Soon.

John snatched her round the waist and held her close.

"I am ever yours, my dearest," he whispered, "My heart stays in Braintree." They clung to each other.

"My dearest, my dearest," John murmured into her ear.

"May God protect you all," Abigail said, her voice breaking. She bit her lip to keep back the tears.

Johnny climbed into the sleigh and snuggled under the rug that

Joseph brought from the attic. After running a gentling hand along the mare's flanks, Joseph climbed up into the driver's seat and took up the reins.

"We'll miss the barge out, Par," Johnny said eagerly.

"They stand and wait for us, John Quincy," John replied. "There is no one else."

After kissing Abigail hard on the mouth, John climbed in and settled himself on the cracked leather seat beside his son. Joseph slapped the reins against the mare's rump. The sleigh took off with a lurch, pushing its occupants back against the seat.

"Goodbye, Mar!" Johnny shouted.

"May God be with ye!" Abigail cried, lifting an arm in salute.

My heart may burst, she thought. She watched as they disappeared behind the hissing veil of snow.

The following morning, Abigail trudged through the drifts to the top of Penn's Hill to watch the *Boston* weigh anchor and scoot out of the harbor under reefed sails into the teeth of a gale.

Four days after their departure, Abigail left Charly and Tommy with Patty and walked the four miles between Braintree and Weymouth Parsonage. The snow had stopped, leaving sculpted ledges and caves along the ditches in the road, but the wind continued unabated, howling through the naked trees like an evil spirit. Wrapped in her tattered old cloak, Abigail covered the ground with long, determined strides, her mind on the frigate that carried John and Johnny.

As she rounded her father's barn, she scanned the yard. It looked mournful. The fence had not been painted since her mother died, and the pear tree was unpruned, its unruly branches scoring each other as they whipped in the wind. Half-rotting cabbages, now frozen, dotted the garden. They should have been root-cellared months ago, she thought ruefully. Coming up the walk, skidding in the slick-packed snow, she was surprised to see the door opened wide by Nabby.

"Mother! I should have come to see you if you hadn't come today. Oh, Mar! There's news."

Abigail stomped the snow off her brogans, shook the hem of her cloak clean and stepped into the hallway. Seeing Nabby's face, her heart began to pound.

"What news?" she asked.

"Daughter!"

Reverend Smith came into the hallway. Abigail suddenly saw him as bent, stooped with the years and cares. Will I, too, bend beneath the weight of loneliness? She shuddered. God does not give us more to bear than we are able, she reminded herself, willing away the self-pity.

"Come in to the fire, Abigail. Warm yourself. Nabby, fetch your mother some hot wine."

"But Grandfather," Nabby protested.

"Go along, now, do as I say."

Blood thumping in her ears, Abigail went to the fire, and turned to face her father.

"What news?" she asked.

"It may not be news, Abigail," Reverend Smith said, gravely.

Out with it! Abigail wanted to scream.

"Cousin Isaac heard something from one of his captains."

Cousin Isaac, a childhood friend, was quietly making his fortune in shipping while John spent his years in service to his country.

Reverend Smith coughed and stared at the floor for a moment, then blurted: "They say the frigate *Boston* was captured by a British man-of-war, that John and Johnny were taken prisoner to New Hampshire."

Abigail's stomach lurched, but she stood by the fire, hands still stretched out behind her toward its warmth.

"Has this report been in any way confirmed?" she asked, astonished by the calmness in her voice.

"Not to my knowledge. It is rumor only, Abigail, but I thought you would want to know."

She nodded dumbly, her mind working.

"Cousin Isaac has nearly twenty ships sailing this coast. Surely, he can..."

"He is already sending to every port he can for more information," her father hastily added. "He should have confirmed news in a few days."

The old man studied his daughter's face, watching her struggle with the fear, the hope, her mind sorting out possibilities, alternatives.

"I will not tell the little boys," she decided. "Not until we know for certain one way or the other. There is no hurry to alarm them. It may prove a false report."

Reverend Smith nodded in agreement. "Nab can stay here. She is very worked up about it, Abigail. She has not your strength."

"She is young, Father," Abigail replied, her mind meanwhile searching for other avenues whereby she might learn something concrete. "She will season."

"It is a rumor," Reverend Smith repeated.

Abigail nodded. "Yes. And rumors are an abundant commodity right now. It may yet prove false as so many others have," she asserted, gathering strength. "But if true, we must find a way to obtain their release."

For seven days, Abigail worked at home, only half-hearing Charly and Tommy's lessons, dropping stitches while she knitted in the evening, writing disjointed letters to friends, praying for news. On Saturday, she was making a bed in the boys' room when she heard hoofs pounding along the road. She peered out to see Cousin Isaac bring his mount up so short that it nearly crashed into the gate. Jumping off, he slapped the reins against the post to tie them then ran up to the front door. Her heart in her throat, she clambered down the steps and met him in the front hall.

"It's untrue!" he shouted without preamble, seizing her by the shoulders. "I've just had word from a frigate that passed the *Boston* en route to France. They were pounded mightily by the storm, and they were *chased* by a British man-of-war, but they outran her. They are safe!"

"Oh thank God!" Abigail cried. "Come in, Cousin. Come warm yourself with a hot drink. Patty! Patty!" she shouted, going through the drawing room door toward the kitchen.

"Yes M'am?" Patty met her in the hallway, eyes wide and fearful. "What's happened?"

"Mr. Adams and John Quincy are safe!" Abigail cried, eyes shining. "Make Mr. Smith a grog and be liberal with the rum!"

Isaac Smith had followed her through the drawing room, and closed the door behind him.

"Oh, I nearly forgot. I have a letter from John," he said, pulling a small, sealed paper from his breast. "The seas were calm enough to exchange letters when the *Patriot* passed."

"Was it one of your ships?" Abigail asked, taking the letter from her cousin.

"No, it belonged to a friend -- and rival," Isaac said, smiling. "But I had cast a wide net for information of Cousin John, and my net came back with that." He pointed to the letter in Abigail's hand. "Do not stand on ceremony, Abigail. Read it now."

She ripped opened the seal, and read:

My Dear Friend, There is but a short time to scribble a few lines to you and send it back via the Patriot. I pray this may reach your hand safe to let you know of us. On the way out of the harbor, we were accosted by a man-of-war, but as she was a sluggish vessel and the Boston so maneuverable, and skillfully handled, we easily outran her. It was the storm more than the chase which laid me low. I puked from the time we left harbor until yesterday, and am only now regaining my appetite. Johnny does well. His sea legs were sturdier than mine, no small gratification to him, I can tell you. I will write on landing. Always yours yours yours. John..

A tear stood in Abigail's eye, but she brushed it away impatiently. Isaac Smith had watched her face as she read, the smile spreading unconsciously as she reached the last line.

"I thank you for bringing me news. And this," she said softly, folding the letter again.

The door opened and Patty skittered in carrying a large steaming mug.

"Patty, put on your cloak and go to Weymouth. Let Nabby and Reverend Smith know that John Quincy and Mr. Adams continue safely on their way to France."

"Yes'm," Patty nodded, handing Isaac the mug. "Anything else?"

"Yes. Invite them to come for dinner and stay the night."

"Yes'm." Patty nodded and scurried out of the room again.

"You will stay, Cousin," Abigail said, turning to Isaac who was gingerly sipping at the steaming grog. "We shall make a celebration with what meager stores we can offer."

"Gladly, Cousin," Smith replied, his back to the fire.

She pushed away the thought that the two still had many treacherous miles still to cross.

Chapter 11

That never-ending flight of future days.
Paradise Lost John Milton Bk II line 221

"It has been three months, and I have had no word from John,"
Abigail whispered to Mercy Warren, who sat beside her in the stern
of the long skiff.

The May breeze rustled through the laced folds of Abigail's cap,
and kicked up a pleating of ripples on the water. In the bow, Nabby,
Charly, and Tommy clustered together on the narrow thwart,
chattering and pointing at the swooping gulls, speculating on the
destination of the outward bound vessel that was gliding past
Peddocks Island under full sail. Leather chafing gear creaked in the
oarlocks as the sailor, shirt-sleeves rolled to his elbows, silently rowed
the party out to where Isaac Smith's frigate *Adams* lay at anchor.

Hurt that they had been left behind while Johnny embarked on
the adventure of his life, Tommy and Charly had persuaded Cousin
Isaac to allow them to visit the vessel he had named in honor of their
father.

"It is only that the mails have miscarried," Mercy responded
softly. "Mr. Adams and your son have surely arrived safely or you
would have heard by now."

Once she had recovered from the worry that they had been
captured at sea, Abigail was faced with a new fear. Assassination.
Not long after learning that the rumor of John's capture was false,
another rumor began circulating: that Benjamin Franklin had been
murdered by an assassin. It had proven false, but false only because
Franklin was not dead. There had indeed been an attempt.

"Yes, I would surely have heard had they not arrived," she
agreed, sotto voce. "But I want a letter from my friend. Charly! Sit
down before you go overboard!"

"I'll mind him, Mar," Nabby said to her mother, taking her eight-
year-old brother by the arm and yanking him back to her side.

Abigail continued, softly, to Mercy. "To lose John to the furies
of a storm, or disease would be hard enough. For him to be

deliberately stolen from me by the hand of man would be more than I could bear."

"Hush!" Mercy told her firmly. "God will protect our dear Mr. Adams -- AND your Johnny."

"The water's COLD Mar," Tommy cried gleefully, holding up the blue hand he had been trailing overboard since they had left the wharf.

"Keep your hands inside the boat, Thomas Boylston," Abigail retorted, unimpressed with his revelation.

"You don't want a shark to come snatch it off, do you?" Mercy asked mischievously.

Tommy's eyes widened in horror. "There ain't no sharks in here, are there, Mar?"

"You never know," Abigail replied.

The sailor, head down, smiled.

Abigail cast her eyes across the harbor. Fishing vessels poked among the shore reeds like ducks. Several frigates, some with makeshift cannon ports exposed, lay at anchor. Mercy, eyes still on Abigail's children, sighed.

"Yours will never give you cause for such pain as mine," Mercy remarked wistfully.

"Is Winston still at home?"

Mercy nodded, sighing. "My husband seems able to manage him. God help me, Abigail, I cannot! And so I impose on your hospitality -- to escape my eldest son. I cannot bear to see him in such a condition. And Winston's fits frighten me. When his mind turns, he threatens to harm me. Such hate! It's been over a month since his regiment sent him home -- to rest, his captain said. Captain Jester was being kind. We later learned Winston had threatened to kill a young soldier who would not follow his orders," Mercy said. "They fear him."

"Is it still the drink?" Abigail asked, thinking of her brother, Will, four of whose six children had been farmed out to Mary and Betsey to raise. The eldest, Louisa, remained with Reverend Smith. Will's wife and youngest child lived in squalor in a shed behind a friend's house.

"Not so much now, though when he does it seems to make it worse. He says he drinks to silence the voices in his head, but...." Mercy stopped, shaking her head.

Three boys, gleefully naked, leapt from North Wharf, their joyous cries lost on the breeze.

Abigail put her hand on her friend's arm. Anger, helplessness, disappointment, heartbreak -- she had felt all these things and more over Will. Hard enough to grieve for the lost promise of a brother. How much keener must be the pain, Abigail thought sadly, when it is your child whose life is in ruins.

Mercy sucked in a deep breath. Crisp and salt-laden, it seemed to cleanse her, and she brightened.

"I will not dwell on such things as I cannot change," she said firmly. "It is enough to enjoy your children, your company, dear Abigail, and this outing. More is not granted."

Deftly, the oarsman turned the skiff into the wind and brought it alongside the *Adams*. He shipped the oars and reached for a knotted rope that hung down beside the rope ladder. The children in the bow had all stood, waiting to scramble up the ladder, but Mercy looked doubtfully at the distance she and Abigail must climb in heavy skirts.

"We are not yet SO old that we cannot scramble up and down one more ladder," Abigail said.

"Perhaps you are not, Mrs. Adams. But I have a much greater weight of years," Mercy laughed.

Eagerly, Tommy sprang to the ladder and scrambled up the side like a monkey. Abigail watched, heart in her throat. At the top, he grabbed for the rail, but in his eager hurry, missed. It took only a split second to imagine him crashing down into the boat, snapping his neck on the gunwale, gone. But out of nowhere, a brawny sailor snatched the child's wrist and yanked him unceremoniously aboard the *Adams*. The captain who had come to welcome his distinguished visitors, looked at Tommy sternly.

"You do not do things in haste aboard ship unless need be," he said. Leaning over the side to call down to Charly who had begun his ascent, he called: "Take care, boy, and see if you will make a better sailor than your brother."

Chastened, Tommy stood beside the blocky captain, head drooping like a rain-soaked daffodil.

"Here, lad, stand here beside your brother," the captain said, after Charly had scrambled over the rail. "I am sending down a bosun's chair for the ladies."

Nabby, standing, was reaching for the ladder, the folds of her skirts and petticoats clutched in one hand, when the captain shouted down, "Stay, Miss. This ladder was never meant for the fairer sex. The chair will bring you up."

She stopped and steadied herself on the vessel's hull as three sailors lowered a wooden seat fixed swing-like to a halyard. When it had reached the level of the skiff, the oarsman stood and helped Nabby into it. Pulleys screeching, the bosun's chair was raised until it cleared the rail, then lowered to the deck where Nabby slipped out and primly straightened her skirts.

Seated on a thick coil of line beside an open hatch, an ancient sailor with a scar that ran the length of his face mended sails. A boy of about twelve stood beside him chewing a cud of tobacco. The youth's clothes, patched and frayed at the cuffs, looked as though he lived in them.

While the captain was directing Abigail's boarding, Tommy and Charly had sidled over to the boy who stood, jaw thrust out, squinting at them knowingly.

"You work on this ship?" Tommy asked, awestruck.

"Sure. I been workin' her since I was your age, I reckon," he said, nodding to Charly. "Me Par couldn't feed all of us. Warn't no fault of his, though. Ten mouths is a lot to feed, 'specially in these times."

"They let you chew tobacco?" asked Charly enviously.

"Yeah. Who's to say no?" the boy wanted to know.

"My Mar'd have a fit if I was to chew," Charly muttered, eyes wide.

"Well, mine ain't here," the boy observed.

"What do you do?" Tommy asked.

"Oh, most anything -- lend Cook a hand, splice lines, haul sheets. Sometimes I climb to the topmast and help with the sails," the boy boasted. "I can get up there as fast as any of the men - faster'n some."

"I reckon I could get up there fast enough," eight-year-old Charly countered, eyeing the netting of lines that ran to the crow's nest.

"I dare you!" the boy whispered.

Charly glanced at his mother, who was being brought like cargo over the port side, then darted to the starboard side and sprang to the rail.

"Don't do it, Charly!" Tommy, who had followed his brother, whispered urgently, "Mar'll skin you!"

"She'll have to catch me first," Charly replied.

He began climbing, hand over hand, toward the crow's nest on the after mast. Tommy, mouth gaping, watched his brother scale the knotted ropes as though he had been born to the sea -- until he reached the top. Unable to pull himself into the crow's nest he made a fatal mistake. He looked down.

The deck, eighty feet below, seemed to sway. His limbs felt like rubber and a lump rose in his throat. Terrified, he shut his eyes and clung desperately to the lines.

Abigail had introduced Mercy to the captain when Tommy came over to her and pulled on her skirt.

"Mar?"

"Don't interrupt, Thomas Boylston," she admonished.

"But Mar," Tommy persisted.

"Thomas Boylston..."

"Mar Charly's stuck up the mast," Tommy said, pointing skyward.

"Dear God!" Abigail breathed. "Charles Adams! Come down here this instant!"

"I can't Mar!" Charly wailed, teeth chattering.

He tried to scramble farther up into the crow's nest. He slipped, dropping suddenly two notches on the rigging. For a split second, Abigail saw his body broken and bloody on the deck, but his arm caught in another notch.

"Riggins, Marley!" the captain bellowed. "Make a hammock of that sail and catch the boy if he falls. Jones, climb up there after him."

"Aye, Cap'n!"

Jones, who had been staring at Nabby since she had been brought aboard, hoisted himself up onto the rail.

"I can't hold on Mar!" cried Charly. "I'm gonna fall!"

"No you won't, Charles Adams. You just hold on tight," Abigail shouted up to him, her panic sounding like anger. "I will not lose you, do you hear? Hold on."

Seaman Jones clambered up the rigging two squares at a time, but Abigail could see Charly's hold giving way, the ropes inexorably slipping through his wet-palmed grasp. Mercy held Abigail's hand, silent. All eyes were trained on the boy who dangled above them.

Her heart beat against her temples. Please God, please God, please God. Just as Charly began to slide again, Jones reached up and grabbed his wrist.

"Gotcha now, Boy," he said, gruffly. "You need some more practice afore you climb so high!"

Jones dragged Charly around to the outboard side of the rigging and pressed his body against the boy's, holding him against the netting. Charly, too terrified to even look at his savior, merely nodded, head against the rope.

"You're all right now, Lad. Just come down. I won't let ye fall."

Hand under hand the two descended until Charly reached the rail where he was grabbed by rough hands and plonked on deck.

Abigail, who had come to stand beside the sail the men had spread out to catch him, took Charly's arm and shook him, rough in her angry relief.

"You could have fallen and killed yourself!"

"Not a sparrow falls, but He sees," Charly, struggling to regain his dignity, unwisely quoted the piece of Scripture he had heard so often on his mother's lips.

Had they not been in such a public forum, Abigail would have smacked Charly's face for his impudence.

"You will sit here, Charles Adams, until this visit is finished, and nary move from that spot," she said through clenched teeth.

"Yes, Mar," Charly muttered, head drooping.

"I thought you said she'd have to catch you," Tommy taunted quietly.

"My sons need their father's hand," Abigail said later when she and Mercy and the captain sat down to a meal in his cabin.

"If ye don't mind my sayin' so M'am, I would think your hand was plenty strong," the captain said.

The setting sun lit the harbor by the time they were rowed back to shore.

"Real coffee!" breathed Mercy. "Oh such luxury! And that scuppernong!"

Abigail smiled.

"It was generous of the captain to give us each a bottle."

"Yes, but you got coffee beans, too!" Mercy teased. "There are certain advantages to being Mrs. John Adams."

The breeze had died. The sounds of carriage wheels and street hucksters floated out across the water. Charly, eyes fixed on the receding bulk of the frigate, sighed.

"I want to go to sea, Mar. "

Abigail watched her son's face, shining as he imagined himself a hero in a battle against the sea.

"And when are you leaving, young sir?" Mercy asked.

"As soon as Mar says I may," Charly replied seriously.

"Your father and I have other hopes for you, Charles Adams. You needs must finish your education before you make such a choice."

"I know I was meant for the sea, Mar," Charly repeated, his gaze unwavering.

"I miss my friend when the boys begin to set their sights upon such a course," Abigail groaned to Mercy.

"Take heart, Abigail," Mercy replied, laughing. "Charly has not even left Boston harbor yet."

The summer of 1778 seemed endless. Prices skyrocketed. Farm hands that would have been glad of work at £20 a year in 1777 now demanded £14 a month. Bread went from 4 pence to 4 shillings a loaf. A pair of cartwheels cost Abigail £60 - ten times what she had paid only a few years before. Desperately trying to prune the budget, Abigail dismissed her hands and rented out the fields, retaining only one horse and two cows. Patty, whose wages were but a meager share of the meager income, remained. But for each burden lifted, there was another to take its place. Nabby was now in school in Boston, another expense. Tommy and Charly were still at home, but Abigail planned to enroll Charly at Haverhill the following year under the tutelage of Betsey's husband, whom Abigail was gradually coming to respect.

She had finally gotten Hayden out of the house, but had been obliged to pay a share of his first month's rent at his next lodging to do it. Taxes were due. She sold things: pins, cloth, and ribbon that John had sent her while in Philadelphia, household goods, cheeses, fruit, whatever she could find to raise ready cash without borrowing.

But worse than the perpetual worry over money was the

loneliness. In the evenings, she sat by the fire writing letters to her 'dearest friend,' tears smearing the ink. She pled for a description of his voyage, for details of his days and the people he met, for affirmations of his love. At times, grief at John's absence overwhelmed her discretion and she poured her heart onto the paper, despite the chance of the letters being intercepted.

Finally at end of June a letter arrived written in John's familiar scrawl. Eagerly she broke the seal, only to find five hastily scribbled lines, just enough to assure her of their safe arrival in France and of their plans for settling at Passy and enrolling Johnny at M. Le Coeur's pension school. Five lines. No more. The delight at touching the paper John had touched three months before was diluted by the clinical stiffness of the dispatch.

Summer dragged into autumn. Drought increased the price of wheat fourfold. The days, grew shorter and shorter, reminded her of the years going by without John.

Finally, in October two more letters arrived. She devoured them, searching for reassurance of his love, of his longing for her. But instead of yearning, John wrote of the beauty of France, of the fascinating newness, of the charm of the French, of the wit and intellect of French women. She, stuck in provincial Braintree, could not compete. He had forbidden her to come then taunted her with the world from which she had been exiled.

"I know his heart is mine by right, by free gift. I hold possession of what they cannot rob me of," she tried to reassure herself, pounding bread dough with her fist.

Outside, the November wind cut through the orchard's naked limbs and whipped the branches of the forsythia against the house.

"I would even consent that the French women should practice their FORMs as he calls them, on him," she continued, mauling the dough. "They throw their arms around a man as they speak. They even kiss Dr. Franklin with great frequency and freedom, apparently. But I WISH he would send me some free expression of his ardor for ME!"

Mercy, who sat at the table, sipping a cup of hot tea, smiled. "Men cannot express the sentiments closest to their hearts. They seem to feel it is vulnerability."

Abigail sighed. "But to me? I think he could unbend a little in his letters. It is all I have of him for I know not how long. He loves the ladies. I have always known that, though I have never *really* feared for his fidelity. But reassurances never come amiss," Abigail cried, taking up the dough and thumping it back down with a force that made the table shake.

And she had heard that French women were adept at terminating unwonted pregnancies. A man could hide his infidelity with a willing partner.

"You are a woman blessed in love, " Mercy said gently. "You and John have a rare bond."

Do we? I always believed so. Abigail thought. But he is so far away. And men have... needs.

The door opened and Patty blew in carrying two full buckets of milk. Kicking the door closed behind her, she dropped them on the table then worked her hands together for a moment to bring back the circulation.

"Powerful cold today," she observed. "I half expected the milk to freeze as it dropped to the bucket."

"'T'is bitter," Abigail agreed, glancing at the girl's blue lips. "I reckon I'll have to rise this dough nearly *in* the fire."

"'Tis chill today even in here. But consider the poor souls on the *Somerset*," Mercy said, shaking her head at the thought of the British gun ship that had gone down on Nantucket Shoals. "I hear the survivors are marching to Boston to turn themselves over as prisoners. How bitter that must be."

"Thirty-eight saved, Mr. Wormsley down the road told me," Patty put in as she warmed her hands by the fire. "All the rest drowned. I can't for the life of me understand why anyone would go to sea. Shall I start more bread, Mrs. Adams?"

"Yes. That crust is the last we have," Abigail said, nodding to the partial loaf covered with a towel that sat on the shelf over the dry sink. "Mrs. Archer says it was forty that was saved. And that no one would give the survivors a dry cloak or wrapping -- in this cold! Inhuman. Poor souls dragging ashore soaked through, icicles hanging off them. They may be our enemy yet that does not give us reason to treat them like animals. No, worse than animals. You would not deny an unfortunate beast."

"Feelings are hard against the English," Mercy said, sipping at her tea pensively. "I wonder at your charity. They would have taken Mr. Adams and his son prisoner, or worse, had they been able."

"God demands our charity," Abigail retorted. "And, those poor souls may have more in common with us than we can guess by the color of their clothing. Merit is not sewn into the stripe of a flag. If these poor wretches merit our sympathy, I will not withhold it."

The door burst open and Tommy and Charly clattered into the kitchen, faces rosy with the cold. Tommy, a muffler wrapped around his ears, rushed over to his mother.

"They're comin' here!" he cried. "Mr. Tanner says so. He sends word ahead and wants us to help feed 'em!"

"Feed who?" Abigail asked, putting the mound of dough into a greased wooden bowl and setting it on the hearth to rise. "Who's coming?"

"The prisoners from the *Somerset*!" Charly cried, rubbing his hands together. "They're comin' by here on their way to Boston. Mr. Tanner says he got word from a Mr.... what was the name, Tommy?"

"I don't know! They're comin' anyhow! " Tommy burbled. "British soldiers! Will they be carrying muskets? Had I better get Par's rifle and stand guard?"

"Don't be stupid!" Charly snapped. "Mr. Tanner says he needs to help find food for 'em and would you help feed 'em, Mar?"

"Feed British prisoners?" Patty exclaimed, indignant. "Why should we waste our flour and apples on them I should like to know?"

"Because we are Christians," Abigail shot back. "Run tell Mr. Tanner I will, Charly."

"Yes, Mar!"

"Will they kill us, Mar?" Tommy asked, face puckered in fear. "Shall I get Par's rifle?"

"No. Now stop interrupting, Thomas Boylston. Charly!" Abigail called as her son started out the door again. "How many men does Mr. Tanner reckon?"

"He didn't say. Shall I find out?"

"Yes. And don't tarry. I'll need your help."

"Yes'm."

Charly bolted out the door followed by six-year-old Tommy.

"Wait for me, Charly!" Tommy cried, turning and racing after his brother.

"Mrs. Adams! Ain't ye afraid they'll murder us all?" Patty cried, eyes popped open so wide the whites were visible all the way around the irises.

"I doubt they'd have the strength, or the inclination. They're probably frozen through. It's a wonder they can walk," Abigail said, hands on hips, ruminating over her stores.

"I don't like it anyhow," Patty muttered, head down.

"What shall I do, Abigail?" Mercy asked. "Organize me."

"Start another few loaves. I'll scour the pantry to see what we have to offer," Abigail said, pushing another large bowl across the table to Mercy. "Patty, get Mrs. Warren the gingham apron -- it would be a shame to spoil that lovely dress -- and then bring in a cheese and a crock of pickle. "Let's see... we'll need to stir up the fire in the parlor, there will probably be too many to keep them all in here. Look sharp, Patty or I'll send you off to Boston with them."

"Yes'm," Patty grumbled.

The ragged troop came up the frozen road three hours later. Gaunt, eyes hollow with resignation, they limped along on frostbitten feet, ears wrapped against the cold in rags and bandages.

Tommy and Charly flattened against the wall, gaping, as the sailors filed silently through the kitchen door to huddle by the hearth.

"There are twenty here, Mrs. Adams," said the farmer who directed them with gruff kindness. "Mrs. Coffin off great Orchard Farm took in t'other twenty. 'Tis hard going to find vittals for 'em, bein' enemy seamen and times bein' so hard."

"Granmar Adams said she wouldn't have no Britisher in her house while her son was fighting against...." Tommy tried to inform his mother but was cut off by a yank on the sleeve and a hissed warning from his older brother.

"Sit ye down, gentlemen," Abigail said, indicating the long table that held plates of sliced cheese and pickle. "There is bread, and new butter coming. Charly, find some more mugs or teacups," she ordered as the men shuffled dull-eyed to the table.

"Yes'm."

The boy trotted off.

Mercy stood at one end of the kitchen table, apron wrapped around her middle, cutting thick slices of warm bread and passing them around, hand to hand.

A lean young man, hands mottled blue and black, hunched over the table, holding a slice of bread as though between flippers. Charly, who had put a broken crockery mug and several chipped teacups on the table at the sailor's elbow, stared.

"Why are your hands like that?" the boy blurted.

"Frostbite, Lad," another sailor, his mouth crammed full of bread, replied. "Cold's cruel to a body. Thankee, Mistress," he said to Mercy who had handed him another slice. "'Tis like manna from heaven."

"Charly, don't just stand there, pour out that ale and pass it around. These men are froze nearly half to death," his mother ordered, bustling in from the parlor with empty pitchers in both hands. She quickly filled the pitchers from the kettle that hung over the fire then strode back out through the hallway.

Patty poured more warm ale into the mug at Charly's elbow. Carefully filling the cups he had found, he passed them to waiting hands along the table. There was little conversation, only the sounds of chewing, cups being filled and gulped down. One stringy sailor, chewed absently, staring into the fire.

"What happened?" Charly finally asked him.

"Happened?" he repeated dazedly. "The storm...cold, like a shock right through me soul. Crashin' and timber smashin'. And screamin', screamin'..." he trailed away, pain in his eyes.

The man beside the young man nudged him.

"Leave off, Owen," he said softly, through a mouthful of bread and cheese.

Patty paused and poured more ale into Owen's mug, a look of pity on her small, pinched face.

"Charly, don' t be botherin' the man," she said softly. "Here. Pass around this plate Mrs. Warren just finished cuttin'. Go on, now. Others need some."

"I lost me brother," Owen said, tears starting, as Charly moved down the table, carrying the plate past grabbing hands until it was empty again.

"Leave off, Man," the sailor beside Owen urged again. "We've got food and warmth for now."

Putting his head down on the table, Owen began to cry softly. His hands, the bread still folded between them, had dropped to his lap.

Charly stopped dead, watching.

"Here son, is there any more of that stuff?" called a burly man whose eyebrows seemed to explode from his forehead.

Wide-eyed, Charly nodded and returned to Mercy, who pulled three more loaves from the oven and began to slice. When Charly returned with the steaming slices, the man grabbed two and slathered them with butter from the dimpled mound Abigail put on the table.

"Don't pay him no mind," the sailor told Charly, nodding toward Owen. "See, poor Owen warn't no real sailor. He and his brother just got grabbed up in a press gang. All they could talk about was gettin' back home." He took a bite and chewed with relish before continuing.

"Some men warn't never meant for sea. The fear freezes 'em. We was caught in a hellish storm off Nantucket -- a real graveyard it is, black and wild. Next thing I knew, we was poundin' on the bottom, timbers crackin', men screamin', sea pourin' in."

"But how were you saved?" Charly asked in horrified fascination.

"I was pitched over by a big sea that came roaring over the side. Thought it was me end. But I came back up splutterin' and spewin' out saltwater. See, I can swim, not like a lot of others who just go down. Somebody must 'a launched a lifeboat 'cause just as I thought I'd go down with the cold -- you know your joints freeze up quick in them icy waters -- I was dragged aboard."

He stopped for a moment and watched Owen, down the table, his shoulders heaving. "It's his first wreck, see. Yer first is the toughest."

Charly's eyes widened. "You've been shipwrecked *before* ?"

"Sure. I been at sea since I was not much oldern' you." the man said, grabbing for the cheese plate. "Been in four shipwrecks, I have. I must have the luck of the devil cause I keep washin' ashore." He chuckled tiredly at his joke.

"But why do you keep going back to sea?" Charly asked incredulously.

"Some were never meant for land, boy," the sailor replied matter-of-factly, eyes on Owen. "He'll lose those fingers sure. I seen it before. I lost this one," he held up his right hand, missing the pinky, "to frostbite, must be ten years ago now. These, " he put his left hand in front of Charly's face, "got tore off in a block. I learned quick, though. Didn't do *that* again."

"Charly, bring that plate back and I'll put more bread on it," Mercy called from the other end of the table.

166

Obediently, Charly returned and watched as she layered another sliced loaf onto the chipped platter.

"Do ye still want to go to sea?" Mercy asked softly as she lifted the plate up to Charly's waiting hands.

Wide-eyed, he only shook his head. No.

Chapter 12

In worst extremes and on the perilous edge of battle
Paradise Lost Milton Bk I line 275

1779

Finally, on the second of August the following year, *La Sensible* sailed into Boston harbor carrying Joseph Stevens, John, and John Quincy Adams. John had been recalled. But he was immediately elected to the Massachusetts Constitutional convention and, as a "sub sub committee" of one, he began writing the new state constitution.

Although he had professed his yearning for home and hearth, his recall and his absence from Congress rankled. John ached to return to the center of events. After long and heated argument in Congress, he was asked to return to France as minister plenipotentiary. John Adams, the blunt, opinionated, upstart lawyer from Braintree was to begin negotiations in prelude to hammering out a peace with Britain.

This time, it was nine-year-old Charly who begged to accompany his father. The thought of going to school with his big brother in France, away from the stiff strictures of Haverhill, presented a wealth of possibilities in his mind. Though it was the need for paternal guidance that John used to quell Abigail's objections, the truth was that he had missed his bright-eyed, laughing son.

They are being taken one by one, Abigail thought. Those I most love are leaving me. I remain. Alone.

"I don't want to go back, Mar," twelve-year-old Johnny said quietly.

He had come into his father's office where Abigail was compiling lists in preparation for the voyage. She looked up at the son who stood so still before her. Johnny had grown during the eighteen months he had been away -- taller, broader, leaner in the face, with a sensitive perception in his clear blue eyes. She could begin to see the man that would emerge. Sighing, she put down the paper, stuffed both hands in her apron pockets and looked at him steadily.

"Ye cannot think it is easy for me to send you away again so soon after your return," she said, practically.

Johnny shook his head.

"Then ye must know I urge you to return with your father for what I believe to be your good," she continued, searching his face for a reaction. "You are growing into a man, John Quincy. I cannot teach you to be a man. That is a father's job."

He nodded again.

"Then what ails ye?"

"I do not want to go," he repeated.

"Why?"

He drew a deep breath and cast his eyes around John's cluttered office, studying the books that lined one shelf, a regiment of learning.

"I do not want to leave here," he said simply.

"Braintree?"

"Massachusetts, Boston, Braintree. My friends…" he stopped, unsure how to persuade his mother of his yearning to remain where he could put down roots, make long lasting connections independent of his parents' scrutiny. "My friends in the Latin School will not know me in time. I will be alone in Braintree."

"Nonsense!" Abigail cried, shaking her head at what she saw as youthful parochialism. "You make friends wherever ye go, John Quincy. Your father has said you were the delight of every company from here to Paris and back. You cannot confine yourself to a farm for your whole life. There is genius in you. You must share it. There are opportunities by which you will benefit yourself and others."

"I missed you, Mar," he said softly, a pleading look on his face.

"And did you think I did not long for you, my strong right arm? How much did it cost me to send you off with your father, to lose the company of you both for so long? Johnny, it is too few who have before them such an opportunity. And I know how you helped Par. His letters were full of the joy of the benefit you were to his mission. I would not deprive him of that help. Would you?"

Johnny dropped his gaze to the floor near his mother's feet. The toes of her shoes were scraped and worn, the dress faded along the bottom where it swished past the barn doors and table legs each day.

"This time Par will have Mr. Dana and Mr. Thaxter with him,"

Johnny reminded her, referring to the secretary and the equerry John planned to bring.

"Charly is to go, too," Abigail replied. "He will need your guidance. You can help pave the way for him."

"Par can do that," Johnny insisted.

"Par will be engaged in his office, John Quincy. I do not understand. You were so full of your adventures and the delights of France when you first stepped off the ship."

"Yes," Johnny agreed, reluctant to confess the exaggerations he had made for the sake of being a hero in his brothers' eyes. "But I had forgotten the delights of home."

"They will, in all likelihood, be here when you return again," she said.

"I could be a help with Tommy," Johnny persisted, "be the man here with Par gone."

"Tommy will not suffer for the lack of male guidance for another year or two," Abigail retorted, smiling slightly. "Enough, John Quincy. Your father has decided he wants to keep you with him; it is too great an experience to deny. You cannot know at your age what you might be giving up. Letting you go again is not easy for me. Trust that what we do, we do for your sake."

"Yes, Mar," the boy murmured, defeated.

He longed for her to embrace him. He had seen French mothers touch, pat, and even embrace their sons with unabashed affection and been consumed with envy. He longed for such warmth. He could never remember his mother ever touching him.

"I pray that when you are grown, you will thank me for sending you," Abigail said, returning to her lists. "Be off now, and help Charly prepare. He has not your sense and foresight, and without your experience to guide him, who knows what he will pack."

John Quincy turned and trudged out of the room.

November 13th 1779, a bare three months after father and son had arrived home, they loaded up the cart again and drove to the wharf in Boston. A crisp breeze ruffled the harbor and stood the flags at attention on their masts. Charly, who was crushed between the gunwale and his father's bulk, cast restless eyes around the horizon at the scudding clouds. He asked one question after another, but Johnny and John remained silent. Abigail stood on the small pier, watching the party being rowed out to the ship. John Thaxter, Johnny's onetime tutor, sat beside Frances Dana in the bow, a wistful smile on his face. Charly, turning back to the pier suddenly, cried out: "Pray the ship don't go down, Mar!" his voice a thready piping on the breeze.

At the words, Abigail's stomach convulsed, and for a moment, she could hardly breathe. She bit her lip and waved, nodding.

"Not a sparrow falls..." she murmured, trying to reassure herself.

Though she was worried for all of them, it was John Quincy who tore at her. Motionless, a look of sadness mixed with yearning in his blue eyes, his gaze never wavered from her face until the skiff reached the vessel's side and they began to climb aboard. As he stood, her throat constricted and she almost shouted the words that would have recalled him, but she bit them back.

He is John's son, too. she thought. More his than mine, now. One by one, they all leave. On the ride back home on John's mare, she thought her heart would crack.

"I'm glad they didn't set off in this," Nabby said, sitting down at the kitchen table beside her mother, who was surrounded by a pile of paper and the open ledger. "It's hardly stopped snowing for six weeks."

"I wonder if they've had these storms out to sea," Abigail muttered, dipping her quill. "If not, they should be there by now, or at least have made landfall."

"Well, at least they haven't roads to deal with. I worry about Grandfather Smith alone at the parsonage in this weather," Nabby said. "Suppose he needed us -- how could we get to him? The roads are impassable."

"I will ask Mr. Belcher to go see him tomorrow if the wind lets up," Abigail agreed, holding the quill above the ledger thoughtfully. She had wrestled with her anger at his betrayal of her mother, of his vows as a clergyman. His sin had fractured her faith in men, to add to the fears she had for her own home, but in the end, the love the daughter bore the father won out. She returned to a comfortable worry over his health and his welfare. "Did you notice he seems older suddenly? More...frail?"

"Grandfather Smith? Perhaps. This winter's been a hard one.

Grandmother Susanna told me yesterday it's the worst one she can remember. Even sitting by the fire, her hands are so crippled with the cold that she can hardly work."

"Have you been to see her today?"

Nabby shook her head, the wisps of ashen blond hair that had escaped her cap waving like strands of gossamer. Another gust rattled the windows in their frames and the curtains lifted. Outside, the January landscape was uniformly white. Drifts had piled up and spilled over the fence between the two Adams houses. The cloaked trees, branches bent nearly to the ground, groaned under the weight. A footpath, sunken between three-foot icy walls, had been maintained between the two houses with constant trampled use.

Abigail ran her hand over her forehead and reached for another billet from the pile.

"Are we very bad off?" Nabby asked quietly, noting her mother's knitted brows.

"Not so bad as some. I only want actual money for the taxes, the rest we can barter or trade for. But I need aplenty for the taxes," Abigail replied, not looking up from the clutter of figures. "They want fifty dollars for the acre your father owns over in the next county, and sixty for the two and a half acres of meadow out here. I fear our tenants will not manage to pay their share - and then what?" Abigail spoke half to herself.

"How can I help, Mother?" Nabby asked, leaning closer.

"You do help, Nab. I don't wish to worry you, but you need to know how to manage. I pray that the things your father promised to send me will arrive with dispatch, then we can sell those for ready cash and we should be taken care of until the next round of taxes comes. What I most want to do is find an extra two hundred dollars for Mr. Belcher's seven acres at the foot of Penn's Hill. Your father has always coveted that grove."

"Shall I sell some of my fripperies?" Nabby asked tentatively, praying the answer would be no.

"Your fripperies?" Abigail laughed. "You mean the little bits of ribbon and feathers we have put on your bonnets? No, Nab. Never. I have some handkerchiefs that usually bring a good price, and a few of those French gingham fans. We'll go to the merchants in Boston the next opportunity and see what cash we can raise with what we have. A young lady needs certain fripperies -- if not too much."

"Thank you, Mar."

"In fact," Abigail confided, "I want something for myself that I have never had..." she hesitated and looked at her fourteen-year-old daughter.

Nabby's taste for the luxuries in life, however modest, was something that Abigail enjoyed, despite her Yankee frugality. Nabby would never laugh at her mother's desire to have some symbol of John's rising star. Nabby waited, her eyes dancing expectantly.

"I wish a carriage, a truly fine one with leather seats and smooth wooden traces," Abigail confessed, her hands resting on the ledger.

"Oh Mar!" Nabby exclaimed. "How wonderful that would be! Why of course you must have one. The wife of John Adams, SHOULD go round in a proper carriage, one that would let others know how esteemed and fine she is."

Abigail blushed at Nabby's calculating so precisely her own unspoken pride.

"You would spoil me if you could, Nabby," she said, her tone half-appreciative, half-admonishing. "Still, I must confess that I would wish an occasional indulgence -- and indulge the children I still have with me. It helps to make up for your par's absence."

"Oh it would be so elegant!" Nabby cried, nearly breathless at the possibility of riding beside her mother in a carriage, showing off the beribboned bonnet she had just made.

"Of course," Abigail continued soberly, "the expense of both boys at school in France, and your father's living expenses, may preclude such a design."

"You'll find a way, Mar," Nabby said.

""You're a comfort, Nab," Abigail told her. "Put on your cloak and go see Grandmother Susanna. I should think she is ready to send Tommy home. And I needs must hear some more *Rollins* from him before the sun gets too low and he runs out of fire."

"Yes, Mother," Nabby said, rising.

"Take your knitting; see if you can finish that sweater. Grandmother will probably want you to sit with Mr. Hall a while. Poor soul. I fear we'll be having a funeral before the year's out."

"It's Uncle Peter I fear for," Nabby remarked as she tied her cloak around her shoulders and stuffed her knitting into a bag. "Aunt's consumption is getting worse. Grandmother says she worries about the children taking it from her."

Peter, who had finally married, had moved to a house not far from Braintree with his wife, who proceeded to have four children in five short years. And she was pregnant again.

"Yes, it would leave Brother Adams's children to your grandmother's care," Abigail mused. "If she still has the strength."

"Grandmother may be aging," replied Nabby firmly, "but her strength never ebbs."

Nabby wrapped a scarf around her head and pulled her cloak tightly around her before opening the door.

"What would I give for some of the temperate French climate Par has so often extolled!" she said as she slammed the door behind her.

Abigail found the money not only for the taxes, but for Mr. Belcher's seven acres, adding it with pride to their modest landholdings. If John could not attend to their fortunes, she would do it. In truth, she found the challenge of buying and selling, the careful searching for better property, for greater fortune, for cash to keep ahead of the taxes even in these strapped times, to be both spur and pride in her own capability.

1780

In spring, there was finally a stream of letters from John. Descriptions of the harrowing overland journey from Spain where their leaking vessel was forced into harbor were followed by complaints of his superfluousness to the ministry in France. Negotiations with the French were, as always, frustrating. John felt the Count de Vergennes was plotting against not only America but against him personally. Finally, in August, he conceived a commercial treaty with Holland that would give America independence from French loans. Taking John Quincy and Charly out of school, he left with both boys and Frances Dana for Amsterdam.

Abigail learned of this change in October, just after Mr. Hall died. The following week, Peter Adams's wife died of consumption, three days after the birth of her fifth child.

"I will endeavor to stay as long as they need me," Susanna said, tying her bonnet firmly under her chin with veined, claw-like hands.

174

"You always have a place here with us, Mother Adams," Abigail said.

"In truth, I would as lief stay here," Susanna replied. "Five children, one a newborn, will be no easy matter. And I will miss my Nab," she said, studying the granddaughter, who held a place in her heart that her own three sons had not. "But my duty lies with them. There is no one else."

An October breeze swept through the browning leaves with the promise of an early winter. Eight-year-old Tommy held the reins to his mother's new carriage, working hard to maintain his dignity. He had convinced his mother he could drive back alone from Uncle Peter's house.

As Susanna stepped into the carriage, the leather straps that sprung the frame to the wooden box creaked and crackled with new life. Tommy reached a hand toward the old woman, but she ignored it, grasping the back of the seat and pulling herself up.

"You are still too small a twig to bring up an old limb like me," she snapped at him. "Are you certain he should drive home alone, Abigail?"

Abigail ignored her mother-in-law's sharpness. Mr. Hall, her devoted husband, has died and now the numbing responsibility of five small children on her brittle shoulders. She is propelled forward by will alone, Abigail thought. As am I.

"I will be a sight for the neighbors in Minister Adams' carriage!" Susanna said with satisfaction, admiring the new paint. "Though there will be some who will say you've let John's position go to your head, Abigail."

She gives with one hand and takes it back with another.

"I would not willingly incur the envy of our neighbors," Abigail replied, not entirely truthfully. "Yet I will not always be curtailed by idle tongues. Let them say what they will. I will enjoy my carriage and so shall you. OH! I almost forgot! Nabby, run inside and get your father's last three letters for your grandmother. I had a packet yesterday from the Marquis de Lafayette. I nearly forgot in the bustle."

"The Marquis de Lafayette? Will he come here? I would be very sorry to miss meeting such a man," Susanna said, eyebrows raised at the high flown circles to which her son and daughter-in-law had risen.

"Sadly, no. He had not the time. And I fear the only way I shall meet him is if the siege returns full force to Boston, which God forbid!"

"Still, I should like to meet him before I die," Susanna said. "I regret not being able to accompany you to meet General Washington and his lady when they were in Boston."

She wants to ride on her son's coattails, Abigail thought. The Boylston pride will out.

"Are you sure I won't need a whip, Mar?" Tommy ventured. "Par's mare is a bit slow to move at the reins these days."

"You won't need a whip, boy," his grandmother said. "Now let us be off."

"Remember, Thomas Boylston, what you have been entrusted with."

"Yes Mar."

Tommy slapped the reins against the mare's brown flanks and the carriage lurched off at a walk.

"I will come next week with Patty and Esther to clean the house. You need not trouble yourself," Abigail called to Susanna's back.

The old woman, sitting bolt upright in the carriage, raised a gloved hand in acknowledgment but continued to stare straight ahead.

Peter Adams' infant daughter died. Susanna put it down to the lack of a mother's breast. Despite her having found a wet nurse, the baby did not thrive and by January was buried beside her mother. Abigail had had no letters from either John or the boys for six months.

The war was up and down; sometimes the colonies could be seen to be winning, at other times it seemed the twin bludgeons of poverty and exhaustion were beating the American troops into the ground. Finally, cash dwindling, Congress demanded the colonies feed the army. In Massachusetts, the quota was divided among the towns. Braintree's obligation was 40 thousand-weight of beef -- or the money to purchase it.

But money was impossible to find. Thanks to both the general loss of confidence and the British counterfeiters, Congress's paper currency was worthless. It had been printed once then rescinded, so that overnight all those who had scraped together the taxes, dollar by hard-won dollar, learned that their hard-won cache was now worthless. They must begin again. And did. Then Congress rescinded the currency again, this time nearly bankrupting the hearts of the colonists. But the people fought on, planting, harvesting, feeding their stock and scratching for new ways to cling to what they had.

John was in The Hague. In July, Abigail learned that four more ministers were appointed to France to aid John in his duties as minister plenipotentiary. It was rumored they were to smooth over the fractious words he had spoken to Vergennes. Her indignation at the insult and her certainty that Dr. Franklin's duplicity were at bottom of this ungrateful slight knew no bounds. Being deprived of John's companionship and help was one thing, being disparaged and unappreciated was quite another. And, she had had no letter from John for nine months. Her logic told her he sent them, but they never reached her hands. Vessels sailing from Holland were constantly attacked by British privateers and men of war. Henry Laurens, an American minister on his way to France, had been captured and sent to the Tower of London. Abigail prayed that it was only John's letters that miscarried, not him and their sons.

"Mother?" The voice was unmistakable. John Quincy!

"Son! Where are your father and brother?"

"They are coming, never fear, Mother. I am home!" Abigail seemed to see him through a veil.

"Oh, Johnny! John! Oh John! Is it you? Where is Charly? I still cannot see Charly!"

"Mar?"

A new voice. The veil dissipated, all grew black for an instant.

"Mar?"

It was Tommy, standing over her bed, gently prodding her awake. Caramel sunlight blotched the bare boards of her bedroom floor.

"Mar, you were shouting. Are you all right?" Tommy stood in his nightshirt, barefooted in the stuffy room.

"Yes, Tom, yes. I just dreamed that your father and brothers were coming home, but I could not see Charly. They said he was coming, but I still could not see him."

She sat up in bed brushing the wisps of hair out of her eyes and back under her nightcap.

"You reckon they're safe?" he asked quietly, his eyes round.

"I pray so. It was so real. I wish I could have stayed asleep a bit longer -- to have enjoyed the pleasure of the sight of them, their voices," she said wistfully. A clatter below brought her back. "Is Patty astir this early?"

"I reckon. I was in bed when I heard you cry out..."

"Never mind. Get up. There is work to do," she said, swinging her legs out from under the light covering on the bed. "Well, go on, Son. Don't stand there gape-mouthed!"

"Mar?"

"Yes, Tommy."

"Do you really reckon they're all...safe?"

A chill went down her spine, but she shook it off.

"Get dressed."

Prophetic dreams? Bah!

But she could not shake the veil that had come over her. It was so real, so clear. Pray let there be word of their safety.

By the time Mr. Brush, a Boston merchant to whom she had sold some of the cloth and ribbon John sent her periodically, stopped on his way from Philadelphia to Boston the following month, Abigail had forgotten her dream. She had been leaning across the wall to pick some of the herbs growing in Susanna's front yard and saw the heavy gelding trotting up the road carrying its thickset passenger.

"Mistress Adams!" Brush hailed her as he reined in his horse at the gate. "And how do ye on this beautiful day?"

He swung off the horse, surprisingly graceful in his movements, and carelessly tethered the horse to the hitching post.

"Middlin' well, Mr. Brush. I have a small store of things from the last little shipment from Holland that managed to escape mishap."

"I cannot do with gingham this time," Brush informed her, coming around the horse's rump to smile down at the small, determined woman with her arms laden with fresh-cut herbs and flowers.

'Tis a pity she is so stiff-necked, he thought. I would quite enjoy a romp with her. I wonder she does not find her pleasure elsewhere while her husband has so long deserted her. Ah, well. There are other mares to breed. Her company and her stores are good.

"There is a surfeit of gingham," he told her. "I would take any linen you have, and woolen things -- calaminco, Jersey, what have you."

"I will rummage through my chest," Abigail said, holding the gate wide. She liked this big, open-faced merchant with the booming voice and ready smile. "Come have some refreshment while I bring down what I have. I fear at least one shipment from Mr. Adams has miscarried, or rather been embezzled. Another arrived so sodden and damaged that it is not salable. But I do have some linen and a fine piece of wool."

She installed Mr. Brush beneath the maple in the side yard, then went in and laid the herbs on the table. After giving, Esther, the young black maid she had taken on orders to feed Brush, Abigail went to her room to pull the small chest from beneath her bed. By the time she returned, Brush was downing his second glass of raspberry shrub, and leaning back comfortably in the chair Esther had brought for him. When he saw her, Brush leapt to his feet and took the chest from her, then laid it on the ground near his chair.

"May I?" he asked, reaching for the hasp.

Abigail nodded. He rummaged in the chest stuffed with cloth, handkerchiefs, fans, gloves, and other trinkets, pulling out several ells of linen and some Belgian lace. Although his manner was the same as always, there was something about him that made Abigail hesitate. He had something to tell her. Finally, he sat up, folding the cloth in his hands, and looked Abigail in the face.

"Have ye had word from your mister, lately?"

"I have heard no word in nearly a year," Abigail replied matter-of-factly. "What you see is my evidence of his safety. I did hear that Mr. Temple had a packet of my husband's letters for me, but was forced to throw them over the side on orders from Mr. Adams when they was boarded by a British privateer," she said.

"Then perhaps ye have not heard?" he began slowly. News was spread by whoever carried it through the colonies. Rumor and truth alike.

"Heard?" she said, pushing away a chill that swept over her.

"Your son has been appointed secretary to Mr. Francis Dana," Brush began, watching her face carefully. "Mr. Dana has embarked for Petersburg in Russia as emissary of America. Your elder son, ... is it John?" he asked, trying to remember the name.

"John Quincy."

"Yes, that's it! John Quincy speaks French so well that he is to act as Mr. Dana's interpreter."

Abigail relaxed.

"Mr. Dana is a prudent man, and a good one. I could wish John Quincy in no better hands," she said, imagining the honor done her eldest son, the treasure of experience he would store for his future. "And when did they depart Holland?"

"Sometime mid-July from what I understand," he replied.

"And what of their journey. Do ye know anything of that?"

"They reached Paris safely and continued on, but that is a much as I know."

"Good. Well, may God protect them and supply their mission, " she said. "And what of my husband and other son?"

"From my information, Mr. Adams is still in Holland. His health continues only fair. He does not like the damp climate. But he grows very fat nonetheless, they say."

Abigail laughed. "I will not be able to put my arms around him when he returns, then?"

It was the first time she had remarked on the intimacy between husband and wife. Brush shifted uncomfortably and looked over the woman who stood before him, her figure firm, carriage erect.

"And my other son remains at the University of Leyden?" Abigail continued.

Brush drew a deep breath then raised his eyes to hers.

"The *South Carolina* lists a son of John Adams aboard the passenger manifest as having shipped for America on the 10th of August," he began.

Abigail's heart leapt at his tone.

"Mrs. Adams, the vessel set off in a storm..." he paused when he saw the blood drain from her face. "They fear it lost."

Chapter 13

Tears, such as angels weep, burst forth
John Milton Paradise Lost Bk I Line 619

1781

"Lost!"

"I'm sorry, Mrs. Adams," Brush was saying, shaking his head. "I wish I had better news. They was overdue for word, you see. Two other vessels they knew of foundered in that storm. Some of the papers have reported the *South Carolina* missing..."

His voice was like a murmur of bees. Abigail heard the sound, but could not discern words. A picture flashed through her mind of her funny, outgoing, bright-eyed boy, clinging to a broken spar, screaming as the waves engulfed him. The light dimmed and her head began to swim. A hand under her elbow kept her from falling and she found herself sitting in the chair under the maple tree.

"Perhaps it may yet prove untrue," Brush was saying. "Rumors abound these days."

Those words calmed her somewhat. So many rumors were later dispelled. News took time and confirmation longer. Her heart began to beat again, slowly, a hard thumping in her chest. *I pray, Lord, if he be with You, that I may be comforted in that, and if he be yet alive, You effect his return by as swift a messenger as ever put to sea!*

"I might go to my grave happier if I was to see your son alive," Susanna said, as she sat at Abigail's hearth mending a shirt for nine-year-old Tommy.

December 20, the advent of a bleak Christmas. Even by the roaring blaze, their fingers were stiff with the cold. There had been no word of Charly or the *South Carolina* for four months. John's September letter informing her of Charly's departure had arrived in November.

Oh, that we had kept Charly here! He was too young, his health too delicate in that damp Dutch climate. And he feared the sea. My poor boy feared the sea. A quivering sob rose in Abigail's throat, but she pushed it back down by sheer will. *I will not cry in front of*

Mother Susanna. It would only upset her.

"I pray I may see your son alive before I die," Susanna said again, "but I shall not ever see my own son again in this life. Of that I am certain."

She repeats it as a litany. Foolish, Abigail thought irritably. She cannot change what will be yet she plagues me with her dire pronouncements.

"I just know it in these old bones," Susanna continued without looking up from her work. "I would despair of my dear John if I did not know that I would see him again in heaven, and that I was leaving him in your capable hands, Daughter."

Susanna made the statement simply, but Abigail knew it for what it was: a rare admission of her mother-in-law's love and respect. Yet she made no reply. Susanna would have rebuked, mercilessly, any hint of sentiment.

"I wish to know something of Charly, if he be in this life or the next. The waiting, and wondering is interminable," Abigail said as she pulled another stitch through.

"No use to whine over what God directs."

"I am *not* whining," Abigail snapped.

I have never whined, she thought angrily. I have born up with fortitude. She was nearing forty, the age at which her own mother had relinquished Mary to Richard Cranch. The mother of married children. Middle age. Now, my mother is gone and Mary and I are mothers of children who are coming to marriageable age. The generations are passing as surely as the seasons, time spilling out like milk from an overturned pitcher.

Richard Cranch may not recover from his latest illness. I may die without John.

He had been gone for two years with no end in sight. Abigail feared sea travel, especially alone, and could not bring herself to leave Susanna or her father, who was growing daily more frail. But at night, lying alone in her bed, she could almost feel John's arms around her, hear him calling her name softly, yearningly. Sometimes, she dreamt of their lovemaking, the feel of his hands of her body, his joined to hers, hot, insistent, the climax of their passion waking her in a sweat, alone.

The snow had started again, dropping powdery dust over the crusted blanket that had fallen earlier in the month. The sound of horse's hooves pflop pflopping on the hard-packed road brought both women to attention. The rider stopped at their gate. Footsteps crunched up the hard-packed path, then a fist pounded on the door.

"Mrs. Adams?" A man's voice came through the thick door. "Mrs. Adams? Are ye within?"

Abigail leapt from the chair and hurried to the door, opening it wide. Josiah Brush nearly filled the doorway, wrapped in a thick woolen coat, and grinning broadly.

"Good news, Mrs. Adams!" he cried without preamble, stepping into the hall. "Your son is alive and well!"

"Alive? John Quincy?"

Brush shook his head.

"The other."

"Charly? Charly is alive? Are ye certain?" Abigail staggered back against the newel post in her relief. "Thank God," she murmured. "Thank God."

"Your might well say Thank God. From the sounds of it, the Almighty had a great deal to do with their saving," Brush said through half-frozen lips as he unwrapped the muffler.

Abigail led him through the door to where Susanna sat by the hearth, hands clasped in her lap, waiting.

"He's in Bilboa, Portugal, with a Major Jackson who's had charge of the boy since Amsterdam," Brush said, glancing at Susanna before turning his attention to Abigail. "When the vessel set out right away it had trouble, and plenty of it. They set off in a storm and nearly foundered, but they managed to get her bailed out again and go on. But then the crew came near to mutiny. And there was some question of Captain Gillion's privateering. They were fired upon by a British man-of-war. Quite a bit of damage. They were forced to put into La Coruna...."

"La Coroona?" Susanna asked.

"La Coruna. It's in Spain," he said to Susanna, before continuing. "For repairs and for water and provisions. They spent some time there, and then set out on the *Cicero,* another ill-fated vessel. Your son was either under a dark star or under the protection of the Almighty, but they made it to Bilboa -- Portugal it is -- safe and sound. He's there with Major Jackson, who has apparently been looking after the boy's education. They're arranging for their earliest possible passage, taking care to depart on a sound vessel."

"Sounds as though he's had education enough to last a lifetime," Susanna remarked acidly. "They are preparing to set off to this coast at the worst possible time of year. And when do they say he will return?"

"Can't say, M'am," Brush replied, rubbing his hand through his sparse hair. "That's as much as I know."

Abigail stood by the fire, hands over her face, shoulders shaking.

"Sit ye down, Daughter," Susanna instructed. "Mr. Brush, help my daughter-in-law to a chair."

Brush took Abigail's arm and guided her to the straight-backed chair, gently removing her mending before easing her into it.

"I didn't mean to upset you," he said anxiously.

"Of course you didn't upset me," Abigail said, tears dappling her lashes. "I apologize for my state. But you can imagine what my thoughts have been these past months. I dared not hope. I prayed, but I dared not hope. Then to suddenly learn that Charly is safely come to land is relief indeed!"

"You will once again see your fair-haired boy, Abigail. A pity I will not live to see mine," Susanna murmured under her breath.

I refuse to have my joy adulterated, Abigail thought in annoyance. Rising, she went through the parlor door to the kitchen where she found Patty and Esther cracking nuts and chatting.

"We have a guest, " she cried, eyes bright. "One who has brought good news. Our Charly is safe. Find some cake and bring the raspberry brandy!"

Cornwallis surrendered at Yorktown on October 19, 1781. The war for freedom was over. Jubilant celebrations were followed by sober thoughts of what lay ahead. The war was won. A new battle, the one between the southern and northern factions for control of the new nation, now began in earnest.

1782

For Abigail, the joy of winning the war was almost eclipsed by the joy of seeing Charly come home. January 28, five months after he had been reported lost, he finally arrived, coming into the house with a look of wonderment on his face. He studied every corner and crevice, eyes shining, taking in every well-loved detail. At eleven years old, he had grown leaner, gaunt almost, with a droop to his shoulders. Abigail wanted to touch him, but held her distance, uncertain if he would welcome the mother who had sent him off.

By the time Charly finally climbed the stairs to the boys' bedroom over John's office, Tommy was asleep alone in the trundle bed. For the first time in more than two years, Charles Adams lay down safe in his own home. Abigail had followed him up the stairs, listening to the wind howl outside and grateful that she no longer must fight an imagination that painted terrifying pictures of her son's last moments of life.

After kicking off his shoes and stepping out of his breeches and hose, Charly climbed into bed and pulled the covers to his chin. Abigail crossed the floor and leaned down to study him, as though fixing his face in her mind.

"Are ye not forgetting your prayers?'" she said gently.

Obediently, the boy, covered only by his long-tailed shirt, crawled out from between the cold sheets he was just beginning to make warm and knelt on the bare boards. Turning a wan face to the ceiling, he prayed aloud:

"Dear God, please bless everybody here. And please take care of Par and Johnny and Mr. Dana who are all still so far from home. I pray you help them find a good vessel and crew. I would never, if you please, wish for them to live through what I did. And thank you for getting me safe back home to Mar. I'll never go to sea again. Amen."

Abigail's throat tightened and she felt a stab of guilt at the dangers he had passed, but Charly's eyes held no reproach when he crawled back into bed and looked at her. Without another word, he rolled over on his side and closed his eyes.

The time apart from John grew more tedious and difficult. He had been gone for two and a half years. Despite the family and friends that surrounded her, Abigail felt alone. "Oh haste to me!" she wrote John, quoting Penelope. "...*Increasing cares and times resistless rage will waste my bloom, and wither it to age.*" For eight years, first in Congress, then in Europe, John had been away in the service of his country while her life ticked away without him. Graying, aging, she studied her seamed hands at night while she did her mending. How much longer?

Sick of the war, the escalating taxes, and the struggles to meet impossible government obligations, many in Braintree were speculating on land. Longing to provide a 'castle' for her and John, an escape from what she saw as public slights, Abigail began buying 300-acre parcels in Vermont a place apart on which to build a peaceful retreat once John finally retired. By July, she had managed to scrape together enough cash to purchase 1,620 acres of wild land. John was unimpressed. 'Meddle no more in Vermont,' he instructed from Amsterdam. Abigail was incensed.

"I vow you are far more taken with Mr. Tyler than I, Mother," Nabby said vehemently. Her eyes were on the dirt road as they walked through Braintree to the Cranch's house.

"And are you taken, then?" Abigail asked, fishing.

Nabby blushed, but whether from anger or embarrassment Abigail could not tell.

"Mr. Royall Tyler is charming and handsome, there is no doubt," Nabby replied severely, "but he is also without scruple when it comes to promoting his own cause."

"And what cause is he promoting?" her mother replied.

"I believe he woos the mother to gain the daughter," Nabby replied, her eyes on the road ahead.

"If he does, perhaps it is because the daughter is too distant to be approached," Abigail retorted, voicing a concern at Nabby's occasionally imperious demeanor.

At seventeen, Nabby had grown taller than her mother and carried herself with a regal self-consciousness that Abigail found both impressive and slightly disconcerting. While she was not beautiful, Nabby had a ripeness that men found alluring. Young womanhood is treating her kindly, Abigail decided, if she but temper her haughtiness.

A bird flitted across their path and landed on a honeysuckle hedge to trill joyously. The Cranches moved back to Braintree from Boston, a pleasure to Abigail, who often went to their small house to visit. While Richard still survived, his health was precarious.

"I am not unapproachable," Nabby informed her mother, "but I would not wear my heart on my sleeve, neither."

"It was at your age that I first met an ambitious young lawyer, passionate and intelligent, to whom I gave my heart," Abigail said, her eyes on years past and distant faces that had forever changed.

186

"Perhaps you gave your heart, Mother, but your hand came several years later," Nabby reminded her.

"Yes, and your father spent those years proving to me the steadfastness that lay in his heart, although my mother did not approve."

"How ironical; this time, the mother approves but the daughter does not," Nabby remarked.

Though she frowned at her daughter's sauciness, Abigail made no reply. She was indeed taken with the Cranches' new boarder, Royall Tyler, a young lawyer who had recently begun a law practice in Braintree. Although at twenty-five he had already squandered half of a substantial inheritance, his remorse was so appealing and his charm so winning that Abigail forgave what she might at another time have considered a character flaw. Tyler flattered Abigail, made her laugh at a time she sorely needed attention and laughter. He was a drink of cool water to a traveler in the desert.

Abigail and Nabby strode side by side, nodding to the few acquaintances they passed in the street, following the shade when they could. A zephyr ruffled the sweet-scented phlox. Abigail lifted up her face, enjoying the feel of the air on her cheek.

My bloom is gone. I am faded. She glanced at Nabby, a blossom in its first flush. I pray prudence does not cause her to miss the love of her life. Her head rules where her heart might to better advantage, Abigail thought, forgetting that her own arguments to her mother had been based not on passion but on prudence.

They turned the corner past a dry pasture populated by a few bony cows, then continued down the narrow road to Richard and Mary Cranch's house. The picket fence that enclosed the garden was badly in need of paint. It would be a while before Richard was able to work, if indeed he were ever strong enough to take up his business again. Abigail went through the open gate followed by Nabby, their skirts rustling softly against the few leggy snapdragons in the flowerbed that ran along the shaded wall of the house. Under the canopy of the maple tree, Richard Cranch sat, knees covered, reading a volume of Molière. He looked up when he heard the sound of their soft-soled shoes on the paving stones.

"Bless us, it's a contingent of Adamses!" he cried, closing the book. His face was still pale and wan, but the energy in his voice made Abigail smile.

"Hello, Uncle Richard," Nabby said, coming across the lawn to kiss him on the cheek.

"Where is Mary?" Abigail asked.

"Within. Did you come only for her company? Ye would not desert an old friend so soon? At least *you* must stay with me Miss Nabby. Tell me what your day has been while your mother steals confidences from her sister."

"Yes, Nab. Stay with Uncle while I visit your aunt," Abigail said. "Richard, I never dared hope you would be so well again. Mr. Adams will be delighted when he learns of your recovery. He wrote he could not bear the loss of so dear a friend as you."

"Good of him," Richard replied. "He'd hardly miss me as little as he's been in Braintree of late." As soon as the words were out of his mouth, he regretted them.

A look of pain crossed Abigail's face, but she smiled.

"'Tis a good thing *someone* attends to our country's affairs, since you seem determined to laze about the garden."

They had been friends for too long to let such a small thing come between them, but Richard's gentle mockery at John's absence scraped a perpetually raw nerve. While their sacrifices had been made without hope for the country's gratitude, it nevertheless rankled that so little appreciation and so much criticism dogged John.

Stepping inside the kitchen, Abigail found Mary making up a tray to carry to her husband.

"Richard looks well," Abigail said.

"Yes. God has spared him a while longer," Mary agreed, a smile on her placid face. "I had a taste of what you must feel at times, Abigail. I have had nearly twenty good years with Richard Cranch, yet I still want more. What greedy creatures we mortals are!"

"Ah! Speaking of greedy. I have a present for you from John," Abigail said, pulling a length of linen from the basket she had carried from home.

"Oh, Abigail! How lovely! But I cannot accept it. You must need it for your expenses. You could fetch pounds and pounds of currency with this, " Mary cried.

"No. 'Tis a gift from your brother who loves you and a sister who esteems you," Abigail replied, buoyed by the delight she saw on her sister's face.

"Oh 'tis beautiful! I must needs find a place to wear the gown I shall make - no! I should save it for Richard's shirts, or for the girls..."

Abigail shook her head again. "You shan't. It shall be for you, Mary. To enjoy. I will come take you for a ride in my carriage and the Smith girls shall go through the town of Braintree as bold as brass."

The two women laughed at the thought of their doing anything so brazen as to show off their goods. Their father, ill though he was, would never approve.

"Such fine stuff Mr. Adams sends! Can you imagine what the bazaars and markets in Europe must be?"

"Nabby wishes to see for herself," Abigail said. "She has proposed to her father that she come keep house for him. Of course, John must say that it is impossible, at least to come alone..." Abigail hesitated.

Mary studied her sister, waiting. Hard to have your children preferred over you, she thought.

"I wish to go myself, Mary," Abigail said. "I have made the merest *suggestion* that I come to him. He has no one with him now. Charly and Tommy are at Haverhill, and John Quincy is in Russia. I could go look after him, keep him in health..." she stopped and looked at her sister.

Last month she had learned that John had lain ill in Holland for months, fearing for his own life, and although many of their friends knew of it, they had not told Abigail.

"We did not see reason to worry you, Abigail," Mary said softly. "It was not meant as a betrayal, but a protection."

"I would rather not be protected. I will not go forward on false assumptions," she said.

Did my mother know? Was father's secret forever unknown? Or merely hid by well-meaning neighbors? Has John betrayed me? So many temptations. "It is just...I fear so for him, alone. I could help..." she stopped. "Oh I *miss* him so, Mary! Nearly three *years*! It is a very long time to do without your best friend."

"Mary," Richard's voice came in from the yard.

"Oh, I forgot his medicine. Coming, Richard!" she called, taking up the tray and going outside.

Abigail followed her, bringing a glass of ale Mary had left standing on the table. Mary moved slowly, almost heavily, despite her slim figure.

Life weighs us down, Abigail thought. She is forty-one. Richard fifty-six. No longer young though not so old as I used to think. Mother died at fifty-six.

Thirteen-year-old Billy Cranch came around the corner of the house, a fishing pole across his shoulder, and five shining scup dangling from a line of hooks clutched in his fist.

"Look, Mama! Dinner!" he cried triumphantly holding the dripping fish aloft.

"Well done, William!" Mary praised. A year older than Tommy, Billy looked frighteningly like his wayward Uncle Will, and was, as Will had been to Elizabeth Smith, the great joy of Mary's life. Abigail only hoped that this Will, despite the physical resemblance, would prove a better man than his namesake.

"How do ye, Master William?"

"Tolerable well, Aunt. Fish are biting. That always puts me in a fine humor." He sat down at his mother's feet, took out a knife and began to clean his catch on the lawn.

"Oh, Billy! Not here, you'll get fish scales all over us. Take then to the back of the garden and take a basket to put them in so they don't get dirty. Clean them onto my cleome. It's doing poorly."

"Yes, Ma." The boy obediently took up his catch and headed for the small flowerbed twenty yards away.

"I'll bring a basket, Will," Nabby said, leaving the company and going into the house.

"Our children are growing, Abigail," Richard observed, his eyes following his son fondly. "I pity John the time he loses with them."

"Sister needs no reminding," Mary chided.

"Abigail knows I mean no unkindness," Richard returned.

"John is only too sensible of what time he cannot regain with his family," Abigail replied sharply. "I would wish us all together, but if he were not to stand by his duty to his country, what manner of man would he be? Certainly not the John Adams I married."

"You must go," Richard persisted. "We could keep the boys. Abigail, I can see the longing in your face every time I look unto it. Could your passage not be arranged?"

"I have written, posing the suggestion to John, but Congress dithers. Some days he has a position in France, others he is being recalled. I wait and hope but each vessel arrives without my John. I dare not embark on my own without knowing he would be waiting at the other end. We could pass on the ocean and be yet another year apart."

"I make a bargain with you: If John once write and give his approbation, do not stick at the boys. We will keep them and make arrangements for their education. You must go. And Nabby with you," he added, seeing Royall Tyler come through the gate.

"Mrs. Adams! What a pleasure to find you here!"

With long, graceful strides, the young man crossed the garden and bowed to Abigail who had seated herself on the ground near Richard. "I concluded my business early, and hoped I might call round to the house in Braintree I love best. But I see you have come to me instead."

"They came to me," Richard said flatly.

"Richard!" Mary hissed.

Tyler's board money was welcome. And Mary, worn down at their penury, would not have a steady income jeopardized for the sake of pride. Despite Richard's initial fear that Tyler would sweep young Elizabeth Cranch off her feet, he showed little interest. Mary suspected that Richard's resentment had as much to do with what he perceived as a rejection of Elizabeth as with his distrust of Tyler's character.

"Supper will be fish -- look what our Billy has caught," Mary said hurriedly.

If he noticed any hostility, Royall Tyler gave no sign. His ebullient good nature never faltered as he greeted everyone in turn.

"Ah! Miss Adams!" he cried to Nabby, surveying her firm, full figure appreciatively, unaware that his lust was so obvious. "My compliments."

"You are filled with compliments, Mr. Tyler," Nabby retorted archly. "Which ones do you intend to convey?"

"She has a ready wit, Madam," he laughed, his eyes still on Nabby. "Like her mother."

Richard rolled his eyes.

"Take your medicine, Mr. Cranch," Mary said firmly, pointing to the bottle on the tray.

As the young man went to the foot of the garden where Nabby stood over Will, who was covered in fish scales, Richard whispered, "If John were here, he would not approve, Abigail."

191

"John is *not* here, and I do," Abigail replied.

But as the spring warmed, so did Nabby's affections for Royall Tyler. Though he did not completely abandon Abigail, without the glow of his persistent attentions to cloud her assessment of his character, Abigail could see the darting glances to other young women, hear the insinuating lust in his voice when he flattered them. She could imagine all too clearly the temptations before him as he rode the circuit courts. His wife would need to be more forbearing, more casual, than she knew her Nabby to be. Tyler was charming, but, she began to realize, he was no John Adams.

Despite her misgivings, Abigail held her tongue. Tyler's ready wit and smile were still a balm to a quiet household. Tyler kept most Sundays with Abigail and Nabby, walking to meeting in the morning for the two-hour service then coming home in the afternoon to eat a meager midday meal, walk the lanes, read from the Bible and discuss politics. The Adams household was dwindling. They paid only one domestic now. Will Smith's daughter, Louisa, now lived with them, refusing to take wages for the constant services she performed. Charly and Tommy were at Haverhill where they studied under Betsy's husband, Robert Shaw.

Though Abigail still enjoyed Royall Tyler's company, she had begun to fear the effect of soft afternoon breezes scented with honeysuckle and lilac might have on Nabby's resolve. She recognized longing in her daughter's study of Royall's slim, muscular form. In May, Nabby spoke of marriage.

"Mama, Royall has said what a fine wife I would make for a young lawyer. He says he can take me with pride amongst all society," Nabby informed her mother. "Indeed, I enjoy the parties and the fine clothes the ladies wear despite these hard times."

They were shelling early peas under the budding maple, throwing the shells into a burlap shack to later be strewn amongst the cornrows. The tendrilled branches of a willow, a fine cascade of green like the wild hair of some transplanted sea goddess, waved in the breeze.

"Life is not all parties, Nab," Abigail said carefully.

She knew if either Nabby or Tyler suspected she did not favor their match, they would stop seeking to her advice.

"How well I know!" Nabby sighed, shaking her head as she

pushed a thumb into the seam of another pea pod. "I miss Par."

Abigail put her hands in her lap. *She is a woman. Soon she will be married and gone. John will have missed half her life. His latest letter imagines her to be a child, still within his control at a word. She will listen to us, but she is nearly free of our grasp.*

"I miss him too, Nab. More than you can yet know. But it is a comfort to me to know that his work is more than important. It is desperately needed."

"It is *some* comfort," Nabby agreed. "But I wish him home. I wish him and Mr. Tyler to meet." She paused for a moment, looked at her hands, then at her mother. "Royall has breathed a word of marriage in the spring, Mar."

"The spring!" *She was startled, but worked to hide it.* "I would not give my consent until your father is home."

"But Mr. Tyler urges me, Mar," Nabby said. "He has such a...passionate nature. I fear if I make him wait too long...."

"Time will only test, not break his resolve -- if he will be a *true* husband. A marriage is not all passion, Nabby. If you father could not wait, think what a string of bastards he would have left in his wake!"

"Mar!" Nabby cried, shocked. Her mouth dropped open as she stared at Abigail's head bent over the small mound of peas in her lap.

"You should understand what a man can be, Nab. I would not send you a lamb to the slaughter."

"I believe I know a bit about life, Mar," Nabby said, squaring her shoulders. "I hear of scandals, of the pain and embarrassment inflicted on innocent wives."

"You can hear and yet not imagine," Abigail said, pouring the lapful of shelled peas into a crockery bowl that sat in the grass between them. "Seeing another's pain is but a faint glimpse of our own. We mortals have so little imagination."

"Do you suddenly disapprove of Mr. Tyler?" Nabby asked.

"No, not disapprove," Abigail replied slowly. "I merely point out that to try a man's mettle is better policy *before* the bans are read. You may save yourself many a sleepless night. Marry in haste; repent at leisure. I would not have you repent."

Platitudes! Nabby thought in exasperation. *I cry out my heart and she responds with platitudes!*

"I should not repent a marriage to Mr. Tyler," Nabby insisted.

" I do not say you would, Daughter. I merely point out that time will not change either your feelings or his if they are of the lasting kind. You are not yet eighteen, Nabby. I was twenty when your father and I wed."

"Not quite twenty," Nabby corrected, her eyes on the peas.

"Shy by one month! " Abigail rejoined. "It seems but a moment now. Time scampers and darts so."

"Not when you are waiting for your love," Nabby said softly, looking at her mother.

"No," Abigail agreed. "Not when you are waiting for your love."

Chapter 14

The rising world of waters, dark and deep
John Milton Paradise Lost BK III line 11

1783

In November, Abigail received John's yearning letter, asking that she come, despite uncertainty, expense, and danger. *'Come to me this fall and go home with me in the spring. Come with my dear Nabby. I am so unhappy without you,'* he wrote.

Yet, now that he urged, she delayed. There were obligations, complications. The farm, sorting out the boys, the money. And neither was certain that, even if she came, he would be there once she arrived. Congress was dithering over appointments to ambassadorships and delegates to hammer out a treaty with Britain. They were considering John's merits when a letter from Benjamin Franklin arrived listing John's manifold faults as a negotiator. John's blunt tongue, his loudly voiced suspicions of Vergennes's motives and machinations, his open dislike of Franklin disqualified him as a candidate -- according to Franklin. It was a bald attempt to have John recalled. But instead, Congress appointed John head of the American mission in France, and dispatched urbane Thomas Jefferson to join him.

The year dragged on. John sent pleading letters; Abigail temporized. How could she leave his mother? Her father? Who would see to them? Her life was not hers alone.

Suddenly, in October, her father, Reverend Smith died, almost secretive in his leave-taking. Of Suzy, fruit of his own broken vows, he never spoke. Abigail never asked. The last words she heard from his lips were spoken the day before he died. *I had only one son and he failed me.* Abigail had made no attempt to comfort him. To the end, she resented the place of a son in a father's -- and a mother's -- heart. The next day, Nabby found her grandfather dead in his study, the book of Revelation open on his lap.

Four years had passed since John, Johnny, and Charly had put to

195

sea. Charly had been returned safe – at least so he seemed -- but John and John Quincy remained separated from her by three thousand miles of ocean.

So many miles and so much time. Nabby is proof of that time. John will not know the young woman she has become, and I no longer know Johnny. He is a different person, a man whose interests and character I will need to study in order to know. And John. Will he have changed, after all these years of cares and sickness? How will he see me? Would I still hold his heart? Or has some clever Frenchwoman, who has not the cares or the years, stolen that which I hold most dear?

She longed to go to John, but the sea stood between them. That vast, fathomless expanse that could swallow a vessel as readily as a whale could swallow a minnow.   It was winter, a time when no one save the most hardy or most desperate put to sea. She held back. The months slid by.

Still, prodded by John's insistent letters, she planned. Little by little that spring, she parceled her obligations out to friends and family.   She hired her father's freed slave, Pheby, now married, to live in the Braintree house as caretakers in her absence. Tommy and Charly, now nearly twelve and fourteen, were returned to Haverhill. Cousin Isaac Smith would take up part of her financial affairs. Richard Cranch was sufficiently recovered to watch over the rest. She engaged two servants, borrowed two hundred dollars from Isaac Smith in exchange for a bill drawn upon John in Europe and began to pack.

The one loose end was Nabby.   She was growing impatient to marry Royall Tyler. Abigail, concerned at what the match might hold in the years to come, yet reluctant to open a breach between herself and her only daughter, hid behind John's refusal to consent -- until the letter.

1784

In March, a letter from John dated January 25, suddenly altered the terrain. John had reconsidered the marriage. A lawyer son-in-law was better than a farmer or a tinker. His own experience and contacts could help young Tyler. John Quincy could eventually enter his new brother-in-law's office. John had, in his imagination, spun a web of familial connections that would bind Royall Tyler to the Adamses and to Nabby. Let them marry, he said, and leave them in charge of the Braintree home.

You have tangled the matter, Abigail thought with annoyance. Nabby believes your consent to be mine as well. Yet I can no longer freely give mine.

She sat in John's office and stared out the window at the horse-drawn cart loaded with firewood that lumbered past. April. The apple trees outside were in bud. I must be sure to leave instructions for combating the caterpillars. A knock on the door interrupted her reverie.

"Mar?" eighteen-year-old Nabby's powdered head leaned in at the door. A bonnet dangled from her hand. "Patty said you wanted to speak with me."

Abigail's heart beat faster, and fear shot through her. Too young, she thought, too young. Yet my refusal could lose my daughter in one stroke. Will she defy me?

She hardly let herself remember her own mother, Elizabeth Smith, and her single halting attempt to outline the pain in store for a wife when her husband's lust overcomes his love, when yearning and need erase, at least momentarily, compunction and guilt. That conversation, Abigail had realized much later, hinted at suspicions if not certainty of her father's secret. At the time though, Abigail was too caught up in her own conviction that without John, her life would be empty. She had been right...and wrong.

"I did, Nab," Abigail said. "Sit ye down."

Obediently, Nabby took a seat opposite her mother.

"I have decided to go to your father," Abigail began.

"So I imagined, with all the preparations you have made," Nabby said.

Abigail hesitated only a second before adding: "I have further decided to take you with me."

Nabby's blue yes flickered for an instant, but she remained immobile.

"Why is that, Mar?"

How can I make her see? Make her trust my judgment?

"I believe Royall Tyler loves you, Nab," she said, choosing her words, "and that redemption from past sins is possible. His repentance is genuine, but is it lasting? Is he truly converted to virtue?"

"If he is not, I could complete the conversion," Nabby said quietly.

"A woman cannot change a man," Abigail said, but stopped when she saw the resistant look that had come over her daughter. "When your father and I were courting, my mother asked that we wait, to test whether or not he was steadfast."

She did not mention John's attentions to the Quincy girls, the fearful pangs she suffered before John settled on her alone.

"If you and Mr. Tyler were to be separated for a time, and if during that time, your feelings for one another did not alter, then I shall stick at nothing. You shall have the finest wedding we can muster. Only let me ask this test. If your love for each other is of the lasting kind, it will serve to strengthen it. If it is not..."

"If you believe that is truly best, Mother, I will submit," Nabby interrupted, her full lips drawn. "But on our return, I ask your unreserved blessing."

"That you shall have," Abigail replied, flooded with relief at Nabby's apparent acquiescence.

Neither woman spoke of the possibility that Tyler might wed another in the interim. Neither mentioned the tiny rift that had just been opened between them.

"When do you propose to leave?" Nabby asked.

"I have contracted with Captain Lyde to sail on the *Active* at the end of May - several weeks hence."

Nabby's eyes widened.

"So soon? Have you told Grandmother?"

"No. And I would wish you to keep it from her. Parting from our friends and going to sea is enough distress. Mother Adams's anticipation would enlarge those fears. I would shorten the time of her fretting."

Abigail's voice had unconsciously taken on a callused edge. Resentful of her mother-in-law's Cassandra-like predictions, assailed with guilt over leaving her, she wanted to put off what she feared would be a scene.

"Mother..." Nabby began.

But Abigail cut her off.

"I wish it this way, Nab. You may tell Mr. Tyler. I would not want to make your parting from him any more difficult than I know it will be."

Nabby's faced reddened.

"Aunt and Uncle Cranch know, as do the Shaws," Abigail continued. "But do not tell your Grandmother."

"As you wish, Mother," Nabby said without inflection, putting the bonnet on her head and giving the ribbon a savage jerk.

She studied her mother silently for a moment. Abigail could not read the look: anger, resentment, resignation, disapproval? All or none may have been mingled in that impassive stare. Standing, Nabby turned toward the door.

"Does Elizabeth Cranch yet know of this?" she asked Abigail, her back to her mother to hide the tears.

"Not unless my sister has broken a promise to me. Is that where you are bound?"

Nabby nodded without turning around.

"Tell your cousin," Abigail advised, her voice softening. "She has been a dear friend and can hold her confidences."

Nabby's head bobbed again, silently. Taking the doorknob, she pulled it open and shut it hard behind her.

Despite the discretion of those who had been told, word of their departure seeped out, slowly, like syrup. But by virtue of a kind conspiracy among neighbors, friends and trades people, it never reached John's mother. The news was Abigail's to tell.

Dressed in her new calico dress, its matching bonnet trimmed with the scarlet ribbon John had sent from The Hague nearly two years before, Abigail stood, heart pounding, at her mother-in-law's kitchen door enveloped by the sweet scents of white-blossomed privet hedge and purple iris. The fragrance of bread baking wafted through the windows. Home, Abigail thought suddenly, her throat catching. This is what home smells like. Will I ever see it again?

When Susanna opened the door and saw Abigail, her face fell. The fine lines that together made up the jigsaw of her countenance sagged. Tears started down her cheeks and she clung to the door handle for support. She knew.

"O why did you not tell me you was going so soon?" she cried. "This is my last leave. I shall never see you again!"

"Mother Susanna!" Abigail cried. Her resolve nearly undone, she threw her arms around the old woman, stifling a sob. "Do not say such things!"

"'Tis true! 'Tis true!" Susanna insisted. "I shall be in my grave before you return. Carry my last blessing to my son. And may God keep you both well in this life."

Abigail was in agony, unable to soften her mother-in-law's pain. She was, Abigail knew, being forced to watch, powerless, as the last of what she held dear deserted her. Life is one long leave-taking. Perhaps if I had prepared her. No, it would have been months of mourning, of recrimination and guilt.

The sun was high overhead, beating uncomfortably on Abigail's back and splashing onto the freshly scrubbed boards of Susanna's kitchen. Hearing footsteps coming through the grass, Abigail turned to see Nabby, her face pale and tear-streaked.

"Mr. Fields says we must be off," she said dully, casting a pitying glance at her grandmother.

Abigail nodded, unable to speak.

"No! I cannot bear it!" Susanna cried, clasping Abigail to her.

"Grandmother," Nabby said, gently taking her grandmother's arms from around her mother's neck. "We must go. Aunt Mary will be your daughter until we return. Elizabeth Cranch will be your granddaughter. They will see to your needs. Pray, grant me a favor and see to mine. Miss no opportunity to remind Mr. Royall Tyler of my love for him. Look to my interests on that head and I shall ever be grateful to you."

"If you had been able to stay with me, Nab, you could mind your own interests there," Susanna spat out.

Nabby glanced at her mother, but made no reply.

"I will write as soon as we are shipboard," Abigail said, itching to be away from the scene. "And at every other opportunity. I shall be as careful as a daughter in that."

"You have ever been a daughter, Abigail," Susanna replied regaining some of her composure. "Elizabeth Smith gave you up reluctantly, but I was the richer for it."

Tears caught at Abigail's throat at the unexpected words.

"Keep the home fires burning, Mother," Abigail managed to whisper before turning toward the carriage that waited at the side of the house.

"When you return, there will be another tending the hearth," Susanna said to her retreating back.

Nabby embraced her grandmother silently then turned to follow her mother. The ride to Boston seemed endless. Although Mary Cranch chattered animatedly in an effort to ease their wretchedness, neither Nabby nor Abigail was able to speak except in half-uttered fragments. At each bend and rise in the road, they cast their eyes wistfully backward across the rolling green landscape as though seeing it for the last time.

But when the *Active* weighed anchor and scooted out of the harbor under full sail, Abigail grew excited.

Mile by mile we are moving closer to England. After six long, lonely years, I will finally see John.

The passengers were below, stowing their gear in drawers beneath the bunks. Despite her fears of the sea and the cramped strangeness of living aboard, Abigail did not feel alone. Jobe Field, brother to Abigail's maid, Jinny, had hired on as part of the crew. Another Mrs. Adams, an acquaintance of Abigail's, was joining her physician husband in London where he had been living since the beginning of the war. Six other passengers, all men, occupied the great cabin, a room about fifteen feet square flanked by bunks in which the entire company dined and sat. The four women, Mrs. Adams, Abigail, Nabby, and the maid, Jinny, occupied the only two staterooms.

The vessel had just begun to roll, when a young seaman in a stocking cap poked his head through the door to the main salon and said: "Cap'n says to put on yer sea clothes, ladies. We're at the sea buoy and the wind's kickin' up."

Nabby, who shared a cabin with the other Mrs. Adams, came into the stateroom that Abigail shared with Jinny. The young maid, homesick as soon as they departed the pier, had stayed on deck to watch the harbor dissolve into the receding blue of Boston.

"Do ye reckon we'll be seasick?" Nabby asked, teeth chattering despite the warmth as she sat down on the edge of the wooden rail that edged one of the two narrow bunks.

"I hope not," Abigail replied, still stuffing clothes into a drawer. "I am more worried about the cow than us. I have heard it said that a cow may die on a rough voyage."

The ship was rolling more markedly with each passing moment. Through the small cabin window, Abigail watched the last jagged rocks of the harbor's entrance disappear astern. The few books that they had brought and pushed onto the shelf over the bunk began to flop back and forth rhythmically. The odors of potash and oil, the twin cargoes lashed in barrels in the hold, wafted up from below mingling with the dank smells of sweat, salt, and vomit, the residue of another rough crossing. Abigail bustled around the cabin in an effort to stave off an increasing lightheadedness. Nabby, teetering on the edge of the bunk, swallowed hard.

"Mother, I believe I may be sick soon," she whispered through clenched teeth.

"Hold on, Nab. If you vomit on the floor, we shall find it impossible to get a footing."

"Mar, find a bucket!" Nabby cried urgently, holding her head as still as she could and staring fixedly at the bulkhead in front of her.

Abigail made for the companionway. The ship lurched, sending her crashing against the bulkhead.

"Mrs. Adams."

One of the passengers, Dr. Clark, stumbled across the salon and caught hold of her arm.

"Thank you, Sir. We need a bucket. Quickly!" Abigail spat out between teeth clenched against the bile rising in her own throat.

Gripping the doorjamb, she watched the doctor weave back across the broad cabin, his head nearly grazing the overhead. He grabbed the leather bucket that hung from a hook just inside the great cabin door and turned to lurch back.

I know how Jonah must have felt, closeted in the deep, dark inside cupboards of the whale, Abigail thought. Dr. Clark thrust the bucket at her with unintended vehemence when the vessel took a plunge into the trough of a wave.

"Thank you," Abigail managed to breath before falling headlong across the bunk where Nabby still sat rigidly upright. When the young woman saw the leather bucket, she snatched it and vomited into it violently. Clambering upright, Abigail braced both feet against the drawers beneath the bunks, holding the bucket with one hand and gripping the edge of the bookshelf with the other.

The sounds of the crashing waves and the groan of timber on timber increased with each passing moment. Metal clattered in the stern lockers. Head throbbing, Abigail suddenly puked into the bucket, nearly falling into its vile contents before she had finished.

Dr. Clark, his face ashen, came in. When Abigail began to vomit, he held her by the shoulders to keep her from falling.

"Are you all right now, Mrs. Adams?' he asked gently.

"I think...," she began, then a wave of nausea engulfed her and she shut her mouth and swallowed hard.

"Lie down, Madam," he said, taking the bucket from her hand. "Mr. Spear!" he called to a slim man of about fifty who was struggling to push an overfull drawer back beneath his bunk. "Can ye find Mrs. Adams's manservant? We're in need of some help."

The other man nodded and attempted to rise but was pushed back into the bunk again as the ship pitched forward.

"Here, let me help you," Dr. Clark said, taking Abigail by the arm and easing her down onto the bunk.

Gratefully, Abigail submitted. Taking the bucket, the doctor opened the window to heave the contents out. As the bucket emptied, a wave sloshed through the narrow opening, soaking his sleeve and splattering the books with salt water. He managed to slam it shut again just as another wave washed over the glass.

Nabby had fallen back onto the bunk, exhausted. Abigail lay down on the bunk opposite and shut her eyes hard against the throbbing in her head.

Mr. Spear appeared in the doorway, clinging to the opening for support. His nose wrinkled involuntarily at the smell, and he turned back toward the salon for a fresh breath.

"Mrs. Adams, I could not find your manservant," he said, taking a handkerchief from his pocket to cover his mouth and nose. "I have sent one of the crew to continue the search."

It suddenly dawned on Abigail that she had not seen Jinny since they had come aboard.

"My maid!" she cried, trying to sit up. "Jinny is no sailor. Where can the child be?"

"She's up top," came a familiar voice.

"Jobe," Abigail breathed leaning out of the bunk, then falling back and closing her eyes again.

"Jinny was afeared she'd get sick right off, so I lashed her to the rail." Jobe smiled grimly. "She's probably soaked through, and throwin' up, but she's still aboard."

"When you can, bring her down here," Abigail instructed. "By main force if need be. T'will not be pleasant, but will be safer for her in the end. We'll help her change to dry clothes. I would not have her die of cold."

"I'll try, though I doubt she'll be willing to leave the fresh air, however chilled she be," he said, squeezing in beside Dr. Clark and wedging the bucket beside the bunk.

Mr. Spear had managed to propel himself as far as his bunk in the salon, where he collapsed, breathing heavily.

"Where has Jeremiah got to?" Abigail continued, her head on the pillow, eyes closed. "We'll need his help."

"Young Jeremy Trott is no better than the others aboard," Jobe observed, eye on the bloodless face of the doctor who stood beside him, swaying and clinging to the doorframe. "He was hanging off the back rail puking heartily when last I saw him."

"Mind he doesn't go overboard," Abigail said weakly.

"Yes'm. I'll do my best," Jobe replied. "The old crewmen say a bit o' salt pork on a string followed by salt biscuits help...."

Nabby lurched to a sitting position to heave into the bucket again, gripping the narrow wooden rail with white knuckles.

"Mention nothing about food for the now," Abigail whispered.

"Cap'n says you've got to keep your strength up. He told me to keeping eating no matter what. If you don't mind my sayin' so, Dr. Clark, I reckon you could do with a lie down. You look a mite peaked."

The Doctor nodded, a tiny muscle in his jaw working convulsively. He eased himself out of the stateroom and staggered back across the salon to fall into his own bunk.

"I'll get Jinny and Jeremy below," Jobe said, eyeing the doctor's unsteady progress, "then I'll find something to eat, just in case."

The women fell back on their bunks, their strength gone. They lay there for two days, retching long after there was nothing to throw up. With the exception of the captain, Jobe, and several other crewmen, everyone aboard was sick. The decks ran with vomit. The entire ship stank. Finally, the wind abated until there was a fresh westerly that scudded across the deck and into the portholes, clearing the stench from below and bringing everyone topside to behold the wonder of the vast sea.

Abigail dragged herself up the ladder and, upon seeing the sun for the first time since they had boarded, gulped in great drafts of fresh salt air. A seaman, wan but mobile, was passing.

"The salon and both staterooms are in a scandalous state," she informed him, grasping his sleeve before he could escape. "Be so good as to collect a gang of men and scrub it down with hot water and soap and vinegar."

The sailor, unaccustomed to receiving orders of any kind from a woman let alone orders given with such assurance, stared open-mouthed for a moment before nodding in agreement and scurrying below.

Nabby, who had followed her mother topside, made her way to the rail to gaze out over the undulating expanse of blue-green. Straightening her back, Abigail crossed the deck with a surefootedness that surprised her, to stand beside Nabby at the rail.

"It's beautiful, Mother, isn't it?" the younger woman breathed, a wistful glimmer in her eyes.

"How great and marvelous are His works," Abigail agreed, quoting Psalms, her eyes on her daughter's round face.

She wishes Mr. Tyler were here, Abigail thought, guiltily. Yet a tiny voice that she dared not acknowledge whispered in her ear. She will remain with you a while longer. You will not lose her yet.

"Mrs. Adams?"

She had not heard the captain approach. The waves, spilling along the hull in graceful rhythm, had covered his footfalls across the deck. Captain Lyde's hat sat squarely on his balding head, his blue eyes mere slits between the sandy fringes of his lashes.

"I am glad to see the whole company recovered," he said clinically. "We had to kill yer cow. She was too much battered."

Abigail started at the abruptness of his words, but said nothing.

"I'll have her butchered, if ye've no objections, Madam," the captain said. "None," Abigail replied, turning her face toward the open sea.

Although they went through one more nor'easter on the American coast that sent all passengers scurrying below again for two days, the voyage was good. Abigail, observing Captain Lyde's ability, and the respect evident between captain and crew, felt confident in the safety of the ship. And the passengers, with only one exception, had become like a small family of brothers and sisters, each solicitous for the welfare of the others. Although Nabby had not once mentioned Royall Tyler, her wan face and silence spoke volumes.

I wish she would confide in me, Abigail thought sadly. It is for her good, not mine that I asked the separation.

On the fourth day out, Abigail found Dr. Clark and Nabby engaged in quiet conversation on deck, his silver head bent toward her.

Later, when Abigail asked him about their chats, the doctor had merely said: "Her heart aches. It will mend, dear lady. But meanwhile, I can be an uncle to her, an ear she need not fear will betray. I do not judge, only listen."

Abigail's heart jerked at the realization that her daughter not only blamed her for her misery, but had in fact told someone of the betrayal. She wanted to justify her decisions, to tell the doctor her side of the affair, but her pride prevented it.

As the miles rolled away beneath the hull, her thoughts turned more and more on what was ahead. At seventeen, Johnny had passed more adventures than many men twice his age. Two sea journeys, a year as secretary-interpreter at the Russian court of the Empress Catherine, Leyden University, Paris. An envious resume. She had no fear for the changes in her son. But John. What would he see in her after all these years?

Although she was not fat, her chin had developed the hint of a jowl and the nose had taken on the long, sometimes disdainful look of a magistrate.

I have aged. What bloom there was has faded and died.

On the 18th of July exactly one month after their departure the *Active* made landfall. The fog clung like a wet veil, wrapping the edges of the rocky Irish shore in thick layers of white. Running more by instinct than instruments, the captain struck south, hoping the fog would lift before they had edged their way around to Portsmouth. By Monday, a gale had blown up out of the southwest. Under double-reefed topsails they ran downwind along the southern coast. The next afternoon, the white cliffs of Dover hove into view.

The rain was coming down in gray sheets when Captain Lyde, flanked by the English pilot, ordered the anchor dropped in Deal Inlet. They had come safe to the other side of Atlantic.

The passengers stood on deck in little knots, making plans for the next stage of their journeys. Abigail stood on the deck, studying the beach, as bald as Nantasket. White sands, subdued to gray in the gauzy mist, was unbroken by wharf or pier. How shall we land?

Leaving a small group of men who surrounded the pilot, Captain Lyde came across the deck to where Abigail stood.

"Some of the gentlemen are discussing disembarking here, Madam. They will take a small bag with them, then wait for their luggage to be brought up the Thames."

"Where can they land, Captain?" she asked, scanning the broad, barren beach.

"Right in that little hollow," he replied, pointing to a small, very slightly protected curve in the otherwise straight ribbon of sand. Waves poured from beneath the vessel to the shore where they broke like a lace ruffle along England 's hem.

"Is it safe?"

"'Tis difficult to say for certain," the captain replied, squinting. "What appears a light chop from here may in reality be a strong sea. The pilots have come through it once, they will know best whether or not it can be done."

Nabby emerged from the after companionway, her cloak drawn tightly around her, and came across the deck to her mother.

"We are completely packed," she said, her eyes shining. "Dr. Clark says he's goin' ashore. Can we go too?"

"So it's been decided?" the captain asked, his voice offering neither approval nor disapproval.

Nabby nodded. "The pilots say 'tis certain they can land us safe without getting wet, and they say a trip up the Thames is a tedious affair. Dr. Clark says he will stand us to the pilot's fee if we decide to go."

"'Tis kind of him to offer," Abigail said, mulling over the decision to risk the trip ashore against waiting for perhaps another week to reach London by water. "But I can pay our passage."

She studied the shore for a moment, then the captain's expressionless face.

"What would you advise, Sir?"

"I would not presume to advise you, Mrs. Adams. I can understand your eagerness to reach London by as quick a route as possible. This may be it. Perhaps you will be dry, perhaps not, but I doubt any real harm will come to ye or I would say so."

"Then we shall go," Abigail decided. "We can leave Jeremy in charge of our things and take Jinny and some small bags with us. Go see to it, Nab."

"Yes, Mother."

She strode across the deck to the men who stood on the lee side preparing to set the small pilot vessel off. "Dr. Clark!" she cried, pulling at the sleeve off one lean figure bent over the rail.

He looked at her, smiling.

"Mother says we're to go ashore too!"

"Good. T'will be yet another hour before the pilot boat will be brought back out, but you can get your things topside now if ye will."

"Yes! Oh, yes! I shall see my Par!" she cried, almost to herself.

By the time the pilot vessel had returned, cases had been brought on deck and stacked in a cairn on the port side. Several had been tied together with coarse lengths of hemp through which the halyard would be knotted for a makeshift lift.

Once the baggage had been stowed aboard, the women were lowered to the waiting arms of their fellow passengers. As soon as her feet touched the jouncing deck, Abigail knew the ride ashore would be rough. Strange how differently the smaller vessel moved, even protected from the wind in the lee of the ship. Dr. Clark, Mr. Spear, Mr. Foster, and Colonel Norton had each braced themselves against the masts.

"Hold fast the women!" The captain of the pilot boat barked as each one was lowered aboard. One by one, Mrs. Adams, Nabby, Abigail, and Jinny, skirts billowing, were disentangled from the bosun's chair then delivered to the waiting arms of one of the four men braced against the masts. Heads bent against the spray, they cast off from the ship, each woman clinging tightly to the waist of her protector.

As soon as they cast off and emerged from the protective bulk of the ship, Abigail realized that the pilots had lied in anticipation of the extra passage money. The waves, rolling six-footers that crested and spilled down toward shore in a boiling foam, lifted the vessel and slewed her sideways, threatening to yank the helm from the pilot's grasp. The spray smacked them in the face, even hidden in the folds of the men's coats. As they turned again for shore, another wave caught up behind them and broke over the stern. The sea poured in, and one crewman, a young boy, snatched the leather bucket near the helm and began bailing furiously. The vessel had begun to squat down in the seas, lolling sluggishly.

"Keep bailin' Harkness!" the captain shouted. "One more like that an' you'll niver see yer mother agin!"

"Quiet man! You'll frighten the ladies!" Colonel North shouted over the thundering waves.

Harkness bailed furiously, staying just ahead of the next sea that broke over the stern, and the vessel finally righted itself, hanging for a long moment on the crest of a wave, then skating down into the trough again. Jolted, frightened, Abigail clung to Mr. Foster praying for their safety as they slogged toward shore. After what seemed hours, the boat crashed aground in a terrifying grinding of copper bottom on sand.

The men immediately clambered over the side, determined to drag the boat up before the waves could drag it back out to sea again.

"Nay! Nay!" the captain shouted. "Ye needn't trouble yerselves! She'll come ashore by and bye!"

Unheeding, the shaken men, covered to their chests in roiling surf, gripped the gunwales of the pilot boat and, struggling for a foothold, hauled for all they were worth. Another incoming wave lifted the vessel, and the men with it, and thrust them further ashore. The climb over the side was more difficult, especially in heavy skirts, than the boarding, and they were all soaked by the time they trooped up to the little inn on the cliff top.

But Abigail was too elated to care. England! They had crossed the wide ocean and were alive still! Soon, her arms would be wrapped about the thick waist of her dear, dear John.

Chapter 15

..how awful goodness is, and..virtue in her shape how lovely
John Milton Paradise Lost Bk II Line 846

1784

They reached London on the 23rd of July, but neither John nor John Quincy were there. John Quincy, who had spent a month waiting for their arrival, was finally called back to The Hague by his father. Instead, John's secretary, a charming, bright-eyed young man, who cast a keenly appraising glance over Nabby, arrived to greet them at the ship's offices.

John's young assistant, Arthur Smith, had engaged rooms for them at Osborne's New Family Hotel, where they would wait for the *Active* to wend its way up the Thames with the rest of their baggage. He arranged to exchange some of Abigail's American dollars for English currency, then guided them through the labyrinth of decisions attendant upon such a journey.

"Ye shall not want for company I warrant," Smith was saying as he looked out the window at the people, cloaked and hooded who bustled along the street below in a chill July mist. "There are many Americans in this city who will be anxious to entertain the wife of Ambassador Adams. Mr. Adams deeply regrets that he cannot be here himself to meet you, Madam."

It had been a bitter disappointment to be forced to wait for John again. Abigail crossed the large room to seat herself at the writing table.

"I had hoped to have seen Mr. Adams by now, I confess. It is hard to have come all this way and still be denied. I would behold him face to face."

Smith straightened. A light came into his eyes and he smiled gleefully.

"But you *can* behold the Ambassador's face," he said.

Abigail sat up, staring in disbelief.

"How?" asked Nabby from where she preened in the bedroom. Appearing at the sitting room door, she put her hand to her hair, smoothing it one last time.

"I shall take you to Mr. John Copley's studio," Smith said triumphantly. "I have already had instructions to present you to the Copleys at the first opportunity. He has done a painting of Mr. Adams. So, while Mr. Adams cannot see you, you can see him."

"Yes, oh yes, Ma!" Nabby cried.

Since coming to London, Nabby had shed the lethargy that she had worn like a sodden cloak since leaving Boston and grew daily more animated. Abigail could not decide whether the change was due to anticipation of seeing her father and brother again, or Smith's attentive company. She darted a shrewd look at her daughter, then agreed.

"If I cannot have Mr. Adams in the flesh, I would relish a preview in paint," she laughed.

Copley's studio was some distance from their lodgings. Struggling with rheumatism and unaccustomed to walking hard road for the month they had spent aboard, Abigail was exhausted by the time they climbed the marble steps to ring the bell. The servant, who at first told them that Mr. Copley was out, bowed and disappeared behind the door when Smith asked him to be sure whether he was out to Mrs. John Adams.

"*Out* in London does not mean what it does in Boston," Smith explained with a knowing smile. "*Out* means unavailable to callers but not necessarily out of the house. Mr. Copley must be working. But I feel sure he will see *us*."

Indeed, when the servant returned, he swung wide the door and with a dour 'Follow me, sir,' led the way up a set of dim stairs to a drawing room, lit only by the bank of windows at the artist's back. John Singleton Copley, clad in velvet breeches and a paint-spattered linen smock, laid down his brushes and palette and strode across the room to meet them.

"My dear Mrs. Adams!" he cried, taking her hand and bowing over it with a flamboyance that Abigail found both flattering and slightly suspect. "You do me too much honor. I would have sent a chaise for you."

Abigail smiled. It was hard to believe that this bewigged, velvet-clad, thoroughly English gentlemen was Boston-born and bred.

"I do not mean to interrupt your work, sir," she said.

"Not at all. Not at all. I am delighted to have Mrs. Ambassador Adams come calling."

"I have brought Mrs. Adams and her daughter to see Mr. Adams," Smith explained. "The original has been detained in The Hague."

"Oh, certainly, certainly. You must stay to dine with us, Madam. My wife will be the envy of London. We have been the first to entertain the famous Mrs. Adams, wife to our American Ambassador. Cecil!" he cried to the servant who was slowly turning to go. "Tell Mrs. Copley we will have honored guests for dinner."

"As you say, sir," the man nodded without enthusiasm.

The party followed Copley who led the way to a dark corner of his studio where a large painting, its subject indiscernible in the gloaming, stood against the wall.

"Can you help, Mr. Smith?" Copley asked, bending to grip the huge canvas and nodding toward the windows. "We would wish to present Mr. Adams to his wife in the best light possible."

Together the two men carried the painting to where the oblique northern exposure cast a steely light over John's full figure.

"North light is the best in which to paint," Copley explained in the silence as Abigail and Nabby studied the painting. "Mr. Adams commented on the dimness of my studio, but it casts no shadows, exerts no undue influence on the color. I find it to be a bit gloomy, but the best way to accurately portray my subjects. It makes me look more carefully for the light within. What think you?" he asked, finally when he could bear their silent scrutiny of his work no longer.

Her throat constricting, Abigail gazed at the picture of John longingly. It was him to the life -- older, fatter, his double chin betraying a dimple where the jowl had begun to set itself, but her own dear John Adams. The robust, proud carriage, the broad hands that had roamed eagerly over her naked body, the determined set of his shoulders, all flooded her with longing. Had she been alone, she would have laid her cheek against the paint, tried to draw out some flicker of warm contact with him. Instead, she remained impassive.

In the painting, John stood before a globe, his broad stomach covered by a dark green velvet waistcoat, nearly touching the table before him. With his right hand, he pointed, subtly, toward the maps spread open on the table. His eyes leapt off the canvas to hold her in their gaze. 'This,' he seemed to say, 'This is what we have made our sacrifice for, what we have given so many years of happiness and prosperity to bring forth.' But when she blinked and looked again, his

212

expression seemed to have changed. His eyes held desire; the tiniest of curves at his mouth spoke of his hunger for her, and he was taking a step forward to embrace her.

"Think you it is a good likeness?" Copley repeated, his eyes darting from the painting to Abigail's face. "Mr. Adams sat last year, but I have been putting touches on it since then. He cuts a dashing figure does he not?"

"It's wonderful!" Nabby burst out, tears standing in her large eyes. "Can it really be our Par? He looks so...so...statesmanlike, as though he could govern the world. Does he not seem so to you, Mother?"

Abigail was struggling, unable to speak without betraying a choking sob that threatened to rise up in her throat. She felt suddenly envious of the time Copley had spent with John, time she had forfeited.

"He *is* a statesman," Smith broke in, perceiving Abigail's distress. "He is viewed with respect and even awe in some quarters."

"Awe! Oh, Mother!" Nabby whispered, wiping a tear with a gloved hand.

Copley stood beaming.

"I see that Mrs. Adams is affected by the likeness, too. I venture to say without too much conceit, that I have captured the man."

"Indeed, Mr. Copley," Abigail finally managed to agree, her eyes still fixed on John's beloved face. "You have indeed captured the man."

For a week, a constant stream of visitors and invitations leavened the long wait for news of John's plans and the arrival of their things. But Abigail was restless, irritable. To have come so far and still be separated made her ache with impatience. Friday morning while Abigail and Nabby sat at the writing table, Jinny burst into the room.

"Oh, Madam! Madam!" she cried, breathless.

"Calm yourself, Jinny, what is it?" Abigail snapped.

"Young Master," she panted. "Mister John Quincy is a-come."

Nabby started up, flushing with excitement. "Johnny? Here? Where is he? I must fix myself for him."

Nabby scurried into the bedroom, but Abigail remained rooted to the chair, her mind churning with images of her eldest son -- the chubby face, narrow shoulders, diffident ducking of the chin, all ghosts of a departed past. At a knock, Jinny rushed to open the door. A well-dressed young man carrying a small satchel stood in the narrow hall.

"Can this be...?" Abigail began, rising.

He strode across the room and threw his arms around her.

"Oh, Mar, my own Mar! It has been so long!"

The brow had broadened, become more defined. He had grown six inches and gained not a pound. Gone was the shy slouch, the plump youth. For a moment, she was dumbfounded at this stranger, who was her flesh and blood. Her head reached his chin, and for a few seconds, she relaxed into his unexpected embrace.

"My dear son. My dear son," she murmured. "I would not have known ye."

At the sound of voices, Nabby had hurriedly put herself in order.

"John Quincy? Johnny!" she shrieked, coming from the bedroom, then running across the room to throw her arms around her brother and cover his face with kisses. Abigail stood back, watching her two children with misted eyes.

"Nab, I would have known you anywhere." Johnny laughed, picking his sister up off the floor in a bear hug.

"You are no longer a boy, John Quincy," Abigail observed shaking her head, bruskly wiping away a tear.

Johnny smiled, pleased. " I should hope not! Neither is Nabby a girl. You have changed and yet not changed, Nab."

"Well, you look an altogether different person," Nabby said, touching his sleeve affectionately. "I have sorely missed you, Brother."

"And I you," her brother said, beaming. "Par waits anxiously for your arrival, Mar. He wishes you to come to The Hague. I am to buy a carriage, then we shall cross the channel and ride down to Paris in leisurely fashion. Par says it is the first journey he has ever looked forward to in his life."

"How is your father?" Abigail asked, still unable to take in the years that had passed and the changes they had wrought.

"He is well. He has suffered from the climate in The Hague, but now enjoys perfect health."

"We have had colds since we set foot on this rainy shore," Nabby laughed giddily.

214

"It is always the way when Americans first come to London: a month of colds and then you become accustomed to the climate. The Hague is damp as well. But Paris!" Johnny said, breathing the word out as though it were an incantation. "Paris is not only beautiful, but completely congenial. It has gloriously warm days and mild nights...."

"What keeps your father in The Hague?" Abigail cut in, dragging her son back to the only subject of which she wanted news. The weather mattered not at all.

"Our country's business," Johnny said without elaboration. "He misses you more than I can say, Mar. He said he was twenty years younger when he learned you and Nabby had landed safe. He works very hard, but he takes exercise and remains as fit as ever. He says he longs to share the curiosities of the journey between the Netherlands and Paris with you. And, he says to do as you will about clothes, spare no expense so long as you are outfitted properly, as ought to be the wife of the American Ambassador. I am to see to it." Johnny grinned.

It was when he smiled that Abigail's heart caught for a second. The eyes held the same bright mischief they had when at age seven he dunked Charly's head in the milk pail. But nothing else remained of the boy she had sent to Europe so many years ago.

Time, ah time! she moaned inwardly. Its passing is marked in our children. Our lives would seem endless were it not for the milestones our children pass before our eyes.

They did not meet John in The Hague. There were more delays. Jefferson's early arrival in France changed everything. Abigail felt as though Congress and The Fates together conspired to keep them apart. They were now to wait until the carriage was outfitted then make directly for Paris. In a week of hurried planning, they ordered a carriage and scoured the shops for a few articles of clothing that would serve until they reached the world's fashion capital.

"Mr. Smith says he will be leaving for America to see his family as soon as we depart for Paris," Nabby said as they entered their rooms on the 7th of August, nearly two weeks after they had arrived in London.

They had left John Quincy at the carriage-maker, inspecting the last coat of paint.

"Indeed?" Abigail responded, raising an eyebrow as she pulled off her gloves.

She had hoped for some small word, some indication of Nabby's feelings, but her daughter had not mentioned Royall Tyler since their departure, and if she felt any attraction to Smith, she declined to acknowledge it.

"Mr. Smith has been very helpful. I find him a very charming man, do you not?" Abigail asked slyly.

"Mother," Nabby said ignoring her mother's fishing expedition as she cast her eyes around the rented sitting room. "Something has been changed here."

Abigail stopped and looked. Had there been a thief? London teamed with pickpockets and cutpurses.

"There," Nabby said, pointing. "Look on the table."

In the middle of the writing table sat a hat with two small leather-bound volumes sticking out of its top.

Abigail's heart leapt at the possibility.

"John?" she called, her voice soft with hope and the fear of disappointment.

A short, stout figure appeared in the doorway of the bedroom.

"John!" Abigail breathed. She stood frozen for a moment, taking in the sight of him.

With a squeal of delight, Nabby flung herself into her father's arms. Her large, ostrich-plumed hat was pushed askew, pulling strands of hair with it. John embraced his daughter, but his eyes were on Abigail. After a moment, he released Nabby, and held her at arm's length.

"You have become a handsome woman," he told her with approval. "You are a virtuous woman, too, I trust."

"I pray so, Par," Nabby said, reaching both hands up to restore her coiffure.

"The price of a virtuous woman is far above rubies," John said, releasing his hold on his daughter to move toward Abigail. "I have sorely missed thee, Wife."

In four strides, he crossed the floor to where she stood, took her in his arms, and buried his face in her neck.

"John, John," Abigail whispered, clinging to him as though to life itself.

For a long moment, they stood together, each nourished by the sweet taste of the other's presence. Nabby stood silent, tears standing in her eyes as she watched her parents. Abigail rubbed a palm over the shoulder and back of John's broadcloth coat, feeling the muscle, the vibrant warmth beneath the fabric. His heart, pounding against her chest, was a comforting throb, the same ardent pulse of twenty years before. Holding her tightly, John kissed her on the cheek, once, tenderly, then again and again, like a man long-starved. Finally, wiping away the tears, Abigail leaned back to search his face for some indication of what he saw in her.

"I have grown old during our separation," she ventured.

"There is more gray indeed and perhaps there are more lines about the eyes," John agreed bluntly, "but the face is even more dear to me than when we parted. How I have missed my dearest, truest friend!"

He pressed her close against his chest again. "Now my life will be complete."

But more trials awaited him in Paris. Congress, after having read his 'Peace Journal', a diary that exposed John's raw vanity and ambition, launched an acrimonious public debate over his ability to negotiate peace. Humiliated, impatient at being denied what he considered his earned right, John alternately paced and ranted, meanwhile praying for the commission to the Court of St. James back in England.

Even though John fretted, Abigail reveled in their renewed life together. Finally, she could look across the room and see his face, scowling over a book, to be sure, but there in the flesh. Even if she did not ask his advice, knowing it was available was comfort enough.

Together, they settled into life at Autieul, a rambling, rundown manor on the outskirts of Paris. The gardens spread out from the dwelling and meandered through glades populated by classical statues. Here John walked every day for hours while Abigail struggled to bring the proud little company of French servants to heel.

Money was a constant problem. French life was expensive. Everything cost more than in America. Abigail felt obliged to outfit the entire family in Parisian fashions as became John's rank. The servants pilfered. Congress, with little enough money to spare, and even less inclination to part with what it had, refused to acknowledge many of their expenses.

But while Abigail grumbled at the prices, the impossibility of making the cook wash dishes, or the upstairs maid dust the downstairs rooms, she nonetheless gloried in the company of her family and the delights that Parisian life offered. The ballet (scandalous but intriguing), the way French men had of making a woman, however matronly, feel fascinating, beautiful, the mild winter that treated her nagging rheumatism with more kindness than the harsh New England frosts -- all seduced her.

And to sit together as a family once more, breakfast together, to walk in the afternoons, spend evenings enlivened by Thomas Jefferson's engaging company gave Abigail a peace she had not known for years. John's irascibility was no impediment. They were together. For that, she was grateful. And, she had the satisfaction of watching a deeply loving friendship develop between Nabby and Johnny who spent part of each day reading, writing letters, and talking together of their lives and dreams.

It was all as Abigail had imagined it should be. After their time in Europe, they would return home to Braintree. John would take his place in Massachusetts politics, perhaps the State Supreme Court, farm his patch of soil, and write his papers. Statesman emeritus. Nabby would marry, under their watchful eye, Royall Tyler, a prospering lawyer whose character would have had time to temper and polish. Abigail disregarded, for those happy moments of reverie, the fact that the stream of Tyler's letters had dwindled like a drought-parched brook. They would find a suitable young woman for John Quincy after he had begun his career. And she was, with each arrival of the post, receiving good reports of the progress of Charly and Tommy. Life was good.

Abigail was happy, but John was not. In bed at night, nestled beside her, one hand absently playing with the lace on her shift, he vented his frustration.

"Have I not served my country well all these years?"

"You have indeed, John."

"Then why must they dissect my character -- and so publicly?"

"As you dissected the pie tonight looking for the bean?" Abigail asked, a teasing effort to lighten his mood.

It was January 25th, 1785. King's Day. Custom prescribed that a large bean be baked into a meat pie. Whoever found the bean in his slice would be proclaimed king or queen for the following day. All of his or her dictums must be obeyed.

"Can I not be respected at least by my family, for one day?" he demanded as he rolled over onto an elbow and looked her full in the face.

"You *are* respected by your family, John. And not just for one day, but always," she replied with asperity.

She ran a hand down his face, feeling the coarse stubble that the little valet, Henri, would painstakingly razor off in the morning.

"Why can the Congress not accept my nomination for the Court of St. James and be done?" he asked. "I am fed to the teeth of drawing up commercial treaties."

"But who better to draw them, dear friend," she said soothingly. "You and Mr. Jefferson are an unbeatable team. You see what came of the Declaration of Independence. These treaties will determine if our country is to stand on its own, or if Europe will dissect it like the King's pie as they look for the bean."

"To be sure, to be sure," he agreed impatiently. He sighed and rolled over on his back to stare through the gauze canopy at the friezes on the high ceiling.

"John," Abigail continued, "no one has earned the honor more than you. And no one would be better suited to negotiate with England. But honesty, sacrifice, and honor do not always win friends. Pandering and deception seduce those without discernment," she reminded him, referring to what they both saw as Franklin's backstabbing. "But a man's gifts make room for him. Congress will, later if not sooner, recognize your qualifications to the position. Of that I am certain."

"Do ye truly believe so?" he asked longingly, turning once more to look into her dark eyes.

"I do. And Mr. Jefferson believes so, too. You heard him tonight. He said they cannot deny your abilities and your longtime service, that no one has a stronger claim. He called it perfect symmetry. We declare ourselves independent from England, then return -- how did he put it? -- shoulders back in pride, to negotiate as an independent people. Mr. Jefferson does not flatter, nor does he lie."

"No, Tom Jefferson is indeed one of the great friends. But he could be misreading the brain of Congress," John sighed.

"The honor will be yours in the end, Husband," Abigail said

again.

John ran his warm fingertips down the length of her cheek and thoughtfully, sensually, over her lips as he studied her face.

"You have ever been a strength to me, Abigail. What a wondrous bargain I struck in my wife, Wife," he said, wrapping both arms around her and drawing her close. The bedclothes rustled as he moved toward her, pressing his body against her.

"Have a care, Husband," Abigail warned. "My sister is pregnant at forty years old. We are too old to begin another family!"

"We are too young to give up the pleasure of our marriage bed," he replied, pressing his mouth against hers and drawing her hips toward him.

1785

The appointment came through in May. Drought parched the lawns, and the withered flowers were mere stalks. Jefferson brought the news, striding up the drive with a farmer's lanky, easy grace. John, on his way to walk through the arbors to inspect 'his' lands, stopped at the triumphant expression on his friend's face.

"You have finally received the position you deserve!" Jefferson shouted as he closed the distance between them.

"Ambassador to Great Britain?" John asked, wanting to leap for relief.

"Aye! You shall negotiate peace between the mother country and her newly independent child," Jefferson crowed. "I have the seal of the American Congress here in my hands."

He waved the paper before John, and pushed it at him for inspection.

"I have not sought the honor," John said suddenly, bending his head to read the document that would take him into the presence of America's onetime enemy, His Majesty the King of England.

Amused, though not surprised at John's abrupt insistence on having been called to the post without seeking it, Jefferson reassured his friend. He knew John Adams well, understood the continual war between his personal ambitions and his sense of duty. Jefferson knew too, that John needed constant confirmation that he was indeed a statesman, not the scrabbling, office-hungry politician his enemies had drawn in the American press.

"It is your abilities and honesty that have ever called you to office," Jefferson assured him, generously.

A broad smile spread over John's face, and he reached out a hand to Jefferson.

"You are indeed a friend, Tom," John said, joyfully. "I will do my utmost to fulfill your confidence in me, and the grave duty to which I have been entrusted."

"There was never a doubt," Jefferson agreed, taking John's hand.

The two men stood together by the newly renovated fountain, its sparkling waters murmuring like so many voices of affirmation. Though she could not hear their words, Abigail had caught sight of Jefferson as he approached, and waited by the upstairs window. Seeing John's jubilant expression, Jefferson's head thrown back in hearty laughter, Abigail knew.

"Congress has done it," she whispered, pride and relief welling up. "They have sent him to the Court of St. James."

The joy of the appointment was adulterated by John Quincy's departure for America to attend his father's alma mater, Harvard College. John mourned the separation. Together he and John Quincy had spent long nights of study over geometry, philosophy and religion. John Quincy was not only his son and secretary but his alter ego. John had found few pleasures in life more satisfying than grooming his son for the great life that he imagined for him. John Quincy would be, John believed, the embodiment of all the virtues that he and Abigail could instill polished by diplomatic grace. A second John Adams, but better. John felt as though he were severing his right arm.

But it was Nabby who mourned most. She and Johnny had rediscovered one another at a time in their lives when they were growing away from their parents. The prospect of London without him left her bereft. Her mother's anxious curiosity about the contents of Tyler's increasingly rare letters served only to tighten Nabby's resolute silence on the subject of love. She would never again share her heart with Abigail. And now, John Quincy, her treasured confidante, was leaving.

The day before John Quincy left Autieul Nabby rapped softly on her brother's chamber.

"Yes?"

"It's only me, Johnny," she said, coming into the room.

Johnny stopped packing and sat down on the bed. "I had hoped to see you alone before I left," he said, watching her come across the room slowly, almost gravely, her head bowed until she reached him.

"You are the best friend I have ever had," she began, then choked back a sob.

"Nab," Johnny said, embracing her, then bringing her down to sit beside him on the bed. "'Tis not forever."

"It could be, John Quincy. But what is hardest is this: it will never be the same for us again."

"No?" he asked.

"No. We shall never be so close again. And there are so few to whom I dare open my heart," she said, looking at the tips of her damask shoes.

"Mar would be your confidante if you would let her," Johnny ventured, knowing her response.

Nabby gave him an exasperated look and shook her head.

"Mother judges where she does not understand. She listens as a mother, not as a friend."

"She cannot help it, Nab. But she loves you very much."

"I do not doubt her love. But we shall never again be friends."

"Do not be too harsh with her," Johnny said gently. "If she is heavy-handed, it is perhaps because she has felt the weight of being both mother and father to you -- and to the boys."

"She has one set of rules for herself, another for everyone else," Nabby replied, holding her full mouth in a thin, firm line. "She was married at my age, but sacrifices my happiness to keep me by her."

"If Royall Tyler is indeed the paragon you say, he shall be waiting at the dock the day you return, like a race horse at the gate. If not, perhaps Mar was right," Johnny said, gently.

He was unprepared for the look of naked misery Nabby turned on him at the mention of Tyler.

"I fear he has forgotten me, Johnny," she whispered, eyes brimming. "Not a letter for months, and those few I had before then were so scant as to be mere notes, hardly the work of a lover."

"Perhaps his practice grows; he is busy. And you know the uncertainty of the mails," he urged, though it sounded unconvincing. "I will pay Royall Tyler a call immediately I return and will discover that he has been engrossed in cases until the wee hours, that he has been riding the circuit and making influential connections far and wide that will ensure the two of you a prosperous life together."

A ray of hope dawned across Nabby's pale face.

"Do ye really think so, John Quincy? That I could readily forgive. And he warned me on our departure that his missives would not reflect his heart, that he was no letter-writer," she add.

"Yes. I'm certain that's it," he assured her, relieved that he would not be forced to part on a note of despair. "There never was a correspondent like Par or Mar for sheer volume. In comparison, everyone's output looks weak."

Nabby nodded, a smile crossing her face as she gazed at her brother.

"I shall sorely miss thee, John Quincy."

"And I you, Nab," he said, hugging her tightly.

Abigail, accustomed to matter-of-fact separations from those most dear, was not prepared for the tearful farewell the eight French servants gave them. Gaspar, the butler, who had weekly polished the long hallways with brushes tied to his feet, doing figure-eights and pirouettes when he believed no one was watching, stood at the head of the little company, a look of grim resignation on his sweating face. Slowly, John and Abigail made their way down the row, addressing each one, shaking a hand, accepting a curtsy. Sniffles could be heard behind lace handkerchiefs, and, at the end, Collette, the upstairs maid who had dressed Abigail and Nabby's hair, bawled.

"Calm yourself," Abigail said brusquely, startled into emotion herself. "Collette, ne plurais pas."

The girl, her head bent into the handkerchief the downstairs maid had handed her, blew her nose loudly and then looked up.

"O, Madam! Je vous manquerais!"

Touched at the girl's loyalty, Abigail patted her on the hand.

"I will miss you, too, Collette. Here," she said suddenly, turning and walking to the carriage. She reached into the cab and grasped the handle of the birdcage, which sat at Nabby's feet. Pulling it out, she came back and presented it to the girl. "Voila! Des oiseux remplierais le vide!"

"O, Madam! Merci, merci!" Collette said, taking the cage by its gilded handle.

"Let us be gone, John," Abigail, said, turning her back on the little troupe. "We have said our goodbyes, now let us be off."

She marched to the carriage and climbed in beside Nabby, flopping down onto the banquette, her ankles already swollen from the heat. John made a few self-conscious remarks, raised his hand in salute, as much to the gardens and estate as to the servants, then stepped into the carriage and dropped onto the seat opposite the two women. He gazed once more out the window at the parched grounds, then reached up and rapped the top of the carriage with his knuckles. The carriage started with a lurch, picking up speed until the sound of the horses' hooves clopping on the hard road mixed in rhythmic accord with the creak of the leather springs and the metal-belted wheels as they rolled toward Calais.

"I am thankful Tom Jefferson was not here today to say goodbye," John said, finally. "I fear there would have been floods rather than freshets of tears."

"And so there would," Abigail sighed, her eyes on the limp blooms of the flowers that passed by the carriage window. "It is hard to leave a place knowing that all likelihood you will never set eyes upon it again. And I shall miss Mr. Jefferson more than France."

"Ah, but God willing, Mr. Jefferson we shall see again," John said as he settled back to watch the countryside slip away. "One is never parted from a true friend."

Chapter 16

Live while ye may yet, happy pair
John Milton Paradise Lost Bk IV Line 533

1785

"Stop fidgeting, John. I have never fastened a sword before," Abigail snapped. Between fatigue and the cramped space they shared in the only available rooms in London, she was irritable.

Parliament was in session, adding a mob of Parliamentarians to a city already clogged with celebrants of the King's birthday and spectators of the Handel Festival at Westminster Abbey. Peace had opened men's pocket books, and every room in London had been taken. But Abigail and John had bigger worries than lodging. Rumors circulated that the king would refuse to receive an ambassador from America. *The Public Advertiser* castigated the upstart country's effrontery. Although it was not the welcome they wished, it was the one John and Abigail had anticipated.

In Arthur Smith's place, Colonel William Smith, former attaché to General Washington, had been appointed by Congress to be John's new secretary. Smith, whose appealing insouciance opened doors, found lodging for them in the Bath Hotel in Piccadilly then called on Lord Carmarthen, Secretary of State for Foreign Affairs, to announce John Adams's arrival. The response, happily, was warm. Lord Carmarthen invited John to come see him at home immediately. Of course King George would receive the American Ambassador, John was told.

"His Majesty indicated that although he was the last to agree to a separation of our nations," Lord Carmarthen told John over tea, "he would be the first to welcome renewed friendship between them."

John's audience with King George III was to take place in his Majesty's 'closet' the following Wednesday.

"I cannot see how I shall manage to keep from falling on my nose before the king!" John shouted, pulling away from Abigail and trying to buckle the offending sidearm himself.

"Father, let me try," Nabby said, sweeping across the room.

"Hold still, John," Abigail said, hands on hips as she watched him twist before the mirror, fumbling. "Let Nabby do it."

"I shall forget my whole speech in this fluster," John growled as his daughter gently pushed his hands away and completed the fastenings.

"You shan't," Abigail retorted. "And I wish you'd stop saying so. You'll give yourself an apoplectic fit."

"Mother," Nabby started to correct her mother's sharpness, thought better and instead tried to soothe her father. "You have memorized every word of your speech perfectly, Par, and besides, it is spoken completely from the heart. How can you forget those sentiments?"

"You are right, Nab, of course," he said, turning to view himself from behind. "It is just that this is such an honor, to be the first of my countrymen to stand in His Majesty's presence in a diplomatic character. I pray I do no dishonor to myself or to our country."

"You have not so far and shall not today," Abigail said. "Now stop all this fretting and let me see you."

Obediently, John faced his wife and daughter, arms spread. He was gird in the finest material with the plainest cut Abigail could devise, a means of marking him as republican aristocracy. He looked like an exceedingly well-to-do burgher, complete with new wig and silver shoe buckles.

"I look a toad," John moaned, noting their amused smiles.

"You look no such thing," Abigail said, insulted. "I have outfitted you perfectly: you are the dour republican with exquisite taste."

"You look magnificent, Par," Nabby pronounced. "His Majesty will see in you a gentleman, a balance of simplicity and finery."

"Oh?" John said, turning around again to study himself in the mirror. "I hope so, Nab. You see me through different eyes from those the king will cast upon me. But I hope you are right."

A knock sounded on the door.

"'Tis nearly time, Mr. Adams," Colonel Smith said, poking his head through the door.

"What do you think, Mr. Smith?" Adams demanded, fists on hips.

"I think Ambassador Adams perfectly represents our new

nation," William Smith replied. "His Majesty will see in him reason, dedication, and dignity, if you don't mind my being so frank."

"Well said, Colonel Smith," Abigail observed. "You see, Mr. Adams. A universal verdict."

"It is only your excitement that makes you anxious, Par," Nabby said.

Smith stifled a smile.

"I am not excited!" John burst out. "I am weighing the gravity of the moment, and worried lest anything I do reflect badly on our country. I speak not for John Adams, but for America."

"Of course, Par."

"Yet John Adams the man must admit he is somewhat pleased to be making the excursion," Abigail remarked shrewdly.

"Indeed," John agreed, still surveying himself in the mirror. "But I must shove the man aside, and consider only the country."

"May the man not take pleasure in the honor?" Abigail persisted.

"Not enough for anyone to remark upon it. Well? Is everything in place?"

He turned around slowly.

"It is," Nabby declared.

Abigail, her head tilted critically to one side, nodded in agreement.

"I wish you to remember everything of today, Mr. Adams, even the small things. Most especially the small things," Abigail said. "Since I cannot witness this, I charge you to commit everything to memory for a report."

"I wish I could see you there, Par," Nabby murmured. "I would be as quiet as a mouse, but would swell with pride when you were presented to the king."

John's eyes were on the wall, his mind on scenes not yet played.

"I wonder how he will receive me."

"I don't mean to hurry you, Ambassador," Smith urged, "but time is getting on. Traffic at this hour is usually very thick. It would not do to keep His Majesty waiting."

"Just so," John nodded, taking up his hat and heading for the door.

Smith stepped aside for John, darted a warm glance at Nabby then shut the door behind them. Abigail and Nabby listened as the sound of their shoes on the uncarpeted hallway faded. The two women went to the window and peered out to the carriage that waited at the hotel entrance. Neither John nor William Smith looked up to Abigail and Nabby who watched anxiously from above. As he hefted himself up the step, John's sword caught on the door. For a moment, he struggled to disentangle it from the framework.

"That may be a very long ride," Abigail observed as Smith deftly realigned the sword, helped John into the carriage, and stepped lightly into its shrouded interior.

"Par will be wonderful. I know it."

John had been elevated to near-perfection in Nabby's eyes; she resented her mother's casual treatment of her distinguished father.

"You know it, and so do I," Abigail replied, guessing what was in her daughter's mind, "but John Adams does not yet know it, and will not be convinced until he has done with today. He needs not reassurance, but a flint against which to strike so he does not strike sparks at court. Argument cements his ideas and feelings. Many on this side of the Atlantic, both American and British, would fan the coals of discord once again. If your father can move through the Court of St. James without being burnt, he will be something of the asbestos kind of Ambassador."

Falling silent, Abigail watched the back of the carriage slide into misty obscurity.

The audience with King George went well, better than John had hoped. The two bookish, middle-aged men, tired of the strife between their countries, discovered that, despite the chasm of breeding and station, they were kindred souls. John spoke his piece without forgetting a single line and listened intently while King George echoed the sentiments and hopes for the future.

Abigail and Nabby's audience with Queen Charlotte the following week was not so successful. Left to wait in line for four hours in a crowded room while the queen received her visitors one by one, Abigail stood knees aching, ankles swollen, and chafed at Her Majesty's disdainful manner and the foolishness of waiting upon royalty.

But their daily lives were far less influenced by protocol than by the negotiations over hotly disputed commercial treaties, fishing rights, and the struggle over American debts to British businesses.

Unfortunately, John negotiated from a position of weakness. America was nearly bankrupt. The states squabbled jealously, each worried over its own rights. Many delegates stopped attending Congress altogether. The new nation couldn't agree on its own joined interests, and had no power to protect them in any case. Like hyenas circling exhausted prey, the British Navy snapped and tore at American vessels and encroached on America soil, while His Majesty's Foreign Secretary uttered bland assurances in diplomatic drawing rooms. John's task was formidable.

Despite John's difficulties, Abigail enjoyed England. They had moved to a large house in Grosvenor Square shielded from the home of the infamous Lord North only by the tree-filled common. Abigail initiated a lively correspondence with Thomas Jefferson in France, buying damask and diaper for his table linen in exchange for the French figurines, shoes, and lace he purchased for her. John Quincy had arrived safely in America. And Nabby began a friendship with Colonel William Smith.

The September evening was clear, promising a chilly night. Silver dew clung to the grassy commons and sparkled in the light of carriage lanterns.

"'Tis a bit low-cut do you not think, Nab?" Abigail asked, smoothing a stray tendril into place under her lace cap as she looked in the mirror.

"'Tis not nearly so low-cut as the gown Mrs. Copley wore last week to the Duchess of Devonshire's party," Nabby retorted leaning down to check her coiffure in her mother's mirror.

"You do not wish to seem immodest," Abigail reminded.

Twenty-year old Nabby's figure, voluptuous, alluring, was a source of both consternation and envy to Abigail. At Nabby's age, Abigail had had no enticing curves, and even then had lacked the graceful stride of her daughter, whose progress through a room brought many appreciative male glances.

"I do not believe I am immodest," Nabby asserted quietly, her eyes meeting her mother's in the mirror.

"Of course you are not. But in our position, one must be especially careful not to appear what one is not. Besides, it is chill tonight."

"Pardon, Mrs., " Sybil, the housemaid, padded through the door on soft-soled shoes, carrying a pitcher of water for the washstand. "Colonel Smith is waiting."

She poured water into the basin, and set the pitcher on the stand.

"That be a mighty fine dress, Miss," Sybil said to Nabby admiringly. "The cut suits you."

Nabby darted a triumphant look at her mother, smiling. "Thank you, Sybil. Is Colonel Smith in the drawing room?"

"No, Miss. He be waitin' in your Father's office. Said he had some business or other to do there."

"I shall go down and keep him company until you are ready, Mother," Nabby announced, turning to the door without waiting for agreement.

"'I shall only be a moment..." Abigail began, still hoping to persuade Nabby to tuck a piece of lace in her bodice to hide the ripe breasts that spilled over the décolletage, but Nabby closed the door on her words.

Sybil made much of straightening the shawl flung over a chair, all the while casting sidelong glances at Abigail's face.

"Colonel Smith is a fine figger of a man," she observed.

"He is a worthy gentleman," Abigail agreed stiffly.

Despite the habitual closeness in which she and her servants in America had lived, she was not prepared to gossip with the English hired help.

"I fink he fancies Miss Nabby," the girl persisted.

"He pays her the deference due her as the Ambassador's daughter."

"Oh no, Mrs.! I'm sure he pays her every respect!" the poor girl cried.

Abigail sighed, cast her eyes to the ceiling, and rose.

"That is what I meant," Abigail said, exasperated. "We shall be late tonight, I expect, Sybil. You need not wait up for us, but do see to it that all the ewers are married to full pitchers tonight. And be sure to remind Jane to finish taking the spots out of my red silk gown. I will need that tomorrow night for Lady Salisbury's."

Yes, Mrs.," Sybil said, making a stunted curtsy. "You have a nice time."

"Thank you."

The girl's familiarity stemmed, Abigail knew, from a yearning to be part of a life she could only view from behind the glass partition of class. Abigail enjoyed England, but the rigidity of the class system both fascinated and repelled her. Despite a natural inclination to view herself as part of the American aristocracy, she was unwilling to accept birth as the sole criterion for enrollment. Intelligence, ability, service, these things and more were, to her republican mind, the elements of true class distinction.

Abigail left the chamber in a swish of taffeta and lace. By the time she had descended the two flights of stairs to John's small office at the back of the house, Nabby and Colonel Smith were deep in conversation. They fell silent when she entered the room. Although the fire burned low in the grate, Nabby's face was flushed.

"Good evening, Madam," Smith said in a voice slightly too ebullient.

Rising, he bowed to Abigail, the lace at his neck and on his cuffs tumbling away from his coat.

"It is a fine evening. September is often foggy, but the stars are out tonight. I was just telling Miss Adams what a fine walk I had from my rooms."

William Steuben Smith, a slim, graceful young man from a socially prominent, though not wealthy New York family, was the picture of charm and breeding. Apparently eager to please, his temper never strayed from urbane, at times, even fawning. From the time he had first set eyes on Nabby, he had treated her with a special deference, asking her opinion, always looking to her comfort.

Nabby had at first accepted all these attentions with a calm that had bordered on detachment. But when she received word of Royall Tyler's engagement -- to a Quincy woman of greater means -- she began to show signs of interest in Colonel Smith. Several times recently, Abigail had interrupted them talking quietly, heads together. Abigail knew, too, not because Nabby had told her, but because John Quincy's last letter had made mention of the fact, that Nabby had returned Tyler's letters and his miniature. *I was right to insist on her coming with me,* Abigail thought with relief. *I was not clinging.*

"Have you ordered a hansom, Colonel Smith?" she asked.

"I have, Mrs. Adams. It awaits us."

"Will Mr. Adams be able to join us?"

"He said he doubted it. I stopped to take a few letters to him at Lord Carmarthen's. They were closeted together in his lordship's study, discussing fishing rights on Georges Bank when I left. Mr. Adams charged me with escorting his two lovely ladies," he looked at Nabby, his eyes gleaming in the flickering candlelight.

Nabby returned his gaze with undisguised warmth.

There is a more passionate heart beneath the cool exterior than I had imagined, Abigail thought, a little startled at the nakedness of her daughter's attraction. Yet has she leapt too fast into this new attachment? Is it a yearning of the heart and flesh or a salve for hurt pride?

Despite Abigail's reservations, John thought highly of Smith. Though he was not quick-witted, Smith was charming and was adept at smoothing the feelings that John had ruffled. It was a valuable commodity in diplomacy -- and in life. He also knew that Nabby was not the intellect her brother John Quincy was, so would not want a bookish husband.

"We have waited just long enough to ensure you will not have a table on the first round of cards, Madam," Smith was saying. "I know how distasteful gambling is to you. We will be in time, however, for the vittals -- no small consideration at Lady Talbot's."

"Even if I could stomach the loss and gain of money I had not earned, the Adamses have none to throw away," Abigail moaned. "The time has come for us to return the hospitality we have received -- our country's honor demands it -- but how shall we pay for it?"

"Mr. Adams suggested tonight that he could plan a 'bachelor's party,' Smith replied. "That way, the guest list would be divided in half, men only, but the hospitality would be repaid. And, he reckons, with only men present, he could attempt to further America's diplomatic interests without being thought a bore before the ladies."

"A sound plan," Abigail nodded. "though what we shall feed them, I do not know. Well, the English custom of the division of the sexes will benefit us this time, though I wish the ladies could be present for the after dinner conversation over cigars and brandy. I loathe being relegated to discussions of fripperies and children."

"I doubt anyone could relegate you to discussions of fripperies and children, Mrs. Adams," Smith laughed.

"Well, perhaps not," Abigail demurred, flattered. "But there are so few ladies here, who are informed enough to discuss the philosophy of nations."

"Except Mrs. Dr. Jebb," Smith said, seeing that he was winning her.

"Except Mrs. Jebb," Abigail agreed with a nod. "She is a great politicianess."

"I expect Mrs. Jebb will be on hand tonight, Mrs. Adams. Perhaps you will be excused entirely from cards."

Nabby rose from her chair and took a step toward the door to promote their departure. Seeing her move, Abigail glanced around the room.

"I will stop and tell Mr. Spiller to let the fire go out here. Do you think Mr. Adams will wish to work when he returns home tonight?"

"I doubt he will be in much before 1 o'clock of the morning," Smith replied, shaking his head.

"Then I will tell Mr. Spiller to let the fire go out," she repeated. "And to be sure there are not any more candles burning about the house than are absolutely essential. If we are forced by our station to support a platoon of servants, we must make economy somewhere!"

The evening was like many others in London. Every public room of Lord and Lady Salisbury's house was packed to capacity with the aristocracy gambling, drinking, laughing, and flirting beneath the golden glow of a thousand candles.

Mrs. Jebb was indeed in attendance, seated on a sofa sipping Madeira and surveying the room with languid interest. When she saw Abigail making her way through the crowd, Mrs. Jebb's face lit up.

"My dear Mrs. Adams!" she crowed when Abigail came within earshot. "I feared I would be bored to tears tonight."

"And I too, until Colonel Smith assured me we would see you," Abigail replied, sitting down beside Mrs. Jebb.

"Is Colonel Smith here as well?"

"He is. He and my daughter have gone to fetch us something to drink. There are certain advantages to advancing years," Abigail smiled.

"You are no older than I, Mrs. Adams," Mrs. Jebb admonished with mock indignation. "And I certainly do not assent to being described as a lady of advancing years."

"But I have a daughter of marriageable age, now. That as much as anything attests to my decrepitude," Abigail said without believing it.

Marriageable age, but not yet married. I am not old yet, she thought.

"Your daughter has cut quite a figure these last months," Mrs. Jebb said. "Yet I warrant she has eyes for one alone."

Abigail started.

"I don't think Nabby's heart is engaged if that is what you mean," she responded.

"She could do worse," Mrs. Jebb continued, shrewdly eyeing her friend. "The young man is ambitious. He has ideas."

"Has he?"

"Indeed! He regaled me one whole evening with his plans. I believe *that* one will go far, Mrs. Adams."

"He has charm enough for two young men, of that I am sure," Abigail conceded. "But a mother must be reassured that there is more than charm."

"I believe his feelings for your daughter are sincere," Mrs. Jebb said kindly, patting Abigail's hand. "I understand your concerns, Madam. I am a mother myself, after all."

Abigail looked at her friend in silence. Like Mercy Warren, Mrs. Jebb spoke her mind, but unlike Mercy, who had begun to make cutting remarks in her letters, Mrs. Jebb seemed to judge kindly. She truly wanted the best for her friends.

Abigail thought of the last letter she had received from Mercy reeking of self-congratulation and riddled with oblique references to the reputation the American Ambassador and his wife were gaining for frugality. Mercy had intimated that it did our country no good turn to be perceived as tight-fisted. To add salt to the wound, her sister, Betsey Shaw's last letter was filled with concern for the Warren boys' unwholesome influence on Charly and Tommy. Mrs. Warren is very free with her advice, Abigail thought angrily, but she had best look to her own home first.

She looked across the room to see Nabby and Colonel Smith approaching carrying three glasses of punch.

"They cut a very fine figure together," Mrs. Jebb said confidingly.

"They do," Abigail admitted, her eyes on the two smiling young people pressed shoulder to shoulder in the crowd.

By the time John returned that night, Abigail had been in bed for an hour, tossing restlessly. He crept into the room carrying a candle that he rested on the top of his dresser.

"I am not asleep John," Abigail told him, rising on one elbow.

"You have let the fire go out; it is chill in here. Economy, economy, thy name is Abigail," John groaned.

"I must save where we can," she said, mildly hurt at the criticism. "Have you been all this time with Lord Carmarthen?"

"No," he replied wearily, taking off his coat and laying it across the chair. "I have seen Johnathan Sewall tonight."

Abigail sat up. "Johnathan Sewall? And how is he? Was he...cordial?"

Johnathan Sewall and John Adams, once friends, had parted ten years before over their opposing views on America's independence. At the time, John had described the rift between the two of them as the sharpest thorn on which he ever set his foot. Shortly before the war, Sewall had moved to England.

"Yes. In that respect, it was the same old Sewall, bless him. But he is rather shabby. Down and out. He is finding it more difficult to sustain himself here than at home. It is more expensive, and he is unable to earn much. But he will not come back to America, he says. He does not look well. But his eyes and his smile are the same old Sewall," John repeated, thinking of his friend's animated conversation over late-night suppers of apples and beer.

"John...," Abigail began, frowning.

"Yes, my dear?' he said, blowing out the candle before climbing into the bed beside her and sliding down under the quilts.

"Were you aware that Colonel Smith may have designs on our Nabby?"

"Designs?"

"Well, intentions, then. I have begun to notice the looks that pass between them. I believe Nabby shares his interest. And I am not the only one to have noticed."

"It would surprise me if he were not to come to me before the year is out to ask for her hand," John said matter-of-factly, swinging his arm behind his head to stare into the darkness.

"You knew of this?" Abigail asked indignantly.

"My dear, I would be a very poor father indeed if I had not marked the eagerness with which Smith asks my evening comings and goings. He is always at the ready to escort my ladies on their evening rounds."

"That alone cannot have been the cause of your knowledge. Colonel Smith is a man who likes a throng."

"No. It is not only that. But there is a look that steals into his eyes when he mentions our daughter. I remember it well," John said, turning toward her.

"Is Nabby filling the void left by Royall Tyler, or is she truly interested in Colonel Smith the man?"

"My dear, you do not give your daughter enough credit. I would say that in the affair of Tyler, she kept her head more than the mother. She will not give her hand where it will not be appreciated."

"I wonder if you do not see your only daughter through rose-tinted lenses, John. There is a very warm heart that beats beneath that cool exterior. She sees other young women marrying. She may fear her time is passing."

"I would give my approbation to a marriage with Smith," John said after a few moments' silence. "By reputation his family is good. General Washington spoke well of him. He is not a blazing intelligence, but he will get on in this world, I believe. And I would see our daughter happy. For her that means marriage," he said.

His last statement silenced her. She knew that John suspected her of clinging to Nabby. And suppose I am not ready to step into the shadows of the older generation? That only proves my own vitality. Why should I be eager to have my children grown? Mother-in-law. The name alone suggests matronly plainness. Next thing to Dowager. Then followed Grandmother! It is all passing too quickly. The years are going too fast. So many years of my youth, lost to separation, to sacrifice. I will not be pushed into old age so soon.

Chapter 17

So dear I love him that with him all deaths I could endure, without him live no life.
John Milton Paradise Lost Bk IX Line 832

1785

Despite his interest in Nabby, Colonel Smith left for Europe the following week. He made much of his mission -- to carry correspondence from John to diplomats on the continent, correspondence that could have gone by other means -- but he eagerly anticipated this opportunity to tour the continent alone.

"When you get to Berlin, be sure to see the military reviews," John told him, as they stood together in the hallway the morning of Smith's departure.

"I will, sir," Smith said.

"Will you see General Lafayette?"

"I hope so. I contracted the utmost respect for him during the campaign in Virginia -- a tremendously able general, and very genteel company. I would be sorry not to renew so valued an acquaintance."

"Well, I pray that you may enjoy those sights and friendships on the continent as may benefit you, but do not tarry overlong. I need you. Your services allow me to spend more time at His Majesty's court and thereby further our nation's friendship. But I would not stand between you and the education traveling imparts."

"Pray don't let him think you don't want him home right away, Par," said Nabby, who stood in the dining room doorway. "His company will be sorely missed even if you can do without his penmanship."

Smith crossed the floor to Nabby in three long strides, the muscles of his lean legs working beneath the fabric of breeches and stockings. Taking her soft, white hand in his, he looked earnestly into her eyes. Her face tilted up to meet his, mouth parted enticingly.

"The tattoo in Berlin is over by the 20th of this month. I will fly back to where my heart is happiest as soon as I have done my business in Paris. Six days will I stay, no more," Smith said, bringing his lips down to her hand.

At the touch of his warm mouth on her skin, Nabby's face flushed. Abigail, who stood silent at the foot of the stair, saw both the hunger and the sweet fondness in that contact.

I have already lost her, she thought. I must let her go with grace. May God grant her a happy life.

Ten weeks later, they had still had no word of Colonel Smith.

"I have written to Mr. Jefferson, Nab," Abigail was saying as she watched the young woman yank thread through sampler. "He knows everyone who will have seen Colonel Smith. Mr. Jefferson will send word as soon as he has news," Abigail said.

Since the beginning of October, they had been in daily anticipation of Smith's arrival. When no word reached them by mid-month, they began to be alarmed. Now, in mid-November, they imagined the worst.

"Surely, even if he were sick, he would have got word to us somehow!" Nabby moaned.

With each day that passed, she became paler. It was too much to bear, losing one lover to inconstancy, another to who knew what? Longing for the electric touch of his hand on hers as they rode through Hyde Park, the reassuringly amorous looks he cast at her when her parents' attentions were diverted, Nabby fretted. Her appetite waned. Surely, she was not meant to die an old maid?

Abigail struggled to keep up her daughter's hopes though her own were growing dim.

"Perhaps the mails have miscarried. We have had ample evidence of that possibility in our lives," Abigail said reasonably in a litany she had perfected during the passing weeks. "We know he told Colonel Miranda that he was considering visiting Vienna. Perhaps he has gone there. It would be a pity for him not to take advantage of perhaps his only visit to the continent. A young man must seize his opportunities where he finds them."

Ah, but what opportunities, she wondered, casting a pitying look at Nabby.

"You must not fret yourself so," Abigail continued. "You will make yourself sick, and then what will he return to? A hollow-cheeked melancholy damsel who has not the power to welcome him home."

"I would be cured this instant were he to walk through the door!" Nabby retorted sharply. "He should not have been away so long without word unless he has fallen ill or had some other disaster befall him. He could not be so cruel as to omit to write were he able!"

The girl burst into tears, hiding her face in her hands.

Lately Abigail had begun to long for the early years of her marriage, when her children were young. They were growing away, their troubles beyond her ability to mend them. Recent letters from John Quincy had an oddly superior tone, and Betsey's letters raised new concerns about her bright-eyed fun-loving Charly. Though he was the darling of everyone he met, his love of parties and of boon companions had begun to sound like some distant, but familiar warning bell.

"Now, Nab... Nab," Abigail said soothingly, patting the young woman's heaving shoulder. "Tears will not do. Think on your brother, John Quincy. He left us in May and we knew not until September that he arrived safe. And think on Charly! All that time had passed -- it was not reasonable that so much had happened shipwreck, pirates, and yet that he could still be alive, that his letters could have miscarried, but he was and they did. He was returned to us safe. And how long did I wait for word from your father on his first voyage? Nearly a year. Use that to measure this fear by."

Abigail waited for the girl to regain her composure. Nabby looked up at her mother. She could see on Abigail's face, jowled and netted with fine lines, a mother's sympathetic pain. But she saw no understanding of the fear and grief that a young woman felt at the loss of a lover and with it the possibility of home and family. Once ensconced in marriage and motherhood, Abigail seemed to have forgotten the fretful yearning a maiden feels. She will never let me go, Nabby thought dismally. She is sorry for my pain, but not for the postponement of my departure.

"The best remedy," Abigail said, "is occupation. Mrs. Siddons is playing Desdemona at Covent Garden. Pray let us send round to the Copleys to make up a party and all go tonight. I shall send Prudence with a note. If Colonel Smith is not back by Sunday, we shall ask Rev. Dr. Price to offer a special prayer for his safe return this and every Sunday until he is restored to us. The rest must be left to Providence."

Nabby sucked in a deep breath, brushed tears away from reddened eyes, and nodded. "You are right. Tears do little good. I just feel overcome sometimes. Perhaps an evening out would divert my attention."

"Good, " Abigail smiled in relief. "Go find Prudence, and have her take round a note to Copleys' house. We shall see what we can conjure for tonight."

Nabby shut the heavy door behind her, leaving Abigail with an inexplicable sense of loss.

William Smith did not return that week or the next. The Adamses had no word. He simply appeared in mid-December with a friend, Major Dockhard, in tow. Abigail suspected William of using the Major as a buffer between himself and her indignant questions. Striding into the house, his face bright with excitement at his adventures, Smith won Nabby over again with the heady wine of his presence. Eagerly, he regaled her with stories of the courts through which he had passed, the people whose acquaintance he had made or renewed, the connections that would advance his prospects.

He seemed to feel no need to make excuse for either his absence or his long silence. Nabby forgave him the pain of her fears in the joy of seeing him again. And John, busy as he was with negotiations, appeared undisturbed by his secretary's extended holiday. But Abigail, whatever excuses and assurances she might voice, had misgivings.

"He is a young man who must make a place for himself in this world," John said reassuringly the week following Smith's return as he and Abigail sat in his office by a fire, sipping brandy. "Not an easy thing to do on his own, I can assure you from experience. He needs to feel on a par with Nabby's family. Her father is an ambassador. Her brother is better traveled and more experienced than most Americans of any age. Perhaps Smith only wishes the same advantages for himself."

John peeled an apple with his penknife as he spoke, his concentration apparently more on the gleaming peel that snaked across the back of his hand than on Abigail's concerns.

Holding one hand knotted with rheumatism toward the small, leaping blaze in the grate, Abigail studied John's forehead. Broad and furrowed, it rose from his brow in a crest as though the brain beneath were struggling to escape. His eyes were more sunken, the cheeks more prominent beneath the thinning flesh, and the sharp Yankee nose had taken on a beak-like quality. His age was, she knew, merely a reflection of her own. The damp had stiffened her joints and the steep stairs left her breathless, a stabbing reminder of her own mortality.

"You have made your place without such advantages," she finally replied.

"Yes, but my place is hardly assured," John responded around the bite of apple he had taken. "And our children's fortune is in their own hands. They will ever struggle to make enough money for their own needs if their parents are anything to judge by. Young Smith has tastes for the finer things. He studies how those tastes are to be satisfied."

"Well, perhaps," Abigail agreed, sipping at the warmed glass pensively. "Mr. Jefferson thinks him a worthy man, as does General Washington. He is indeed a very likable character. But does it not concern you that he did not write once though he was gone so much longer than he had planned -- not to our Nabby, nor to you, his employer?"

"He told me he wrote, that the letters must have miscarried," John said, stuffing another wedge of apple into his mouth and offering one to her.

"Did he indeed?" she replied stiffening, leaving John's offer unacknowledged. "And why was I not told?"

"Did I not tell you, Madam?" John asked, leaning back into the depths of his chair. "I thought I had, or that he had. It was certainly no secret."

"I should think not!" she cried, leaning forward to close the distance between them. "He owed our daughter an explanation for his prolonged absence and silence. He owed you one as well."

"He gave me one," John replied without elaboration.

"And may I know it?"

"Colonel Smith mentioned to me before he left the possibility of extending his tour. Since his return, we have talked. He made some valuable contacts for us in his peregrinations and said he was loathe to disengage those acquaintances too abruptly."

"He did not mention anything of the sort to me or Nab!"

241

Abigail cried, her mouth dropping open at John's obtuseness. "Why in all the time he was gone did you not mention that possibility?"

"I did, but neither of the ladies would believe poor John Adams," he replied.

"John! You did no such thing! How can you be so unfeeling?"

"Abigail, I *said* as much to you although I warrant your attention was diverted at the time, and subsequent murmurings did not penetrate the veil of tears that had descended over the house. Your focus seemed to be on his over-hopeful prediction to Nabby of the time required to accomplish his task. He and Nabby are together now, and happy. He seems to have explained everything to her satisfaction."

"Has he indeed? Has Nabby said as much to you? She has not said so to me!"

"Perhaps a young woman does not confide everything to her mother," John suggested.

"Not confide? I have been her greatest confidente all these months! And why should she not tell me what is in her mind?"

"Did you tell your mother?" John asked.

Abigail glared at him but said nothing.

"Nabby is happy. That is my concern," John repeated.

"And you think that is not mine also?"

"I think the mother will sorely miss the daughter's company when she marries," he answered. "And that is understandable. But it may cloud the mother's judgment. I have seen Nabby sad too long. Her prudent disposition is married to a passionate heart. I would not forestall what I believe will be a match that will bring her the same kind of happiness meted out to her mother."

His rebuke, however muted, hurt. That he should think her capable of such selfishness after the years she had sacrificed for the sake of duty, that he could consider her capable of turning a blind eye to Nabby's happiness for the sake of her own, was painful, even cruel.

"You do me an injustice if you believe that I will not let her go," she said, biting off her words. "I am merely concerned for her welfare. A woman's lot in life depends almost entirely on her husband."

"You appeared to feel no such qualms at the thought of another's serious attentions. William Smith has had no silver spoon that he has plucked from his mouth and thrown away like a spoiled child," John replied, referring to Royall Tyler's squandering of his inheritance. "Smith must make his own place. To do that, he will learn what sacrifice is, as will our Nabby. But she is equal to it. As was her mother. And it is clear that she and Smith hold the tenderest feelings for each other; you have only to look at them together to know what beats in their hearts. Come, dear Wife. Let us have no cross words. What the Lord ordains, man should not disdain."

"The rub is discovering what is divinely ordained and what is concocted by man alone," Abigail grumbled, sipping at her brandy and staring into the fire.

1786

Nabby became Mrs. William Stephens Smith on June 12, 1786. As Abigail stood beside John in their Grosvenor Square drawing room, her eyes fixed on the couple kneeling before the Bishop of St. Asaph, she suddenly thought of her own mother who had stood with such stolid resignation at her own wedding nearly twenty-two years before.

That day, Elizabeth Smith had been forced to watch the departure of the most delicate, most fretted-over of her three daughters, relinquishing her to a man she could barely tolerate. Her disapproval had quivered through the ceremony that October day, like the anticipation before a storm. But the years had considerably altered Elizabeth Smith's opinion of her son-in-law.

I knew John Adams's worth, Abigail thought, despite my mother's fears. Perhaps, this is the same. A mother finds giving up a daughter to be the giving up of a friend. And she knows more of the struggle of a marriage, of the secret inequalities, the cruel possibilities. Nabby is no longer mine. Is this what my mother felt? Or did she also worry what sort of life I would have at the hands of such as man as she believed John Adams to be?

The bride and groom made a handsome pair. Nabby stood with quiet assurance beside Colonel William Stephens Smith. Straight and lean as a reed, his clothes fitted him perfectly, accenting the well-muscled form. His manners were impeccable, his charm infectious. He had prominent friends and acquaintances and advocates in every quarter. His easy friendliness stood in sharp contrast to John's brusque manner. What would Elizabeth Quincy Smith say to this match, Abigail wondered?

The bishop finished the ceremony, pronouncing them man and wife and gently closed the Book of Common Prayer. As William Smith planted a chaste kiss upon Nabby's rosy mouth, the old cleric smiled.

"I have rarely been more happy to have officiated at the joining of a couple," he pronounced, gazing upon the two glowing faces before him. "This marriage has the best prospects for happiness of any I have ever seen."

At his words, Abigail was flooded with relief. It was as though in answer to an unspoken prayer, Elizabeth Quincy Smith had spoken from heaven through the Bishop, had wrapped a reassuring arm around her aging daughter's bowed shoulders.

The new young couple did not fly far from the Adams nest. Their house on Wimpole Street was close enough to allow a return to Grosvenor Square every evening for dinner, a gradual weaning that eased the pain of separation. Abigail enjoyed the Smiths. Their joy was a bittersweet reminder of the first years of her marriage. While the years had been fraught with struggle they were also filled with passion and pleasure.

Ten months later, On April 2, 1787, Nabby presented John and Abigail with their first grandchild, William Steuben Smith. Abigail, overcome at becoming a grandmother, took to her bed.

Even so, she delighted in the baby. Relieved of the daily cares of feeding and diapers, the responsibility of molding character, she took more pleasure in the rosy toes, sparkling eyes and bubble-lipped gurgles than she had in her own children in those frantically busy years of childbirth. Little Will Smith proved that life is not only loss but renewal.

Yet despite the proximity of the Smiths, the rounds of country tours and parties, Abigail longed for Massachusetts. She was beginning to feel alien to London life. Her sisters' letters, filled with the pleasures of their lively children, the shared excitements and secrets of youth at its most winning and vulnerable, shot pangs of homesickness through Abigail. She could almost see Betsey Shaw's daughters' assault on John Quincy in his cramped room in Boston, bent over a book, dressed only in a dirty wrapper. She could hear Charly's carefree laughter and the music of the Scottish songs she had sent them for evening revelry, could smell the roasting apples while they all played the fireside games at Christmas. And she had missed John Quincy's resounding success at the Harvard graduation. His oration had been published in the new Columbian Magazine. She wanted to share in his accolades, confirmation of her motherly success.

Coupled with the longing was the catalogue of wrecked lives strewn through their family and those of their friends. Mercy Warren, that dear and trusted friend, had lost one son to disease in Spain, another to a life of deception and squandered opportunities. Her own brother, William, had been accused of counterfeiting after deserting his family for the whiskey bottle and had died, alone, of black jaundice. Mary Cranch's brother-in-law, Robert, was virtually living in the streets, begging drink. What would guard her family against such heartbreak? She knew that the line between triumph and tragedy is as thin as an angel's wing.

Her sons were now nearly men, past her grasp. John Quincy was studying law; Tommy and Charly, both enrolled at Harvard, were prey to the beckoning evils that surrounded the college. She could only write admonishing letters and pray. In London, watching her grandson Willie Smith crawl with trusting innocence toward the fire, Abigail felt overcome by the fragility of life.

John, too, was ready to go home. The negotiations with England had stalled. He spent his time touring the countryside and writing *A Defense of the Constitutions of the United States of America*, a thick tome that would distinguish itself as the first American treatise on government, but whose apparently pro-monarchy stance would dog him. His only official duty in months had been a frantic last-minute trip to Amsterdam to renegotiate the loans before they expired. Frustrated at his uselessness, John applied for release. Finally, after a long wait for the letters of recall and praise, release came.

1788

On April 20th Abigail and John set sail on the *Lucretia* bound for Boston.

"T'will be nearly ten years since I have set foot on American soil," John said, carefully blotting the letter he had been writing in their small cabin. "I ache to see my apple trees and the little house in

Braintree."

"Ye shall be happier in the new house," Abigail replied bluntly, dismissing the notion of ever returning to their small Braintree home. Instead, she had purchased by proxy the old Borland house that Royall Tyler had once considered for his new Quincy bride. It was almost twice the size of John's Braintree birthplace and boasted sweeping fields and orchards. "'Tis a wren's house compared to Autieul," Abigail continued, preening a little, "but 'tis still much larger than our old Braintree home."

"I fear Europe has whetted your taste for expansion," John retorted. "You will no longer be a satisfied republican, but instead a dissatisfied monarchist longing for your palace."

"I shall be satisfied so long as my children are well, and you are happy," she replied tartly.

"And I will be satisfied," John said, "now that I will finally be able to oversee my own acres, tend my manure pile, read my books, and write my letters."

"That is an old refrain," Abigail reminded him. Sitting on the bunk, eyes on John, she swayed gently with the vessel's motion. "And one that, however sweet to my ear, strikes a false note somewheres."

"Do you doubt my heart is in Braintree?" he asked, indignant at her skepticism.

"I do not doubt your love for me and for our country," she replied, dropping the mocking tone. "And I do not doubt that your services will be sorely needed at this, our country's beginning."

"I will not be asked," John said miserably. "Many able and cunning men have spent years making a place for themselves. The climb to prominence is slippery indeed and there are many who would gladly grease the pole at the first sign of my attempted ascent."

"The cream rises to the top of the jug, John," Abigail reassured him. "It can do no other, regardless of the shakings and jostlings to keep it down. You have your piece to add to our history. Besides," she continued, mouth curved in a wry smile, "as much as I treasure your presence, I would not for all the world endure the company of a man kept from his life's work. And make no mistake, Husband. The making of our country is your life's work."

"I would not be so bold nor so presumptuous," he said, but his eyes glowed. "There are many able, nay, brilliant men amongst those

246

in Congress."

"Aye, and there are many grasping and petty men too," she rejoined. "You are of the brilliant sort and your work, whatever there be to do, will be waiting for you on your return."

Chapter 18

Unless an age too late, or cold climate, or years, damp my intended wing
John Milton Paradise Lose Bk IX Line 44

They sailed into Boston Harbor on June 18 to the sound of
cannons booming a welcome. From Castle William all the way into
the inner harbor, they were surrounded by a flotilla of wellwishers in
all manner of craft joyfully shouting the name of Ambassador John
Adams. John, who had anticipated coming home unsung and
unappreciated, was delighted at the outpouring. While his stern
morality whispered "Vanity, Vanity; all is vanity," his heart soared.
He was not forgotten.

The country was in political turmoil, the government tottering
under the Articles of Confederation. A group of the nation's
founders had convened the year before to effect a second revolution,
this one bloodless. They used the Massachusetts Constitution, which
John had helped to write, to construct a new United States
Constitution. Despite his democratic model for Massachusetts, many
distrusted John, if not for his intellect, then for his ambition.

His apparently monarchical bent, evident in *A Defense of the
Constitutions of the United States of America*, had pricked fears that ran
the gamut from Congress to the taverns. Having painstakingly
thrown off one king, the people would not tolerate another.

Nevertheless, John was elected to Congress as soon as he
returned, but deeply wounded by the public criticism, he declined the
office. Instead, he went home, unpacked his books, and with John
Quincy, published a series of anonymous responses to the attacks.

Abigail, burdened with making the house fit for their expanded
collection of books and furnishings, had her own battlefield. She
engaged a small army of painters, carpenters, and masons to enlarge
the new house, which, though twice the size of their Braintree home,
seemed small when compared to Autieul and Grosvenor Square.

The decisions and constant overseeing were tiring. She felt
brittle, vulnerable. Rheumatism and occasional light-headedness
hampered her. John, fighting joint pain, aching teeth and recurring

248

eye infections, all of which produced foul temper, was little help. Additionally, Susanna Adams Hall, who had, contrary to her own dire predictions, survived to see her son's triumphant return, was failing. Abigail felt mired in age and infirmity. And she missed her grandson, Willie Smith.

Colonel Smith and Nabby had settled in Jamaica, New York, bosom of the Smith family circle. There, Nabby discovered her husband to be a different man from the one she had known in England. She had seen his ambition, but not his overweening pride; his hopes, but not his improvidence. Determined to earn a fortune and thereby live in the style to which his social pretensions entitled him, Colonel Smith embarked on a series of land speculations. Additionally, to Nabby's acute embarrassment, he openly badgered any and every contact for a high post in the new government. She had believed he was like her father -- ambitious, despite John's life-long protestations to the contrary -- but wholly principled, willing to work for his honors and earnings. The Colonel William Smith she saw now looked only to the main chance.

Yet her pride dictated silence on the subject. Instead, she complained of her in-laws' criticisms and suggestions. Abigail chafed at what she saw as insults to the Adams honor. She wanted to be sure her only daughter was treated with the respect due her family name.

"Mrs. Smith has spoiled her children, particularly her sons," Abigail remarked as she examined the paint samples -- splots of color on broken shingles -- for John's new upstairs office, a recently built addition.

"Has Mrs. Adams never spoiled her sons?" John teased absently, lifting his eyes from the paper he was writing and pushing his spectacles down to look at her over their rims. He sat at his massive desk, hunched like an old scrivener and surrounded by a clutter of papers and books.

"I have never allowed my sons to expect something for nothing, to consider place without considering duty," Abigail shot back, holding a dark green sample to the light of the south window where the sun streamed onto the newly varnished floor.

"Is our Nabby happy?" John asked, his constant refrain.

"With her beautiful little boys, certainly. How could she not be?

They are so healthy and lively. I was so afraid the baby would be puny after the ordeal of its birth -- a servant for the midwife indeed!" she spluttered, referring to Nabby's telling no one of the labor pains she was suffering with her second pregnancy until too late to summon help. Nabby and a young servant girl had managed the birth between them alone, both terrified, but in the end, mother and child were safely delivered.

"If I understand correctly, Nabby was in part at fault for having held her peace when she should have set the wheels in motion," John said.

"She was too close to her time to be left alone," Abigail insisted. "I would that Mrs. Smith, genial as she is, had treated Nabby as her daughter, not her daughter-in-law. There is a clannishness in that family."

"As there is in many families," John reminded her.

"I would never deal that way with the wives of my sons!" Abigail cried indignantly. "They will become our daughters, too!"

"That remains to be seen, my dear," John responded evenly, his eyes perusing the letter he was writing.

Abigail glared at her husband's curved back. I have had enough of a fulltime John Adams, she thought. God help me, I wish you gone back to government. You tread on my intuition, re-argue my decisions. In the years gone by, you have lost a connecting thread to our lives, an understanding of the currents of our being.

She knew his absence from their lives stemmed from his preoccupation with his own, and his failed hopes. But she was convinced that time would vindicate him, that he would triumph in the end. She was not so certain that life would treat her children as kindly.

Charly was now out of her reach, yet she grasped fearfully at the few pieces of his life she could see. He was not a bad student, but his heart was not in the study of the law. And he lacked both the confidence and the seriousness of John Quincy. No matter how short of pocket money she tried to keep him, Charly always managed to find some friend who would stand him to drink at the taverns in Boston. Fleetingly she glimpsed traces of her brother Will: wasted opportunities, wasted life. Part of her wanted Charly home, to be continually under her surveillance, yet she knew he could not make a career for himself in Quincy.

He is delightful, but not steady. People like him, sometimes too much, she thought. He chooses his companions with an eye to pleasure rather than character. If only John could somehow take Charly under his wing. But that is not possible now, not while he himself flounders about the course of his own life. And he holds his younger sons to a different standard than he did John Quincy.

John saw Charly's nightly carousing as evidence of a fun-loving spirit. John envied the ease with which his two younger sons attracted and kept people near them. He would never admit the possibility that the friends they chose might be undesirable. Many were chosen from the finest families in Boston.

Charly needs must be thrust on the world and make his own way, Abigail told herself sternly. A bird cannot fly stuck in the nest.

"I don't know if Nabby is happy..." she murmured.

John grunted, but said nothing, dipping the pen into the half-full inkwell at his elbow and scratching something over the page. Deciding on a green reminiscent of the rich, placid pine forests of Europe, Abigail came back across the room and put the sample shingle before John.

"This is the color I will have for this room," she said, still holding the others in her hand like playing cards.

John looked up from his work and squinted at the paint splattered on the wooden square.

"Restful," was his terse comment.

"It is a bit dark," Abigail said, explaining her reasoning, eyes still on the shingle, "but t'will bring out the warm color of the furniture and there is sufficient light in this room..."

"What makes you think Nabby is not content?" John interrupted.

"A mother's instinct. Colonel Smith is often away, leaving Nabby alone with the boys."

"I was often away in those early years of our marriage," John observed, "yet you did not seem unhappy."

"I was unhappy at your absence, but not at what you were about," Abigail replied.

"And what, pray tell, is Colonel Smith *about*?"

"Well, he's off *renewing acquaintances* so he says, and searching for investors for his land speculations," she said uneasily, knowing the words sounded less than ominous to someone who did not harbor a nagging doubt.

"It sounds to me as though he's about trying to keep his family fed and clothed."

"Perhaps..." Abigail could see the conversation would have no satisfying end.

John refused to credit her suspicions. His need to believe Nabby well situated overrode any credence he would assign to her fears, particularly since he knew he could do little to alter his daughter's life.

Abigail understood John's need to believe their children safely launched. His own worries overshadowed all other concerns. She sighed and, still standing at his elbow, stuffed the discarded paint samples into her large apron pocket.

"There," John said, dropping the quill back into the inkwell and broadcasting blotter over the page. "What a joy it is to converse with a true friend!"

"And what true friend is that, Husband?" she asked, reaching for the quill to mark an X on the chosen paint sample.

"Benjamin Rush," said John, blowing the grit off the page and folding it carefully before sealing it. "He has written me of his confidence in my ability and my disinterested devotion to our country. *And* of Hancock's unsuitability for office beyond what he now holds."

"THAT we have known for some time," Abigail remarked sourly. "John Hancock's position as governor is due far more to the money he casts around like so much grain to feed the voters, than his dubious ability. He is too easily swayed by what is popular rather than by what is right. You should have been governor, John."

Abigail had spent many years trying to assuage John's self-doubts and despairs over how the world viewed him, and she had grown weary of what she saw as neglect by a fickle populace. So much sacrifice and so little real honor. And the money was beginning to worry her again. The improvements to their new home were costing more than anticipated and their savings were running low.

"Rush says *I* should be next vice president, though everyone knows the honor of president must go to General Washington," John continued, testing her reaction.

"While I respect General Washington," Abigail remarked dryly, "I do not think he should be the only candidate for the office. With only one candidate, there is no real election. Having just got rid of one king, we do not want to make the office of president an hereditary one. There are others at least as qualified for the post whose experience rests more on diplomacy and law than battle."

John's eyes gleamed.

"You have ever been a ruby to me, Wife."

"I speak the truth to you, Husband, as ye well know," Abigail retorted. "And while I do not seek to leave our sturdy New England climate ever again, still I know you cannot remain a farmer from now to the end of your days. Visiting your mother, mending fences, forking manure -- these pastimes are worthwhile, but not worthy of your talents. And we need to pay Charly and Tom's tuition fees. "

"Ah, but forking through the manure is what I have done best!" John laughed.

"Manure tends to spatter those nearby, whether they are forking or not," she warned. "You have been besmirched in the newspapers despite your unspotted character."

"I will not trade words with you today, Wife," John said, pushing the chair back and standing. "I needs must post my letter and be about my farmer's duties."

Abigail watched him cross the room with a spryer step than he had mustered in recent days. He needs to return to the fray, she sighed.

1789

By a slim majority of votes, John Adams was elected Vice President of the new United States of America. He left for New York in April of that year with a cavalcade in tow and made his way into the heart of the new government. He was grateful not only for the position, but for the employment, yet was soon chafing at the job. The vice president required much silence and tact, both of which he lacked. Stifled, frustrated in his attempts to influence the course of the new republic, he was reduced to lecturing the Senators on protocol and jurisprudence, creating a sea of ill will.

While John was immersed in politics, Abigail was immersed in family. Charly, soon graduating from Harvard, would need employment. Apprenticeship would be best, she decided, a foot on the path toward his future law career. She remembered the stories John told of his days apprenticed to John Gridley, chafing at the constrictions of a junior position. It is difficult for John to pull in harness with anyone of a mind other than his own. But Charly needs constrictions. Perhaps, a serious, plodding John Gridley could help steady him.

Yet instead of a quiet law office in Boston, John arranged for Charly to be apprenticed to Alexander Hamilton's law office in New York, a post he felt would benefit Charly by its sophistication and proximity to the halls of government. Abigail had qualms. There will be more temptations in New York than in Boston, she reasoned, and fewer family to stand watch. But times were hard. Beggared by the war and the economy, families lived hand to mouth, many thrown out of their homes. Those in government were besieged, inundated with job requests. Family members and friends, especially, attempted to use their connections to secure government posts. Nineteen-year-old Charly was lucky to have a job at all, John reminded Abigail in his letters, silencing her objections.

Louisa Smith, daughter of Abigail's dead brother, Will, now supplied some of the place that Nabby had left on her move to New York, but the young woman's feeling of being a supplicant, a hanger-on weighed her down. She moved through the house as though afraid to disturb even the air.

Her father refused to love her -- his own flesh -- so she feels entitled to no one's love, Abigail thought, sadly. I cannot undo the years. Still, I may try.

In June of 1790, crotchety with the constant opposition to his counsel, and hungry for her comfort, John sent for Abigail. In order to settle debts before she left, Abigail was obliged to sell the oxen at half their cost, a loss she resented as much as the work of packing yet again. Furniture and books must be crated, the house let, lists made to direct the operation of the farm, schedules arranged, and passages paid.

Abigail wiped the perspiration from her face with the tail of her apron. The last of the chairs were on their way down the road toward the packet in Boston harbor that would deliver them to the Vice President's residence in New York. All was in readiness -- except for Charly.

He should have been home two days ago -- or at least sent word, Abigail fumed. She was folding a dress into the trunk in her room when she heard a horse pounding up the road. Looking out, she saw Charly, coattails flying, hat stuffed between his thigh and the saddle, clear the crest of the hill and wheel the frothing animal around to stop in front of the stable door.

Furious, relieved, she dropped the dress onto the bed and hurried down the stairs and out the back door toward the stable, her stiff joints objecting all the way. Charly stood beside the horse, holding the reins and laughingly trying to calm the animal. Sweat poured down his flushed face, and he staggered as the horse pulled him off balance. John Breisler came out of the stable and snatched the reins from Charly's hands, soothing the animal.

"There old lad, there, now," Breisler murmured in a deep bass. "No need to git yersel' all lathered, is there? Calm yersel', that's it, calm yersel'."

He looked at Charly scornfully.

"This animal's been run too hard for too long, Master Charles. No animal should be treated with such disregard."

"You're right, John," said Charly. "I was a brute to have galloped him so far. But I was in a lather to come home. Mar'll have my hide."

"I'll have it in any case!" Abigail shouted breathlessly, coming up behind her son. He was taller than she by nearly a head, and slimmer than when she had last seen him. His clothes, covered in dust, looked as though they had been slept in.

"Where've ye been, Charles Adams?" she cried, both fists planted on her hips. "I told ye to return here by the 12th. You're two days late and I've heard not a word from you. I've been worried half out of my mind! What explanation can you offer me?"

Her chin jutted defiantly, as though ready to take whatever blow he would deliver, but she was unprepared for his quiet, almost sober reply.

"And why should two days matter to you, Mar? I was lost for weeks and weeks on the way from The Hague, and did ye worry then? What sort of welcome did I get? Jubilation? NO! 'Ah, It's only Charly come home again. Ah, well, here he is. Time for bed now.'"

She reeled, open-mouthed, as though he had slapped her. Having quieted the horse, John Breisler led the animal through the stable door without a word. Charly had been drinking, of that she was sure. His eyes were bloodshot and his speech, though quiet, was slightly slurred. It is the alcohol talking, she told herself. He cannot hate me so much!

For one long moment, they locked eyes. The rage, drawn from some deep well within him, was written plain across his features. Bewildered, hurt, she stared for a long moment. Finally, she drew a breath

"I was worried about you, Charles," she said finally, not specifying whether she meant during the past two days or during that other time so many years before, when she had tried to make her peace with the loss of her son. "Where have ye been?"

"Clearing up some things at end of term," he answered vaguely, ducking his head as he dusted off his breeches with his hat.

"Did you not think to send word?" she asked, marveling at the steadiness of her voice. She had expected a quiver to run through the words, betraying the terror and hurt she felt.

"No," he replied evenly, looking at her once more. "I did not."

"Charly?" Louisa's soft voice broke the tenseness between mother and son.

She had come out of the house at the sound of the horse and walked to the stable. Despite her reluctance to interfere between her strong-willed aunt and her favorite cousin, she could not contain the joy she felt at his arrival.

"Louisa!" Charly crowed, wrapping his arms around her and swinging her up off her feet. "You are a full woman, now, Cousin!" he cried, a little too loudly. "Mother, what do you feed the girls Braintree that they grow into such beautiful blossoms?"

Louisa allowed herself to be swung up without protest, a shy smile spread across her normally somber features. Abigail watched in silence. A chasm seemed to be opening beneath her son's feet, and she was powerless to stop his fall.

They all left for New York the following morning, their luggage tied onto the carriage like so much flotsam. The ride to Boston, where they left John Breisler with his wife Esther, too sick to come, was nearly silent except for Charly's periodic reassurances to Louisa, an effort to allay her fears of the sea journey from Providence to New York.

He has such a good heart, Abigail reminded herself. He always has -- so willing and kind. Perhaps I am making too much of youthful high spirits. He has less of his father's seriousness, more youth than John Quincy ever had. Perhaps I am too worried. He will outgrow it in time, given more serious and directed pursuits. She willed herself to believe it, but at her heart tugged the memory of Mercy Warren's son Winston, often drunk and brawling.

The Warren boys! she pursed her lips unconsciously. They have had no good influence on my sons. Their roisterous behavior has endeared them to their Harvard classmates, but they have dragged Thomas and Charly into more than one drunken spree.

Abigail had not seen Mercy for several years, though they had continued to correspond. At young Charles Warren's death in Spain, Abigail had sent a letter overflowing with sympathy and sorrow for a mother's loss, but she had since kept Mercy at arm's length.

"Do you remember the day we went aboard the *Adams* and you climbed into the rigging?" Abigail asked suddenly, interrupting Charly who was regaling Louisa with a whispered rendition of the latest bawdy song traveling through the Harvard student body.

"Eh?"

"The day we went into Boston and lunched aboard the *Adams*, Uncle Isaac Smith's frigate," Abigail repeated.

"Oh, yes," Charly agreed distractedly.

"We went with Mercy Warren..."

"Her son has just been arrested for public drunkenness," Charly laughed. "It was lucky I was just a little ahead of him round the corner," he murmured to Louisa who pretended to find it amusing.

Abigail's eyes opened wider and it was on the tip of her tongue to say something disparaging, but she checked herself.

"You do not spend time with the Warren boys any longer, do you?" she asked.

"Time?" Charly asked, winking at Louisa. "Not much. I am busy with my studies, after all."

"You will be busy in Mr. Hancock's office, I warrant," Abigail said, hearing his sarcasm but ignoring it. He is out of my hands, she thought sadly.

The journey to New York was a grueling one for Abigail, although the sail down Narragansett Bay from Providence was glorious. A stiff westerly breeze pushed them along the rock-etched shore and gaps in the trees revealed an occasional house. But once they rounded Point Judith, the breeze came east and the boat rolled and pitched uncomfortably. To Abigail, who lay miserably seasick in her bunk for the entire trip, it seemed that the vessel crawled along the shore, destined never to reach land.

But to her surprise, Charly became her ministering angel. He bathed her head in vinegar and herbs coaxed from the stores of another passenger, spoon-fed her a thick gruel, which she immediately threw up into the basin he held, and read to her. There was more than duty in it. There was love. Despite their disagreements, Charly was a loving person, whose heart was touched with pity for every suffering soul.

Chapter 19

Led Eve, our credulous mother, to the tree of prohibition, root of all our woe
John Milton Paradise Lost Bk IX Line 644

"All ye who will not repent will face hellfire!"
The Congregational minister's voice ended in a squeak that
hinted he was on the verge of tears over his sinning flock. The
Adams pew, five from the pulpit, was full. Nabby and Colonel
Smith had moved from Jamaica, into the Adams's New York house,
Richmond Hill, shortly after Abigail's arrival, an opportunity for the
Colonel, anxious to be placed in government even in the temporary
capital, to be nearer the seats of power. Their two young sons, Willie,
nearly three, and John Adams Smith, one, were sandwiched between
them in the pew. Together, they alternated whispers and threats to
keep the boys subdued. It was the first time both boys had attended
church since little John Adams Smith had recovered from smallpox.
The boys' exuberance at being let out of the house was almost
uncontainable.

Thomas Boylston Adams, seventeen -- on holiday from Harvard
-- had come to New York with his father earlier that December.
Gaunt, he huddled in his coat, bony hands tucked under his armpits
against the cold.

Too much study, too little fresh air and physical labor, Abigail
thought. He is out of balance.

But it was Charly who most concerned her. Nineteen-year-old
Charly, wrapped in a thick greatcoat, sat beside his cousin, Louisa, his
head rocked back slightly on his shoulders, eyes glued dazedly to the
pulpit.

"Our son overdrunk himself last night -- again," Abigail
murmured to John.

"What's that?" John asked a little too loudly. She had jerked
him from a reverie over a Congressional debate, and he had
momentarily forgotten where he was.

"I *said*," hissed Abigail, trying to drag his mind back to his family
and the present, "that Charly has overdrunk himself again. His look

is glazed."

"And whose would not be with this ranting?" John replied indignantly, not bothering to lower his voice and thereby earning the disapproving stares and some vigorous shushing from those within earshot.

They fell silent for a moment until the other churchgoers had returned their attention to the minister.

"Aye, I mislike these bullying, howling sermons as well as you," Abigail finally whispered in agreement, "but we needs must be civil!"

She thought longingly of the reasoned marches through Scripture that always sent the Braintree faithful home with fodder for a quiet day of meditation. This New York Protestantism was a take it or leave it attack, more like a cold water immersion than a call to the Table.

"We must find another church, Mrs. Adams," John mumbled grumpily. "I am subjected to verbal assaults enough in Congress. On Sunday I need peaceful persuasion and spiritual sustenance."

Abigail sighed. A difficult year.

Fifty-four-year-old John was besieged on all sides, and his health suffered. His punishing schedule exacerbated the trembling in his hands and a recurrent pain in his chest that came upon him during Congressional debate. Additionally, Congress had only recently voted him a salary. The amount, John felt, was insulting as well as impractical: less than half the president's annual $25,000 stipend though the position of vice president required just as much entertaining and attendance at formal functions as that of the president.

Never free from financial worries.

Abigail had traded three heifers and ten sheep to Cotton Tufts in exchange for his payment of Charly and Tommy's quarter bill at Harvard. Additionally, she had sold the field John bought on their arrival home from Europe, and sold one of the Vermont tracts that she had bought in the hope of peaceful retirement. She juggled the debts and income with deft skill, but their finances remained on shifting sands. In a black mood over money, John wrote to each of his sons to forget about going into the country's service and instead, learn a trade.

Yet he would not give up his self-appointed position as Protector of the Union. Though as vice president he was forbidden to debate, he alternately lectured the session and engaged in back room politicking, trying to extract compromises that would balance the personal ambition, greed, and jealousy of the regional interests gathered uncomfortably together in Congress. He was beside himself with frustration, but could not desert the new country he had worked so hard to midwife.

The nation commanded his full attention. He was as absent to Abigail's private concerns as if he were still in The Hague. Frustrated at his distraction, she reminded herself that they were nonetheless together. And, though she missed Braintree, she loved *Richmond Hill*, their New York home.

The shabby but expansive old manse sat on a rise on the edge of the city that looked down into the blue-black waters of the Hudson. Surrounded by thickets and hollows, home to a hundred varieties of bird and beast, it offered broad scope for her grandsons' play. Inside, she converted the large second floor hall to a drawing room where she served teas to the senators' wives, held grand dinners, wrote letters, and watched John read to his grandsons.

Having children and grandchildren under her watchful care gave her a sense of purpose. With diligent attention, she might still improve the lives of her children, offer corrective advice, use her experience to prevent her offspring's mistakes. But Nabby, longing for a grand home of her own, chafed. She had exchanged the suffocating bosom of the Smith family on Long Island for her mother's loving, but tenacious grip.

The minister finished his sermon by sending the collection plate around for the second time, much to John's chagrin.

"I'll not be fleeced again," he grumbled as the plate made its way up and down the full pews. "If we were paying for the quality of the sermon, I should ask for my offering back."

"SHHH!" Abigail warned, taking the plate over John's objections and quietly passing it on without adding anything to it. "Ye have not the luxury of considering nothing for the opinions of your fellow men."

The minister dismissed the congregation with a final blessing and stern warning for the week ahead. Rising, the Adams family joined the stream of people shuffling out the front door under the pastor's baleful eye.

"And how should I shake his hand after that?" John snorted.

"You will shake his hand as a Christian and a man of reason, if nothing more," Abigail replied, exasperated. "It is not necessary for you to love him to wish him well."

"Like that self-salesman Mr. Hancock who spews insincere compliments far and wide? " John retorted.

"You need not pour forth compliments in order to be civil. And as far as that goes, you have had your own back on Mr. Hancock," Abigail reminded him.

Hancock had given a dinner in President Washington's honor, but neglected to invite John until the last minute, an oversight -- or intentional slight -- that John could not forgive. John had accepted but had not gone as a deliberate insult to his host. When he later ran into Hancock in the streets of Boston, he had tendered neither apology nor explanation and did not offer to shake the man's hand, a gesture one step removed from a slap in the face.

"I could *not* have gone to his home and smiled and conversed civilly all the while knowing that Hancock wishes to set himself up as monarch of Massachusetts," John replied, somewhat more quietly. "I might have openly insulted him. I did not wish to be the cause of an ugly scene in the house of my host, especially with President Washington in attendance. Hancock tries to build a kingdom in Massachusetts. He uses the representatives to further his power, but I cannot help him there so I am no use. Blast the man. The union is so fragile. He could fracture it with his demands."

John's anger at Hancock was political, but it was personal, too. He had once, despite Abigail's mistrust, considered Hancock a friend, and could forgive neither a betrayal, nor his own misjudgment.

"Hancock is not the only friend who is not a friend, to us or to the union," Abigail replied.

"Mistress Warren's machinations and treatises will have far less effect on the nation than will Hancock's bid for power," John said flatly. "And it turned out that she did not write that scurrilous poem."

"Nevertheless, she has been heard to speak against you. She has openly doubted your intentions, your integrity," Abigail retorted. "I could forgive her, perhaps, but I could never trust again."

In truth, I cannot forgive, she thought. There are too many things, the influence of her corrupted boys, her condescension, her slights. I thought we were friends.

When John reached the church door, the minister reached out his hand, his lips stretched into an unnatural smile in an effort to hide his anger.

"Ye were in competition with me for the attention of the congregation, Mr. Adams."

"Not competition," John retorted, ignoring the hand that hung between them. "Deafened, merely, by the tinkling cymbal and sounding gong."

The minister opened his mouth to reply, but John passed on. Coloring, Abigail quickly shook the hand that still dangled like a day-old cod and followed John down the brick walk toward their carriage. Charly, who had come out of the church behind his parents, stifled a laugh at his father's irascible exchange with the preacher. With barely suppressed rage, the minister cursorily continued through the line of Adamses, only defrosting when he reached the next family.

"Par really let him have it, didn't he?" Charly sniggered to Tommy and Louisa as they went down the walk three abreast.

"Don't let Par hear you," Tommy warned. "His temper is as bad as I've ever known it. The whole way down from Braintree he shouted at the horses and swore over what he termed the fools and blockheads in Congress."

"It's Mar I need to steer clear of," Charly said, dropping his voice. "She's on a rampage about my drinking. I don't see as I drink any more than Par does. Why, he starts the day with hard cider and small beer and continues from there."

"But Par never, ever, loses his head," Tommy reminded him. "He would never have been caught pissing right in front of Mrs. Quincy's house the way you were."

Charly turned to his brother with a sharp intake of breath, but held his tongue. Louisa, eyes on her feet, pretended not to hear.

"Mar would be scandalized," Tommy continued, baiting his brother.

Charly opened his mouth to bite, but Louisa took each young man by the arm and, with forced gaiety, deliberately changed the subject.

Abigail and John climbed into their carriage. Taking up the reins, John waited sullenly for Nabby and Col. Smith to climb in with their sons.

"Gammar! Gammar!" young Willie Smith cried as he scrambled

up into the carriage, "Papa's takin' me hunting today!"

"Hunting?" Abigail snorted. "You are far too young. And on Sunday? It is not fitting."

"Surely that is for his parents to decide?" Colonel Smith replied evenly.

"You may not kill my birds, Colonel Smith, " Abigail retorted, her tone acerbic, "and most especially not on a Sunday."

"Did the lad say we were planning to kill *your* birds, Madam? I have had an invitation from our neighbors, the Palmers, to come shooting this afternoon. It would pleasure me to take my son. I was his age when I was introduced to the manly sport. Now it is his turn."

"I do not approve," Abigail pronounced. "Nabby, do you hear what your husband has planned for your little William?"

Nabby looked long and sharp at her mother before replying through pursed lips.

"Colonel Smith may surely decide for himself what is best for his sons."

She is defending a decision she does not approve, Abigail decided.

"They are your sons, too, Nabby. You have let your husband and his mother spoil these boys too long. You have a say in their raising."

"Then I say let their father have charge of them," Nabby replied curtly, and turned to look over the fields and sparkling waters of the sound to the blue slab of Long Island.

Abigail was jolted at Nabby's defection. The following week, the Smiths moved out of *Richmond Hill*. In letters to friends and family, Abigail explained the move as the result of the cramped living quarters, but she was cut to the quick and mourned losing the daily oversight of her darling grandsons.

If the Smiths were gone from the household, they were not gone from the fold. Invitations to the Vice President and his wife often included Colonel and Mrs. Smith as well as their niece Louisa Smith and Tommy and Charly when they were in residence. Only twenty-three-year old John Quincy remained outside the New York social swirl. In Newburyport during his final year studying law with Theophilus Parsons, John Quincy was, much to his parents' chagrin,

264

busy falling in love with sixteen-year-old Mary Frazier.

"He cannot think to marry the girl!" Abigail insisted as she bustled through the house with Louisa Smith close on her heels.

"But Aunt," Louisa said gently, picking up the pieces of paper that were slipping out of Abigail's basket of note cards. "John Quincy has not yet mentioned anything of marriage in his letters, has he?"

Her breath made ghosts in the chill hallway. The dozen fires barely took the edge off the penetrating cold of the dim February day.

"No, not to us, but I hear from others..."

"Then you need not fear," Louisa interrupted calmly. "John Quincy would never marry without your and Uncle John's permission. You must know that."

She caught up to Abigail, and laying a hand on her aunt's arm, looked her full in the face.

"Johnny is far too young to consider such a step," Abigail repeated, flushed with anxiety and exertion. "Why, he is only just now finished his study of the law. His practice is not even yet begun. We do not yet know his prospects; to be sure his possibilities are great, but one cannot count chickens before they hatch. He cannot bind himself in marriage, with children perhaps soon to follow. He cannot afford it."

"Does not the same prudent and caring son you raised know this?" Louisa asked reasonably. "He cannot help what he feels, but he will not *act* without your approbation."

Abigail smiled. If we could not save brother William's sons, at least we could save this daughter.

"You have a hand that smoothes troubled waters," Abigail said. "I shall miss you sorely when a young man comes to carry you away."

"I doubt that shall happen, Aunt," Louisa replied, a little wistfully.

She did not miss the trace of relief that flitted for a second over Abigail's face.

"Nonsense!" Abigail cried, her ebullience an inadequate mask for her thoughts. "There will be a young man sooner than you think."

Neither was fooled.

By August, the government was packing in preparation for the move from New York to Philadelphia while the new national capital city, the result of a compromise hammered out between the northern and southern factions in Congress, was being built on the Potomac. New Yorkers were in mourning. Their population was already less than the 40,000 souls in Philadelphia; they feared that New York would wither and die once the lucrative bustle of government was gone.

The receiving line snaked out the hall and into the road. Invitations to the President's farewell ball had been as coveted as pieces of gold. It was a last chance for the famous and infamous of New York to see and be seen. Sweating in their thick finery, they filed like communicants past President and Mrs. Washington and Vice President and Mrs. Adams. Broad smiles diminished noticeably once guests passed the Washingtons and moved on to greet the Adamses. As vice president, John could neither further a career, nor grant a favor. His position, as he often complained to Abigail, was as fettered as that of a draft horse. He plodded, unable to determine the course or alter the speed of events. It gnawed at his pride.

But despite his frustration, he loved being surrounded by the chatter and burble. Each state occasion was new, a precedent set for future generations. Together, they were making history for the new country. Abigail too was enjoying the splendor of the evening. It was a visible sign of how far her husband -- and she -- had come from their provincial roots. Even Grandfather Quincy had not traveled in such wide circles, had not seen such sights as they had seen, taken part in such momentous decisions. If she was forced to play Portia, to defend her husband from the spiteful accusations of the envious, she could also bask in his prominence. The position had been paid for with long years of sacrifice and hard work, with each twinge of rheumatism as a reminder of the cost.

At forty-five, she felt and looked like an old woman. Her body had thickened. Dizziness, frequent headaches and erratic monthly blood all foretold change of life.

I will not be sorry to be free of the fear of childbirth, she thought. Betsey Shaw, a new mother at forty -- and to such a large baby -- healthy thank God, but too dangerous. I have enough worries. My children are growing up. Yet, somehow, I never

266

imagined they would grow away.

And Nab. My Nab. We were such friends. Now her letters reveal nothing, accept nothing. There is no exchange of hearts, no confidences between us. And in the widening breech stands Colonel Smith. He demands all of his wife's attention and devotion. Too many babies too soon. He is too passionate; he knows no restraint.

She would not accept that Nabby was a willing partner in that passion.

Though her husband was gone much of the time now, Nabby had had three sons within four years. Her rosy face had taken on a gray pallor; her body, thickened with childbearing, was stuffed into clothes that no longer fit her. And she rarely smiled. There seemed to be no joy in her life.

On the surface, it could have been the same marriage that Abigail and John had had in the beginning. The separations, the swift increase of responsibilities, the struggle to make a name and a place, to fulfill a destiny. But beneath the similarities, there was a difference. It was John's abilities -- not his charm -- that had made their way, his principles and his work, not a glib tongue that had earned his place. John was a middle class Yankee through and through. Smith was an aristocrat without a fiefdom.

Abigail could imagine Nabby's loneliness -- Smith's job as a marshal seemed to keep him away but never brought home any money -- and the shame of being unable to keep up with the people in her social circle. But it was not until she stopped to see the new baby, Thomas Hollis, that she saw the mire into which her daughter had sunk.

Coming in the door, she was hit by the stench of childbirth, unwashed linen, and a full chamber pot. The larder was nearly empty. Colonel Smith, the maid informed her, had been gone these ten days. There was no money for food. He had not yet seen his new son. It had twisted Abigail's stomach to see his neglect, but she was determined to hold her tongue when she saw her daughter.

Still weak from the birth, Nabby reclined in her bed on pillows, her face gray beneath the flush of her cheeks, her pinched look a mixture of determination and fear. Abigail smiled and cooed over the baby, who lay like a Botticelli cherub under the gifts of Smith family linen that Nabby received from her mother-in-law. Abigail pretended not to notice the shabbiness of the room, the ragged, unwashed bedding. Just before leaving, she stocked the pantry with apples and hams, cheese and butter bought from a local farmer, a gesture she and Nabby could both pretend she had not made.

Now, standing beside Martha Washington, Abigail's stomach somersaulted again when she thought of Nabby and her grandsons. As they waited for the late-arriving guests to make their way up the long stairs to the ballroom and through the receiving line, Martha Washington smiled at Abigail across the expanse of John Adams' brocaded vest.

"It seems even those whose sentiments are against the move to Philadelphia have condescended to join us tonight," Martha Washington observed.

Abigail raised an eyebrow and scanned the ballroom. Women dressed in the latest European fashions adorned with jewelry that sparkled in the candlelight mingled with those wearing carefully reworked draperies and fashions that had been ten years out of date. To save money, increasingly more people were going out without wigs, even to the most formal occasions, preferring instead to powder their own hair. The economic downturn had taken its toll on the pocketbooks of wealthy and poor alike. The revolution that had brought political independence had not produced the prosperity so many had hoped.

With a few exceptions. Washington's household was, Abigail noted with a mixture of admiration and envy, well appointed. Glasses, serving pieces, food, all were plentiful and of the best quality. But, as she saw a serving girl stop to surreptitiously swig from one of the glasses on her tray, she felt a certain satisfaction that even the Washingtons were saddled with drunken servants.

The receiving line ended and John immediately excused himself to corner John MacClay, leaving Martha and Abigail standing side by side, surveying the scene like two generals assessing the progress of a great battle. Martha opened a fan of lace-cut ivory and waved it gracefully before her face as she watched yet another servant stagger from the kitchen under a haunch of roast venison.

"Do you suppose the servants in Philadelphia will have the New York disease?" Abigail asked, following Martha's gaze to the young man who, after laying the venison on the table, had taken a glass of punch and downed it in one gulp before exiting again.

"New York disease?"

"Drunkenness."

"Ah. Aptly put. I certainly hope not, Mrs. Adams," Martha replied, frowning. "It has been such a trial to hover over their every move for fear of their purloining silver or breaking glasses. We do not have such problems in Virginia."

A slave will fear to do what a paid servant will dare, Abigail thought, but said only, "I am hopeful that in a Quaker community, the standards of behavior will be higher."

Catching a movement by the punch bowl, she saw Charly, powdered blond head bent toward a young woman whose back was turned toward them. She breathed a sigh of relief when she saw that he held no glass in his hand.

"I am moving closer to my children and grandchildren," Martha remarked. "But the change will put more miles between you and your family. It will be hard for you, I believe."

Abigail nodded, her eyes still on her son. "One needs must let the young ones go, but it is such a world that we often wonder if we have adequately prepared them for what they will face."

"No parent raises a perfect child. But the apple does not fall far from the tree. Of that I am convinced. Your children come from sturdy oaks, Mrs. Adams."

"It is kind of you to say so, Madam," Abigail said, turning to look the older woman in the face. "I find myself wishing two things at once: to see my chicks well launched from our nest and for them to remain with me."

Martha chuckled then followed Abigail's involuntary glance toward the punch bowl.

"Your Charly has begun to show signs of maturity of late," Martha remarked. "Perhaps a woman's gentle touch?"

The hint that Charly's behavior had been noticeably errant, coupled with the suggestion that its improvement could be attributed to a young woman's influence, stung Abigail. Particularly as the young woman was Colonel Smith's younger sister.

"Sally Smith is very young. I wonder if she has the strength of character to influence him," Abigail responded. "She is a fine girl, of that there is no doubt," she added hastily. "But they are both young. There is time enough for him to be influenced, as you say, by a woman."

"Indeed," Martha replied, noting but not remarking upon

Abigail's sudden sharpness. "Do I understand that Charly is to stay in New York?"

"Yes. He is boarding with Colonel Smith and our daughter while he pursues his law career. I hope the bustle of a household does not distract him too much."

"Or the beauty of a young sister-in-law?" Martha murmured.

"Indeed."

"Perhaps the comfortable situation of a family will be more support than distraction," Martha said. "A young single man may fall into so many unwholesome ways."

Abigail looked across the room to where Charly stood, head bent close to Sally's, laughing conspiratorially.

"Perhaps."

Chapter 20

*Fame, if not double-faced, is double-mouthed and with contrary blast proclaim
most deeds*
John Milton Samson Agonistes line 971

1791

Charles Adams did indeed mature in New York. His
responsibility, his widening circle of friends and contacts, his
circumspection and generous nature were all lauded in Nabby's
autumn letters to her father and mother in Philadelphia. Abigail was
relieved.

Though she complained of her children's leaving, her household
was still full of family. In addition to Louisa, Tommy had come to
Philadelphia to serve his law apprenticeship. Additionally, to lighten
Nabby's burdens, Abigail and John had brought her second child,
three-year-old John Adams Smith, to live with them. Handsome,
precocious, he could be as charming as his father, the Colonel -- and
as high-handed. His favorite game was to play "Fosses" with his
grandfather. Often, after dinner, Abigail would find John hitched to
the boy's dinner chair. Johnny Smith drove the aging Vice President
of the United States all over the living room, shouting "Go foss, go
foss!" while the chair's legs scratched up the floors and dragged the
rugs into knots. If servants looked askance at little Johnny Smith's
tyranny, his grandparents did not. It was a delight to have a
grandchild in the house. There were other considerations besides the
rugs.

Invitations and social obligations rained down on them as soon
as they arrived at *Bush House* outside Philadelphia. A regiment of
callers began to arrive before the paint was even dry on the walls.
Added to that, the entire household came down with a variety of
illnesses.

Bush House was naked to the wind and weather on a hill
overlooking the Schuylkill River, a mere muddy creek compared with
the magnificent Hudson. The land had been all but stripped of trees
during the British occupation. Heating the tall-ceilinged rooms was a

constant chore. The fireplaces consumed forty cords of wood their first winter.

Christmas of 1790 brought Charly from New York and John Quincy from Boston, but the holidays were subdued. Abigail, still battling an intermittent fever, spent part of each day in bed. Tommy, who had been nearly crippled with rheumatism, lived in a reading chair beside the fire. And though John Quincy and Charly were there in body, they seemed absent in spirit. Despite his having severed the relationship, John Quincy's heart remained in Newburyport with Mary Frazier, and Charly yearned to be back in New York on his own. Abigail missed Nabby and her other grandsons. Their lives seemed fractured, out of tune.

In the spring of 1791, Abigail persuaded John to go home. She wanted to renew herself. Blessed time away from the constant demands of public life. Long conversations with Mary and Richard Cranch, walks through the orchard and gardens, visits with old friends, all cloaked in the familiar scents of barnyard and salt air; it all promised a longed-for sense of peace. She contacted her Massachusetts managers with instructions. The tenants of their Braintree home were to move to other lodgings. Mary Cranch was instructed to buy kitchen utensils, cooking pots, and tools, and have tables and beds made.

Though the Philadelphia weather was mercurial -- an eighty-degree day in March was followed by a northwest snowstorm, a change that worked cruelly on her joints -- and Tommy was still unwell, the thought of home lifted her flagging spirits.

Braintree, Summer 1791

"The trees are setting a very nice crop of apples this year," John informed Abigail as he came through the back door.

The fragrance of mock orange clung to him as he pitched his hat onto the table and flopped down in the chair farthest from the low fire that burned in the hearth. The summer had so far compensated for Philadelphia. Warm weather and rain had brought a profusion of blooms. The earth smelled rich, fecund. Inside, the air was spiced with the scent of mugwort and tansy, vervain and sage and juniper that hung drying from the ceilings.

"I wonder you don't have Jeremiah make up the fire outside

instead of heating the kitchen," John remarked, drawing a bare forearm across his sweaty brow.

"Pheby prefers to be indoors out of the sun, even in the heat of summer," Abigail replied, going to the pantry and pouring a mug of ale for John. "I have had so many vexations from the cooks in southern parts, I am willing to accommodate the whims of a good one."

She handed John the mug, then folded her arms across her chest as she looked at his flushed face.

"You are pensive Mr. Adams. Pray, what is on your mind?"

"I was mourning the loss of a friend," he said quietly, looking out the kitchen window to where the yard cast down into a hollow toward the orchard.

The apple trees glowed green in the sunlight.

Abigail cocked her head and put her hands on her hips. "Mr. Jefferson?"

He nodded. "If he had not sent that second letter..."

"Mr. Jefferson cannot admit his own ambition," Abigail snapped. "He pays much lip service to his own reluctance for office, yet he curries support for himself and his views. And he sacrifices your honor in the scramble. That, I cannot forgive."

In the spring of 1791, James Madison enthusiastically sent Jefferson a copy of Thomas Paine's unpublished new pamphlet, *The Rights of Man'* with instructions to read it then send it on to the Philadelphia publisher. Jefferson, then Secretary of State, was delighted with it. Paine's idealistic reliance on reason and education to produce the best of all possible governments coincided with Jefferson's optimism about mankind in general. But it contrasted sharply with John Adams's belief that men, craven by nature, required subduing. Though the disagreement was born of differences in temperament, the two men viewed it as a battle for the soul of the republic.

After reading the pamphlet, Jefferson had sent it to the publisher with a note explaining why the copy was coming from him rather than its author, Paine. He added that it was good to see a rebuttal of certain 'political heresies' that had recently sprung up, a none-too-veiled reference to John Adams's *Discourses on Davila* and what many viewed as John's persistent monarchical bent. The publisher used Jefferson's private note as the book's very public forward.

To John, it was betrayal. Jefferson had been a confidante, privy to John's inner-most thoughts and internal debates. That his trusted, much-valued friend could distrust him and his motives was a wound that went through John's soul.

John Quincy, zealous for family pride, took up his father's defense in a series of articles published under the name *Publicola*. But rather than restoring John's reputation, they fanned the fires. A faction bent on replacing John Adams with John Hancock as Vice President then took up the fight. In the midst of this published feeding frenzy, Jefferson wrote John a long conciliatory letter, vowing that he had not wished his remark to be public, that he had always considered their disagreements to be honorable and private.

John, anxious to reconcile, returned a letter assuring Jefferson that the friendship was intact. But Jefferson's second letter blamed *Publicola* – and unknowingly John Quincy -- for unnecessarily keeping the dispute before the public, an accusation John could not swallow. He refused to reply. The ranks of John's friends were thinning noticeably; he mourned each desertion.

"I do not believe he meant for his remarks to be printed," John said wearily. "But he believed them, that is what rankles. That he could know me so well, and yet believe me to be so grasping of power, so calculating, so utterly devoid of concern for my country and its government! I have spoken my mind most freely to him and yet he misunderstands me. It is painful."

"For all his southern charm, Jefferson is not without striving. He would make himself a name, and do it by climbing over you, if necessary. Many would. Hancock..." she said, but John snorted dismissively. She paused and continued in another vein. "You have worked hard to ensure the health of our new government. Small minds do not see it. And they may never. The public is a fickle mistress. But God knows your sacrifice. And He knows your heart. You cannot trust in the hearts of men."

For all the years of service and sacrifice, we shall reap only bitterness, she thought. Yet we have done our duty and shall be vindicated in heaven if not on earth. Small recompense down here, but something.

John looked at his wife, whose face had gone red during her speech. She will never let me down. It is comforting to have that much ensured in this life, he thought.

"The public may be a fickle mistress, my dear, but you have ever been a faithful one to old John Adams."

He reached a plump arm around her waist and pulled her to his side, patting her rump affectionately. The door flew open and little Johnny Adams Smith marched in, pushed himself between his grandparents, and climbed up on his grandfather's lap.

"Jeremiah will not do as I say!" he cried, round face flushed in fury.

John chuckled indulgently. "And what is it that you say he must do?"

"I want him to hitch up a foss so I can drive the carriage round to the front. And he won't. He must do as I say. He's only a black boy."

Abigail started.

"And what makes you say so?" she asked, her voice low.

"It's true, ain't it? He's only a dumb black boy and he's our servant and must do as I say."

"Jeremiah is a servant, not a slave," Abigail snapped, hands on hips as she leaned closer to the frowning face of her grandson. "He is not dumb, but quite clever, and he does not take orders from spoilt little boys."

Johnny folded plump arms over his chest and stuck his chin out defiantly.

"I say he must!"

"Well you are wrong, my boy!" She snatched him off John's lap and smacked his backside several times before pushing him off toward the hallway. "You go upstairs to your bed and do not come down until I call you."

Instead of crying, the four-year-old looked momentarily stunned, then, his face becoming a mask of intractable fury, glared at his grandmother.

"Get yourself up there right now, John Adams Smith before I take a switch to you!" Abigail bellowed, pointing in the direction of the hallway that led to the boy's little upstairs bedroom.

Johnny looked for a long moment at his grandfather, debating whether or not to try to enlist his help, but John Adams carefully studied the spider that wove her web in the corner of the window. No help there. Unrepentant, Johnny turned and stomped off toward the stairs.

"He grows more difficult as he grows older," Abigail remarked, her face still set angrily.

"He is just a child, Abigail. Life will temper his temper and mend his ways for him," John said mildly.

"You would never have said so had that been your son rather than your grandson. I think you are too soft on the boy."

"I will not live forever," John replied. "I would have my own flesh and blood love me if the public never will."

Abigail sighed. While she understood John's reluctance to discipline Johnny, the boy was becoming almost more than she could handle. She laid the blame for the boy's insidious notions of inborn superiority entirely at Cololnel Smith's doorstep.

On their way back to Philadelphia that September, they returned Johnny Smith to Nabby's care. Colonel Smith was once again away, this time in England. He was, Nabby assured her parents, making powerful acquaintances in hopes of securing for himself an appointment to the Court of St. James, a fitting post for the son-in-law of the first American Ambassador to Britain.

Though he sent home glowing reports, Colonel Smith was passed over for the position in favor of William Short, a friend of John Quincy's. Furious, he blamed his father-in-law. Still determined to improve his fortunes and position, he returned to America and persuaded a group of wealthy New Yorkers to back him in yet another get rich quick scheme, a speculative business to sell western land to the English. Becoming the sole agent, he was to return to England for several years. But this time, if only to spite his parents-in-law, he wanted Nabby and the boys to accompany him. Nabby, reluctant to leave her few friends in America, nonetheless dutifully made plans.

"I cannot but believe that the emetics and leeches are only weakening her," Nabby said, fists on hips in unconscious echo of her mother.

Before leaving for London, she was visiting her parents, who were once again at *Bush Hill* in Philadelphia for the Congressional session. To her horror, she found her mother too weak to leave her bed, bled and purged every other day by Dr. Benjamin Rush.

Nabby leaned closer to her father, who was bent over a book on the desk in his study. Haggard from lack of sleep, John reluctantly peered at his daughter. He felt inadequate to make decisions of the domestic sort. Accustomed to haranguing Abigail from a distance on matters about the farm, he realized he was lost without her councils. He needed her flint against which to strike.

"Your mother has great confidence in Dr. Rush," he repeated, but his voice lacked conviction. "And he is my friend. I would not wish to offend him by calling in another method of cure."

"You must decide who is more important, Par," Nabby persisted. "Mar or Dr. Rush. She has been ill for weeks. I have no doubt of his fidelity, but I question his method. You can see for yourself that his cures serve only to weaken her. She is unable to rise for a day or more after each of his bleedings. It cannot mean he is helping. She needs to husband her strength, not be continually depleted."

Nabby had grown more agitated with each point in her argument and finished by leaning forward, palms on his desk.

"It is this infernal Philadelphia weather," John responded, dodging his daughter's prodding. "Three quarters of the year we must either melt or freeze. I have never known winters so hard in New England. There is something here that seeps into one's bones and takes hold. The climate, I fear does not agree with your mother."

"I agree, but that is not the point at this precise moment. How can I go to England wondering all the while whether your letter informing me of Mar's death will soon follow?"

John started as though she had slapped him.

"I do not believe it is as serious as that!"

"No? LOOK at her, Par! Her skin hangs about her -- our Mar who was *never* slim! Her face is gray. She cannot rise. I cannot but believe, with only good intent, that he is hastening her end!"

John was jolted. His usually long-suffering daughter had never spoken to him this way before, and it frightened him. From the porch, pounding footsteps approached, then the front door burst open admitting his grandsons William and Johnny Smith, followed close on their heels by their little brother, two-year-old Thomas Hollis.

"Mama! Mama!" five-year-old William shouted. "Johnny's teasin' Tom. He says he's gonna throw him in the muck pile if he don't stop followin' us."

"I am not! And besides, he's bein' a pest!" Johnny countered angrily.

Little Thomas Hollis toddled up to his mother, arms up, wailing.

Angry at being interrupted, Nabby picked up her youngest son and slung him on her hip, murmuring "hush, hush" as she scowled at the two older boys. "Where is your father?"

"I don't know," William said, chastened at her tone.

"He's gone down to look at a hoss, I fink," Johnny answered.

"Gone down where?"

"Don't know," Johnny shrugged.

"You boys will wake Gammar with all your shouting. She needs her rest. Here. Take Thomas Hollis with you to see if Jeremiah has come back with the wagon."

"I don' want to!" Johnny whined.

Thomas Hollis clung to his mother's shoulder in anticipation of being put down with his bullying older brother again.

"None of that," Nabby said sternly, when she felt the child dig in his fingers. "I must speak with your grandfather. Johnny, you will be kind to your little brother or I shall cut a birch whip tonight and show you what kind of harvest disobedient little boys reap. Now go outside, all of you."

"Yes, Mama," William said quietly, his head slightly bowed.

"But Mama...!" Johnny began plaintively.

"I mean it, John Adams Smith. Do not make me more cross than I am at this moment. If you value your skin, do as I say without argument."

"Come on," William whispered, tugging at his brother's sleeve.

"Here, Thomas. William will look after you," Nabby said gently, putting the boy on the floor firmly and disentangling his fingers from her clothes.

"Mama!"

"William, take your brother's hand, there, that's right. Now outside all of you, and don't shout so. Gammar needs her rest."

The three boys turned reluctantly and marched outside again, banging the front door behind them and muttering about the unfairness of life. John had watched the exchange, seen the look of exhausted resolution on his daughter's face. She is worn, he thought. Perhaps all is not well with them.

"You must find another doctor, Par," Nabby began again.

"Your brothers have not expressed distrust of Dr. Rush," John faltered.

"My brothers are not here," Nabby retorted. "Par, you cannot let friendship stand in the way of Mar's health."

John hesitated, then said almost meekly: "I will consult with your mother. She should have her say."

"She will say that she loves Dr. Rush, I have no doubt," Nabby replied disdainfully. "It does not mean that his ministrations are effecting her cure. Par, I cannot stay and nurse her myself. Colonel Smith has arranged for us to leave for England in two weeks' time. I have heard countless good reports of Dr. Physick. At least see what he has to say about her condition. Promise me that."

John sighed deeply.

"I will consider it, Nab," he muttered finally.

"Good," Nabby said, convinced she had won her point. "That will rest my mind."

Nabby prevailed. In the end, fearful of his daughter's uncharacteristically dire predictions, John had sent for Dr. Physick, a noted Philadelphia surgeon, who prescribed healthful herbs and decoctions, but forbade purgings and bleedings. With the onset of spring, Abigail was able to take the air once more and recovered more of her strength. But, certain that the Philadelphia climate was the culprit, and unwilling to repeat the experience, she decided not to return with John after their spring pilgrimage home. In September, John left for bachelor quarters in Philadelphia, while she stayed in Massachusetts.

"He said to tell you it was for the Duchess of Braintree," Mary Cranch said, smiling as she laid a basket on the table. A large halibut stuck out from beneath its newspaper wrapping, mouth and glistening eyes wide as though it were desperate to get a glimpse of its new surroundings. "He pulled it from the sea this morning."

"How generous are our neighbors!"

Abigail sat in the east-facing drawing room in a shaft of sunlight. She was too stiff to curl her feet under her as she had done as a child and instead, rested on a footstool covered with a light rug. When did her limbs grow so unyielding?

The day was clear and warm, filled with birdsong, and the faint echo of George clanging away on the anvil by the barn where he made ready to shoe the horse. A cart clattered by outside, its wheels a single contemplative reminder of bustling Philadelphia.

"Indeed. The neighbors are kind," Mary said, smiling as she pulled off the kid gloves Abigail had sent her from New York. "But your largess reaps its rewards. There are many hereabouts who were always mournful at your departure. You send a basket when the neighbors are in need, remember their troubles. They find it good to have their old Mrs. Adams back."

"Old Mrs. Adams, Eh?"

"Oh, Abigail, you know I did not mean..."

"No. I know. I merely tease you, Sister. We are both old grandmothers several times over. But I feel younger in Braintree."

Abigail sucked in a deep breath of air and with it the rich perfume of spring in bloom. She looked out the window to the trees that cast quivering shadows over the dirt road in front of the house. A rabbit scampered out of a hollow and darted underneath a thicket of wild brambles. Boston Harbor was obscured by mists and by the newly built houses that dotted what had not long before been unbroken forest and field.

"Braintree has changed somewhat in these past years," Abigail remarked.

"'Tis no longer Braintree," Mary reminded her.

The council had voted that spring to break the parish in half. The south parish in which John's mother, Susanna, now eighty, still lived retained the name Braintree, while the north parish had been named Quincy after Mary and Abigail's grandfather Colonel John Quincy -- no small source of pride.

Mary untied her bonnet and put her gloves inside its crown before laying it on the table. "How does it feel to have moved from Braintree to Quincy without having shifted your furnishings?"

"It is the simplest move I have made in my life so far," Abigail laughed. "It is also satisfying to have it named for Grandfather. Nice to be so closely connected to such an illustrious man."

"You are married to an illustrious man," Mary said. "The time will come when things are named for John Adams."

"It is hard to imagine it," Abigail replied acidly. "There are many who have no love for the Adamses."

"No one is universally loved," Mary reminded her gently.

"Especially no one in public life."

"But to have Washington run again for office unopposed yet have so many trying to take John's place in the vice-presidency is a sharp thorn indeed. Why may not John Adams run unopposed for *his* office? It is a slap."

A honeybee flew by the window and stopped to sip nectar from the stray honeysuckle vine that climbed up the side of the clapboard house, the buzzing of his wings audible in the quiet room.

"John is contemplating keeping bees," Abigail murmured as she watched the creature hover, its attention completely absorbed by the flower.

How wonderful to have but one purpose in life, she thought as she watched the bee, and to know when your job is well done!

"He could be happy were he to come home," Mary observed, carefully avoiding the word *lose*, "John loves being the country farmer."

"Yes," Abigail replied, looking at Mary. "But only for a time. He buys fields when we cannot rent out the ones we own, tends his trees and his manure piles, but public affairs are his meat. He cannot stay happily away from the center. He must be part of the decisions, see to it that they are well made. Then it falls to me to shore up the Adams finances, scouring the countryside for tenants."

"John was ever a visionary, Abigail," Mary said. "You have been the practical one. A good match, a real partnership."

Abigail beamed. Her marriage, for all the sacrifices, had indeed been the union she had prayed for in her youth. If it had been hard, if the time apart had been stolen from their personal joys, she had reaped a marriage that was the envy of many who had sacrificed less.

"I think all the Smith girls made good matches," Abigail replied, trying not to sound smug.

Mary smiled, remembering Abigail's early opposition to Betsey's husband Mr. Shaw.

"Tell me the news, Mary. What of our friends and neighbors?"

Mary came across the room to pull a chair from its place by the southern window and sit down, her skirts gently rustling over its sides.

"You probably have as much news as I. Cousin Sam Adams came by and stopped for a night last week."

"What did he say?" Abigail asked, eyes narrowing.

Mary looked guardedly at her sister, trying to calculate her thoughts. Abigail had begun to see opposition and enemies around every corner.

"He is well...." she began.

"Sam Adams has roused people against John. And wrongly, wrongly," Abigail said a little feverishly, shaking her head. "John holds the selfsame opinions as he did from the beginning. He has not changed. It hurts him that Cousin Sam has been heard to speak in the taverns as though John is a traitor to the government."

"Methinks Cousin Sam's grasp of the details of government is not so strong as John's," Mary said soothingly. "Sam Adams sees things painted in broad strokes. There is a time for that and then a time for attention to detail -- John's specialty. Sam Adams still rouses the masses, but he shouts in part out of habit. He is no longer clear what he cries against. But it is not against his cousin, John Adams, the man. Sam Adams still loves John. I told him you would be home soon. He has promised to call. He and John will smooth their differences, never fear."

"Always the peacemaker, Mary," Abigail said. "I have not your gift for gentle persuasion."

"There is another who wishes to make a visit as soon as your health allows," Mary began, avoiding her sister's eyes. "Mercy Warren has written asking when you will be home, and asked particularly to know when you would be receiving."

"Has she?" Abigail raised one eyebrow.

The day thirteen years before when she and Mercy had visited the *Adams* anchored in Boston Harbor came flooding back to her mind. How close were we then. How treasured and trusted a friend was Mrs. Mercy Warren. But things change, or perhaps times change us.

"I have not seen her," Abigail murmured, "since before her son Charles died, and Winston ..."

Winston had been embroiled in one scandal after another. Most recently he was being pursued for a $2,000 debt and had attacked and caned his pursuer. The result was a lawsuit against him for assault and battery. Mercy refused to acknowledge her son's dishonesty, blaming the accusations instead on the ignorance of his accusers.

"She wants to renew the old ties," Mary prodded.

"She wishes to reach the ear of Vice President Adams, possibly gain a post for a son, not renew old ties with me," Abigail said cynically.

"There was a time when you were the dearest of friends," Mary reminded her.

"There has been much water over that dam," Abigail replied, cutting off any more discussion.

Mary sighed and let the matter drop.

"Where is my Elizabeth gone to?" Mary said finally. "I asked her to find Pheby and have her cook this fish."

As though in answer to her summons, the door to the drawing room opened and a tall, slim young woman with lustrous brown eyes and brown hair entered.

"And how are you feeling, Aunt?" she asked, coming to peck Abigail on the cheek before going to the table and picking up the basket.

"Tolerable well, my dear. Where are your children?"

"I left them with Pa in the post office. I thought I would come out with Mar for a while without having anyone hanging onto my apron strings," she laughed.

"Do not complain of those light burdens," Abigail said, forgetting the constant cares of small children in her longing to be younger. "It is over all too soon."

"Perhaps," Elizabeth acknowledged, "but there are times when it seems unending. Would you like tea, Mother? Pheby is fixin' to make a pot."

"Yes, Elizabeth. The Smith girls shall take tea together," replied Mary.

"Yes," Abigail agreed. "As it was in the old days. All we need now is sister Betsey Shaw."

Chapter 21

Before mine eyes on opposition sits Grim Death, my son and foe."
Paradise Lost Book II Line 803

1792

The November election was heatedly fought. John was attacked unceasingly by Jefferson's anti-Federalists. Though Washington ran unopposed, even he was pilloried in the press – 'King George,' 'The figurehead on the throne,' 'The monarch who dare not call himself king.'

But it was the vice presidency that was the bone over which several contentious candidates snarled. John, resentful that he should be forced to scramble for the job, was weighed down with ailments. He had lost a number of his teeth that summer to pyorrhea, and was even more afflicted with a trembling in his limbs and infections in his eyes. And he worried over Abigail's still precarious health. Refusing to campaign, he went home to Quincy. Others fought for him. Though Hamilton had no love for John Adams, he hated Governor George Clinton, the next closest contender, and so politicked hard for John's reelection. Ironically, those John had once considered friends were arrayed against him. Mercy Warren's husband, James, actively campaigned against him. And Dr. Benjamin Rush, their former physician, jumped ship and landed on the decks of Jefferson's Republican vessel.

If his public life was disintegrating, at least his family was whole. John Quincy, practicing law in Boston, frequently rode the six miles to his parents' Quincy home to spend the evening with his father discussing politics and philosophy and how best to make a name for himself in public life. Charly, who had made a success of his apprenticeship, was just beginning his law practice in New York. He had won his first case, a feat neither his father nor older brother had managed in their beginnings. Tommy was in Philadelphia happily studying for the bar. And Nabby had come back from England.

The Smiths returned triumphantly, coffers apparently full of money as a result of Colonel Smith's enterprises. The family had moved in the highest social circles in both France and England. Smith's estimation of his own worth rose in proportion. Although John was distressed and embarrassed by the Colonel's boasting he was nevertheless relieved to see his only daughter in less straitened circumstances. And the time spent with his grandsons was a balm to his bruised soul.

Campaigning wore on. Finally succumbing to both Hamilton's and his son Thomas Boylston's worried blandishments, John rode south to mount his own defense, arriving in Philadelphia just before the election. He won by a neat margin, though not wide enough to salve his battered ego. Too unwell to travel, Abigail remained in Quincy while John spent a lonely winter in bachelor quarters in Philadelphia at the nation's temporary capital.

"Sally is older than Mar was when you and she were married," Tommy said, watching his father pull contemplatively on an after-dinner pipe. "I believe her and Charly's feelings for one another are very strong, and of the lasting kind."

He leaned back comfortably in his father's compact study, stretching his feet toward a roaring fire. His father, seated in the enveloping wing chair, huddled beneath a blanket and studied the embers in the grate, a frown on his face.

"If their feelings are indeed enduring, then it will do them no harm to wait until Charles has established himself in his practice. I was a good deal older than he when your mother and I married. We were obliged to wait on your grandmother's blessing."

Tommy took a breath to say something, but his father, ignoring him, continued.

"Charly cannot afford to take on a wife, and very possibly children, so early in life. He is only twenty-two. He needs must be free of encumbrances to pursue his career. If he saddles himself with debt to find lodgings suitable for a family, he will never be able to get out from under that yoke."

Tommy, mindful of the promise he had made to Charly, sighed. He had been so happy to see his brother apparently launched on an even keel. Ready to believe it had been due to Sally's influence, he had agreed to help press the matter of their engagement with their father. Tommy loved Charly dearly, and yearned for a guarantee to his brother's happiness. Perhaps Sally was that guarantee.

285

"You admitted yourself that Charly is doing very well," Tommy said, taking another tack. "I believe Sally can take a certain credit for that. They have honored your desire that they spend some time apart."

"Charles has indeed taken his life in hand. And I see him now launched on a very happy and prosperous course. Yet it is but the work of a moment to destroy it all. It would do his mental state no good were he to suddenly take on a burden that he could not possibly carry right now. The two lovers may endure this separation now so that their later marriage will endure. Waiting will only help, not harm them," John finished firmly.

You have forgotten a young man's longings, Tommy thought, but he could tell the conversation was at an end. Adept at gauging his father's temper, he knew he would gain no ground by pressing.

Reluctantly but faithfully, Charly honored his promise to his parents not to see Sally Smith, but her absence left a bleak hole in his life. He wrote of Sally only when his father, longing for assurances that his son was bearing up well, asked about her. But when John did ask, the misery that poured out of New York startled him in its intensity. Still, Charles Adams was attending to his new practice and trying to be a dutiful son. John and Abigail had faith that in time, he would see the wisdom of their request.

1794

"If this rain picks up, it will ruin everything," Abigail muttered to Mary as they jolted along the rutted road to the Quincy town wharf.

The March sky was gray, reminiscent of the chill veil that had perpetually cloaked London. The air still smelled of winter, cold and barren. Behind them rode George in the farm wagon, head bent under the weight of an oilcloth cape. All around them was the evidence of the difficult economic times. Fences gaped, wires strung between rotting posts were rusted and broken. Barns were nearly stripped of paint, raw boards exposed to the elements. Houses looked disheartened, untended. Cash was scarce and the countryside looked as though it were in a chronic state of disrepair.

"Perhaps we can cover all the furniture with the tarpaulins we brought," Mary offered. "And we can up-end the chairs so the water won't leave marks on the fabric."

286

"It is almost fitting that my furniture should be ruined on its last leg home," Abigail moaned. "I feel I have spent half my life in peregrinations of the country's doing and at the end of the journey will have nothing but nicks and bruises to show for the effort."

"You have had a life many in this very town would give their farms to have had," Mary retorted, suddenly brusque. "You have conversed with the most important people of our time, kings and queens and heads of state. Your husband has had more than a fair hand in the making of the country we now struggle to keep going. Despite the hardships, you have been blessed in so many ways. And you complain of a few sticks of battered furniture!"

Abigail started. She had never heard Mary's tone so peremptory. Was it a simple rebuke? Or did she envy her worldly sister? Abigail had never once considered it, although she was suddenly forced to admit to herself that she had taken secret satisfaction in the excitement of her own life when compared to her sisters' more mundane domesticity.

"You are right, Mary, of course! I was whining," Abigail replied humbly. "Forgive me. I am weary of the separation from John. You would think, after thirty years of marriage, that one would grow sanguine at a husband's absence. But I want his company now more than ever. Conversation by letter does not substitute for his warmth in bed. Our time together on this earth grows short. And John is my very dearest friend and companion."

"Of course," Mary said, putting her hand over Abigail's. "I forget sometimes how difficult it is for you to endure such separations. You have always managed things so well. I have my husband always with me, and the burdens of family and home are never wholly on my shoulders as they are on yours."

The two women rode on in amicable silence, the rain increasing to a steady tattoo on the roof of the carriage, until the stiff black fingers of the Quincy wharves hove into view.

Cheeseman's coastal packet sat at the dock looking like a broody hen -- black and plump and settled heavily in the water. She was a solidly built cargo vessel, reliable, and, because she was armed, less inviting to the British privateers who had begun to hover over the coastal waters like so many hungry gulls.

Despite the dismal day, the wharf was full of activity. People milled about awaiting cargo. The crew shouted orders to one another as they pulled crates from the vessel's hold. Boxes, unloaded and awaiting delivery, crowded the wharf. Merchants stood in what was now a heavy rain, inspecting the wares they had ordered while streams of water cascaded off the gutters of their hats.

"I dread setting foot outside the carriage," Abigail remarked, grimly surveying the scene.

As they pulled up to where the dock met the land, she leaned out of the carriage and called to George.

"Go see when they will unload my furniture, George. It should all be marked. Mrs. Cranch and I will wait here."

"Yes M'am," George said, climbing down from the wagon and striding hunch-shouldered to the end of the dock.

They watched as he consulted the dockmaster, who stood beneath a small umbrella supervising the unloading. The dockmaster pointed a finger toward a clutter of crates that had been shoved off to one side of the dock, and they could see George nod, glance in their direction then point toward the cart. The little dockmaster made a sweeping motion with his arm that they could not interpret. George nodded again and walked back through the jostling crowd of people and vehicles toward the wagon.

"He says he wants us to wait until they finish with this load, then they'll be room for me to take the wagon down and collect your boxes," he told them.

"Is that mine all of it standing in the rain?" Abigail asked in dismay.

George nodded, adding almost apologetically. "Dockmaster says it was the first thing unloaded. It's been standing out since this mornin'."

"Ohhh!" Abigail breathed in exasperation. "Look at that! It'll all be ruined!"

George nodded noncommittally. "I'll just get the wagon turned round and in place so's I can get down there soon's he give me the word."

The furniture was considerably damaged. The red velvet sofa Abigail had bought at Passy had a large blotch that oozed over the back and spread down onto the seat, and most of the tables were marred with whitened stains that spread like fungal growths. No amount of oiling and scrubbing helped. As frustrated as she was at the damage, Abigail took it as a sign that after the bruising journey through public life, however marked they might be by its travails, their travels had ended. They would spend their time, once John had finished his term as Vice President, at home.

1795

" '*Charles is as fat as a squab*'," Abigail read aloud, as she stood by the bright window in John's second floor study.

Mary sat in John's favorite chair sipping gingerly at a steaming cup of tea.

" '*His practice is improving. I found him seated in his office amidst a triumvirate of clients with whom he was conferring*'."

It was April. Betsey Shaw's husband had died suddenly, the year before, and Abigail had added that family to her list of those she worried over and helped to sustain.

"That's good, news," Mary murmured, ducking her head to the cup again.

"Yes," Abigail nodded agreement, her eyes continuing down the page she held in her hand. " '*But he has sad eyes.*' -I don't like the sound of that, Mary."

"He must still pine for Sally," Mary said. "Charles was ever a sensitive soul."

"Sensitive, yes. And..." she stopped.

There were times when, against her will, her mind jolted back to the little boy who had been so ill and so homesick that his father had put him on a ship to cross the ocean with a virtual stranger. He had spent five months enduring one hardship and frightening experience after another in an effort to return to his home. She remembered his face when she first saw him again, seated in the wagon beside Cotton Tufts, his eyes like saucers. She remembered, too, the silence behind that haunted look. Except for the drunken outburst before they left for New York a decade later, he had not once spoken of the ordeal. Disturbing. Did I do wrong? she thought again. She shook herself free of her musings. What is done cannot be undone.

Mary watched her sister shrewdly. She could guess her mind. "We make the best decisions we know how to at the time," she said.

"I should never have let Charly go, but he was so attached to his father, and so mournful, morose even, at his absences..." Abigail replied pensively. "And I worried that he was reaching an age when he needed a man's presence. I did not want him to grow up clinging to a woman's skirts."

"There, my dear," Mary said softly, putting her hand on Abigail's where it held the letter. "What you did, you did for the very best reasons. Do not chastise yourself. There is no way to know what things might have been had he never gone at all. Look at brother William."

Abigail looked up sharply at the mention of their dead brother's name, then stared out the window to the three willow trees that stood in a row along the hill, the tendrils of their limbs coated in the pale green of early spring.

"Of course, Charles is not William," Mary hastily added when she saw Abigail's face. "Any more than is my Will, who has a great fondness for drink. I merely mean that we as mothers can only do so much to mold what clay God has given us."

"I know," Abigail nodded, sighing deeply. "I know. Your Will, our brother William, Charles, the lines between charm and dissipation are fine."

"And Charles is being very circumspect from all reports," Mary continued, hopefully. "He has honored his parents' wishes not to see Sally..."

"I believe he sees her," Abigail broke in, an agitated note in her voice.

"Do you? On what authority?"

"A mother's heart. I know my son. He cannot indefinitely do without that which he hungers for, any more than he could do without home at nine years old. He thirsts for her. And they move in the same circles. It would be very strange were they never to meet, were sympathetic friends never to arrange dinner parties with both invited."

A horse turned the bend at the top of the hill and cantered along the road. The portly rider sat his mount uncomfortably, elbows out, squirming in the saddle as though he had ridden a long way. Abigail came closer to the window and watched, squinting over her glasses. A bald head, surrounded by a fuzz of gray hair suddenly brought her heart into her throat.

"John! Oh Mary! It is my dear husband!" Abigail cried.

Tears starting in her eyes, she dropped the letter unheeded to the floor and rushed across the room and out the door to clatter down the long flight of stairs. Fifty-nine-year-old John, saw her through the window, and galloped to the gate. He flung himself off his horse without even bothering to tie the beast, hurried up to the porch and through the door. He met Abigail at the bottom of the stairs.

"Wife, wife! My pretty little wife!" he crowed, taking Abigail into his arms and burying his face in her shoulder.

Abigail wrapped her arms around his neck and stood, clinging to him, as though he were her anchor in the storm. She could feel his heart thudding through the layers of shirt and waistcoat, and hear his eager breath in her ear. The warmth of his body beside hers tonight, she thought with a little thrill in the pit of her stomach. How can we stand to be apart so often for so long?

Finally, still pressed close to him, she tilted her head back and looked at his face. Without the wig, his bald scalp shone blotchy, glistening with sweat that sat like dew drops in the fringe of hair that surrounded the back of his head. The beaked nose looked russet in the darkened hall, his cheeks had sunken where the teeth were missing, and his shoulders seemed more stooped than she remembered. But his eyes. His eyes were the same fierce blue that had always made her heart pound.

"Mistress Abigail, I believe you owe me a thousand kisses. I have been sorely in want!" John said in echo of the note he had delivered to her in the hallway of the Weymouth Parsonage a lifetime ago.

"You would think you were just married rather than an old couple who are entering their third decade together," Mary's voice teased from the landing at the break in the stairs.

John looked up, smiling, without releasing his wife. "I feel suddenly that I am that young man again," he roared, squeezing Abigail's waist. "It is a secret that the young do not know: the years increase the desire."

He lunged for her again, and covered her face and neck with kisses.

Mary chuckled. "I believe I had better leave the Adamses before I am scandalized completely."

She began to turn and climb the stairs in pursuit of her bonnet, but John stopped her.

"Wait, Mary. I have news. Great news that I want to share with you, too. The President has appointed John Quincy to be Resident Ambassador to The Hague."

"John!" Abigail cried, tears starting in her eyes.

"That *is* wonderful news, John," Mary agreed. "I will carry it home. But now I shall take my leave."

She turned and mounted the steps in search of her hat.

"Oh, John. That is good news," Abigail cried. "Does John Quincy know?"

"Yes, I wrote him that it was a possibility some months ago, but he was under strictest orders not to breath a word. He has only now been confirmed. And in what may be my proudest moment, *I* read out the appointment for confirmation."

She waited, knowing there was more. He still dragged out a story, made her wait for the most important pieces.

"He was approved unanimously!"

"Oh, John! What a glorious moment!"

To have their eldest son crowned with such an honor, and to have John there to share the joy of it with her was bliss.

Mary's footsteps sounded on the stair.

"I am descending," she shouted ostentatiously. "Make yourselves presentable."

Ignoring her teasing, John still held Abigail, but dropped one arm to touch Mary affectionately as she passed.

"It is good to be home. Commend me to your husband, Brother Cranch, and tell him I look forward to his company at his earliest convenience."

May 1795

"I shall finally mend the single omission in the Adams ledger. All have crossed the Atlantic but poor Thomas Boylston -- until now," Tommy said, stuffing a forkful of chicken salad in his mouth.

Family crowded around the table in the low-ceilinged dining room. Betsey Shaw, Mary Cranch and her husband, Richard, drawn and weak after another long bout with fever, Louisa Smith and Tommy Adams elbow to elbow, crushed in between Mary's daughter Elizabeth and her husband whose children cavorted in the twilight outside -- all were present to share in the expanded fortunes of the family. John Quincy, serious at his place beside his father at the head of the table, watched the company with devouring eyes as though he were memorizing each face to carry with him on his journey.

"I wish to propose a toast," John began raising his glass.

"Wait, Mr. Adams, not everyone has a full measure," Abigail said.

"Don't trouble yourself, Aunt," Louisa said, rising. "I shall fetch another bottle or two of wine. We cannot let our glasses run dry on such a night as this."

The young woman smiled and glided out the back door toward the kitchen where she pulled two more bottles of sherry from their rack in the pantry and came through the cool, dim corridors to rejoin the party.

The candles in the all sconces cast a benedictory glow over the company. A cooling breeze floated in through the windows, carrying with it the sounds of the children's shrieks of laughter as they played "hosses" on the stone wall in front of the house. Setting one bottle on the table before her uncle, Louisa opened the other and poured a golden measure into John Quincy's glass.

"We shall miss you," she said simply.

For a second, she thought she saw a tear in his eye, but his voice was robust when he responded.

"I shall miss you, too, as I shall all of my family. I shall be in sore want of my father's evening lectures," he said. "But I have my orders, and a reading list from him longer than my arm. That will sustain me if not advise me."

"It will advise you if you read it aright," John put in.

"I shall endeavor to read it with your voice in my head," John Quincy said. "I aim with this appointment to not only serve my country but to set myself on a course."

John nodded, pleased. "Comport yourself with all propriety, seriousness, judgment, and your career shall be assured."

Thomas Boylston watched his father. Nearing sixty, burdened with a wearying struggle to keep the northern and southern factions from shattering the country, and still beset by enemies in Congress, John nonetheless took joy in every day. Raising his glass, he waited for the table to fall silent.

"To the next United States Ambassador to The Hague, John Quincy Adams. Your health and your prosperous endeavor!"

"To John Quincy," ran in murmurs around the table as though

in response to a prayer.

The Adams family triumph was short-lived. John returned to Philadelphia far sooner than he had anticipated. John Quincy and Thomas had already sailed for The Hague when word reached John that he was needed. John Jay had negotiated a treaty with Britain in an effort to keep America out of the war between Britain and France, but when it had been presented to Congress, it aroused a storm of protest. The treaty had failed to address the Americans' most pressing concerns: privateering and the impressment of American sailors by the British vessels that thronged the coastal waters like so many sharks. It was an oversight that would mean economic disaster for American shipping and commerce.

This time, with her health improved, Abigail decided to accompany John as far as New York. There, she would stay with the Smiths and see her new granddaughter, Caroline Amelia. On the 26th of May, 1795, they set off from Quincy by coach. Although most of the roads were still the rutted dirt highways of a rural backwater, the fields filled with wheat, barley, oats, and clover promised prosperity to come.

Jolted to her teeth, Abigail watched through the coach window as the green countryside rolled by.

"We should be a poor people indeed if we could not make something majestic from what had been bestowed upon us," she remarked.

They arrived at the Smith house in New York exhausted from the long journey and the flea-ridden accommodations en route, but overjoyed to see their daughter and her children. Little Johnny Adams Smith, now nearly seven, met them at the door with a howl of delight. Running out to the carriage, he flung himself at his grandfather with a shout.

"Grandpa, Grandpa! It's been a long time!"

"Not so long as it has been since you've seen your Grandmother," John said, extricating himself from his grandson's grasp and making way for Abigail to lean down and stroke the little boy's sweaty forehead.

"Hello, Gammar!" Johnny panted in excitement. "You're to sleep in my room. William and Thomas Hollis and I are sleeping on the floor in the pantry!"

"You are!" Abigail said with mock surprise. "Isn't your mother afraid you'll steal all her stores in the middle of the night?"

"I never thought of that! William, William!" Johnny called to his older brother who came through the door to help with the baggage. "Gammar says we might steal everything from the pantry in the middle of the night. Maybe Mama will let us stay outside after all!"

Worried that she had rekindled an argument Nabby had already quelled, Abigail pretended not to hear Johnny and turned to smile at William. Quiet, serious, William looked much like his handsome father, but carried himself just as John Quincy had at his age.

"You've grown into such a fine big boy," Abigail praised. "It won't be long before you'll go off to Haverhill with your Uncle Shaw."

"He shan't go to Haverhill," Colonel Smith said, plopping the last of the carpetbags down from the back of the carriage. "He shall follow in my footsteps."

Abigail exchanged glances with John, but said nothing.

"Carry your grandparents' bags upstairs," Colonel Smith instructed his two older sons. "Where is your mother?"

"She's putting Caroline down, Papa," William said softly, not meeting his father's eyes.

He's afraid of his papa, Abigail thought.

"Go tell her to come out and greet her parents."

There was palpable tension in the household. It wasn't until dinner that night that they learned why.

"I've lost three ships to privateers in the past two months," Smith finally confessed, carving the half-eaten venison haunch that Nabby had brought cold to the table.

He sawed savagely at the meat as though it had been personally responsible for his reversal of fortune.

"But surely you did not put everything into those vessels?" Abigail cried despite her resolve not to criticize.

Smith shot her a sharp look, but continued to slice and lay meat onto the platter before him.

"You do not get wealth by investing a few dollars here, a few there," he told her. "Big rewards require big risks."

"But your family...!"

295

"Mar!" Nabby hissed, miserably.

"I came back from Europe wealthy. I made it once, I shall make it again. The tide flows in and out. We are just now at an ebb. The tide shall come in again," Smith asserted, cutting off further conversation.

Although little Johnny seemed oblivious to the atmosphere around the table, William sat beside his mother, eyes glued to his plate.

"William," Abigail ventured, searching for a way to change the conversation. "Tell me what you are reading, now."

"I am reading a copy of Addison's *Spectator Papers*," the boy said softly, looking into his grandmother's eyes for the first time since their arrival. "Uncle Charles gave it me."

"Uncle Charles got married!" Johnny crowed.

John and Abigail froze. John's face looked like a boiled beet, and Abigail stared at her daughter in shock.

"Is this true?" she demanded.

"How dare he?" John roared, finally finding his voice. "We expressly forbade his marriage."

"If I do not mistake, Charles is of age," Colonel Smith said calmly, chewing a piece of venison.

"Par, please don't be angry! " Nabby pleaded, turning to her father. "Charly loves Sally so much. He held out as long as he could. And there are such temptations in the city! You do not know. " Her words tumbled one over the other in her anxiety to stem her father's mounting fury. "Sally is a good woman, kind, sensible, sweet. She is a very good influence. Charly has been quite abstemious in her company," she said.

"He did not even have the temerity to do his duty and at least inform his parents himself!" John shouted, refusing to be mollified.

"Par..."

"No! It is too much to be told off-handedly by a child who knows a thing that we by honor and affection have a right to know first!"

Abigail sat listening to her husband and daughter volley across the table. She felt as though she had been kicked in the stomach. Secret. He had married Sally in secret. How had her children come to be secretive? Are we such fearsome parents? Or they such heedless children?

"Par, Charly loves you so much, but he fears your wrath -- and your good opinion of him. "

"So he proposes to ensure my good opinion by shirking his duty to me and his mother, by deception..." John blustered, as hurt by Charly's secrecy as he was angered at what he believed to be his imprudence.

"He honored your wishes for a long time. But he feared Sally would not wait for him forever. She is, after all, twenty-six." Nabby pointed out. "Older than I was when I married Colonel Smith..."

John gave Smith a sharp look but said nothing.

Nabby, well aware of her father's reservations about her marriage, tried another tack.

"Par. Go see them before you go to Philadelphia. Let Charly know you still love him, that you give him your approbation. His practice is doing well, now. They have a very nice little house..."

"You have been there?"

"No," she said hastily. "He has written. But it sounds very trim and neat, not extravagant at all, but very suitable for him and Sally."

John had flung his fork down and now sat sullenly staring at his plate. The children sat through this exchange quietly. When John threw down his fork, four-year-old Thomas Hollis slipped off his chair and ran to his mother, burying his face in her skirt.

"Come Thomas Hollis," Abigail said, reaching out for her grandson. "Come see Gammar. Grandpa's an old bear, but he doesn't bite."

Chapter 22

For solitude sometimes is best society and short retirement urges sweet return.
John Milton Paradise Lost Bk IX Line 249

1796

"He wants to be president!" Abigail cried in dismay, staring at the letter in her hands. "He says not, but I read it in every line!"

The February storm covered Quincy with a gray pall. Six inches of snow already lay on the ground, and the new layer was quickly filling ruts and smoothing the jagged edges of the last storm's snow piles that the workmen had built around the yard in an effort to clear paths between house and outbuildings. The three middle-aged Smith sisters, Mary, Abigail, and Betsey had drawn chairs in a ring around the hearth in John's upstairs study. Although it was only four o'clock, the day was so dim that Abigail lit a candle at her elbow in order to read John's latest letter.

"Mama? Who wants to be president?"

Nearly seven years old, little Abigail Adams Shaw, Betsey's daughter, child of her middle age, sat beside her mother on a stool, working quietly at her stitches.

"Never you mind, Child," Betsey said gently. "Perhaps you mistake him, Abigail."

Abigail shook her head firmly, her eyes still on the letter she held between two trembling hands.

"I do not mistake him. I know him too well. He has been forced to hold his peace as Vice President too long. He wants to be President. Yet he will not seek it. He imagines himself to be like Cincinnatus, called from his farm to lead by the popular will. He walks around and around the center of his thoughts, telling me of Jefferson's ambition, Madison's machinations, of his dire fears for the dissolution of the union. He says, quite rightly too," she added looking from Betsey to Mary, then returning her attention to the words scrawled across the dry page, "that it is the pride of aristocracy in the southerners that threatens the country's dissolution. Whoever is to be elected president may well simply preside over the country's demise."

"He cannot abandon the child he has worked so hard to miwife," Mary remarked. "But if he would be assured of a strong and wise step-parent, he might be content to return to his friend and his farm."

Abigail shook her head again vehemently. "No. He will not be content. From his letters, there is no one to follow General Washington. He cannot leave the country in the hands of Hamilton. And, he sounds..." Abigail hesitated, trying to pinpoint the change in tone. He seemed in the last months to have thrown off his depression, and armed himself for battle. "He is more energetic, like a horse called to service once again. He has languished so in the vice presidency. I can hear him coming out of his lethargy. Listen: *'If I were home',*" she read aloud, " *'I should show you I feel nearer forty than sixty'.*"

Betsey and Mary both sniggered.

"He was ever an energetic man," Mary said laughed.

Little Abby glanced up again, but said nothing as she watched her mother and aunts exchange knowing looks. Her Great-Aunt Abigail's cheeks colored.

"But he is *not* forty!" Abigail continued, sobering. "And neither am I. These old bones have been rattled too many times already over the ruts and hills of public life. To be dragged away from Quincy just when I believed our sentence in the public good to be nearing an end... Oh, I don't know!" she wailed.

Betsey shot Mary a look.

"It would be yet another sacrifice," Mary agreed. "But it would be the highest honor his country could bestow. John deserves this. You would not deprive him of it, nor would you deprive him of the joy he will take in it."

Abigail sighed deeply, staring hard at the letter she held between two knobbed hands then looking into the fire. "I would deprive my husband of nothing," she said finally. "He has earned every accolade. But I would leave Quincy with much reluctance and a heavy heart if he were elected."

The three sisters fell silent for a moment. The fire crackled as a log fell through the andirons onto the brick hearth. Abigail rose, put the letter onto her seat momentarily and, reaching for another log, pitched it onto the fire. Sleet hissed against the windows.

"The office of president will not simply fall into his lap," Abigail continued as she picked up the letter and sat down again. "He has raised many hackles with his principles and his honesty. He cannot woo the masses like Jefferson. He speaks his mind, but only those with understanding will listen. Even if John is elected, he will hardly have an easy time. It will be like trying to tame the tempest."

Betsey smiled and put her hand on Abigail's where it lay in her lap.

"Has John ever had an easy time?" she asked. "This is what John Adams was made for. If it wearies his body, it obviously refreshes his spirit. Forty indeed!"

She and Mary laughed.

Abigail sighed. She knew her sisters spoke the truth. And, despite John's perpetual complaints, she had expected this. It was not only his pride that goaded him. He could not rest content in Quincy while the government that was so much of his life's work teetered like Humpty Dumpty on the wall between war and peace.

Abigail smiled at her sisters' laughter. John's unabated appetite for her was a source of secret pride to them both. "It is all very well to speak of his showing me he feels nearer forty," she said, "but it is another thing to be here in the flesh. Words and actions need to coincide."

Mary and Betsey laughed delightedly.

"They say absence makes the heart grow fonder," Betsey teased. "Perhaps it also enables the suitor to save his strength."

Abigail colored.

"But Abigail is not the Smith sister who continues to produce," Mary said.

Betsey shrieked, and put her arm around her daughter. "My late-life treasure!"

Little Abigail, uncomfortable at the joke she could not comprehend, kept her eyes on her stitches.

"I do not want to be Mrs. President," Abigail announced after they had stopped laughing. "I shall have to mind my tongue."

"Perhaps the languid south needs the pepper and salt of a northern tongue," Mary said.

Abigail chuckled in spite of herself. Her sisters had been stalwart friends. Others had fallen away like so many autumn leaves.

"I do not want to be in the new Capital City," she continued. "I am never as well anywhere else as I am at Quincy. And the climate of public life saps me."

"Papa says the north is a much more healthy country than the south," little Abby put in as she bit the thread in two.

"Use the scissors, Dear," Betsey said, handing her the small silver sewing scissors that had belonged to their mother, Elizabeth Smith. "You will lose your teeth soon enough. Do not hasten their departure."

"For every child, a tooth," Mary murmured. She turned to look Abigail full in the face. "If John Adams strikes sparks, you have been his steel, Sister. He needs you. I do not relish more winters without your company. To sit here together is a great joy to my days. And I worry for your health. But John Adams would make a fine president. He *is* the best man for the job."

Abigail looked at Mary with a mixture of gratitude and wan resignation. The door creaked open, and Louisa came into the room carrying a tray filled with teacups and saucers, two tea pots, biscuits, and pot of jam.

"Refreshment," she said simply, coming across the large room to put it on the table Betsey had drawn into the circle they made around the hearth. "What does Uncle John say?" she asked Abigail, as she poured steaming tea into the china cups.

"He says his country needs him," Abigail replied flatly. "Louisa, here. I will pour the tea. Reach into that cupboard for the brandy bottle. I believe we need some to stave off winter's chill."

The presidential election of 1796 was more barroom brawl than a contest among gentlemen. Washington, who had debated resigning at the end of his term in 1797, suddenly changed his mind, fearful of the factional caldron into which his departure would throw the government. Adams, who had seen Washington's resignation as his signal to step forward, was stricken. Jefferson -- protesting as loudly as Adams that he was not seeking the office of president -- was being put forward more and more forcefully by his friends. Friends and enemies of all parties wrote ferociously, supporting or attacking the candidates both announced and presumed.

To add to the cacophony, the Jay Treaty with Britain was struggling for ratification. Weak though it was, it staved off a war with Britain that America could neither afford nor win. Tired of pretending that the sailors they impressed off American ships had deserted from British vessels, Britain had taken to seizing ships and sailors without bothering to find excuses. Furious warmongers -- in Congress and out -- insisted on immediate reprisals. John Adams, indignant at the affront to American sovereignty, was still realistic enough to see that America, on the brink of bankruptcy already, could not wage another war. Sam Adams, that perennial rabble-rouser, now governor of Massachusetts since John Hancock's death, loudly took the opposite view. He viewed the impressments as acts of war, and John Adams' opposition to retaliation as cowardice. The defection stabbed John, but it did not alter his course.

"Many have forgot the destruction a war visits on everyone," the Reverend Quimby was saying, Grandmother Quincy's china cup poised between the saucer on his knee and his mouth. "The clergy wishes to forestall unnecessary bloodshed. If you would lend your name in support of the petition, it would persuade many of your neighbors to do so. "

"My husband does what he can in Congress to ensure its ratification," Abigail told him. "I have no influence. I have no office, nor title to add weight to my persuasion."

She frowned. I have no formal education, neither, she thought. I should be a laughingstock should I become embroiled in such works.

The minister studied her for a moment, trying to decide whether she believed what she had said, or was fishing for flattery.

"Neither office nor title confer influence," he said finally, his soft voice neither fawning nor urgent. "The name of Mrs. Adams is known far and wide for concern for our community and its people. You are respected both for your husband's principles, and for your own as well. That respect confers influence, Mrs. Adams."

"There will be those who say that 'The Duchess of Braintree' puffs herself up but is nothing but hot air," Abigail rejoined.

She knew the townspeople used the name with malice as often as with affection.

"The small-minded will say what they will, Mrs. Adams," the minister replied. "We cannot let them steer us away from our duty. Mr. Adams has received many an injustice, but he continues yoked in service. We cannot let those with less understanding prevail. You know as well as I the dire consequences of any war, no matter how

302

just, on a people."

He could see by her sharp look that his words had struck home.

"You are right, of course, Sir. It is everyone's duty to help as best they can," she agreed, sipping at her cup pensively. "My hesitation is not for want of conviction. Leave your petition. I shall begin in the morning to canvas the town."

The little town of Quincy had grown in thirty years. A wheelwright's shop now graced the road between Quincy and Braintree. Cottages had sprung up on sections of farm that had once been larger family landholdings. Shops and farm buildings, like wild mushrooms, now dotted the land, and increasingly large herds of cattle grazed on Penns Hill. The town, despite the plodding economy, thronged with people and activity.

Abigail, dressed in russet linsey-woolsey and covered in her old squirrel-trimmed cloak, sat at the reins of the trap. The twenty-two signatures on the petition at her side on the seat had taken just two hours' work. Most of her Quincy neighbors, faced with the prospect of supporting a new boys school in the township, were anxious to avoid the expense of war. The winds of early April still blew chill, but carried the scents of dandelion and redbud and the first shoots of rye, promises of spring. A gust scurried under Abigail's skirts and darted off to run its fingers through the greening grass of the common where a band of forty men drilled.

As she approached, a few of the men smiled in recognition. Pulling the reins, she halted the trap and climbed down, petition in hand.

"Captain Newcomb!"

The militiamen, dressed in ragged homespun, marched in unison, muskets on shoulders, in time to the burley captain's shouted directions. At the sound of her voice, Newcomb and several of the men turned and stopped.

"Captain Newcomb!" she called again, coming across the green to where the band stood in casual formation.

"Madam?" He stood at attention, broad shoulders thrown back so far that the straining buttons of his uniform nearly popped. Slightly younger than Abigail, the Captain was an imposing presence. His manner was no-nonsense, but the eyes were kind.

"Captain, I wish to speak to you on a matter of great

importance."

He inclined his head toward her in acknowledgment and waited.

"Captain, I understand that you have so far refused to sign this petition," she said, making a frontal attack.

The men strained to hear the conversation. They knew that Mrs. John Adams was a formidable force in her own right.

"If it is the weak-minded petition that the clergy have been thrusting on the local folk, you heard aright," he replied.

"Why?"

He leaned back for a moment, as though he could not believe his ears then swept his hand toward Quincy harbor.

"Look out yonder. See all them ships? They's meant to do business, but they can't leave our ports. It ain't right. We're a new country. We need to build ourselves up, to do trade and commerce, to have a way to make a living for our families. Half these boys," he continued, glancing over his small company of men, "would be working on them ships, but they can't get no work. None of the owners will send 'em out for fear of the British seizing ship and men together. They can't feed their families if they can't work."

"They can't feed their families if they're dead, neither," Abigail shot back. "Have you forgotten what a war is? Have you forgotten the privation and disease that followed on the heels of our fight? As I recall, you lost your mother to the dysentery. And Billy," she went on, eyes now on the face of a young man in a torn coat who stood off to one side with his stringy hair hanging down his back in a cue. "Your two brothers and a sister died of the bloody flux, and your father died of the putrefaction of the wounds he received at Bunker Hill. Make no mistake. That is what we are playing with when we entertain another conflict. Permit me to read you a piece of Mr. Adams's latest letter," she said, taking the paper from a pocket in her cloak and unfolding it to read two paragraphs of John's prediction of what destruction would follow the rejection of the Jay treaty. "So, you see, an even better way to help our country is not to prepare for war, but to ensure peace. To ratify the treaty."

Newcomb stood for a moment in thought, the thick brows working like clouds scudding across the April sky before a wind.

"You make a right good case, M'am," he admitted finally. "Mr. Adams really thinks this treaty will help?"

"He does," Abigail nodded emphatically. "It is by no means

perfect. There still will be problems. But it does mean we will stave off armed conflict. Then, we can renegotiate a better treaty without draining our country."

"She makes sense to me, Cap'n," one young recruit said, leaning on his musket.

"Naw. How're them Limeys goin' to listen if we ain't ready to fight?" another young man shouted. "The Adamses will always be all right. They live in their big house, they have fields and money. What about us poor souls who cain't keep body and soul together? We need to stop them Brits from keepin' us from earnin' a livin'."

"Bein' ready to fight, and wantin' to fight ain't the same thing," Captain Newcomb replied. "I fought in our great war. I was away from family for months -- little pay and starvation rations sometimes," he said, his words carrying over the heads of the men who stood before him like a class of schoolboys, listening. "War ain't no fun, nor little glory, neither. Mostly it's dirt and misery."

Abigail waited, listening to the captain's words and gauging the men's reaction. The wind whipped through her hair, ruffling the laced edge of her cap and threatening to pull her bonnet from her head.

"Then why're we out here drillin' Cap'n?" asked one boy whom Abigail did not know.

"We prepare for war, but try to make peace," the captain responded.

"Wise words from a military man," Abigail observed quietly.

The captain stood a little straighter at her comment, but continued to address his men. "If Vice President John Adams, who hails from Quincy, and knows us here better than any of them down there in Congress says we need to have the treaty, then I say I'm for it," the captain decided. "And I think you should all be for it, too."

"Why? 'Cause someone who spends most of his life in high places says so?" asked one young man.

"No!" Newcomb thundered. "'Cause I says if Mr. John Adams, who's worked for this country as long as I can remember says it'll do us more good than harm, then we're for it. You read the treaty, Slocum? You know what it says? You can bet the Vice President's read it, and studied it too. Here, M'am. Do ye have a quill? I'm ready to sign yer petition."

Abigail rushed back to the trap, followed by the entire company of men. She reached for the inkwell and quill that sat on the floorboards, and handed them, along with the petition, to Captain Newcomb. The rest of the men crowded around the trap and watched over his shoulder as he scratched his name beneath the signatures of other Quincy neighbors. After he signed in large letters with a flourish, he turned to his men.

"I say we all sign. What say you men?"

Cries of "Yes, yes!" rose until one man, Slocum, held back.

"I don't sees we gotta sign just 'cause the Duke and Duchess of Braintree say so."

The Captain winced at the slight to the Adamses. Slocum's words raised hackles within the troop. Many of the men remembered Abigail's kindness to one or another relative in times of trouble.

"You goin' to fight the Brits all alone, are ye?" one man jeered.

"If we're all for it, it'll be bound to pass," another said, "and ye won't have no war to fight. Here, Mrs. Adams, if a mark'll do, I'll sign yer paper."

"Come on, Man. We all stand together, come what may. We stood together for war in the revolution and won a new country. Now let's stand together in peace and keep it."

In the end, all forty men signed, even Slocum -- though under protest.

Abigail climbed back into the trap filled with the glow of triumph, and headed down the road toward Braintree and Susanna Boylston Adams's house. John, she decided with satisfaction, was not the only statesman in the family.

The two little Braintree saltboxes nestled side by side like two doves huddled in the curve of the hill, seemed small. Susanna's house looked unkempt. The dead stalks of last year's herbs still stuck up over the stone wall that separated the houses from the road. Abigail shook her head. It's a good thing Mother Susanna cannot see the casual way Peter keeps the farm.

Susanna had been confined to her bed with one ailment after another for a year now. How Susanna Boylston Adams would love to see her son President of the United States, Abigail thought suddenly. It would be the culmination of all her hopes for her firstborn. As Abigail pulled the horse up before the gate, a rider came around the curve of the road, just missing the old apple tree.

More and more traffic had prompted the Braintree selectmen to condemn the poor old tree. It was to be removed, that wonderful hundred-year-old landmark that gave two barrels of good cider every year. John will be unhappy, but Mother Susanna will be inconsolable. Perhaps she will never know, Abigail thought.

Susanna, now well into her eighties, remained alert, but her body no longer answered her commands. Abigail found her on a bed made up in the back room beside the kitchen, sitting up and looking out over the greening fields toward Penn's Hill. When Abigail entered the kitchen, carrying a gooseberry pie that Louisa had baked the day before, Susanna called out in a voice still strong despite the illness.

"Who goes? Peter?"

"No, Mother Susanna. It is Abigail Adams."

After laying the pie on the kitchen table, she opened the door to the narrow room.

"And where've ye been?" Susanna asked sourly.

"I've been gathering names on the petition to support the Jay Treaty's passage," Abigail replied, ignoring her mother-in-law's tone.

The last two years had been difficult ones. Susanna, proud and independent, had fought her physical disintegration every step of the way, but was losing the war. She took each defeat as a failure of character, and so had capitulated with very bad grace.

"Oh? And whose idea was that?"

"Reverend Quimby requested it, but it is in John's cause that I work," Abigail replied. "I persuaded Captain Newcomb to sign, and he persuaded the rest of his company. I got forty signatures right on the Quincy common."

"And will forty signatures make a such difference?" Susanna asked, turning her gaze out the window to stare again at Penn's Hill where she and John's father had gone on picnics a half a century before.

"I believe it will," Abigail said. "Or I should not have spent the time. I brought you one of Louisa's gooseberry pies. Let me cut you a piece."

"Gooseberries! In April? Not possible!" Susanna dismissed the notion.

"Dried gooseberries. You like them," Abigail reminded her.

"Dried?" the old woman snorted. "They wither away to

nothing, like me."

"You do no good talking like that," Abigail said.

"I have lived past my time," Susanna complained, unheeding. "You lost your young Susanna, she that might have lived. And here am I, a useless old woman, still clinging to life. It is hard to fathom what goes on in the Almighty's mind."

The sudden mention of her dead child caught Abigail unawares, and she sucked in her breath, tears starting in her eyes. Susanna had unearthed a pain that Abigail had worked hard to bury years ago.

"The trials of life seem endless at times," Susanna continued. "And just when you have had your cup filled with them, you must accept still more before leaving.

"Perhaps it is to make the leaving easier to bear," Abigail suggested, making no attempt to varnish the truth of her mother-in-law's approaching end.

"Perhaps," Susanna nodded.

"You have lived to see your son in the second-highest office in the country," Abigail suggested, trying to turn Susanna's mind to something less morbid.

"The SECOND highest," Susanna fastened on the word. "He should be president."

The wrinkled chin poked up angrily.

"I believe he may yet become president."

"Do you?" Susanna's eyes widened. "I hope so. He certainly deserves to be. And you deserve to be Mrs. President."

"I am not sure what deserving has got to do with it," Abigail replied. "Willy nilly, if John is elected, I must button my tongue to my teeth and go. I do not want to leave Quincy."

"And why not? Your children are no longer here. Only I and your farm, a mere piece of land, remain."

"I love my bit of land," Abigail said. And I love you, too, she thought, but did not say the words.

"It will be here long after you are gone on," Susanna informed her. "Take your place in the light while it shines."

"Shall I bring you some tea?"

"Later. First, tell me: What news of my grandchildren and great-grandchildren?"

"I brought a letter from John Quincy. He will return to The Hague soon. He has been in London helping with diplomatic matters concerning the Jay Treaty. According to his letters, he has spent a goodly amount of time with the Joshua Johnsons."

"Johnsons?"

"Yes, old friends. Mr. Johnson is the American Consul. He has seven daughters," she said by way of explanation.

"Seven? Do you not fear John Quincy will find at least one flower among that many thorns?"

Abigail almost laughed, but her mother-in-law's temperament had been so mercurial lately, she dared not.

"I believe the Johnson girls are accomplished and charming. John Quincy is nearing thirty. His career is becoming established. I do not fear so much his finding a wife, provided it is one who will support his career."

"Homph!" Susanna grunted.

"The daughter of a man already in diplomatic service must be accustomed to such a life. John Quincy could certainly do worse."

"Like Charly?" Susanna asked pointedly.

Abigail's heart leapt, for what reason she could not determine. It was as though something in her soul flickered constantly around the possibility of disaster where Charly was concerned.

"John said he found Charly well on all fronts when he last visited him and Sally in New York," Abigail replied.

"You should never have let him go," Susanna said firmly, her mouth pulled into a determined line.

"There was nothing for him in Quincy," Abigail said.

"I meant to The Netherlands. He was too young. Not strong enough to make such a trip."

Abigail felt as though the old woman had kicked her in the chest. She could not get her breath. Her heart raced, and she thought for a moment she would faint.

"You never said a word, not then or in all the years in between!" Abigail finally burst out.

"'Twas not my place. And you never asked my opinion. But you should know, 'twas not right."

"If 'twas not your place to say so then, 'tis certainly not now!" Abigail cried, rising from the chair she had pulled near her mother-in-law's bed.

"I say it only that you might give Charly, that young boy who came home alone so many years ago, the benefit of your love and

309

repentance. He will have need of it before he's through, I'll be bound."

"My repentance!"

Abigail turned and stalked out of the room, banging the door behind her. Peter was just coming in the back door as she walked through it without word, got into the trap, and set off for home.

Chapter 23

Give me the splendid silent sun, with all his beams full-dazzling!
John Milton Give me the Splendid Silent Sun. I

1797

John Adams was elected second President of the United States by three votes. Even without Hamilton's scheming, it would have been close. John Adams as vice president was one thing. Adams as president was another. Hamilton tried to alternately coerce and persuade electors to vote for Thomas Pinkney, a man he believed he could control. His attempt failed. But its result was a bitterly close election.

As President of the House of Representatives, it fell to John to read out the Electoral College's final vote in February of 1797. He, John Adams, was president; Thomas Jefferson was vice president.

It was not until after the election that John began to tally the cost of the necessary presidential accouterments: house rental of twenty-seven hundred dollars a year, carriage, horses, livery, household. In addition, since all the furniture and fittings of the current president's house belonged to George Washington, John was faced with buying plates, cutlery, glasses, furniture, and drapes. The salary of which he had such sore need began to evaporate. Fortunately, Congress voted fourteen thousand dollars to buy furniture for the new presidential mansion, a permanent national investment.

The inauguration, his hour of triumph, John attended alone. Abigail remained in Quincy, John Quincy and Thomas in England, Charly and Nabby in New York. Only faithful John Breisler, the servant who had been with him for nearly twenty years, was present for the historic first transfer of power from one President of the United States to the next.

"He writes again that I must come!" Abigail told Louisa as she read through John's weekly letter.

It was late April, 1797. The forsythia had lost its bloom and

311

showed long tendrils of pale green where the leaves had begun to show. "He says he doesn't care what I do with the house and farm, just come," Abigail sighed. "He makes it so difficult. How many times a day do I long to fly to him, leave every responsibility, to have him hold me in his arms. But I cannot leave. Not yet. I *cannot* leave things in uncertainty. The farm, whatever he says, must be attended to. It will be our only source of income upon his retirement. Without it, we should have nothing in our old age to fall back upon. And Mother Susanna. Daily I expect to have word from Peter that she has left us. I am the only link in Quincy she has to her oldest son. How can I, in good conscience, leave when she is at the threshold of her final leave-taking?"

Louisa smiled indulgently. "Uncle John knows as well as you do your obligations here, Aunt. But he yearns. I know many and many who would willingly spend their lives apart though they were wed. You know how Uncle depends upon you."

"Perhaps," Abigail said, unwilling to acknowledge her niece's compliment, though it was a point of pride that her husband remained devoted while the husbands of beauties had strayed. "He writes that he has a cold that will not leave him, but will he take the tonic I send? No. Will he take care to wrap up when he goes out, or to take an umbrella when it rains? No. I cannot be in two places at once. I cannot attend to everything."

"Do not fret yourself," Louisa said calmly. "All things in time as you often say to me. Mrs. Hall's time draws near. And you must stay with her. Take his calling for you to be what it is, the yearning of a loving heart. You will go when it is time."

"Yes, yes," Abigail nodded agreement.

She is ever a comfort, a daughter I might have had, Abigail thought.

The two women threw shawls over their shoulders before going out the back door toward the barn. James, the young black servant, had drawn Abigail's carriage out and readied the horses. As the women approached, he spread both feet in anticipation of the horses jostling.

"Good morning, James. How go your studies?" Abigail asked as she pulled herself up into the carriage and reached for the basket of bread and homemade jam Louisa held up to her.

"Tolerable well," James replied.

Abigail looked at the young man sharply.

"What is it, James? Is there something amiss at school?"

"No M'am," he replied, not meeting her eye. "You a'goin' to see Mrs. Hall?"

"Yes."

Louisa climbed up, pulling up her skirts from where she had trodden upon them.

"How does Mrs. Hall?" the youth asked.

"It shall not be long now, I fear," Abigail replied. "She had a spell of fighting for breath yesterday while I was there. I thought we should be laying her out today, but she is of very sturdy stock."

"Yes'm. She is that," James agreed, standing patiently while the women settled themselves. Leaning back, he looked at the side of the carriage, which until three days before, had been graced by the newly painted Quincy coat of arms. Abigail had had the herald painted as soon as John had been elected president. When she wrote him of it, he was horrified and insisted she remove it.

"'Tis a pity the arms had to go," James said, his eyes surveying the spot where they had been. "They dressed it up mighty well."

Abigail nodded and slapped the reins on the horses' rumps. The carriage started with a jolt. She guided them through the gate and down the dirt road.

"It *is* a pity Uncle John insisted you take them off again," Louisa agreed when they had gotten out of James' earshot. "I loved the colors. And it did make the carriage look... distinguished. I must confess I enjoyed the looks of our neighbors as we drove by. 'Tis no sin to be proud of our *worthy* ancestors."

"Exactly my feelings," Abigail agreed, thinking of the many sly, even cruel comments about her father and ne'er do well brothers that Louisa had been forced to endure over the years. "It does no one any harm to be reminded you are of the distinguished Quincy line. We are given enough of the bitter in life to temper our pride. I cannot see the harm in claiming what is one's own. Your Uncle John feared the wrath of a jealous populace. So," she sighed in resignation, "off came the coat of arms."

The spring day was soft. A warm breeze moved over the face of the countryside rustling the new leaves of the sycamores and locust trees and carrying with it the exuberant trill of nesting birds. The steady clang of hammer hitting anvil echoed in the distance.

But despite the sounds outside, John's mother's house was still. The dog that was Peter's constant companion was nowhere to be seen, and there was not a sound of life.

"Shall I stay with you, Aunt?" Louisa asked.

"No," Abigail shook her head, handing the reins to her niece. "Take the bread and jam to Mrs. Cranch. Let her know where I am."

As Abigail climbed down from the carriage, the front door of Susanna's house opened and a young woman came out to empty a bucket of slops into the street near the horses' hooves. Mrs. Peter Adams had dark circles under her eyes, and her skin was drawn tight over fine bones. It bespoke a tightening of her soul. The unrelenting work and the lack of appreciation Peter showed her had slowly drawn out all the sap of her life. She glanced at her visitors with a look of weary resignation. She had never liked Abigail, and made no effort to hide the fact.

"How does our mother-in-law today?" Abigail asked her sister-in-law.

"Poorly," she answered, watching the last drop of the bucket's contents hit the dirt of the road before taking up it up by the handle again. "She doesn't know who I am. She's been spendin' all her energy just keepin' breath in her body. I don't know what for..." she muttered as she trudged back to the house with the empty bucket hitting her thigh.

"Life may be hard, but I haven't yet had a day I am not glad to see," Abigail muttered sanctimoniously -- and inaccurately -- as she climbed down. "Some do not know how to be grateful for their blessings." Raising her voice, she called to the other woman's retreating back. "I shall be able to stay until dinnertime if ye want to leave our mother-in-law to me for a while."

Peter's wife ignored the offer and walked into the house.

"It takes little enough to be civil," Abigail remarked acidly to Louisa.

"It has been hard to share her mother-in-law's house," Louisa reminded Abigail.

Sighing, Abigail nodded as she watched Louisa turn the horses slowly toward Weymouth.

It did not seem possible, Abigail thought, looking at the two Adams houses turned conspiratorially toward each other like two gossiping old women, that nearly thirty-three years had passed since she began her life here as a new bride. So many memories both bitter and sweet. God teaches us compassion by experience, she thought.

Shielding her eyes from the sun, she marched around to the kitchen door and stepped into the dark interior. The house smelled of death. A stale heaviness clung to the air and, for a second, Abigail had the urge to run back out into the warmth of the sunshine. But the urge passed. She was practiced at pushing aside what she wanted.

As she came into the sickroom, she was struck by the sound of Susanna's rasping breath. Dragging close the chair that had sat by Susanna's bed for almost three years, she sat down heavily and leaned over her mother-in-law.

"Mother Susanna?" she said, raising her voice to overcome Susanna's deafness.

The old woman, stringy arms lying limp at her sides, appeared not to have heard. Peter's wife had been right. All the energy she had remaining for this world was focused on drawing in and letting out breath. The nonstop huff-puff was like the blowing of a laboring horse.

"Mother Susanna!" Abigail almost shouted, leaning over her mother-in-law. The old woman stared straight ahead, her eyes unfocused, her vision turned inward.

"Susanna-Boylston-Adams-Hall!" Abigail shouted in the old woman's ear. The eyelids flickered, but Abigail could not be sure it was from recognition or only a fluttering at the disturbance her voice had made in the concentrated battle for life.

Abigail took the old woman's hand. It was cool, the skin gray, like washed silk. Tenderly, Abigail held it between her hands, stroking the bony fingers, watching the veins pulse faintly.

"I have learned to love you," Abigail said quietly, making no effort for the old woman to hear her. "I never thought I would. I wanted my home to be my own, not a part of yours. I wanted to have John to myself. I did not understand then the bond between a mother and son. Now, I have come to know it all," she continued, almost in a whisper, tears starting down her cheeks. "You bore John Adams. Hoped for him, prayed for him, and loved him. We both love him, you and I. I would have loved you for that alone, if for no other reason. I shall miss you."

The old woman's breath changed. It began to slacken, each

intake growing perceptibly shallower. The frown that had knitted her brow slowly melted and her face wore a look of innocence and ease. For a second, Abigail could almost glimpse that young woman who had married John's father so long ago. Then it was gone. The skin around her eyes darkened, the breaths came slower, the effort to continue abandoned.

"Goodbye...." Abigail whispered, searching the old woman's face through a fog of tears.

Susanna Boylston Adams Hall gave two quick gulps, expelled her last breath, and was gone.

Momentarily, Abigail looked down at the lifeless body of her mother-in-law. The fiercely possessive mother who had feared she would never live to see her cherished firstborn son return from Europe again, had not only welcomed him back home but lived to see him elected to the highest office in the land. Susanna Adams Hall could leave this earth in peace. Her dreams for John had been abundantly fulfilled.

Abigail was waiting outside the front of the house by the time Louisa returned with the carriage. She left money with the servant woman who came in at dinnertime to prepare Susanna's body for burial, and left word with Peter's wife that she would return to help make funeral arrangements the next day.

Three days after they buried John 's mother, Mr. Faxon knocked on the front door. Abigail was busy packing when Louisa came in to fetch her.

"I've shown him into the downstairs drawing room."

"What does he want?" Abigail asked, folding a kirtle into the bottom of her battered, water-stained trunk.

"He would not say," Louisa replied. "Only that it was of utmost importance."

"Did he indeed?" Abigail said, eyebrows raised.

Faxon, a lean man with a pockmarked face and greasy hair, who was a governor of the town's new school, sat on the edge of a velvet chair in the drawing room. He rose hastily when Abigail entered.

"Mr. Faxon?" she said coming across the room to stand before him. "You wish a word with me?"

"Yes, M'am…" he stopped for a moment, flushed, and stared at his feet.

"Come Mr. Faxon, I am in haste over my packing. I must attend to my husband. What is your business?"

"It is the Negro boy, James," the man managed to stammer out.

"James? What has he done?"

"He can't go to the Quincy school any more, M'am. The school will break up if he continues."

"Break up? Why? Has James misbehaved?"

"Misbehaved? No, nothing like that, M'am. He's...That is to say.... the other boys refuse to go to school with a Negro."

"Refuse? Indeed? What boys?"

"Well, the others.... They say they shouldn't have to go to school with a black-faced boy."

"They go to church with him," Abigail pointed out tartly. "They don't object to going to dances with him. Pray why should they object to schooling with him? He has sat in this very room with me while I taught him ciphering and letters. He has sat in that very chair," she continued, pointing to where Faxon had been sitting. He looked stricken. "Do you object to staying in this drawing room on account of that?"

"Sartinly no, M'am!" Faxon stammered. "It's just the others..."

"Pray send *the others* round to discuss it with me if they wish. Meanwhile, I'm sure you'll excuse me to attend to my packing. Good day, Mr. Faxon, " she said and swept out of the room.

"Imagine the nerve of the man!" she said to Nabby the following week as she recounted her confrontation with Faxon. She and Louisa had left Quincy with James and Mrs. Breisler and her children at the end of April to join John in Philadelphia. They were stopping for several days in Eastchester with Nabby and her children. "He tried to pretend it wasn't him all along that objected!"

"Really," Nabby commiserated, but her voice was distracted.

Colonel Smith was once again away. No one seemed to know where. Abigail was distressed to see the condition of Nabby's life. Besieged by creditors, yet still trying to live the high life, Colonel Smith kept two horses, spent days on end gaming with his brothers then left for long journeys, which he told Nabby would once again secure their fortune. Nabby, grown fat and haggard at thirty-two, struggled to maintain her spirits and raise her children, but her prudent, sensitive nature warred with her circumstances. She maintained a tight-lipped silence on the subject of her husband. Abigail dared not pry. She spent three uncomfortable days pretending not to see the obvious misery. Conversation was tense, calculatedly light. Helpless to alleviate any part of her daughter's and grandchildren's pain, she ached for them.

It was with relief that she took her leave and traveled into New York to stay with Charly and Sally and their new baby, Susanna Boylston Adams.

"The Smiths wish to see you while you reside with us, " Charly said, while Sally rocked their new baby.

Little Susanna Boylston Adams was born just before her great-grandmother Susanna's death. Charly named his firstborn in honor of a grandmother he had dearly loved, a gift to his father, his token of love and respect.

"We have planned a dinner, a family entertainment on Thursday," Charles continued. "There will just be us and Sally's parents and perhaps her sister, so we can speak freely."

Abigail thought in passing that she might find it harder to speak freely with the parents of Colonel Smith than her son imagined. Once he had forgiven Charly his indiscretion, John's sole comment on his son's marriage to Sally Smith, Colonel Smith's sister, was that they were forced to endure a second alliance with that weak family.

But Sally and Charly seemed well. Their rooms, a suite of four chambers in a building not far from Charly's office, were modest but well appointed. Frugality and prudence, in stark contrast to Nabby and Colonel Smith's home, appeared to reign. Abigail approved.

Charly was very happy, delighting in his new daughter, proud of his home, his growing practice, his small, blond wife. Abigail arrived at Charly's office with Louisa and the rest of her retinue that morning. After installing Mrs. Breisler and her children and James in a lodging house, Charly drove his mother and cousin to his home.

He has gained his foothold on life, Abigail thought. He will be well. And Sally is handsome, a matter of pride to a man. Perhaps it will be a better match than Nabby made.

She watched her daughter-in-law cooing to the baby. Her cheeks were flushed a becoming peach, and she had managed to regain her slim figure almost immediately after the birth. Sally favored her brother, Colonel Smith in face and figure, but appeared to be content to live a simpler life. Pleased for her son, she was also envious. They are at the threshold.

"You have a handsome baby," she observed, proud that her own blood ran through the child's veins, too.

Charly flushed in pleasure at his mother's rare compliment.

"She's a very good babe, too" he agreed eagerly. "She hardly ever cries, does she, Sally?"

"Hardly ever, " Sally replied absently, her attention still focused on her child.

"And my practice is going along, well, Mar," he said. "I have more clients every week. I'm starting to get a real reputation."

"Just so you don't get a swelled head with it." The words escaped her lips before she even considered what they would cost her, or her son.

She could never seem to speak to this the tenderest of her children without inflicting some kind of pain. It was like the unconscious urge to touch a wound.

Charly's face fell like a collapsed soufflé, and he looked out the window, scowling.

"On, no!' Sally cried, rushing across the room to touch her husband on the arm, a gesture of comfort and support. "Charly's the least conceited of men. You should know that better than anyone, Mrs. Adams," she said, her voice gentle, but the rebuke plain. "He is a very good lawyer, with good prospects. Each client sends another client. It speaks very well of his abilities and his manner, don't you agree?"

"I do agree," Abigail said, both chastened and relieved at Sally's loyalty. "Charles has good prospects, a good family, and a good wife. And I am mightily glad to see it. It has been some time since I have seen your mother, Sally," Abigail went on, deliberately changing the subject to neutral, incidental things. "I remember the last time we spoke together, it was about miniaturists in the city of New York. Her opinion was that they have grown so numerous and skilled that they can rival any on the continent."

The May light still glowed around the west-facing rooms where Charles's little family, together with his mother, his cousin Louisa, and his parents- and sister-in-law all sat on chairs around the drawing room. Sally had made a small dinner spread out buffet style on the table, and Charly had ordered up a quantity of wine and spirits from the local tavern.

"Charles's practice is growing by leaps and bounds," Mrs. Smith gushed. "We are so pleased to see our Sally so well situated."

Abigail flushed with pride and relief. She had noted Charly's flushed face and red-veined nose with alarm, but at Mrs. Smith's words, her fears suddenly seemed groundless. She let herself relax and enjoy the flow of conversation around her.

The Smiths, who traveled in educated and highly social circles, relayed the latest New York gossip, both political and social. Abigail was particularly keen to know the tenor of feeling about John's election to the presidency. And, as always, Mrs. Smith had conveyed whatever sharp message she had with a diplomatic touch, softened by assurances about John's inimitable character. Louisa sat in a chair near the window, a plate of potato salad and ham on her lap, as she spoke animatedly with Sally's father. Abigail could see where Colonel Smith got his magnetism. Louisa was flushed with pleasure at the older man's attention as the two leaned together deep in conversation.

When the landlord knocked on the door in a transparent effort to be introduced to the wife of the President of the United States, Charly ordered up quantities of oysters and more wine, growing more expansive as the evening wore on. Abigail watched him, his face flushed, eyes bright, as he surveyed his domain. He had not sat down, walking round the room with a bottle in his hand as he continually refilled glasses.

Little Susanna, to her parent's delight, was the unofficial guest of honor. Surrounded by doting grandparents, an elder cousin who devoured her with the greedy look of one who hungers for her own children, and her parents, she was hardly allowed to sleep, passed as she was from one set of eager arms to the next.

"We have been introducing Charles to many here with influence," Mrs. Smith said. She leaned toward Abigail who sat on a rush-seated chair beside her, facing the bank of windows. The sun, melting beneath the line of roofs and chimneys, filled the room with a rosy glow. "It has certainly not hurt his practice, I can assure you. It is the influential who bring law business."

"I'm sure you're right," Abigail acknowledged, suppressing irritation, and slight jealousy at Mrs. Smith's smugness. "But I'm also sure that were Charles not qualified, they would as quickly leave him."

Mrs. Smith smiled benignly, but there was a look of sharp assessment in her eyes. "Certainly. We see his practice increasing so rapidly that we believe it will not be long before The Young Charles Adamses are able to move to more accommodating quarters," she continued.

"It seems to me the quarters here are more than accommodating as they are," Abigail responded, with a brittle smile.

The Smiths' pretensions to grandeur, she thought, is the ruination of Nabby's marriage. If Charles can only maintain his Adams prudence, at least he and Sally will be all right.

"I will wait a bit to see how my business goes before we search for new quarters," Charles smiled to his mother-in-law in a deliberate attempt to break the sudden tension between the two women. "We can stay on here at least through another child."

"To be sure," Mrs. Smith agreed amiably. "I was merely looking ahead in the life of a successful lawyer."

Abigail's heart caught. Another child?

"Sally is not pregnant again so soon?" Abigail breathed, having caught a look of glittering pride on Charly's face.

"'Tis too soon to tell," he replied, swigging down an entire glass of wine and pouring himself another.

Sally blushed furiously and made a show of taking the baby from her sister Anne to lay her in a cradle to sleep.

"Oh, you are not with child again so soon, are you, Sal?" her mother asked, eyes widened in anxiety. She knew too well the demands of a man, as she glanced at her husband, head still bent conspiratorially toward Louisa, and the results to a woman. Too many men kept their wives pregnant, only to seek amusements elsewhere. "It is hard on a woman to have one on top of the other if she can prevent it."

Ducking her head in embarrassment, Sally tucked the blankets around little Susanna and murmured, "As Charles said, 'tis too soon to tell."

She stood and shot Charly a look of reproach, then leaned down and picked up a plate of deviled eggs from the table and offered them to her mother. The room fell silent for a moment except for the sounds of the carts going by outside, and the gentle whisper of the curtains blowing in the warm May breeze.

"Hold up your glasses," Charly said suddenly breaking the awkward silence, his arm holding the bottle of champagne aloft like a salute wobbling slightly. "We shall have a toast. To my father, President John Adams."

Murmurs of approval buzzed through the small drawing room, and the guests held up their glasses for Charly to refill them one by one. When everyone held a full measure, he turned to the gathered company and held his glass in the air.

"To my father, John Adams, new President of these United States of America. May he continue to serve his country as he has, even to the sacrifice of his family, and may he yet receive the reward due that sacrifice."

A chorus of "to John Adams!" sounded in automatic response. But Abigail had not taken her eyes off her son. A bead of sweat slowly made its way from his temple down his face like a droplet of blood oozing from an open wound.

Chapter 24

The world was all before them, where to choose
Their place of rest, and Providence their guide.
John Milton Paradise Lost Bk XII Line 646

1797

John met Abigail and her party on May 8, twenty miles outside of Philadelphia. Extracting her from the retinue, he sent the Breislers, happily reunited, along with Louisa and James on into the town. Together in the new carriage, John and Abigail set off to a tavern in Bucks County, Pennsylvania where John had arranged a dinner for the two of them, a single night of solitude together.

"'Tis a fine evening," Abigail sighed contentedly.

The carriage wheels hardly sounded on the soft earth of the roadway. She leaned back in the dark of the carriage's interior into the crook of John's arm, eyes on the thickets of wild rose and honeysuckle that flowed by outside. She felt young again, glad to be alive and beside John after so many months of separation.

"I sorely missed thee, Wife."

"Thee? Hast Quakers made such in-roads into thy language?" she asked playfully.

"Nay," John laughed. "But the Quaker ways are good ones. Kind, sober, hardworking people. I would there were more Quakers, or at least more Quaker sensibilities amongst the Congress. Alas, there is so much faction."

"Never mind, John. Rest a while. Oh, what a beautiful country! We have such a wealth here," she said. "I quite forget it at times."

"New York is not designed to inspire such sentiments," John observed. "How did you find our son and daughter?"

"I am uneasy. Nabby..." Abigail hesitated, deciding how much of her fear and anger to confide. John's burdens as president were heavy enough. "Colonel Smith was away again..."

John snorted. "Trying to make his fortune in one big killing again, no doubt."

"I fear he forgets his family," Abigail said, pursing her mouth.

"Nabby says nothing. She will no longer confide in me -- her loyalty must remain with her husband, but I see the anxiety in her eyes, and the straits in which he leaves them. I gather he leaves very little money with them when he goes off on one of his *journeys*," she spit out the last word. "I cannot fathom how Nab lives, except that perhaps the senior Smiths help to subsidize the household in an effort to keep their son from appearing worse than he is."

John frowned and shook his head. "I did not foresee this for our daughter," he said. "It saddens me to think she is not well situated."

"It is through no fault of her own, I can assure you," Abigail said defensively. "She is absolutely blameless, speaks no ill of the man, never seems to complain of their circumstances. But it is most heartbreaking to see them, the children especially. I wish we could put them with Betsey and the Reverend Peabody in Hingham. Such a good man. My sister is blessed to have found two such fine husbands in her lifetime. With the Peabodys, William and Johnny would receive a proper education. Under their father's tutelage, I fear they will never be half they could be."

"Have you suggested it?"

"I did once, in Colonel Smith's presence, but he was most emphatically against it. Despite my offer to help pay the fees."

"Perhaps if you wait a bit, Nabby will come to persuade him in time -- without the presence of meddling in-laws."

"We do not meddle!" Abigail cried indignantly. "We only mean to help!"

"Do I not know that, my dear heart?" John said. "I mean only to suggest Colonel Smith's perspective. Give Nab time. She may yet place the children with Betsey and her husband."

"I pray so," Abigail said, her eyes on the blue outline of the Pennsylvania mountains. The vistas of the countryside comforted her with their timelessness, their endurance in the face of warfare, famine, privation, and disease. "The whole earth breaths the Divine," she murmured. "I remind myself that not a sparrow falls that He does not see. But it is a bitter thing to watch one's children nearly drowning in difficulty."

"Not all our children are poorly," John said, deliberately turning her attention from their worries to their triumphs. "John Quincy and Thomas make themselves indispensable to their country. I rely on

John Quincy's missives as I do no other's. His sense, his discernment, and humor, the broadness of his education, and the shrewdness of his observations all enable me to see more than I might otherwise. It gives me comfort that I am being truly informed where it is most needed. You can be proud of our son, Wife."

Abigail smiled, and relaxed into John's comforting bulk. He smelled of tobacco and ale, the dust of the road, and the heady fragrance of spring.

"We have been blessed, Abigail," John said softly, taking the hand that lay in her lap. "We have been happy together for three decades and more. And our time together is just as precious today as it was thirty years ago. We have only our own lives to live. We cannot live those of our children, no matter how much we may desire it."

Abigail looked into the old face. The bags under his eyes spoke of many late nights. She rarely looked long in a mirror these days. It was such a shock. But John's face, slowly collapsing in on itself, was evidence enough of the changes the years wrought on them both. He leaned over and kissed her, long and hard, the kiss of youth and passion. For a moment, Abigail wished that they could stop the carriage and make love on the grass in the glow of the setting sun.

The carriage pulled up outside a small tavern in Bristol where John handed Abigail down to the ground. The tavern keeper, dressed in what appeared to be his Sunday best and flanked by his wife and son, bowed and welcomed the President and his lady. He showed the Adamses into a small back room that looked out on a garden thick with newly greening herbs. The dill waved in feathery fronds in the gentle breeze, and clumps of mint and tansy had sprung up from the dark earth. On the table, set with fine china and silver, was laid the beginnings of a dinner. A bowl of dried fruit was flanked by a vase of wildflowers. A basket of bread, still warm from the oven, sat beside a large decanter of wine and two plates, each with its own thick lump of fresh-churned butter.

"I hope everything is to your liking, your Honor," the publican said, bowing again slightly at each new piece of conversation. "My wife's a capital cook. She's got a wonderful roast of venison waiting to be carved, and a large salmagundi made. Of course, 'tis not so nice as it would be further into the season, but we do what we can with dandelion and such, and then..."

"I am certain your fare will be fit for a king," John interrupted. "Your establishment is highly recommended. My wife has had a long journey and would be grateful for some sustenance."

"Aye, certainly, certainly!" the man said, bowing out of the room and clattering across the wide boards toward the back of the house.

"Who recommended?" Abigail asked, sitting down at the table.

The room glowed with the setting sun that fingered through the trees and dappled the grass with gold and rose.

"Mr. Jefferson. We may not agree, but his taste for the finer things in life is unequaled."

Abigail made a wry face.

"How does your vice president?" she asked, sipping the wine John had poured into her glass after they sat down.

"I am certain he does well," John replied sardonically. "I rarely see him, and even more rarely alone. He seems to be of an entirely difference branch of government from myself."

"I hope he does not raise a strong faction against you, Mr. Adams."

"He can only do so much. I believe he is glad not to be President himself right now. He works best as a critic, but has not the stomach for the grind of daily maintenance."

"Odd words considering what a farmer he is reputed to be. What is farming but constant maintenance?"

"You have done well with the farm," John acknowledged, knowing she meant to remind him of her own management. "I would not be so sanguine in my work if I did not know you were in charge of the farm. Thanks to you, it will be a fine retirement."

"We are not there yet," Abigail laughed, delighted at his praise. "There's many a slip 'twixt the cup and the lip."

After dinner, they walked along the river. The sun had dropped behind the mountains and the water shimmered silver beneath a darkening sky.

"You have not mentioned Charly and his wife," John said finally, breaking the comfortable silence that had fallen between them. "How does our New York lawyer?"

"I don't know," Abigail sighed, not looking at him. "They treated me like royalty. I lay in state on Beaver Street while the masses came to call."

John laughed.

"Charles *appears* to be doing well. His practice is growing -- due, Mrs. Smith intimated, to the Smiths' contacts and introductions to the wealthy and influential of New York. I thought that a bit much, but it pleases her to think she has such influence, and perhaps she is in part correct. Sally keeps a pretty, but frugal home. Everything is appointed for respectability and ease, but nothing for show. And she loves our Charly a great deal. But," she sighed, and looked at her feet as they stepped pace by pace along the moss-covered path, "Charly wears a look of anticipation, or perhaps unease. He delights in home and family, but there is a tension about him, a... how can I put it? A feverishness that I can feel more than see, that worries me. He is on the edge of a knife blade. Which side he may fall is in God's hands -- and his own."

John walked on without comment for a moment, bringing his head up to look for the fish that had jumped out of the river, but the surface of the gently moving waters appeared untouched by its leap.

"Charles has always been in God's hands," he reminded her. "We can do nothing for our children now but pray. We must make our own lives, Mrs. Adams. Tomorrow, we will be the President and His Madam. Tonight, I would be just Abigail and John. Let us return to our rooms. I have sorely missed the comfort of you in bed with me."

By the time they arrived in Philadelphia, the Breislers had unpacked, aired the linen, and briefed the servants on Mrs. Adams's preferences and requirements. Relieved of the burden of household in addition to presidential concerns, John relaxed.

While Abigail's presence in Philadelphia lessened John's burdens, it increased hers. Three days after arriving, she held a formal dinner for thirty-two members of the House of Representatives with their wives, and followed it immediately with a reception for the Senators and their ladies. Additionally, she was forced to run the farm by letter, instructing Cotton Tufts on the buying and selling of stock, listing on-going chores for the farm hands, and directing the making of cheese and the gathering of herbs. Her days began at five, when she rose to pray, write letters and read, and often ended after midnight following a round of visits and entertainments. The schedule was grueling, particularly as she was plagued with rheumatism and fevers, but she knew only too well how much more business could be transacted over food and convivial spirits than over desks and papers.

America was faced with strife inside and out. The division between northern and southern interests continued to rule Congressional debate, while the war between Britain and France threatened to engulf the United States. Britain snatched American men and vessels. Congress prepared for war. It passed a resolution to build fourteen men-of-war for their new American Navy, the stick with which they planned to beat the British. They chose three envoys to make the long journey to France and to treat with the new government under Talleyrand. Despite all the preparation, though, Congress adjourned in July without any firm decision about the country's ultimate course.

To escape the recurrent yellow fever that cut a swath through Philadelphia every summer, Abigail and John returned home to Quincy in July. On their way north, they stopped to see Charly and Sally and the baby, then picked up Nabby and her children and took them back home to Quincy.

Nabby still refused to say a word against her absent husband. Unable to speak of her pain, of the disappointment of her marriage, she spent much of her time alone. No one came to visit. Her friends, drawn from the ranks of Colonel Smith's acquaintances, fell away. Though they had swarmed to his table, his hunting parties and excursions, eating his food and drinking his wine while he was in funds, they evaporated when the money ran out.

Unwilling to cause a rift, John and Abigail held their tongues. Instead, they strove to interest their grandsons in books, engaged them on the farm, and tried in every way to lighten Nabby's mood. It was a campaign of kindness that broke down her resolve to obey her husband's dictums.

The summer was short, but glorious. Warm, full days were followed by cool nights, and the Smith children slept soundly. They spent their days racing through the fields, helping the men to pick and load fruit, press cider, feed the stock. Their limbs were lean and brown, and they collapsed exhausted into bed each night. Wariness was replaced by exuberant innocence, a balm to Nabby's heart. When she could see Nabby's softening, Abigail renewed her offer to pay for their education, provided it was at Haverhill.

"You aunt and uncle admirably prepared our sons for Harvard.

Together, she and Reverend Peabody will do the same for your sons," Abigail told her.

And they will be safely out of their father's hands, she thought.

Resigned, relieved, Nabby agreed.

In the beginning of September, Nabby and Abigail drove to Boston and deposited William and John Adams Smith with their Great-Aunt Betsey. Little Abigail Adams Shaw, Betsey's mid-life baby, knew her father, Reverend Robert Shaw, only as a revered but distant memory. It was her stepfather, the Reverend Stephen Peabody, a gaunt, quiet man with a hint of mirth in his eyes, who she now called Pa.

Two ministers, Abigail noted, wondering at the coincidence. Our fun-loving Betsey has married two ministers...but different men from our father.

Reverend Peabody took the boys into his study and sat them down, an effort to limn their past education and plan one for the future.

Nabby, who had worried that her boys would object to the separation, drove away with a nagging fear that they would not miss her at all. As she and Abigail left, she turned to cast a long, melancholy look at the house.

"It is hard to part from your children," Abigail said softly, her eyes on Nabby's face. "Even if it is for their good."

"I will miss their chatter and their company," Nabby said, still hoping to catch a last glimpse of her sons. "They liven the house."

Then, realizing she had left a perfect opening for her mother's barbed comments about her husband, Nabby swallowed the tears that had started down and took another tack. "Of course, it will leave me more time for Caroline and Thomas Hollis. I will be able to attend more to their letters and ciphers until they can be placed properly."

Although she was grateful for her parents' payment of the boys' school bills, she could not bring herself to acknowledge it lest she be forced to acknowledge the reason for that need. But instead of commenting, Abigail merely tendered an invitation.

"Why don't you join your father and me in Philadelphia this year, Nab? I would enjoy having some of my grandchildren with me, and Louisa would be grateful for the company of a woman her own age."

Nabby turned a look filled with love and gratitude toward her mother so naked it almost took Abigail's breath away. In that gratitude, the starkness of her life was clearly written.

"I would like that," she said simply, laying her hand on her mother's. "Thank you."

A week before they left for Philadelphia, Roger Knight, an old friend and neighbor, rode through the gate and knocked on the front door. Nabby, having left her packing for a moment to play with little Caroline, rose from the floor to answer the door.

"Mistress Nabby, is that you?" Knight asked, trying to disguise the shock he felt at the sight of the woman who had aged decades since he had stopped to see her in New York only five years before. "I heard you was in Quincy this summer. Had a nice visit?"

"Yes," Nabby smiled, grateful for the sense of connection that Knight's recognition brought her. "I have liked it so well, I am going to continue it. My mother and father have asked me to join them in Philadelphia this winter and we are right now packing to go."

"Oh?" He looked distracted. "Then maybe now's not a good time? I just came up from south, ye see, and thought I'd stop and visit with your folks. Brought the mail from town while I was about it," he said, removing out four smudged letters from his coat pocket. "Methinks from the look of the stamp, that one's from John Quincy."

Nabby reached for the correspondence.

"I stopped in New York to see young Charles..." Knight began, a clouded expression crossing his eyes.

Nabby looked at him sharply, then nodded. "Come with me, Mr. Knight. I am certain Mar and Par will receive you."

Roger Knight, an enterprising neighbor who had, as a youth during the Revolution, run blockades and smuggled needed goods from one colony to another, had continued his trade, legally, after the war and had built up a sizable business. On occasion, he brought news from outlying parts of the states, enabling John Adams to speak with authority about the feelings of the people on the frontier.

Together, they went through the house, Nabby leading, until they came to the back yard where Abigail was returning from the barn with a basket of eggs on her arm.

"I thought that was Thomas Hollis's job," Nabby said.

"So it is, when I can find him," Abigail replied, smiling

indulgently. "Mr. Knight. It has been quite a while since we have seen your face in these parts. How do ye?"

"Tolerable well, Mrs. Adams," Knight began. "I was just sayin' to Mistress Nabby that I have come up from the southern parts and thought to come see you. I brought your mail, too."

"Here 'tis, Mar," Nabby said, holding out the letters. "Looks like one from John Quincy."

"Yes?" Abigail stopped in a pool of shade, put the basket on the ground for a moment and took the letters Nabby offered. Glancing through, she nodded agreement, then, reaching down, she picked up the basket again. "It will be a great pleasure to his father."

"I...," Knight stopped for a moment and shifted uncomfortably on his feet.

Abigail looked at the man shrewdly. "There is more."

"Yes. I have been to New York."

"Oh?"

She glanced at Nabby, wondering for a moment whether or not he had news of Colonel Smith, but her daughter's expression told her it was something else.

"I stopped to see your son, Charles..." he began awkwardly.

Something in his demeanor caught at Abigail's heart and she gulped involuntarily. She started again for the house. "Come. Mr. Adams is in his study."

They found John standing amidst piles of books scratching his head, one hand on his hip. He looked up when he heard the footsteps behind him. "Ah! The estimable Mr. Roger Knight. And how is trade?"

"Fair to middlin'," Knight replied.

"He has been to see Charly," Abigail said.

John turned to look the man full in the face for a moment, then, clearing a path, he motioned to a chair. "Here, Mr. Knight. Sit ye down. I can see there is something on your mind."

Knight picked his way into the dark, walnut-paneled room gingerly avoiding the precariously stacked volumes, and sat in the chair John had indicated. Abigail and Nabby remained in the doorway.

"Perhaps you would like something to drink?" Abigail asked, suddenly aware of her duties as hostess.

Knight shook his head, his eyes still on John.

"What is it?" John asked, leaning forward in the chair he had seated himself in.

Knight drew in a deep breath, and looked at his shoes uncomfortably.

"Charles is..." he searched for a description, "...not well."

"How not well? John asked immediately.

"I ... I never really saw Charles," Knight began again. "I saw his wife, Mrs. Adams, and then, when she asked me to find him..."

"Find him?" Abigail broke in.

"He had been missing nearly six days when I got there. His wife was frantic, said he had clients who were searching for him, that he had briefs to file, had been missing deadlines..." Knight squirmed in the chair.

"Is he drinking?" Nabby asked from the doorway.

Knight looked at her face, suddenly drawn, the eyes opaque.

"I think so. Yes. I spent the better part of a day searching for him. He has...haunts," Knight said. "I finally kind of got on his trail, and found some of his...friends. It was hard to get help from them. They were mostly... They were not the kind of friends I would have expected of your son."

The image of her brother William Smith, dissipated and surrounded by drunken, surly men in the warehouse on the Boston waterfront, came involuntarily into Abigail's mind. With an effort, she pushed it away and focused on the problem at hand.

"He has fallen in with bad company," Abigail said, struggling to sound calm. "He is drinking. How much?"

"I don't know, not really, M'am," the man replied apologetically. "I don't like to bring bitter news here, M'am. I know ye have enough to occupy your thoughts. And I don't want ye to think I am happily the bearer of bad tidings. But you have been good to me over the years. And Charly was once very kind to me."

Abigail nodded. "Charly has great kindness in him. I believe, sadly, that he also has great demons."

The news of Charly's situation overshadowed the news of John Quincy's marriage, which came in the letter Roger Knight had brought. On the 26th of July 1797, John Quincy married half-English Louisa Catherine Johnson, second daughter of the American Consul in London. Despite her assured words to Louisa about the consul's daughters understanding the demands public life, Abigail now worried that her eldest son had chosen a woman who was accustomed to luxury. Johnson's wife had her own fortune. Their daughters were accustomed to the latest fashions, fine appointments, a spacious home. John Quincy was a young lawyer whose sole income came from his public service.

Chapter 25

Rocks whereon greatest men have oftest wreck'd
Paradise Lost Bk II Line 228

Abigail and John stopped in New York on the way to
Philadelphia in October. What they found was worse than their
fears. Charly was nowhere to be found, and Sally, heavily pregnant,
was nearly beside herself with fear and sorrow. Charly, drunk most
of the time now, had beaten her more than once, then, repenting
almost immediately, lurched out again to try to drown the voices that
warred for control of his mind.

"He's not himself," Sally tried to explain to the Adamses who
stood horrorstruck in her disheveled drawing room.

"He is his worst self," John Adams had muttered, grief-stricken
and filled with impotent rage.

"You must go home to your family," Abigail advised.

She pushed away the image of Charly, her bright-eyed funny,
caring son, smashing his fists into the face, the chest, the belly of his
pregnant wife. The young woman stood in the middle of the
apartment, shoulders bent as though under a great weight, staring at
Abigail with dark-rimmed eyes.

"You cannot stay with a drunken madman."

Sally opened her mouth to protest, but Abigail held up a hand,
determined to say the worst, a punishment -- or exculpation -- for
herself.

"No, I must say it. I am his mother. God dictates that I love
him. I do love him. But I cannot condone this. You cannot stay.
You endanger your own safety and your children's safety. Your
family will take care of you even if your husband will not."

"When he is not drinking, he is wonderful," Sally said, tears
standing along her lashes. "Kind, funny, and a wonderful lawyer.
Why, he won his first case!"

Abigail nodded. Little Susanna, who had heard the urgency in
her mother's voice, stopped playing in the corner and toddled across
the room to pull at Sally's skirts. Sally reached down and patted the
tousled blond head gently.

"He is all that and more -- *when* he is not drinking," Abigail agreed, her stomach knotting. "I do not know what it is...." She bit her lip. She could not bring herself to admit to Sally that alcohol had run through her family like a scythe, indiscriminately felling those in its path. Neither could she breathe a word of the guilt that whispered in her own ear like an icy wind: *your fault, your fault.*

"There is more, Mrs. Adams," Sally said, finally looking square into her mother-in-law's eyes. "His cough, in the morning especially, he coughs like to tear his insides. I don't know what will happen to him if I am not here."

"You must go to your family," Abigail said again, firmly, but more kindly. "I will leave word with the doctor to come and see to him."

"But if Charles comes home and we are not here..." Sally whimpered.

"If he comes home drunk and..." Abigail could not bring herself to say the words: *beats you again.* "You must protect yourself and your children. You have an unborn babe to consider. A woman is most vulnerable when she is with child. For some men, the sight of it..." she stopped, her mind on her brother, Will. He hated his wife for her pregnancies, attacking her with greater and greater fury each time, as though he had had no part the conception.

"Leave word with your landlord where you have gone. If Charles is able to come to you, he will. If he tries to come in an unfit state, your family can protect you. And they can offer peace." Each word was painful, the shards of a broken life, a life which had held such promise. "If Charles comes home sober and willing to change, so much the better. But your first consideration must be for the safety of your children."

"It will break his heart..." Sally whispered, putting her hand to her mouth.

Abigail looked at the young woman, her face bloated with crying and pregnancy. Abigail had not wanted this marriage, had even, she now admitted, prayed against it. But she knew Charly's troubles could not be laid at the doorstep of this union. Sally had tried. And she loved him. She still loved him.

"You must protect your children," Abigail repeated doggedly.

The Adams entourage continued on to Philadelphia in near

silence. John had spent his time in New York searching fruitlessly for Charly, but had succeeded only in discovering the depths to which his son had sunk. At each new revelation, he could feel a tightening in his chest, a restriction of his breathing. He feared his heart would crack. Nabby, seeing in Charly's broken marriage, fragmented reflections of her own, was mired in despondency over her brother and herself. The higher the Adams family climbed, the lower they sank.

Conversation picked up again as they neared Philadelphia. Proximity to the seat of government returned their thoughts to less personal matters. The yellow fever that had thinned the population of the city still clung to pockets in town. As a precaution, the Adamses rented a house outside the city limits to wait until the fever had run its course. They moved back to the presidential mansion at the opening of the Congressional session in mid-November.

The headaches of government pushed family considerations into the shadows. Deluged with decisions, meetings, and paperwork, John was forced to give up his daily exercise. Added to his headaches was a steady stream of invective from Benjamin Franklin Bache, Franklin's grandson and editor of the Philadelphia newspaper, *Aurora*.

John had appointed John Quincy as ambassador to Prussia, and assigned William Vans Murray, John Quincy's former Harvard classmate, to his vacated post in England -- a kind of nepotism that set Bache aflame. Then the Senate expelled William Blount, a Republican, for high misdemeanors resulting from his plotting with the British over an expedition into Spanish territory. Shortly afterward, Tench Coxe, another Republican, was dismissed from his post in the Treasury Department. Though both were duly investigated and ejected by a majority, the incidents were portrayed by Bache as Adams's paranoid but systematic efforts to eliminate all personal opposition. Ironically, John had replaced very few members of his cabinet on taking office, a move that meant he had retained many of the men Hamilton had persuaded Washington to appoint. But Bache preferred to believe in John's yearning to purge the government and so shredded his reputation in the press.

While Bache's insistent stings made life difficult for John, there were too many other things to command his attention to linger over any single one. Furious at America's relegation to second-class status at the hands of both France and Britain, Congress authorized a navy in 1794. As soon as the appropriation was announced, legislators were besieged with bidders. Shipbuilders, speculators, naval architects, contractors, anyone with a stand of wood or a foundry descended on Philadelphia in a scramble to win a lucrative government contract. Rumors of bribery smoldered through the corridors, fanned into flame by the newspapers. At each turn another reputation teetered on the thin line between speculation and hope.

1798

The January countryside beyond the windows was shrouded in gloom, the colors a monochrome. Brittle branches, over-weighted by an early ice storm, were snapped but not quite severed and dangled listlessly like half-amputated arms. The day was fading, leaving only the dim wash of gray sky. John stood at the fireplace, his elbows on the mantelpiece. The letter held between his hands caught the flickering light of the candle.

"Is that from the packet that Louisa brought in?"

John turned around so suddenly, he knocked a candlestick off the mantle. As they bent down together to pick it up, Abigail caught sight of the letter in his hand.

"Do I mistake, Mr. Adams, or is that missive to me, not you?" she asked, indignant.

His sheepish look was answer enough.

"You have opened my mail!"

"I hunger for news from home," he stammered, more embarrassed at being caught than remorseful at his indiscretion. "And Mrs. Cranch's letters are worth ten of anyone else's!"

"That's as may be," Abigail replied, "but they are mine. I do not open your mail, Husband. I expect the same courtesy from you."

For a moment, Abigail could see John's conscience war between contrition and justification. Contrition won -- but just.

"I apologize, Abigail. You are right, of course. But," he continued, still at pains to excuse himself, "I share everything with you -- every detail of government, every decision is yours to examine. I rely on your advice."

"Freely, Husband. You do this *freely*. I do not extort any

confidence."

Abigail put her hand out, demanding.

"Mrs. Cranch says that the cider remains sweet, surprising considering the fluctuating temperatures...," he said, conciliatory. "The fences have come through the freezes well so far..."

Silently, she waited for him to give her the creased letter.

"She writes with more careful detail than anyone else..." he trailed off, relinquishing the letter like a small boy reluctant to give up his stolen cookie.

"There are things," Abigail informed him stiffly, "that are confided between sisters and no one else. They are not for prying eyes, not even yours, my dearest friend. I shall read pertinent passages to you, I shall share Mary's news, but nevermore open my mail."

"But we have no secrets between us," John said, hurt.

"These are not secrets, my dear," Abigail told him, relenting. "They are private matters between sisters only. They are not things for men's eyes."

Though unconvinced, John declined to argue the point any longer. He resolved to be more careful in future. Reaching for a taper from the fire, he lighted the candle that he had replaced in its holder before taking the sheaf of letters stacked on the mantle and coming to sit in a red wing chair close to the warmth of the fire.

"Here," John said, sorting through the letters.

He handed Abigail a collection of wax-sealed envelopes, then turned to open another in his stack.

"Here is one from dear Dr. Tufts," Abigail said, her voice going soft with affection. "Another from Betsey to me, and one from Betsey to Nab. I trust the boys are doing well."

"One from John Quincy -- I had missed it," John noted, holding a discolored envelope toward the light, "you so distracted me."

Abigail ignored him and continued to sort her stack in order of importance. John ripped open the seal and extracted a thick tome.

"John Quincy writes me far more than do my other emissaries," he said, flipping through the leaves.

"Did Mrs. John Quincy include one in that envelope?" Abigail asked.

She was warming to John Quincy's young bride, Louisa Catherine. Though initially opposed to his marriage to a woman who

338

was not only accustomed to the parties at court but was half-English to boot, Abigail gradually softened. She wanted to love the people her children loved. And Louisa's letters to Abigail had just the right degree of deference balanced with an independence that Abigail admired. Additionally, the young woman's apparent distaste for a life of balls and diplomatic functions endeared her, sight unseen.

"A diplomat needs a wife, does he not?" Abigail began, hoping to elicit a positive response from her sometimes laconic husband. "You suffered without a wife to order your affairs, take charge of the daily details of a household. And Louisa appears to love our son as she ought, don't you agree?"

"Umm?"

"John?"

"Umm?" he continued reading.

"I *said*..." she began again in exasperation.

John sucked in his breath sharply, and held the page closer. "No!" it was a whisper, an exhaling of breath.

"What is it?"

Silence. He ran a hand through his thin hair, and looked at her over the rim of his spectacles.

"Mr. Adams! What is it?""

"John Quincy has asked me to find out what has happened to the money he sent to Charly," he said in a quiet voice.

"Money?" A chill went up Abigail's spine.

John nodded.

"Why is John Quincy sending Charles money?"

"It seems that Charly regaled John Quincy with the great profits to be made in stock certificates. And John Quincy, sensible that he will never manage to properly support his family by his diplomatic salary alone, had hoped to find another way to increase his capital. You are always going on about stock certificates and government treasury securities, Wife. He has learned that from you."

"And our son-in-law speculates in western lands. Would you rather John Quincy had put the money with him?"

John fell silent again and ran his hand over his mouth.

"But what about the money?"

"John Quincy sent Charles money to invest -- for his 'nest egg' as he calls it here, his hope for his children's future."

"But how can he have thought that wise?"

Abigail was horrified. Had they neglected to give John Quincy a clear understanding of Charly's current circumstances? No, we cannot have been so circumspect as that!

"Has a letter of ours miscarried?"

John shook his head. "I don't know. The money appears to have been transferred into Charles's hands over a year ago. My dear, we did not know then how bad it was -- one can maintain appearances."

The rheumy eyes looked sadly at his wife.

To think they could have produced one child who was destined to ruin another. Charly had sold his brother's birthright for a mess of pottage...or rum.

"John Quincy has written to Charles several times, he says, but received no answer."

"How much money was it?" Abigail asked, her throat constricting.

"John Quincy intimates it was all of his savings."

"No, no," Abigail wailed, putting her hands to her head.

Her brain throbbed.

"If it weren't tragic, it would be touching," John said pensively, lifting the page up again to read from it. "John Quincy speaks of his confidence in Charly's abilities... his intelligence and shrewd judgment. He says he asked his brother to mind his fortunes while he is minding the country's. John Quincy says that he will never be able to raise a family on the salary he receives in service."

"According to that Bache viper, he receives the kingly sum of twenty-five thousand dollars per annum," Abigail said bitterly. "How can he arrive at such a figure when fact makes it four thousand, five hundred? Does no one care for fact any longer?"

"Nine thousand," John reminded her. "John Quincy's salary now is nine thousand per annum. Doubled for the reasons of his marriage. Still, it will be difficult...." John turned and looked at the leaping flames sadly.

"How bad is it do you think?"

John shook his head staring into the fire.

"I don't know. John Quincy says he has heard nothing from Charly in months. He asks that we send to find out what has happened."

"Perhaps there will be something left. Or perhaps Charly

invested it before..."

"In our discretion, we have done our eldest son wrong," John muttered, hardly hearing Abigail's frantic hopes.

"But we could not know!" Abigail cried.

"We have seen it before," John reminded her, staring hard into her face.

"But Charly is not my brother Will..." Abigail began, catching his thought.

"No. He is not. Your brother was always spoiled, and selfish. Charles is made of different stuff. He has a kind heart, but he has a demon. We have seen that demon take hold and destroy before, Abigail. We have been remiss in not warning our other children."

Abigail's head pounded. "It was not that simple... Warn them against what? Investing money with Charles? How could we know they would think to do so? Why should we have even considered it?"

"We have ever been careful to look to our own," he reminded her, "for work, for help, for helping. It would be un-Adams had John Quincy been considering investment and NOT considered his brothers first."

"Charles is intelligent, capable. And they love him. Of course they would consider him," she said, unaware of the contradictions in her words as she continued to search for justification. "How could Charles rise to their expectations if they had none? How could he hope to redeem himself without the hopes of his loved ones?"

She was crying now, softly, in resignation.

"We have always known that our Charly walked a thin line between happiness and despair."

"Yes, and do you not think his sister and brothers could not see that too?" she asked, almost angrily.

"They had not the experience to see it as clearly as you and I. What we have seen should have been conveyed," John repeated stolidly.

Charly had spent it all. Every last dollar of John Quincy's savings, scraped together penny by penny, had been squandered. It was a blow to all the Adamses, a heartache that one of them could so wholly let another down. It shook their faith in themselves.

But life at the center of government did not allow much time for mourning. The XYZ affair, Talleyrand's bungled attempt to extort money from the American envoys to France, had set off the hawks in America. Now, like Britain, France had begun to seize American ships and sailors. Struggling to solve the problem through diplomacy, America sent three envoys to negotiate with the French. Talleyrand, the French minister, demanded payment from the American envoys for an audience with him. Additionally, he demanded the guarantee of a loan of $10 million, which would accrue interest to both the French government and to Talleyrand himself. The American envoys said they could not endorse a loan, and indignantly refused to pay for a meeting. France's doors slammed shut.

Adding fuel to the nationalist fires were 'foreigners' whose loyalties were divided between the old sod and the new. Irishmen both inside Congress and out promoted Ireland's cause against Britain, something most Congressmen preferred to ignore. In a fit of pique, Matthew Lyon, an Irish firebrand, spat on fellow Congressman John Griswold in the House chamber. For two weeks, Griswold waited for Congress to censure Lyon. Nothing. Finally, he attacked Lyon with his cane on the floor of the House. In self-defense, Lyon snatched up the fire tongs. The two ended up in a brawl on the floor of the chamber. The newspapers had a field day.

Led by the Federalists -- and Hamilton especially -- hawks in Congress and out spoiled for war. Remembering the triumphs that he had shared at Washington's side during the Revolution, Hamilton imagined himself at the head of a glorious army, his victories acting as steppingstones to his own political aspirations. But the southern Republicans, headed by Vice-President Jefferson, searched for ways to excuse their beloved France's betrayal. The struggle over whether or not to declare war became entangled in the struggle for control of the country between the northern Federalists and the southern Republicans. Accusations flew back and forth.

John stood in the middle -- hating the destruction and economic disaster of war, but slowly coming to the realization that, with diplomatic doors closed, the choice was war or capitulation.

In addition, the country was besieged from inside. Spies were as plentiful as houseflies. Counterfeit currency was adding to the increasing problem of inflation. Critics rocked people's faith in their elected officials.

In an attempt to silence what they saw as dangerous lies and threats against the government, the Federalists proposed the Alien and Sedition Acts. Under the articles, anyone who threatened a public officeholder would be fined $5,000 and imprisoned for five years. Those who attempted to defame an officeholder in writing, print, or speech could expect a $2,000 fine and two years in prison. Under these new laws, seventeen newspapermen and officeholders were brought to trial. Their papers and books were seized. Among them was Benjamin Bache, John's long-time fourth estate nemesis. Ten were indicted. Bache died of yellow fever before he could be jailed.

The Federalist view was that the lies not only damaged personal reputations but hindered an officeholder's ability to do his job in a time of national crisis. But Republicans saw the laws as a way to silence criticism, another step backward toward monarchy.

Finally, the southern faction declared the acts null and void. In a set of 'resolves' that were the first whispers of 'states' rights', Virginia and Kentucky both rejected the federal government's authority in what they termed 'matters of conscience.'

Amid the disputes, Congress continued its shipbuilding.

The year was hard for Abigail. She suffered one ailment after another. Coming home from Philadelphia had been ordeal enough. She felt so faint on the trip north in June, that she had been forced twice in one day to stop at taverns, rent a room, and take off all her clothes to lie down before she felt strong enough to continue. She spent the whole of the summer in bed suffering from diarrhea and fever.

Nabby visited twice during the summer, coming each time with Caroline and the three boys, but she was nearly as worn as Abigail. She had grown fat, dispirited, and trudged about the house in ill-fitting clothes. Captain Smith returned home for several months, but lived as though at a boarding house, spending time with his children only when it suited him, then leaving for days together on shoots and mysterious business. Abigail suspected that he occasionally struck Nabby but she asked no questions. Nabby remained as silent as the tomb.

It was Charles who worried Abigail most. During the long, tedious days in bed, she could see him in her mind's eye, running bright-faced across the fields with a fistful of wildflowers, unadulterated joy on the delicate features. That trip abroad all those years ago had changed him. Susanna had been right. It was a mistake.

On the way home through New York, she and John stopped to see him. They met him coming into his chambers on Beaver Street. Abigail hardly recognized him. She stopped and stared, open-mouthed in her shock. His body was bloated, swollen, like the potato-and-stick-men the children used to make on the hearth, pallid and out of proportion. Sally was gone. She had moved with the children back to her family. Charly had made no move to stop her.

The days in bed were hard, but the nights were worse. Night after night she would dream again of Charly, first as a child, alone, clinging to life on the storm-ravaged vessel, then as a man, friends and family abandoning him, like the rats that escape a sinking ship. They leave to save themselves, she thought. But they leave. He has been abandoned. Everyone he loves, gone. His only friends now were hoary-faced men in doss-houses, friends only so long as the money for liquor held out.

Charly. Oh, Charly. Sometimes she awoke, her heart pounding erratically, certain she would die.

By September Abigail was still too ill to travel, and could not face another winter in Philadelphia. In her place, John took faithful, quiet Louisa Smith and his nephew, William Shaw, Betsey's son, and returned to the fall session of Congress.

The fall had always been a lonely time for Abigail, even though in the country, it was the time of greatest abundance. Reaping the rewards of months —sometimes years -- of labor, farmers and housewives alike brought in vegetables, fruits, and grains. Cartloads of apples and sweet-smelling plums perfumed the air. The cider presses were at work. A ride through the village enveloped her in the scents of bubbling jams and pickle, smoking meat and butchered renderings being turned into soap. It smelled of home, of family industry, and bounty. Everywhere she looked, she saw men and women working, putting by for winter, gathering in for the long, cold nights -- together.

In contrast to the glorious smells, she could almost touch the loneliness, that thin emptiness of dark evenings and dim days.

Chapter 26

Earth felt the wound, and Nature from her seat,
Sighing through all her works, gave signs of woe that all was lost.
John Milton Paradise Lost Bk IX line 782

1799

Talleyrand, pilloried in the American press as nothing but a greedy bureaucrat, suddenly realized his rebuff of the American envoys would drive America, however reluctantly, into Britain's arms. Quietly, deftly, he let it be known that were the American envoys to approach him a second time, he would not turn them away empty-handed.

France rescinded orders to attack American vessels carrying British goods. Step by step, the French were retreating from the brink of war with their American allies. In December, Talleyrand sent a letter to President John Adams urging that the American commissioners come to discuss lasting peace.

But in America, the juggernaut for war was gaining momentum, pushed by the Federalists. A tax – though hugely resented by the public -- was levied to outfit the army and navy. Congress authorized a provisional army of 10,000 men and made Alexander Hamilton second in command – raising the prospect of glories on the battlefield -- the first step toward realizing his political dreams.

But President John Adams was about to destroy that dream with one stroke. On February 18, 1799, he delivered Talleyrand's letter to Congress, along with his proposal that William Vans Murray be named as special envoy to France: talk, not armed conflict.

Congress, still prodded by John's own Federalist party, dithered. But John was adamant. And he found supporters. Vote by vote he won a majority over to his views.

Hamilton, the kingmaker who thought he held the reins of government securely, if surreptitiously, in his hands, was furious. He hadn't realized that John Adams was a Federalist in name only. He was temperamentally incapable of being a party man -- ever. Although he was vain, pompous, and protective of his own place in history, John Adams was above all else a principled man. Hamilton had not bargained on that. He had not realized that John Adams, who ached to be reelected, would knowingly throw away his reelection on a point of principle.

But he had. Having struggled all his life to be prominent, respected, and loved, John Adams was knowingly defeating himself. He would not play politics if it meant sacrificing the nation. However much John's vanity wanted glory, his soul wanted right more.

Abigail watched it all from Quincy. The vilification in the press was heartrending. Her beloved John was dissected piece by piece, his motives and honor smeared, his family attacked. Death threats began to arrive.

Hold on, my dearest friend, she prayed. You have ever taken the unpopular side because it is right. Remember Captain Preston and hold on. God knows your heart. Take comfort in that.

While saddened at his distress, at the endless attacks, she was also relieved. His time as a public servant would soon be over. She had supported him, cheered him on for thirty-five years. Now, she wanted peace. And she wanted it with him. She was tired of being alone.

'We have so much to be grateful for, even in the midst of our troubles,' she wrote him that spring. *'There is not a day that comes that I do not look to with a grateful eye. Yet I want your company, my dear friend. I have shared you overlong with an ungrateful world.'*

Ensconced in the broad wing chair in John's study, feet covered with a heavy rug, Abigail read John's most recent letter. She had finally begun to recover. Still not strong enough to work, she nevertheless occasionally made pies and puddings in the kitchen, as much for the satisfaction in making a thing as a desire for her own cooking. She did not like so much enforced idleness.

The second floor office was now two rooms wide. On her written instructions from Philadelphia Dr. Tufts had had men knock out the center wall to make one large room. The fireplace could not heat the corners in winter, but in summer, the sweet-scented breeze blew through the open space like a breath from heaven. The trees had grown taller. The Colleys' house was now obscured by a thicket of branches. Nothing remains the same.

The letter in her hand was dated February 21, 1799. It took fifteen days to get here from Philadelphia to Quincy. The roads must be thick with mud, she thought. Some missives come in five.

The snow had stopped, but a gray pall hung over the countryside, reminiscent of the lowering sky that foretold of a summer squall. Outside young Eli began to clear the walks yet again, the shovel rasping against brick as he pitched the new snow on top of the five-foot drifts he had already piled up. The thud of heavy shoes on the stairs echoed up the hallway. The office door opened and Mary Cranch came in, her face gray, despite wind-pinked cheeks.

"What is it?" Abigail asked, half-rising from her chair in alarm.

Mary held up a hand, and shook her head without replying. She pulled the other upholstered chair closer to the fire and sat, hunching herself under the thick shawl, thin armor. She drew a letter from her apron pocket and handed it to Abigail.

Abigail read while Mary stared into the flames. After a few minutes' silence, Mary rose automatically to poke the fire higher and toss in another log then collapsed back into the chair.

"Ohh, Mary!" Abigail breathed, looking up into her miserable sister's face. "It sounds very bad. Speculation. Again land speculation! What will it bring our family to?"

Mary shook her head. "Ruined. My children are ruined. All their money gone. How can they raise their families? They have worked and saved, trying to better their lives...." tears began to flow down Mary's creased cheek. "Richard and I have scraped by our whole lives. Our - whole - lives. We have pinched and worked and tried to make every penny count twice. And still we have so little. We cannot help them."

She stopped talking and stared again into the fire as though trying to read her children's future in the leaping flames.

"They will begin again," Abigail murmured, looking for some words of comfort, though she knew there were none. Some pains simply must be borne.

Land Speculation; Colonel Smith, Charly, Billy Cranch, and Lucy Cranch's husband, all had poured their hopes and their future plans into one bucket and that bucket had been emptied by unscrupulousness. The money was all gone.

"What will become of them?" Mary asked softly.

"They are in God's hands, Sister," Abigail reminded her.

"They may be in God's hands," Mary replied, a bitter edge to her voice, "But they are our flesh nevertheless. Pieces of our hearts."

"It is a hard lesson, is it not?" Abigail said, reaching a hand over to Mary's arm where it rested on the chair. "How must our Lord feel to watch all mankind's folly? The pain His heart must bear for His children."

As Mary looked up, Abigail could see the resemblance Mary held to their mother, Elizabeth Smith. The firm jaw, the clear eyes. But there was a kinder line to the mouth, a softer aspect to the countenance. Mary had a more forgiving nature.

"We can do only what we can do," Abigail continued, repeating the words she had used so often to solace herself. "When we have children, we are simultaneously blessed and burdened. Nabby has shackled herself to a man whose life has been spent chasing what he considers his by inherited right. Even now he pesters John for a position in the provisional army, one he considers equal to his previous rank with General Washington. He has no idea how many hate him now."

Mary sucked in a long, deep breath and ran her hands slowly over her wet cheeks, wiping off the tears. She gathered herself and settled back into the chair.

"I saw Royall Tyler the other day," she said, wondering again if she had played a part in breaking Nabby's engagement to Tyler. "His last play was well-received. The once unstable young man has come to prominence."

A fleeting look of pain crossed Abigail's face as she thought how different Nabby's life might have been had she married Tyler -- now a successful judge and playwright --instead of the capricious Colonel William Smith.

But despite the sorrows, there were joys. One was Thomas Boylston's return from Europe. Seeing this son, now solid, healthy, and prosperous, was a tonic to both John and Abigail. Thomas delivered Talleyrand's letter to John, spent time with him in the capital, then rode to Quincy to see his mother. It lifted Abigail's spirits to see one son who was so obviously doing well.

While Abigail stayed home, John faced his duties as president alone. He wrote constantly that he missed his 'talkative wife.' He wanted her with him. So did the public. On the heels of John's Feb. 18, 1799 letter to Congress advocating one more envoy to France, the papers contended that if 'the old woman' had been with him, he would never have weakened. *She* would have stuck for war, they said, and forced him to do the same. Many of the papers, and John's supporters, were convinced that Abigail heavily influenced his decisions.

While the support in print soothed her ego, what helped more was the steady stream of love that John put down on paper and sent through the mails. So many other men, after years of marriage were searching for young women to rekindle the fires of their old age and were busy spawning a legion of illegitimate children. But if John had fathered a wrong-side-of-the-blanket baby, the press would have uncovered it by now, she felt sure. She could relax in John's fidelity. He had remained faithful to both the body and mind he loved. Her stitchery had not mattered. Grandmother Quincy and her mother were wrong. A woman could hope for more. Abigail felt something like smugness in the knowledge.

John's decision to send envoys to France one more time threw the government into turmoil. German farmers in Pennsylvania rebelled against the military tax, an armed revolt that resulted in the arrest and conviction of John Fries, the man who had led it. He was sentenced to be hanged for treason. John's cabinet wanted the death sentence to be carried out. But John saw Fries as a man who had acted against what he saw as unfair taxation and pardoned him. The Federalists, who had feared that the uprising showed a growing disregard of the law, were furious. They had been determined to make Fries an example for all of the discontented. Once again, John's independence had thwarted Federalist policy. In retaliation, Hamilton swore to thwart John's reelection.

Although his advisors demanded he stay to campaign for a second term, John left for Quincy that summer. He missed Abigail and his home too much. He spent summer trying to run the government by letter from Quincy. A mistake. Finally, in November, Abigail was well enough to travel. Together with their usual entourage, they made their way back over the pitted roads to Philadelphia. On the way south, they stopped in New York. But

349

Charly was nowhere to be found.

On December 14, 1799, George Washington died. The country went into paroxysms of grief. While they had greatly admired Washington, both John and Abigail were appalled at the bombast and hyperbole used to extol his virtues. He had been a good man. A judicious, rational, man. But he had been a man. No saint, surely, John grumbled. They both knew that John's death would not occasion so many effusions. It stung their pride.

1800

Election year. John, still determined to imagine himself the reluctant gentleman farmer called into public service by public acclaim, refused to campaign for his second term. Yet he hungered for it as some men hunger for a woman. The Federalists, furious at his independence and still smarting from his dismissal of three Federalist cabinet members who had been reporting back to Hamilton, searched for a newer more tractable candidate.

Exhausted by the onslaught of both work and criticism, John grew more and more irascible. As the months wore on and his chances for reelection grew more and more dim, he began his familiar, self-defensive litany of denial. He did not want to serve, he said, he had ruined his health in sacrifice to his country. His words were meant to tamp down his own longing. Each time he had used them before, another office had been offered. For years, his family had listened impatiently to his blusterings. This time, Abigail listened with pity. This time, she knew, no office would be offered.

And, though indignant, she was also relieved. The years of struggle and separation were coming to an end. Each ball, each dinner, each official tea she held, brought her one step closer to that end, and she poured herself into the final year with enthusiasm. Louisa, true to her own prediction, had not married, and remained with her aunt and uncle, the spinster daughter who stood in her mother's shadow, seeing to the details, following up on Abigail's orders, managing the servants. The round of parties and visits was even more hectic than during previous years. Many who knew and respected the Adamses felt they would be seeing them in their official capacity for the last time. They wanted to pay their respects.

Buoyed by the hope that this indeed was their last hurrah,

Abigail's health improved. And, as though in tribute to their last year in Philadelphia, spring came early, bubbling up through the trees to burst into pale green leaf, then verdant bloom. On the 19th of May, 1800, Abigail left for Quincy.

But it was a sad trip. This time, when she stopped in New York, she found Charles at home.

"Mother?"

Abigail was shocked at the figure that stood before her in the doorway of the Beaver Street apartment. Gray, swollen-faced, and unshaven, thirty-year-old Charly looked fifty. The paunchy bulge of his stomach in his otherwise slim figure told of drink without food, his liver unable to keep up with the steady stream of alcohol that had become his diet. She tried to compose herself, to keep from showing her horror, but the shock was too much.

"Mother!'" Charly reached out both hands to draw her into the filthy room. It stank of stale spirits and urine. "Oh, Mar!" He wrapped his arms around his stunned mother, holding her like a little boy yearning for protection.

"Charly..." she managed to gulp, slowly putting her arms up to envelope him, an embrace long overdue. He had not bathed in months and his clothes smelled of vomit.

"Mar, come in," he released her and scurried to get a chair. Pathetically, he tried to clear an overloaded table on his way past it, but simply upset the contents and left it on the floor.

Abigail crossed the room and opened a window while Charly brought her a straight chair and put it near the sweet spring draught that seeped into the fetid chamber. Hurriedly, he brought a second chair, and sat across from her, their knees nearly touching, and reached for her hand.

"I have missed you, Mar," he began, eyes brimming. "I...I..." he stopped and bent double, blubbering into her lap.

Horrified, disgusted, and overwhelmed with sadness, Abigail stroked the dank hair.

"Hush, Charly," she crooned as though to a small child. "Hush, now. Calm, yourself. I am here."

"Oh, Mar! What have I done?" he wailed into the folds of her skirt.

What indeed, she thought. Nearly choked with emotion, she bit her lip to hold back the tears.

"I tried, Mar. I tried. Sally...left. It was the money, and the land... they couldn't find the land and the brokers took the cash, I tried to find them, filed a brief, a complaint, a... I forget... but it was no good. Johnny's money... is Johnny angry?"

He rose suddenly, his eyes wide.

Abigail shook her head, not trusting herself to speak.

"I've let you down, let everyone down...I don't deserve..."

"Hush!" she said, more sharply than she meant to.

Charly hiccuped and swallowed his tears, looking earnestly into her eyes for a moment.

"This is a terrible way to welcome you. I have not... it has been so long...." he rose so abruptly he almost sent his mother over backward. "I haven't offered you anything."

He clattered awkwardly around the room, his movements sluggish, as though his muscles would not obey. He picked up a stained lace handkerchief and found two sticky, ant-covered glasses beneath it. He hastily covered them again. Glancing backward to see if his mother had seen, he continued his fruitless search for something to offer his mother, a pitiful effort at hospitality.

"Charles," Abigail said, reaching out a hand to retrieve her son. "Charly. Don't trouble yourself. I want for nothing, save your sensible company once again. Sit. Sit and compose yourself. A deep breath. Here, come sit ye back down."

Obediently, Charly stopped his futile hunt and returned to the chair, this time falling silent in his realization of what his mother must see.

"You have not..." Abigail began.

"How is Par?" Charly burst out, as though to stave off her advances into his black world, forestall any advice, admonition.

He had so longed for friendly company, had missed his mother so acutely, he could not have borne her censure. He simply wanted to be with her, wrapped in her love.

"Your par is well, considering," Abigail began, studying him, pain written in every line of her face. It is too late. There is no use in recriminations. "His eyes do not plague him as they have, and his teeth are nearly gone so they do not hurt so much. But his heart is sore."

"He is well?" Charles said, eagerly fastening on the positive. "I am glad. I am glad of that. There is much in the papers, they say bad things...I do not like to read them any more. It is too sad, too much anger, sorrow."

He dropped his head again and began to cry.

"Charles," Abigail said softly, stroking his head and thinking of that small, charming boy he had been. It seemed such a short time ago. "Charly, you must come home with me. Quincy will help. The sea air, work on the farm. It will make the difference."

"Nothing will make a difference now, Mother!" he almost shouted, brows furrowed in confused anger. "Nothing! It will end as it ends, and there is nothing for it. If you came for that, you can go!"

He jumped up again and went to the door, flinging it open.

"But--"

"No! I will not be treated like a small child! You be on your way to Quincy. I do not live there any more!"

"Charles!"

The sound that emerged from her throat was an animal cry. Tears streamed down her face, and she put both hands to her cheeks without rising.

He came back across the room, took her by one hand and tried to lift her from the chair.

"Let me go, Charles. Release me, I say!"

He did as he was told, sheepishly, but a resentful look came into his eyes.

"I'm a lawyer, Mother. And grown. I do not take orders, not even from my mother, however worthy a personage she may be."

"I give you no orders, Charles Adams," she said, anger at the accusation giving her a measure of control.

Charles went back to the door and stood with one hand on the knob, waiting, his look cold.

Heavily, she rose and trudged to the door, looking into his face once more before she started out. His eyes, bloodshot and swollen, stared as though at a stranger who had intruded upon his domain. Then a flicker of the old Charly came back, a glimmer of comprehension.

"Perhaps come back tomorrow, " he whispered, so faintly she thought at first she had not heard it. She stopped for a moment, head down, unseeing. "I am not myself," he said softly, reaching a hand up. It did not quite touch her shoulder. The tone was apologetic, conciliatory. "Come back tomorrow."

She nodded, head down.

"Mar…"

"Yes." she dared not look into that face again.

"I--"

She heard him choke -- whether from emotion or cough she could not be certain. She waited while he regained control of himself and he finished gently, "Tell Par that I asked for him."

She nodded again and made her way slowly down the stairs and out into the street.

Charles was not there the following day. She waited for three days, going back to his apartments several times each day, but he had once again disappeared.

In New York, she also stopped to visit Nabby, but the stay was painfully circumscribed. Colonel Smith's regiment was being disbanded, which meant he was once again without income. Nabby was reduced to observations on the weather and reports of the boys' schooling while her mother sat awkwardly playing with Caroline. Heartsick and impotent, Abigail finally left and rode toward Quincy with a profound — and guilty—sense of relief.

John, meanwhile, set out toward Washington to inspect the capital city that was slowly rising out of the swamps of the Potomac. He found many of the public buildings further along in construction than he had anticipated, but the President's mansion was still unfinished. I will never live here, he thought sadly. He set off for Quincy at the exhausting pace of fifty miles a day, desperate for the comfort of his own home.

The presidential campaign was a brawl. The Federalists, led by Hamilton, devised a campaign to repudiate their incumbent president without actually disavowing him. It created a rift within the party that was widened by the Republican discovery and publication of a series of letters characterizing John as jealous, petty, weak, and dishonest.

This, John half-expected. But what almost crushed him was the defection of a collection of old friends, men he had spent long discussion-filled evenings with, in whom he had confided and against whose ideas he had sharpened his own. He felt deserted in his last great battle by his comrades in arms.

Though abandoned by many old political friends, John was not completely alone. A steady stream of legislators and officials made pilgrimages to the Quincy manse to consult with or give advice to the 'old man.' Additionally, Abigail's renovations for the house, the new barn, the annual maintenance to the stone walls and outbuildings all required an army of workmen, keeping the house in a general buzz of activity.

The Federalists may have resented and distrusted John Adams, but the public still loved him. They knew a died-in-the-wool common man when they saw one and appreciated his understanding of their lot as well as his cantankerous individuality. On his annual journeys to and from Quincy, he was met along the way by well-wishers laden with flowers, gifts of food and drink, and other tokens of their respect. While it would make no difference in the number of electors he would garner in the election, their support helped to soothe a badly battered ego.

The summer of 1800 at home served to give John more perspective. Separated from the claustrophobic halls of government, he read the newspapers, conducted business, and read Tacitus, comforted by the knowledge that he was certainly not the first man in history to be unjustly attacked.

By July, Quincy was in the throes of a liver fever that had laid many of the residents low. Though both Abigail and John escaped it, rheumatic fever sent Abigail to bed again. By September, John was forced to make plans to leave for Washington without her. But Abigail, determined to be by John's side, soon followed. She knew he could endure accolades alone, but she could not bear to think of him in the last few months of his presidency alone in that nest of vipers. And, she must see Charly.

Sally had written to let Abigail know that Charly was no longer at Beaver Street. He had been evicted. He was ill, living on the kindness of a friend in a rented room.

By the time she found her way to the rooming house through the maze of muddy New York City streets, Abigail was exhausted. She had left Louisa in their rooms. Unable to bear her niece's pain as well as her own, she had insisted on coming alone. The prospect of going alone through the streets had not seemed as frightening in her hotel room as it did now that she was picking her way, unprotected, through an unfamiliar part of town. Drunks reeled past, now crashing unheeding into her, now staggering into the darkened doorways to refortify or relieve themselves. One, a former servant who recognized her from their days in New York, pleaded for a few pennies. Abigail pressed two coppers into the man's dirty palm and, with a glance over her shoulder lest she be stopped by a crowd of beggars, hurried on. The streets stank of human excrement and urine, rotting vegetables and despair.

"Mrs. Adams!"

The voice came from above. She looked up and saw Sally Adams leaning out of a second story window.

"Mrs. Adams, come into the door, there," she said, pointing to the unpainted door on Abigail's right, "and come straight up here -- first door on your left at the top of the first flight."

Sweating in the close September heat, Abigail came through the door Sally had indicated, and leaned against the jam for a moment to catch her breath. Then, wearily, she started up the stairs, each step bringing her closer to what she feared to face.

"You should not have come alone, Mrs. Adams,"' Sally admonished.

She had flung open the door and stood, staring in disbelief as her mother-in-law, the wife of the President of the United States of America, trudged unaided up the steps of a filthy rooming house, its walls greasy with the palm prints of its hopeless inhabitants. Taking Abigail's arm at the top of the stair, she led her into the darkened room and steered her toward the only chair inside. The room was dim. At first, Abigail thought Charly was absent. Then she heard the bed creak. As though in a dream, the outline of a form came slowly into focus as her eyes adjusted to the dim light.

Her son looked like a cadaver, sprawled on the bed, a splotched coverlet pulled to his waist, his shirt open at the neck exposing a white chest whose bones were outlined in sad relief just beneath the skin. His unwashed hair was stringy. It had been pushed off his face and was damp at the scalp. A bowl of rusty-looking water sat by the bed, a torn rag folded neatly over the rim.

Abigail sucked in a breath to steady herself. The room reeked of death. I have walked into a coffin, the lid half-closed, she thought.

"Charles?" Tentatively, she reached out a hand as she pulled the chair closer.

The wasted figure on the bed made no acknowledgment.

"He may not know you," Sally told her matter-of-factly. "He's been drifting in and out. He knew me yesterday, but today he doesn't. I'm glad the girls are not here to see this."

The young woman had not meant to be callous, but it stabbed Abigail to imagine Charly's daughters, their fading memories of their father framed by the pain of his last days.

"How long has he been like this?" Abigail asked hoarsely.

Sally shook her head. "I've been here almost a week. I don't know how long before that. The friend who pays for this room for him wrote me, told me I should come..." she trailed off, looking sadly at the pathetic figure that her successful, loving husband had become.

"Has the doctor been sent for?"

Sally nodded. "Archie, the friend who pays for the room, has been most kind. The doctor comes daily, out of respect for the President as much as for the money Archie gives him to see to..."

Charly groaned and attempted to turn over. Failing in the attempt, he winced and flopped back on the bed.

"Charles?" Abigail said again, leaning toward her son. "Charly?"

He opened his eyes but stared uncomprehendingly through her.

"Charly, it's Mar," she said, putting a hand on his where it lay limp on the coverlet.

The eyelids fluttered, a connection made somewhere in the recesses of his mind, but he could not focus on her.

"Husband!" Sally called to him, putting her face near his and raising her voice.

Slowly, he turned his head and looked at her, his mouth hung slack.

"Your mother is here to see you."

He nodded, but without understanding. Suddenly he doubled over, racked by a fit of coughing. With practiced hands, Sally dipped the cloth into the water, wrung it out and held it to his mouth until he had finished his fit. When she took it away, it was spattered with blood. Her face a mask, the young woman reached down and rinsed the cloth into the bowl, then folded it over the rim again.

"What does the doctor say?" Abigail asked. Her chest constricted, and she felt as though she were forcing breath through a tiny straw in a frantic effort to keep herself alive.

"He says it won't be much longer," Sally replied, making no effort to soften the blow.

Abigail nodded, silently; her mind was racing, running over the years between his birth and now, catching fleeting, sharp-edged glimpses of him as a child, as a young man, a successful lawyer, the young husband and proud father. Each was like a knife in her soul.

"Are you there?" his feverish voice sliced into the images flashing through her mind and dragged her back to the present.

"I am here, son. "

He appeared not to have heard her.

"Are you there?" he cried again, more frantically.

"I don't know who he's callin' for," Sally observed. "He's been doing that since I got here."

'Has he said... anything?"

"You mean about you or Mr. Adams?"

Sally's bluntness startled Abigail. She had not expected it, though what she had expected, she was not able to imagine now.

"Or anything about... what has most haunted him...of what his demons are made?" Abigail almost whispered the words, fearful for the Pandora's box they might open.

She dared not look at Sally but stared, transfixed, at her son's nearly unrecognizable face.

Sally shook her head, her lip pushed out musingly.

"No. He spits out snatches. I can't make anything of it. He's called for his Grandma Adams a couple of times. He scared me once, with it. I thought, the way he was looking, that she was in the room with us; I looked over my shoulder expecting to see her standing there, but of course there was nothing. But he stopped that, thank God."

"But nothing...else?" Abigail persisted, angry at herself for her own selfish need for relief.

"No," Sally shook her head again. "He said something a couple of days ago about disappointing the family, about being a sorrow to you and Mr. Adams. But most of the time he's been out of his head. He talks a little of his girls, then he seems to get them confused with childhood friends, I can't make sense of most of it," she said again.

Abigail sat by the bed every day for three days, waiting. Only once did he come to himself enough to acknowledge her presence. And in that acknowledgment was contrition and shame, a plea for forgiveness. She could hardly breathe for the pain she felt. I do him more harm than good by my presence, she decided. She thought suddenly of her own mother's love for her brother, Will, of Elizabeth Smith's need to see him as she wished him to be. Abigail thought too of the lies of omission she and her father had told Elizabeth Smith about Will in an effort to protect her from the truth.

I would wish to be so protected, she thought. I cannot bear to watch my son's disintegration.

She watched Sally's patient attendance on the broken man that once was her little boy, the tenderness of her movements and murmurings. It was hard to believe that this was the sister of the foolish, selfish rake that Nabby had married. Abigail was overwhelmed with remorse for her condemnation of Sally's marriage to her son. It may have been the only redemption in Charly's life.

As she left, Abigail reached her hand out to the young woman, noting sadly the dark circles under her eyes.

"If ye have need of anything, call on me. Anything. The post reaches us in a very few days, and if you send it by urgent mail to the President, it will reach us posthaste. My prayers are with you."

Sally nodded without expression and turned away.

Chapter 27

The sum of earthly bliss
John Milton Paradise Lost Bk. VIII Line 522

As she trundled over the roads toward the new capital city, pain jolting through aching joints at each rut, Abigail looked back over her life, scattered like the pieces of an incomplete jigsaw in her mind's eye. So many separate pieces. She had struggled to make them all fit neatly, but there were ragged edges.

Daughter, wife, mother, confidante, friend, farmer, keeper of the flame. Each had rubbed against the next and in that rubbing, stolen away as well as added. She had never gained without losing.

She had already buried two children. The loss of each of those two babes had been hard. In her heart lay those wounds, thickened and grown over with the years, a persistent ache, but scabbed, protected. But Charly. Charly's impending death, as sure as the hand of Providence itself, was a cruel blow. She could now imagine her mother's pain over Will, and understand the love that kept her returning to her cherished son, despite his falterings, his selfishness, his drinking. What hopes did Elizabeth Smith have for Will that Abigail did not have for Charly? And Charly had come so close. Close enough to begin a career, to stand in the light of success. Far closer than Will. She was losing more -- or was she? Perhaps she had misjudged Will. Where was the difference between the two? No. She would not accept that. Her mother had been indulgent of Will, while she had been firm, demanding, had expected success -- or at least striving. And Charly had striven, had succeeded, for a time. By what perversity had he thrown it all away? Elizabeth Smith had never spoken of the part she might have played in Will's destruction. Abigail, too, never voiced her own guilty questions.

She wondered, clinically, if Charly's sudden death would have been easier to bear than this drop-by-drop ebbing away. She had thought him lost all those years ago. She could remember what it felt like. A sword to the heart. Would a swift unforeseen stroke be an easier burden than to be forced to stand by, powerless, and watch her son's gradual disintegration? She had borne both for the same child and still did not know.

The burnished leaves of autumn drifted by the carriage window in a kaleidoscope of scenery. Such contrasts in this world, she thought. Such beauty in the midst of ugliness. She looked down at the stain on her gown, the stain she had deliberately put there. A reminder that it had all been real. Beautiful Charly, at the end so withered and ugly, his regrets and sorrow standing in bitter relief against the pillows. She could still feel Charly's cold, clammy skin beneath her fingertips as she wiped her hands across his fevered brow one last time. Deliberately smearing it on the side of her skirt, she watched as the stain darkened the bright cloth, the imprint of her son's suffering. As she sat in the jouncing carriage, her fingertips strayed to the stain. Charly. I will bury another child. I could give life but I have no power to save it.

The coach reached the crest of a hill and she peered out to see the countryside below, a patchwork quilt of color spread haphazardly over the brown earth. On the left, crimson and green hedgerows of honeysuckle bordered a small farm, its ripe fields like a bolt of golden linen flung out to bedazzle the eye. A man and woman, surrounded by a brood of children, some with tools, others cavorting carefree in the field, raked cut grain into stooks that they methodically rowed up to dry.

The old yearning to have worked daily side by side with John and the children to bring in their harvest, to have seen her children grow, take their places in a growing community, watchful of each other, returned. She imagined the happiness of those provincial neighbors in Quincy and Braintree whose children were born, lived and died all within the space of ten miles, each intimately connected to the lives of the others. That was not our lot, Abigail reminded herself sternly. We have been close, she insisted in answer to her own nagging doubts. We have grown together in community, but that community has been wider than Braintree and Quincy. Our watchfulness has been manifested in prayer. If we have not often shared our days, we have shared our hearts, she told herself.

She saw the farmer stop, homemade rake held with practiced ease as he straightened and swept off his hat to drag a sleeve across his sweaty brow. Jamming the hat back on his head, he stood staring at her carriage, which was nearly abreast of the fields. His wife stopped too, and leant on her rake, the two of them within an arm's reach of one another. They harvest together, Abigail thought, watching them enviously.

The capital city was a quagmire. Men walking in the mucky streets had had their shoes sucked right off their stockinged feet, lost forever in the mire that clamped onto horse, carriage, and pedestrian alike. There were few houses. Congressional wives had chosen to remain home while their husbands took up lodgings in boarding houses and hotels. It might be beautiful one day, Abigail thought as she endured the slow, lurching progress of her carriage, but it is ugly now.

John opened the November Congress in the new domed capital building, the first president to speak to both houses of Congress simultaneously. The first president to govern from the new capital. As he looked out over the Senators and Representatives, their disparate interests and temperaments congealed into the body that would become the conscience of the nation, he prayed that his words would find fallow ground in every heart. Let all those who serve here look not to party, not to expediency, but to the future, to the good of the whole country, he said. He had done that. But he also wanted the office, public acknowledgment for his lifetime of faithful service.

Taxes, recession, the muddled decisions of a Congress riddled with factionalism, public and private frustrations with the Federalist elitist views -- all struck blows against John's chances at reelection. And there was Alexander Hamilton. Without the tempering hand of his mentor, George Washington, Hamilton worked like a thwarted child to snatch the election from John's hands. Gleefully, the southern Republicans watched and anticipated their victory. But John's popular support remained strong. The common folk trusted the old man in the President's House. He was one of their own.

On December 4, the electoral colleges of each state convened to cast their votes. John Adams and General Pinckney ran together representing the Federalists, while Jefferson, John's elusive vice president, had joined with Aaron Burr against them for the Republican party. When the first tallies reached Washington on the 8th of December, John Adams held a single vote lead. There was still hope. South Carolina, Pinckney's home, could put them back in office.

362

"I might yet win a majority, My Dear!" John chortled, coming into the cavernous drawing room. It was damp, despite the huge blaze that lapped up the sides of the fireplace.

Abigail looked up from the list she was making, her heart threatening to choke her. Win? Is that victory? Or defeat?

"Indeed?"

"Yes. Pennsylvania, Maryland, New Jersey, Massachusetts, and Virginia all have returned their votes. I hold forty-seven to Mr. Jefferson's forty-six! With South Carolina still to be counted, we may yet carry the day!"

Abigail studied John for a moment, her pen poised above the tablet, its quill drying in the chill air. Part of her was glad at the possibility for his sake. She wanted the honor as much as he did. But after thirty-six years, she wanted to go home more -- and this time she wanted John by her side.

"Ye may yet," she said quietly.

"You might take more pleasure in the possibility!" John admonished.

Abigail eyed him. Could he not feel as she did that they had given their lives to an ungrateful nation and sacrificed their family in the process?

"My mind is much on our son," she replied.

"As is mine," John said with an exasperated edge to his voice. "But I feared I might be completely routed from this office. After a lifetime spent in service, it was too much to bear."

"Your sacrifices will never be known or appreciated," Abigail replied bluntly. "Your devotion must be its own reward. You cannot by another span of years in this office hope to alter the opinions of those who wish you ill. If you wish to serve another term, I wish it for you. But do not ask me to take pleasure in the sacrifices we make while my heart is breaking."

"Is Charly not my son, too? Does the possibility of his loss not tear at me?" John cried, angry at her refusal to celebrate with him. "But we have more than one son. While one is sinking, two others are rising. For that we can give thanks, and be proud. My reelection would further their careers. That is no small consideration. And may I not hope for continuation in an office, which I hold by every right of duty and honor?"

"Have I argued that point with you?" she snapped, dropping the pen and putting her hands flat on the table to steady herself. "Have I ever done anything but sacrifice with you for the sake of our country? Many and many years have I done without your company, yet I never stood in your way. I have rejoiced at the honors done you, and mourned at the poison flung at you. I have stood beside you when I was able, and always, always in my heart, upheld you. I think I have a right to be treated with the respect due an old soldier of the wars -- one who entered the battle not happily but with integrity, eyes on the cause. But battles bring losses. We have lost much. Do NOT ask me to celebrate those losses."

John stood, lips slightly parted, taken aback at her vehemence. He looked at her and finally saw the woman she had become. Her shoulders sagged. Rheumatism had knotted the slender hands he had once caressed with such joy at the miracle of their smooth white skin. The determined jaw was laced with jowls and the hair had gone silver. When did that happen? At fifty-six she was an old woman. Despite her increasing ill health, John still considered her his rock, indestructible, like the stones on the Quincy shore.

"I do not ask for glory in the sacrifice," he said, chastened. "You *are* an old soldier, but not a common one. You have ever been my general, Abigail, my stay and my guide. I ask only that you, as our marriage vows describe, take joy in my joy, and sorrow in my sorrow."

"I do," she said shortly. "I always have. Yet I take my own joy and my own sorrow as I find them, too. And your joy and mine may not always coincide. I can both rejoice at your triumphs and sorrow for my own losses."

"Would another term be such a loss for you?" he asked, coming over to put his arm around her shoulders.

She looked up at him, bald now except for the fringe of hair that ringed his domed head like the grassy outcrop on a mountain. The lips puckered into his nearly toothless mouth, and the red-rimmed eyes had heavy bags beneath them. At their marriage, she did not even consider the old man he would become nor could she have imagined this bent old gnome had she tried. Neither could she have imagined the love she still bore him, the passionate devotion she still felt for the slowly wasting figure that stood before her.

She sighed deeply, resting her head on his arm.

"I would rejoice for you," she said, choosing her words carefully, "because you wish it so much. But I want to go home. I am tired, John."

He leaned back and reached a hand down, cupping her chin in his palm. Their eyes met, the love in them undiminished since they had stood before her father and said their wedding vows.

"I fear I am no longer fitted for any other thing, My Dear," he confessed. "As much as I love our little farm, I fear I will dry up without the stimulating juices of the political battle. I may hate the fight, but I love it as well."

Abigail nodded, holding his gaze. "I know. But if ye are not reelected, you must reconcile yourself to that other life."

She searched his face as she collected the words to express her hopes for their future together.

"I fear you have not fully tasted the pleasures of that other life. You have taken joy in the farm, the rocks, the walls, the building and bustle of enlargement. But you have been a mere lodger, knowing that you would in time fly off again to another world, another work. You have always had one eye for home, one eye for posterity. When you have both eyes set on one place, you may see more joy and challenge than you imagine. Besides," she continued, her voice sharper in its return to practicality, "you have not built up such a stock of capital that your life in retirement will be one of ease. We have sacrificed more than time for our country. We have sacrificed fortunes that others have made. You must work to keep us going, Husband."

John smiled, his eyes twinkling at her Yankee toughness. "Let us see which way the electoral winds blow first," he said gently. "Then we can plan my Quincy retirement."

Before John and Abigail received word of the final tally, they had news of a different kind. They sat together in their bedroom, Abigail holding Sally's letter in a trembling hand, bent toward the fire.

" *"His last words were to you,"* " she read, as John sat in a heap in the chair opposite, his eyes, filled with tears, fixed on the carpet at her feet. "'*They were spoken a week before he died, then he lapsed into a fevered state where I could discern nothing comprehensible. What he may have said, what words of comfort or contrition, I do not know. But he spread his love about as he could, and asked forgiveness of you both. That he would be a disappointment to you was an arrow that pierced his heart.*'"

Abigail stopped reading and looked up at John, struggling to keep herself under control. Together they had made this son. Now, another hand had taken him away.

"Oh, that I could have died for him!" John wailed.

"We must be sure that Sally is adequately provided for, and the children are educated," Abigail said.

She clutched the letter with whitened knuckles, hands contorted into fists in her lap.

"Of course, of course!" John moaned, his head in his hands. "Oh, my son! Such promise wasted! Evil has taken his pound of flesh, cut out the heart..." he choked.

The door opened softly. Louisa came into the room.

"Uncle?" she sounded almost timid, like the girl who had first come to them so many years before.

John looked up at his niece, who looked bleary through his tears. Louisa crossed the room and put her hand on John's shoulder.

"Uncle, there is a delegation here."

"From whom? What do they want?"

"I believe it is the election," she said softly, bending down to him.

"I cannot see them now!" John croaked. "Send them away! Deputize! Tell them to leave their message and be gone!"

"I will go," Abigail said dully, pulling herself from her chair and handing the letter to Louisa. "Stay with your uncle. Comfort him. It is Charles."

She walked across the broad room and closed the door behind her. In the hallway, she found three young men, the looks on their smooth faces unreadable.

"Madam, we have come to deliver news of the final count in the presidential election," the tallest said, bowing slightly.

He was richly dressed -- Parisian fashions, Abigail noted. I wonder what part he plays in all this.

"I am afraid the President is indisposed," Abigail informed him. Straight-backed, she waited, bracing herself. "I am to take a message to him."

"Mr. Hamilton said..." the young man began, but, seeing the sudden rage in Abigail's eyes, he stopped. "Very well, Madam."

Taking a paper from his breast pocket, he read the results.

"Mr. Jefferson and Mr. Burr are tied with seventy-three votes

366

each. Mr. Adams received sixty-five votes."

Out! Abigail felt slightly faint, though from relief or fury she could not decide.

"There will be a second vote to determine whether the president is to be Mr. Jefferson or Mr. Burr," the man was saying, but Abigail hardly heard him.

Quincy. She almost said the word aloud. It seemed magical, an incantation of hope.

John took the news of his defeat as though it were an afterthought. Charly's death, however expected, had hit him hard. Yet he continued to the last trying to batten down the governmental ship against the Republican storm he believed would follow. It was frustrating. Every day, he could see his influence waning as he marked out the last of his term. His suggestions and missives were looked on in many quarters as a minor, and temporary, annoyance. Through it, he mourned Charly, the injustices and vagaries of life, and the ineluctable workings of Providence.

Streams of visitors came to pay their respects, many smiling with pleasure behind their mask of commiseration. It galled him to receive those who had wished his downfall. But others came in genuine affection and sorrow at his defeat. John Quincy's letter declaring that 'the sober decision of posterity' would one day pronounce John a 'statesman who made the sacrifice of his own interest and influence to the real and unquestionable benefit of his country,' helped to salve John's wounds and lift his eyes toward the future.

For weeks, the Electoral College continued to squabble over which of the two Republican candidates would become president. A simple majority was all that was needed to decide which office each candidate was to hold. On the thirty-fifth ballot, Jefferson was finally declared the winner. By default, Burr would be vice-president.

Jefferson came to see Abigail just before they left for Quincy. Shown into the large room the Adamses used for an office, he crossed the floor and bent to take Abigail's hand and waft a kiss over it, a reminder of the time they had spent together in France, a prayer for reconciliation.

"I came to offer my services to you and Mr. Adams in any way I can, Madam," he said, simply, sympathetically.

"That is most kind."

"It is no more than you and your husband deserve."

Abigail eyed this tall man, grown to such a distinguished, even handsome middle age. He was one year older than she, but carried himself with the ease of good health and fitness. He, too, had suffered loss in his life – his beloved wife, then a daughter -- she reminded herself, but his looks gave no hint of it. The years had treated him kindly.

"Thank you for your letter on the death of our son," she said.

"I share your grief, as does every parent," he said.

"To live is to lose," Abigail responded.

She looked at the face of the man whose companionship had given John such pleasure. My husband misses those he once considered friends.

"I still mourn your Polly's loss," she said, her voice softer. "She would have been proud of her Papa."

Jefferson smiled wistfully. "There is not a day goes by I do not think of her. Your kindness to her in England was a great help to us both. I will always be grateful."

His words, unexpectedly sweet, caught her off-guard and her eyes filled with tears.

"One can weather the stresses and strains of life on this mortal coil," she said, struggling to regain her composure, "but the death of a child, under whatever circumstances it may occur, is one pain from which a parent can never fully recover."

Jefferson nodded gravely, his eyes filling in memory of the children they had said goodbye to so prematurely.

"I wish you and Mr. Adams a happy retirement," he said after a pause.

"Thankee," Abigail replied.

She made no mention of the fact that Jefferson had refused to make John an Ambassador, believing it to be undignified for a former president to go traipsing about the courts of Europe on his knees. Although she had been insulted at yet another rejection, she had also been relieved.

Despite her resentment at the slight, their conversation that day was a step toward healing. Broken friendships, the wreckage of political differences, were strewn through their lives. That the coming years might mend them, even a little, heartened Abigail.

And then it was over. Breisler packed up the carriage, loaded boxes and parcels into the carriage and carts. Unable to face John's public defeat, they left Washington before the inauguration, never to return. Silently, they passed the fields of Maryland into Pennsylvania. The clatter of the wheels on the dry roads and the steady clomp of the horses' hooves were the only sounds they heard for miles. John stared out of the window, lost in thought. Abigail left him alone. She had her own concerns.

She dreaded passing through New York. The familiar roads, the turn toward Charly's home, all were filled with memories, both painful and sweet. Now it was all gone.

"I hope and pray that Mr. Jefferson may not cast our other son out of service," John said as, days later, they finally crossed the stone marker for the Massachusetts line. All the way home, he had mourned his losses. "It would be a wound in my heart to see John's Quincy's prospects destroyed on the basis of mere political expediency. He has a discernment and a gift for thought and decision that will stand our country in good stead if he is allowed to serve."

"I think Mr. Jefferson will ensure that he stays," Abigail said, relieved at John's expression of interest in the future. "He asked most especially after John Quincy when he came to call, spoke quote enthusiastically of his merits and abilities. I believe Mr. Jefferson knows our son is a man well suited to a task."

"Well, I thank Providence for that," John snorted.

He fell silent again, dozing a little until they came to a rise. Waking, as though startled by a familiar voice, he looked down the slope toward the two saltbox houses. The ancient apple tree had gone, felled by his own hand to make way for change.

"All gone but me," John observed.

Peter had died. His widow, remarried now, still lived in the house that John had been born in. She had never been friendly. Her children were strangers to the Adamses.

"No," Abigail corrected him. "You have increased. You have left a generation to carry on. So all is not gone; it is only beginning."

"It does not seem so," he replied morosely.

Will he remain thus? she wondered. He has many years left if his mother is anything to judge by. Am I to be imprisoned by the

369

melancholy of what's past? I will not be shackled to my husband's moods, she told herself angrily. He must look to the future. His new life that is just beginning. Our life together.

"When will you begin your memoirs?" she asked lightly, as though opening a topic they had been discussing for years.

"Memoirs?" he asked, jolted upright. "My memoirs?"

"Surely you have considered the notion?" she continued, briskly. "Your life has spanned one of the most convulsed and exciting eras of our country's history. Your hand in that history is clear. Of course you will put down for posterity your view of events, explain yourself clearly."

John sat up straighter and looked at Abigail. She had stayed by his side for almost thirty-seven years. Her certainty in the future had been his prod. A smile, grateful and warmly affectionate, spread across his face and he leaned over to kiss her full on the mouth.

"I should have been a great fool not to love you," he said.

"You never minded my stitchery," she said softly.

"What?"

"I have had the marriage I wanted."

They leaned together, arm in arm in the carriage and watched the last few miles between Braintree and Quincy roll past. The two Braintree houses slowly fell behind them as surely as the years that had passed, the sharp outline of their rooftops descending behind the treetops. As they climbed the hill toward home, Abigail began to see a buzz of activity along the road. The line of shade trees that stood just inside the walls dividing their house had become discernible.

"Look John," she said, pointing out the carriage window. "Has traffic grown so much since we left?"

John leaned across her and squinted toward the house. "It is not traffic, I believe," he said, a smile lighting his eyes. "I believe our Quincy neighbors have come to welcome us home!"

Although it was a chill day at the end of March, the lawn was spread with tables. Crowds of people milled beneath the beech trees. They could see John Breisler coming out of the carriage house.

"There they are!" the cry went up as someone caught sight of them. "There they are!"

Three men leapt onto horses and galloped the few hundred yards down the hill toward them.

"It is the mayor!" John cried. "And look, there is Billy Cranch!"

370

"I had not thought he was up north!" Abigail cried excitedly. "Uncle! Aunt!"

Billy, now a judge in Washington, had ridden the five hundred miles home to be with his uncle, the man who had given him his start in government.

"The whole town has turned out to welcome you home!" Billy declared. He jumped down from his horse like a boy and came to trot beside the carriage as it lumbered up the last rise toward their home. "Mother has been baking for a week as has every woman in Quincy and Braintree and Boston."

John's eyes filled with tears and Abigail squeezed his arm.

"If the electors do not know what they have lost, Massachusetts knows what it has gained," Billy pronounced.

Up ahead, they could now see Mary's thin form, standing on a chair on the front porch, supported by her son-in-law, Elizabeth's husband. Abigail reached out of the carriage to wave.

"Well, my dear," John said, a hint of his old playfulness returning for the first time in months, "is this what you expected?"

"It is our reward, John. The approbation of those who know us best. It is what we have earned."

"Earned?"

"Reaped, then," she smiled.

"And is that what we had hoped for all those years ago?"

"I don't remember. We have survived. Perhaps, that alone is the fulfillment of what we hoped."

"Is it enough?" he asked, eyes on her as the carriage rumbled to a stop.

She looked across their lands, the house, enlarged for children and grandchildren, the orchard and carriage house behind, the light falling across the fields that would grow this year's crops, the annual promise of renewal.

"It is abundance."

EPILOGUE

John and Abigail had eighteen more years together, continually working at the joint enterprise that was their life. They enjoyed and educated the raucous crowd of grandchildren in their lively household. 'Peacefield,' their Quincy home, became a Mecca for political pilgrims who sought the wisdom and advice of 'the old man.' Thomas Boyston had become a successful lawyer and businessman, while John Quincy went from one political triumph to the next, rewards for their labors.

They suffered loss and disappointment, too, including Nabby's death from breast cancer. But together, they could lighten the other's burdens and multiply the joys.

Despite the loneliness, the struggles, the sacrifice and loss, Abigail had had the life – and the marriage – that she had prayed for, a partnership of mind, body and spirit. In an extraordinary time, Abigail and John Adams had led extraordinary lives.

And through it all, they shared a love like no other, one that stands as a model for us today.

ABOUT THE AUTHOR

Nancy Taylor Robson is the award-winning author of the novel, *Course of The Waterman,* and the nonfiction, **Woman in The Wheelhouse** about the six years she worked as cook, deckhand then licensed mate on a coastal tugboat. As an essayist, journalist, gardener and cook, her work has appeared in *The Baltimore Sun, Washington Post, Christian Science Monitor, Chesapeake Bay Magazine, Yachting, House Beautiful, Southern Living, Coastal Living, Sail, WorkBoat, Woodenboat* and more. She lives with her husband and dogs on the Eastern Shore of Maryland.